T0281855

THE
Last
Israelite

THE Last Israelite

A NOVEL

ALLEN CHILDS

Bartleby Press
Washington • Baltimore

To my Children and Grandchildren

ISBN 978-088400-397-7
ISBN 978-0-88400-398-4 (ebook)
ISBN 978-0-88400-399-1 (audiobook)
Library Of Congress Control Number: 2023941947

Bartleby Press
JACKSON WESTGATE PUBLISHING GROUP
PO Box 858
Savage, MD 20763
800-953-9929
BartlebythePublisher.com

Printed in the United States of America

10 9 8 7 6 5 4 3 2 1

1

The gust of breeze was momentary, as though toying with the Arab merchant vessel adrift in the current of the Red Sea. The smell of freshly turned earth suddenly filled the air, mysterious since they were marooned 100 miles from the African shore.

Eldad leaned on the heavy teakwood railing and turned to his corpulent traveling companion, "We were sailing so well, for six days, then this accursed stillness."

Saul, as pale as Eldad was dark, tightened the wrap of robes around his ample middle against the cold and recriminated against the cold, "Why did we get on this wreck of a boat, without at least looking into the reasons for their telling us that, yes, we could get passage all the way to the north end of the Sea, but we had to leave *right* then, in the middle of the night. They didn't even get all the crew on board."

Eldad laughed at the memory of the drunken crewmen who did make it back on board at Aden. In their haste, the 110-foot shallow bottom teakwood boat nearly rammed into a barge twice its size, after failing to judge the speed of the larger vessel. The crew's screeching was surpassed by the murderous rage of the boat's captain who had briefly been below deck. Some of the crew were slaves, and though they got it the worst, almost all crewmen still nursed welts on arms and faces.

"We're barely moving," Saul complained. "Look at this sail! Looks like it's woven from palm leaves and stitched with coconut fibers."

Eldad grabbed Saul's arm and pointed at the Arab crew on deck. "I wish I understood what they were saying. Look at how agitated they seem."

1

Saul shook his head and shrugged. The two young men knew but a few words of Arabic between them. They had a scribe translate a note asking for passage into Arabic. The captain seem reluctant but brightened at their mention of *zahav*, Hebrew for gold. At the port of Aden, Eldad had been able to trade his golden trinkets for thumbnail sized gold coins, called dinars, these being half the size of the Muslim silver coin, the dirham. Both bore Arabic inscriptions but no images. The light-skinned Jewish scribe in Crater, the old section of Aden, gave Eldad a quick lesson to accept no less than 20 dirhams for a dinar. "And," he cautioned, "this port collects thieves, pirates and cutthroats, even among the Jews."

Now, after six days of a glorious following wind, they drifted with sagging sails, hour after hour, wherever the Red Sea wished to take them. Even this was not as monotonous as the steady diet the crew and passengers were forced to eat: dates and dried fish. Saul had begun to complain bitterly about wanting something green to eat.

"Assifa, assifa!" one Berber-looking crewman said with rising alarm, looking out at the sea. At this, a few of the sailors were derisive, striking exaggerated fearful poses, while the others showed varying degrees of worry, their eyes collectively looking to the south. But there was only the cloudless sky, the strange stillness and the earthy smell.

The boat creaked and groaned occasionally with no visible provocation, as though squeezed from below. They had been sailing for more than one day before Eldad noticed that there were other passengers, but the two older men who wore turbans and the young woman whose face they could not see seldom came on deck.

Now, all three stood before them. The young woman had let her veil drop. Eldad wasn't quite sure if it was an accident, but he was breathless at her stunning beauty. Her large dark eyes gazed curiously at him, but shyly looked away and covered her lower face.

He knew these feelings from a breathtaking encounter with the daughter of Asher's tribal chief. Making matters more awkward, this tribal leader was the teacher of Hebrew and the five books of Moshe, and as the Tribe of Dan's brightest student, Eldad was sent to the neighboring tribal land for scribal training, this being arranged by the boy's grandfather. Sav had need for an excellent and dedicated scribe, as he had their family's oral history to record for posterity. "I must tell only you this story, my precious Eldad," the ancient Sav had told him over a crackling campfire. "There are things no one would believe, and as mysterious as to why I have lived so long."

Sav was never very far from the young Danite's thoughts. Eldad had begun this unfathomably long journey because of the old Sav's story, which he had faithfully recorded on three-foot scrolls of goat leather. On this same leather, cut into smaller squares and bound by thongs, was the young man's copy of an ancient book in Sav's possession. As he traveled, this thin book, tightly sewn in skins made oily with goat fat, was strapped to his side. His thin bag of gold and silver coins was secured beneath the book. He shifted this to air out the underlying skin, and at that moment, had the sensation he was being watched.

As he turned from his vigil of the southern sky, he was only a few feet from a smiling, unveiled face of light brown skin and golden hair.

2

Eldad could not divert his eyes from the now unveiled woman. Perhaps too boldly, he stepped forward, only to be blocked by the larger of the two turbaned men who now stood between them.

To Eldad's amazement, her small hand smacked the man's large upper arm, who promptly feigned a dramatic fall to the deck, his honey-colored turban bouncing off a coil of rope. Now everyone was laughing.

"My brother believes himself to be so terribly funny", the young woman said. "He imagines he springs from 1001 Arabian Nights."

Eldad was stunned. He looked at Saul, whose features betrayed his own confusion. The woman was speaking what sounded like Hebrew.

"I think I understand, but some of what you say sounds strange to my ear. And who are these Arabian Nights? An army?"

"Just a story. Of no consequence."

"This pitiful heap on the deck is my brother Hillel and the other disreputable is my cousin Yosef," she said with mock weariness. "He told me that you two spoke to each other in Hebrew and no other tongue."

Now the sun was high in the sky. She removed, unselfconsciously, her drab outer travel robe to reveal a pale rose silk blouse and flowing pants which clung to her until she loosened the sash, obscuring details from the eyes of the men about her. "I pretend to be a Muslim since I travel in their lands. Their modesty suffocates me." She didn't seem to mind, nor be surprised by the rapt attention.

"Why this boat, this middle of the night...escape?" asked Saul.

Eldad was making a heroic effort not to feast on her every physical detail, while Saul was entirely oblivious to her charms.

"It's a long story," she offered. speaking cautiously. "We noticed that you also left in the small hours of the night."

"Cheap, a whole lot cheaper than other Red Sea boats, that's our reason," The Asherite seemed proud of his sagacity.

"Oh, yes, oh yes, we were ever so smart!" Eldad interjected. "I am Eldad, and this is my friend Saul. And who are...?"

"A moment, a moment...your names tell us nothing of who you are," Hillel interrupted. "Nor what you two are running from."

"It is he who runs, not I, the pure of heart", said Saul.

Eldad could sense that all eyes were expectantly locked onto him. There *had* been a problem of a delicate nature in the Gulf of Aden port city, but Eldad very much doubted Saul would bring that up, not unless he wanted everyone to know....

"Some problem with a money changer, when he weighed the jewelry after we had gone," Eldad improvised, trying to be vague. Saul snorted in private mirth, immediately discrediting any story Eldad was fabricating. Eldad was sure that his ebony skin would conceal his embarrassment, but he felt a bead of sweat forming in the cool air of the Red Sea stillness.

The woman seemed to notice. To Eldad's great surprise, she casually stepped closer to him, her breathing deepening, as though catching his scent.

"From where do you come and why this torturous journey?" she asked softly.

"I'll gladly tell you, but it will take time. Would your guards allow their princess to sit at the front of the boat...in full view, of course?"

She smiled shyly. "My name is Adiva," she said, raising a restraining palm in the direction of her brother and cousin. They stopped moving and said nothing. She swept gracefully past Eldad who followed her to the shade of the motionless foresail where two heavy storage trunks nestled against the teak railing. The palm frond sail scented the stillness with a faint smell of decay. Adiva and Eldad sat on the trunks, a few feet apart. The craning and hyper-vigilance of her traveling family noticeably faded as the two sat down, out of earshot of everyone. Saul pouted at being left out but was soon trading stories with the guardian relatives.

"They are so loving, but they pain me like blisters on my feet," she said with a chuckle.

"Back in Pumbedita, they wouldn't dare surround my every movement, noses fully intruded into my every conversation."

Eldad recalled his grandfather mentioning this place, but the old man would wave his emaciated arms in wide arcs, giving the same location for all distant places: beyond the River Cush.

Eldad asked, "This Pumbedita, is it far away?"

"It is a city on a tributary river of the great Euphrates. I am Babylonian".

"I know of an exile to Babylon, perhaps 1500 years ago, yes?"

Avoiding a patch of sunlight shining through a broken frond, Adiva moved a foot closer to him. She stretched out long and firm legs, covered to the ankles by rose colored silk. He followed her movements from her sandaled feet up to her inquisitive eyes.

"I heard your friend call you 'Danite.' Dan must be your father's name?"

"The legends of my people are very old, and have been passed down by word of mouth from grandfather to father to son, and they say we are of the Tribe of Dan."

"You mean the *lost* Tribe of Dan?" she asked, doubt creeping into her voice.

"I have carefully recorded my Zav's stories of my tribe. When he started telling me these, he somehow mixed in our family's tales."

"You don't believe it?" She shifted and the silk's rustle distracted him. His mind kept wandering to the memory of her stretching and clinching her toes.

"Not all of it." Eldad turned away, looking instead to the mirror-still surface of the Red Sea.

"Zav told me *not* to believe everything some crazy old man says, no matter how I revere him, nor, if a woman, how much I adore her."

Adiva smiled, "And my mother says men always overestimate the women they love and the sages they love to study."

She liked his candor, a surprise from this slightly nervous young man. She had never met a black Jew, and couldn't remember ever meeting a man whose chiseled features and inviting eyes had so arrested her attention. She realized she simply loved looking at him. He pretended a nonchalance, or maybe he, like so many men, didn't notice.

Eldad laughed at her. He hesitated before asking.

"And you, have you been, uh, overestimated?"

Adiva looked directly into his eyes. "Do you mean to ask if I've ever been in love?" The Danite, flustered, blurted, "No, uh. No...I mean yes." She toyed with him. "Dreams have been brought to my doorstep, but never crossed the threshold of my heart." Eldad had been made nearly speechless. He longed to know her better and wondered how. He was lost in his thoughts.

Adiva interrupted. "Now you.... you don't tell stories very well, do you! You won't slip away, so, now, the Tribe of Dan, tell me of the Tribe of Dan. I know the names of some of the other tribes who are lost."

Eldad again noticed a wave of turned earth smell, and a gentle breeze began to inflate the sail in front of them. Two of the sailors popped monkey-like onto the foot thick mast, reaching awkwardly with long wooden needles to thread fabric strips through torn fronds. For the first time in half a day, the boat began moving faster than the sea's northward current.

"By the way," Adiva said quietly, "The boys and I came out on deck because of the crewman's 'Assifa, assifa!'".

Adiva asked, "Do you know Arabic?"

"No, but the people who hear my kind of Hebrew say I use Arabic words sometimes." "We say seh-ah-rah. Isn't that your..."

"Yes, of course, *storm*," Adiva replied. So that's what he was so alarmed about, but everything is so clear and still."

Adiva stretched her arms out on the railing and tilted her head back, eyes closed, in the sunlight now peaking over the growing fullness of the mainsail. She looked momentarily so vulnerable, and Eldad felt protective. But the color of her velveteen skin, the full lips, the long and graceful neck, easily brushed aside *protective*, replaced by other more primitive feelings

"I'm waiting, Danite", she said teasingly without opening her eyes. "Now, please, while the year is still 4668, tell me mysteries of the ages." She laughed and it was so lovely it could have been a song, Eldad thought. He was aware that something within him was racing at a dizzying pace.

"My Sav and the other, younger elders say this is the origin of our people:

For years, the ancient Assyrian empire threatened our people. They made slaves of our people, plundered our land. Our tribe, the Hebrew tribe of Dan, knowing their freedom would inevitably be crushed, left their homeland in waves. They became fierce desert fighters and migrated along the coast of this great sea, to the land beyond the rivers of Ethiopia. Before long, we were joined by other exiles, from the tribes of Gad, Naftali, and, most importantly for me, Asher."

Eldad paused, looking for some sign of interest that he continue.

"Don't stop," Adiva opened her eyes. She pointed to Eldad's rotund traveling companion. "Why is Asher so important to you?"

"Saul's father is most honored among all men of our four tribes. He is our great religious teacher, but he teaches many other things as well. When he was on the threshold of manhood, his father sent him by Arab caravan to the north African coast, to a city they called Kairouan."

Adiva sat up and said, "This city, Kairouan, my father gets correspondence from them and sends replies to the rabbis there. He says this is the land of the ancient civilization known as Carthage."

"How can written documents travel so far?"

"By ship, over the Mediterranean, like the voyage that brought us to Egypt so many months ago. We carried documents to parties in Cairo. Perhaps, I'll tell you about that later."

"Please do. Saul's father was trained at a special school in

Kairouan, and he brought back to our tribes the knowledge of the world beyond our pastures."

Eldad lowered his voice and leaned slightly toward her, "In exchange for the two years as his pupil and guest in his home, his father made me promise to take Saul on this already too-long voyage. Oh, I shouldn't say that, but I have wearied of his endless complaints." Eldad rolled his eyes beseeching heaven, "What bothers me is he's *right* about it all!"

Adiva laughed, again a song to Eldad, and she reached out, touching him briefly on his wrist. For a moment the young Danite could hardly breathe.

Just then, as though he knew he was being talked about, Saul came bounding over to the seated couple, both of whom made motions for a welcome they didn't feel at that moment. The Asherite's intrusion became more tolerable as he bore the news that in the now fading stillness, three of the Berber crew had caught a school of fish in nets. Saul was flushed with delight and making little kid smacking noises. "Two fish, maybe more, for each man!" He bowed to Adiva, quickly adding, "And woman, and woman!"

Adiva poked him in his large stomach. Her brother and cousin strolled across the deck in their direction, the mirth beckoning them irresistibly.

Hillel patted a too full goatskin bag slung at his side, "Through my superior planning and foresight, I have again saved the Sabbath with a midnight purchase of ceremonial wine before we left the port." At the mention of wine, she saw sheepish looks from her brother and cousin.

"I told you to buy *food*, I told both of you!" Adiva flared. The boys just laughed, but an instant later, they wished they hadn't, as the lithe young woman sprang upon them with smacks on shoulders and backs from which they pretended great pain. The two were snorting like hogs, causing further tribulation at the hands of Adiva.

Eldad guessed this affectionate abuse was a well-worn playscape for his three new companions. Adiva stopped beating on them as it was just making the two husky lads laugh more. "We bought some food, too, honored cousin," said Yosef, affecting a serious demeanor. "Dates and dried fish!"

"Oh, *you're* a funny person too, 'eh, just like this one," she said as she kicked at her cousin, missing by some inches. "Our dear father and uncle would surely be horrified by this barbaric treatment of their offspring," Hillel interjected, "If he were to find out...". "Well then," she laughed, "I'm just going to have to make sure you have something to report!"

As if on signal, the Asherite produced two wooden cups, one with a cracked rim. Hillel unstrapped the goatskin bag with some relief. Saul was quick to pry off the cork lid and said, pouring the cup full, "Someone must test this for purity. I shall sacrifice myself for the good of our party!" Before anyone could react, he'd drunk half a cup of the blood-red liquid.

"Should we not say a prayer?" Eldad asked.

"Is that the custom of the Danites?", Adiva asked.

"Yes, as the Torah tells us...." Before Eldad finished this thought, Saul had emptied his cup.

"The nectar of Eden," he said, wiping a dribble from his double chin.

"We shall honor your custom," said Adiva decisively. She gathered them in a semicircle around her, placed her hands over her closed eyes, and sang the ancient prayer thanking the Lord of the entire universe for the fruit of the vine. Eldad was moved by the familiar words but a melody he had never heard. And from a voice he was beginning to treasure.

No one spoke or even moved. But the palpable aroma of cooking fish soon led them all to the back of the boat where crewmen were gutting still squirming fish, passing them to others who carefully placed them in rows on a cast iron grill. Another man did nothing but manage the charcoal in the shallow pan below. A too-old crewman, surely a last-minute addition as were a few others, sprinkled a rust colored spice on the on the sizzling fish. It gave the air around the grill an essence of bitter lemon, spiking the roasting fish aroma which had already caught everyone's undivided attention.

"I can't stand this," said the agitated Saul. He strode to the side of the charcoal boss, then realizing he didn't speak a word of his language, turned beseechingly toward his new companions.

"C'mon, ask him, ask him."

Hillel came to the rescue, or so it seemed, croaking in Arabic, "My eager friend, obviously in the throes of prolonged starvation, wants to know how long." Adiva translated for Eldad, who laughed with her and the four crewmen tending the fish.

The captain appeared through a deferential parting of crewmen standing around the aft deck. His skin, darkened and creased from relentless sun exposure, stretched like parchment over the hollowed coves of his temples. Seeing this, Eldad's years as a trained healer led him to the conclusion that captain Mustafa was gravely ill. *I have seen this in my clan, the old, but sometimes even children. The wasting, how their pitiful images haunt me.*

To Eldad's surprise, the captain bowed with respect to Adiva. He did not understand the words. The old captain asked, "How does the voyage and my crew treat you, daughter of Zemah ben Paltoi?" "We are treated well, captain Mustafa, but my brother and cousin, who sleep in hammocks slung next to slaves, complain of rude behavior from some of the men. Disgusting behavior I don't want to describe."

Captain Mustafa raised his left nostril and lip in a contemptuous sneer, "Animals...they would mutiny if my loyal slaves failed in their vigilance."

"We'll mutiny too, if we don't get some of this fresh fish", Adiva quipped. At this, the captain ordered that she be given the first fish off the grill. His cabin boy produced six plates and soon the five passengers and the captain, each with a whole fish in their plates, sat in the late afternoon sunlight and devoured their first fresh meal in a week. The skin was crisp with a citrus tang, and abundant white flakes of tender fish fell away from bones.

Saul kept filling their two wooden cups, passed them around the five of them. Though he, Hillel and Yosef grew louder over the course of evening meal, Eldad felt still and more reflective. Finishing her second fish with a resounding crunch of its brittle skin, Adiva moved away from the others, as had the Danite, and she sat with him on a low wooden bench. They both sat quietly for awhile. Eldad was relieved when Adiva spoke. "Your thoughts are far away, Danite. Do you think of a special woman?" Eldad was momentarily disquieted by her directness, but at the same time, intrigued. Though he barely knew her, he felt an instinctive trust of this Babylonian mystery. "No," he laughed, "Unless my grandfather has changed a great deal since I last saw him!"

Adiva smiled broadly, but Eldad was not sure she was convinced by his attempt to cover more somber thoughts. "You miss your Sav, don't you?" Her voice was gentle and soft.

"I so fear my voyage will be so long, I'll never see him again." The words caught in Eldad's throat, but he soon recovered his composure. "All my family, Mahali my father, Chava my mother, my two sisters and three brothers, all of them are so precious to me."

Eldad looked at Saul and Adiva's brother and cousin. They were clearly besotted with wine.

He turned back to Adiva. "Your family...tell me of them".

"I am the second daughter of the Gaon of the Yeshiva at Pumbedita." Eldad was candid, "I don't understand, the word "gaon" means haughty pride in my dialect. But I know a yeshiva is a place of learning."

"He is headmaster of the school, but also a religious leader who is often asked to rule on matters of the Torah and the rituals of observance. Gaon is a term they have used for a very long time. To some this word means genius. Perhaps Judah ben Ezekiel who founded the yeshiva 600 years ago *was* a genius. But my father, Zemah ben Paltoi, makes no such claims, except for his brilliance, he is fond of saying, in choosing my mother as his wife."

Do you study in the Yeshiva?"

"No", she replied firmly, "No women in the Yeshiva. Zemah taught everything to his daughters at home. Many girls, most of them, cannot read the Torah. My father did something wholly unusual for my sister and me. I believe he has a rebellious nature he keeps well hidden because of his leadership position in the wider community."

"What did he do that was so unusual?" Eldad asked.

"Through his connections in Baghdad, which is 40 miles east of Pumbedita, he arranged for us private tutors at the great library called the House of Wisdom. The inventors, the astronomers, the linguists and the scribes all taught us as though we were their own, even if we did have to be schooled in a shed behind the back wall of the library."

"Because you are women?"

"No, because we are Jews."

Jews?

Adiva replied, "Yehuda. From Yehudi, the Kingdom of Judah. Israel is no more. After the exile, to Babylon, all that remained was Judea, that is, the tribes of Judah, and Benjamin. We have our Levites too."

Eldad was a little confused but tried not to show it.

Adiva continued. " Now, all the followers of laws of Moses, our Teacher and God's Torah are called Jews by peoples everywhere."

Adiva smiled. They locked eyes. " I guess you are a Jew as well."

Eldad considered this and said," my people do not know this word, Jew, but rather call themselves Israelites.

Adiva continued, "The edicts governing the way we live forbid educating Jews in Muslim schools. Also, decrees forbid Muslims from teaching Jews or Christians. Maybe my father's eminence as a scholar induced the House of Wisdom scholars to teach us in secret for two years, but more likely it was those little coin purses we brought to each lesson."

"Jews are not welcome in Babylon? asked Eldad."

"Welcome? Not welcome, more like grudgingly tolerated. We are forced to wear a yellow square cloth sewn to our clothes. The other so called protected people are the Christians, who must wear blue."

"Protected from what?" asked Eldad.

"From being murdered by our Muslim conquerors. Instead, we *dhimmis,* the non-believers, must accept public shaming. A century and a half ago, faced with annihilation, Christian and Jewish leaders signed the Pact of Umar. In accepting the odious restrictions on our freedom, the leaders had to declare something like, All this we promise to observe, on behalf of ourselves and our co-religionists, and receive protection from you in exchange. And if we violate any of the conditions of this agreement, then we forfeit your protection, and you are at liberty to treat us as enemies and rebels."

Eldad shifted on his seat, disquieted by these words. "What are we not permitted to do in your land?"

Adiva sighed and gazed out on the featureless blue-green waters of the Red Sea. "My mother told me of the irony that at least six of the decrees from the original Pact of Omar were adopted from the laws Christians used to oppress infidels. This pact has changed, or rather been added to by one Caliph after another, depending on how hostile and acquisitive he was. The latest version, which I read as part of my Arabic language studies, is from 850 AD—the Decree of Caliph al-Mutawakkil. Some provisions are no longer enforced, like nailing wooden devils to the doors of non-believer's homes."

"850 AD? Do you use the Christian calendar?" Eldad asked.

"And the Muslim. It is wise to adjust this depending on who is listening, whether you intend them to or not." Her eyes drifted to an unusually ragged crewmen working on the opposite side of the foresail. "This year, 878 AD is 256 AH for Muslims."

"So, the laws for our people in Babylon, are they still so different? You said, 'public shaming'." Eldad looked into her luminous green eyes and wished this conversation would go on long into this night and many others. The edgy feeling on first meeting her was all but gone. He wondered for a moment if the wine had soothed him, but quickly deduced that this feeling had nothing to do with wine.

"Jews must not imitate Muslim dress or mannerisms. As you can see from the outer garments I wore, and my brother's and cousin's turbans, they are all honey-colored. It is the only colored cloth we are permitted to wear in public. Perhaps you can see why I was so willing to relieve myself of the stifling veil and the large wrap, the tent I was wearing over myself. Everything honey-colored, as decreed by Caliph al-Mulawakki, branding us as Jews."

"I saw this in the port city, especially in some quarters."

"Did you see the saddles Jews must use? Two tufted balls attached to the back and only wooden stirrups? That's been brought back to us by our most generous Caliph." Adiva said.

Eldad stood and took her empty plate, and, placing it atop his, he walked a few paces to wordlessly hand them to Saul. Saul was in charge of food, this being an ever-present preoccupation of his. Eldad retraced his steps and sat beside his new friend. *No, something more than a friend*, he told himself.

The parchment-skinned captain reappeared carrying a large spyglass and again addressed the young woman. He looked tense and distracted, making no effort to prevent others from hearing. At first what he said did not match his pressured tone, but not for long.

"The wind favors us, but we lost time during the doldrums. Do you wish to discuss this in my cabin?" Eldad didn't understand but he could see the captain was struggling with his composure. It was more important for him to prevent the crew's seeing that. These were treacherous times and some of the men he'd known only since the voyage began a week ago.

"I need my brother and my cousin to hear you, captain, and the two Africans as well,' she said, motioning with her head toward Eldad and Saul.

The captain nodded stiffly and marched to the steps leading below deck. Eldad signaled the others to follow and in a moment, they had walked through the common hammock area to the three aft cabins, the largest of which was the captain's. Inside contrasted sharply with the disarray and unpleasant smell of the crew's quarters. Maritime scrolls were spread upon a high gloss teakwood desk. A papyrus scrap had numbers and ink stains on it, and after closing the door, he picked it up.

"My calculations, they are different from when we left port." He held them up as though someone else in the room could understand them.

"You gave me your absolute assurance and you took almost three times your usual fee to leave hastily."

Adiva was clearly struggling to remain calm.

But something was wrong. The captain cleared his throat, which he did every few minutes while talking. They all remained standing, and Hillel moved to Eldad's side to translate the captain's Arabic. Captain Mustafa said, "You did not tell me whom you believe to be a threat to your party. I have learned not to ask when such urgency is expressed as you did on the dock."

Adiva asked, "Why does it matter, what threat I saw?"

The captain grimaced and answered through gritted teeth, "Because any *other* threats we left at dockside."

"Other than what?" asked Yosef warily, though he didn't seem to be registering surprise at the direction the captain was taking.

"One of the new men, who jumped on board at the midnight hour, I knew from years ago, fancies himself a spy, and hires himself out to people. Some of these are very bad people but he doesn't care."

Adiva asked, "What has this to do with us?"

"This crewman has confessed he was hired to follow you three after you left the caravan at the city gate. He reported all your movements, including your Sabbath dinner with the banking family, and he was sent to the dock to collect his money. When he arrived, he was simply laughed at by the first mate of a well guarded vessel with three grey sails. They had all along intended to cheat him. One dock worker said, 'If they think you'll make trouble over what they owe you, they won't mind killing you just for that.' They are pirates and slavers as well."

The group in the cabin shifted audibly at this, causing the floorboards to creak. Eldad waited for the murmured translation, but he could already see the gravity on the captain's emaciated face. He looked into Adiva's eyes and saw the reflection of his own dread.

The captain continued, "Today this crewman told me he believes the ship with the grey sails was waiting, perhaps for more information about you three." He looked questioningly at the Babylonians.

Hillel shifted and Eldad noticed he had the empty goatskin wine bag slung over his shoulder, riding his right hip.

"Why did the spy wait so long to let you know about that?" Adiva asked.

"Until the half day of doldrums, he believed our head start was more than enough. Now he watches the horizon every moment for the grey sails."

Captain Mustafa was quiet for a moment then said, "We carry other cargo they would no doubt relish, like the silk and the fresh-water pearls, but those wouldn't be worth their time."

Adiva looked at him steadily and asked, "It's the human cargo, isn't it?"

The captain sighed and walked over to the table of nautical charts and answered, "They are known to hold persons for ransom, if they think them important. Some they shackle and sell as slaves. The unsuited or rebellious do not survive."

The Asherite was now highly agitated, and when Hillel translated these last words, he blurted out "Aleynu lifnot lyabasha!" The captain looked puzzled until the Hebrew was translated into Arabic by Adiva. "He says we must head for dry land".

"We are days from shore, perhaps the same whether we sail east or west," the captain replied, opening his wiry arms in those directions.

Adiva asked, "What do you think we should do, captain?"

The captain did a fair imitation of what he had just heard from Saul and said with some urgency, "Aleynu lifnot lyabasha!"

3

The sea air felt uncomfortably cool when the five of them mounted the stairs to the main deck. It was at least a momentary relief after the closeness of the captain's cabin.

Hillel, the only one with any experience at all spoke to the others. "The captain was already tacking to the west before we went below. I didn't understand. Our progress to the north was brisk for the first time in two days, but now I see." None of the others could tell a change of direction since only open sea stretched out in every direction and he felt the need to explain the source of his knowledge to Eldad and Saul: "I have sailed on two rivers before, the Bedita and Euphrates."

Casually, Adina drifted to the aft of the boat and gave an inviting glance to Eldad who welcomed a chance to follow.

They stood quietly looking out on the blue-green waters of the sea. Finally, Eldad broke the silence. "Are you afraid?" he blurted out.

Adina seemed a little surprised but didn't hesitate. "Yes, as I have been since we arrived at the port city. Still, I cannot understand how anyone except the Netira family knows our business at Aden, nor even who we are."

She smiled, eyes warm and twinkling. "I don't want to seem mysterious to you, though you certainly are to me."

Eldad again felt the pull of her femininity, wondered at her light heartedness. "Tell me about the Netira family?"

"They are an influential banking family who has never lost the caring for their less fortunate landsmen. My father taught all their sons at the Pumbedita Academy, and their daughters in the privacy of their home. They and the ben Aarons, the other prominent Jewish family of the round city, want my father to move the yeshiva to Baghdad."

"*Round* city?"

"That is how Baghdad was built, as a great circular-walled city, four miles around." She laughed as she added, "For all the restrictions on Jews throughout Babylon, 150 years ago they chose a Persian Jew to design their greatest Muslim city!"

"I cannot imagine how far you are from home. You must have some very good reason to risk such travel." At once, Eldad wondered if he was being too inquisitive.

The boat suddenly gained speed from a reassuringly steady wind filling all sails and Eldad was almost knocked off his feet. He wasn't meant to be a sailor, he decided. The scent of turned earth was gone, replaced by colder, dryer air that seemed to come from the desert many miles away. Adiva motioned to her cousin to bring her honey-colored wrap. Eldad was disappointed but tried not to show it. He was pretty sure she had noticed, barely disguising her delight.

"Yosef, what have you learned from the crew?" she asked, enveloping herself but leaving her head uncovered. Saul had come over, too.

"We," Eldad said, pointing to himself and the Asherite, "asked some more questions of the crewman the pirates cheated. He is not an Arab or Ethiopian, unlike the rest of the crew. He is from the great land of China."

"Yes, well, what has he said?" As she asked this, Hillel appeared from below, groggy but looking curious.

Saul spoke up, "He told Yosef he saw the three of you each carry something in a leather case into an elegant house and leave with a large skin bag." Saul pointed to the goatskin bag slung over Hillel's bony shoulder.

Adiva looked about for any crew within earshot, and seeing none, said, "We delivered copies of the Five Scrolls to the rabbinic authority in Aden. There were also direct communications from my father to these leaders, who had submitted religious questions to the Gaon of Pumbedita."

Adiva was studying both Eldad and Saul, strangers until only a few days ago, as though trying to decide whether to trust them.

Saul playfully reached for the bag at Hillel's side, and the tall young man suddenly lurched sidewise, directing the prying hands into empty air. Hillel was silent and unsmiling, clearly a temporary rupture in an otherwise developing friendship.

Adiva eyes darted between her brother and cousin. "I have decided to trust our African friends with information they may need to know."

Yosef's head shook side to side slowly, but Adiva ignored him. "The Netira family has a long-established branch in the port city of Aden. Their banking activities have been highly successful there and they have recently sold most of their ships, plantations, and many other businesses. Though they are bankers who carry and lend gold money, they have no secure way to store wealth of this magnitude."

The Asherite paled, even beyond his winter pallor. "So you get hired to move the gold, to move it home to Baghdad?"

Adiva replied, "We go to Fustat where the Jewish banking families are secure, then on to Babylon." She was quiet for a time. "I am aggrieved if we have put you in danger, but I have a proposition for you."

Hillel started to say something but an icy stare from his sister quieted him.

"I am empowered to hire the two of you stout young lads as extra bodyguards for our party." Yosef looked at the unsoldier-like Asherite and started to laugh, but Adiva would have none of it, striking his chest with her elbow.

"But Adiva bat Zemah, we are not trained warriors." Eldad pointed to Saul. He is a merchant and I, a scribe and herbalist. I know more of plants than I do of fighting. You have to know what you're buying."

Eldad paused. "And what we're protecting."

He instantly regretted doing so, but she just pouted, teasing, "Oh, *I'm* not enough?"

Helpless, Eldad managed a flustered, "Oh, certainly, yes of course!"

Saul nodded enthusiastically. He had a look in his eyes Eldad had seen before in shops and bazaars. Saul would involuntarily rub his hands together, but Eldad had pointed out it that made him look too eager, so only the eyes betrayed the underlying exhilaration.

Eldad took his friend by both shoulders and placed his face nearly at a lover's distance. "Do not, Asherite, I say, *do not* demand to know what we shall be paid. It is a mitzvah to protect travelers, and we are willing..." His expression of mild amusement betrayed his harsh tone, which Saul was slow to notice.

"But, but, I was..."

Eldad cut him off, "to protect our lovely friends for no compensation whatever. It's a blessed thing, isn't it Saul?"

Saul put his hands to his face, a ploy Eldad had seen--the defeated, utterly-ruined-by-the irrational-intransigence-of-the-bargainer face. But now they all laughed, even a grudging Saul.

"As our Asherite guessed, valuables are sewn into the lining of the goatskin. Belts we wear and our clothing also have hidden pockets in odd places," Adiva said, blushing faintly with this revelation.

"The Netiras have devised ingenious ways of transporting their assets from Aden to their family in the Egyptian capital." She stopped, looking lost in thought.

She spoke to her brother, almost whispering, but making no attempt to hide it from the others.

"Hillel, do you remember the slave girl at their house? I caught her lurking behind a heavy drape at one side of the doorway. I thought she was just being attentive to our every request and gave it no thought. Now with all this talk of spies..."

She looked upward. "I feel like the pirates know everything. I am so troubled and uneasy. Even before we undertook this journey, I was told that the Gulf of Aden's north shore was called Pirates Alley."

Vapor from the salty water of the Red Sea hung in the air between gusts of wind that jabbed at the sails. They now seemed to be skimming along the surface, with the waves adding force and direction. Captain Mustafa came up from below and his appearance quickened the pace of crewmen doing routine chores. Most did not look at him directly, unless spoken to. He stopped beside a brawny man, the ships carpenter who was repairing a foredeck railing. Out of earshot, the Danite watched as the captain seemed to be asking the carpenter a question. From somber and attentive, the carpenter's huge, bearded face suddenly erupted in a maniacal grin, and he nodded vigorously.

Mustafa grimaced and placed a finger to his lips, then pointed to himself. *I'll tell them*, was clearly the message.

After the captain had addressed two other groups of sailors, Yosef was able to overhear them talking among themselves. "The captain has said to these men that we are likely being pursued by a larger, faster vessel, he reported, "He is asking who among them is practiced with the sword and mortal combat." He paused, "These are rough-cut men, and most are no strangers to weapons and killing. Some even boast of fights with pirates. Looking at their scars, it's obvious they've been in fights with *somebody!*"

At that moment, Eldad regretted he had no fighting skills. This was certainly not typical of young Danite men, many of whom were required to fight off marauding tribes from other African lands. Tradition had it that their warriors could stay in their saddles a week at a time. Eldad doubted anyone did such a thing.

Except in childhood play, he had never handled spears or swords. He had watched friends of his practice their swordsmanship, wooden swords cracking on one another. When the swords they wielded turned to iron, so many...always too many...were lost in defense of tribal lands: theirs, and those of Asher, Gad and Naftali.

Eldad asked Yosef, "What does he say about the change in direction?"

"He believes we are no more than three days off the coast of Ethiopia but will be better able to tell from the stars tonight."

They had all seen the captain standing on the deck at night with his kamal, the Arab navigation instrument. One end of a string knotted in nine places was held in the captain's teeth, and the other passed through a two inch by one inch card of wood to his outstretched hand. He gave readings of longitude to his cabin boy to write down on a skin stretched over wood.

"Tell them the rest," a worried Saul insisted, "About the water."

"When I filled the goat skin with the fresh water from the barrels," Hillel replied, "I tapped on them as I had seen the cabin boy do yesterday. I know they were full and sloshing around when we started, but only a few inches remain."

"Perhaps it will rain. I know they have a system for catching it if it does," said Saul optimistically.

Adiva said quickly, "It never rains on the Red Sea, or almost never." She could tell the others found that hard to believe.

All of them had immediately begun to feel thirsty at Hillel's news and not encouraged by what Adiva told them. The hazards of Red Sea voyages were known to all of them but the infrequency of these disasters compared to caravan travel made the Sea feel safe. The impending water shortage was a useful focus for worry, diverting emotion from other more disquieting realities.

"We should talk to the captain directly about this," offered Eldad. "First, does the captain know, though I can't imagine he doesn't."

Saul added, "Also, what is our true distance from land, and *what* land." They were all now looking at Hillel, who alone among them knew the ways of the water.

"I'll wait till he has made his rounds of the crew. Perhaps he will be more comfortable talking to me alone," Hillel replied, looking in the captain's direction. The group saw Hillel's eyes widen, and he said, "Something is wrong."

They all turned toward the foredeck where they could see waves of frantic, but purposeless movement among the crew. Crescendos of speech in three languages competed for center stage.

Soon all beings on the ship were straining their eyes at the western sky, where the sunset had begun to appear crushed by a light extinguishing blackness, stretching like a silhouette on a wall from the waters surface to above the horizon. Though distant, it cast a shadow that seemed to divide the boat in half.

From the din of now fearful voices, one word leapt out:

Rami!

Even Eldad and Saul understood. Adiva moved closer beside Eldad, and they looked in each other's eyes for a lingering moment before turning to the west. Even miles from shore, the blackness that did not dissipate over vast stretches of sea closed the narrow sliver of light on the horizon.

From its home in the Sahara Desert, a two-thousand-foot-high monsoon of sand screamed in their direction.

4

"We are headed for those ten volcanic islands of the Zubair Group, Allah willing," the captain answered curtly. Hillel had caught up with him on the starboard side of the boat and thought he had been diplomatic and had simply asked where they were going.

Hillel understood the captain's predicament. He had been in violent storms in the vastness of the Persian Gulf and knew that unless they trimmed the sails the 40′ cedar masts could snap like dried sticks. "Do you trim sails in case we're hit in the night?" Hillel asked to the captain's back.

"No," the captain answered more civilly. "Tell your sister the crew will practice striking the sails once this night. But we must maintain full sail throughout the night."

The captain winced and rubbed at his right side.

The young Babylonian was sympathetic, but felt he had to ask, "The water, I know it is low."

Mustafa shrugged helplessly. "He who was in charge of securing fresh water, he was told to procure additional oak and teak barrels. We were a day gone from port, before I realized not only that had he failed to do so, but...,"

The captain gritted his teeth, spitting out, "The whore's son fled with the silver."

He sighed deeply, his thin shoulders drooping toward the center of his chest. He realized many eyes were on him, even if only Hillel could hear his hushed tones. He straightened and affected a smiling countenance, quite contrary to what he was revealing to Hillel.

"The water supply is meager but limiting the measure for each crewman could cause a murderous mutiny, as they will surely turn on me. There is enough for two days, maybe as many as three if we ration. It is urgent that you say nothing to the crew of this."

Nodding, Hillel asked, "The Zubairs. From your charts and instruments, how far with a steady wind?"

"Allah permitting, steady winds, yes, but we may yet feel the sting of gale force blasts of sand. If it goes around us, we'll use the turbulence at the storms edge to move us quickly toward the ten volcanic islands," captain Mustafa, feigning optimism.

Hillel was not satisfied, "How far and how long?"

Mustafa frowned, but didn't hesitate. "Two days, perhaps more if the winds do not favor us. If you are the sailor you say, you already know the winds that move us so steadily can as well rip us to pieces."

Hillel swallowed hard, feeling his prominent Adams apple bobbing up his spindly neck. "Can you tell the sandstorm's distance?"

Daylight had collapsed with eerie suddenness.

Just as he asked this, everyone on deck felt a single slap of high velocity air instantly covering all their exposed skin surfaces with a fine white dust.

The captain turned away and bawled out orders, but even before he could finish, crewmen had scrambled up the two masts to lower the palm frond sails.

Then suddenly another assault of wind, making the first seem like the brush of a fan, whipped the boat to starboard, slinging a terrified crewman from the top of the main mast into the now roiling sea. In a moment the piteous man was far out of reach of the ship's ropes. The wind howled down the man's cries.

Crewman struggled to protect the still half furled sails not only from the shearing wind, but now the earlier dust had quickly turned to abrasive sand.

Hillel said to his companions, all of whom were shielding their faces with articles of clothing, "Below deck without delay!" Their exposed hands were stinging, and they stumbled toward the stairs that led below.

As Adiva was shaking the sand from her outer wrap, she looked at Eldad and laughed heartily.

"What amuses you?" Eldad asked her. By then the other three men were also looking at him with great amusement. Adiva went quickly to her small cabin and returned with a small, highly polished brass hand mirror which she which she gave to Eldad, saying, "Behold, a new Danite!" Eldad burst out laughing when he saw himself in the mirror. The dust was abundant on his eyebrows, hair and eyelashes, making him look ancient, but what everyone was laughing at, in this otherwise threatening time, was that Eldad was now alabaster white!

For a moment, he posed, pharaoh-like, hands crossed over his chest, his features frozen in the mists of time.

Their temporary diversion was abruptly halted by a thundering jolt felt throughout the ship. Pebble-laced sand shot down the stairwell filling every crevice and every fold of their garments. The ships planking beneath their feet groaned as the ship yawed back and forth from waves of increasing size. Some made it hard to stand, even below deck.

The sand blew through the clothes covering them. Yosef cut down several seaman's hammocks, those woven of dense cloth, and gave each one for additional protection from the relentless blasts. They quickly huddled under these as far as they could from the opening to above deck.

The sound was more frightening than being scoured by sand. They could not cover up the demonic howl of the sand-heavy wind as it clawed mercilessly at men on deck clinging to all manner of tethers. The brawny carpenter, whom the captain believed with good reason to be quite a bit more intelligent than most sailors, had wrapped himself and several other men, captain Mustafa included, in the 40-foot sail.

The salt air of the sea had been replaced by a fine dust infusion which was hard to breathe. Saul began wheezing audibly a quarter hour into their confinement under deck. Throwing off the protective wraps made his breathing even more labored. He hunched down next to Eldad and asked urgently, "The herbs you bought in Aden, will they help me?"

Eldad had already begun thinking about the seeds and herbs he had so patiently sought out in the back streets of the port city, including such staples as meadow saffron and cocoa beans. As herbalists, his father and especially his grandfather taught every aspiring herbal healer such as Eldad and his siblings that they must never travel without their bags of seeds and herbs.

It was the cocoa beans, or rather an extract from them, that Eldad had been taught would ease breathing. It was a very old Danite remedy that had come down through an unbroken tradition of herbal healers.

Preparing the extract under these conditions was nearly impossible. Eldad had to guess how extreme the Asherite's situation was, as Saul regarded any health matter as a life and death issue.

"Put the cloth back over your face, Saul. You can't suffocate under it and we have to filter the dust the best we can."

Adiva listened intently to the words Eldad spoke in his role of healer. She noted Saul seem less agitated, attributing that to Eldad's soothing tone.

"Your in and out breathing, which is more affected?"

Saul coughed a wheezy cough, and Eldad said, "Never mind, I can hear it from a distance: breathing out."

Saul said a muffled yes.

Eldad touched his friend's cheek, "Stop thinking you're going to die because you aren't."

Adiva and the men were all beginning to sicken from the gyrations of the storm-tossed boat. Ten-foot waves crashed over all decks, adding to the misery of the swirling sand.

Snapping noises began to add to the basso groans of the weakening hull.

A phrase from Genesis crossed Eldad's mind, as he strained to see in the night so deepened by the sand and dust of the storm: *Darkness which may be felt.*

The wind was a song of destruction with long, undying notes as it lashed through and around every object on deck. It did not fade, as would a gust of wind, but bore steadily into the resistance of the teakwood boat, moving it over the Red Sea at a speed it could never attain, even full sail.

Hillel shouted to his unseen companions above the menacing wind, "This can go on for hours."

"Don't try to cheer us up so," Saul shot back and followed it with a fit of coughing.

They moved closer to one another, which helped overcome the isolation of the darkness and the howling wind. Adiva, seated in the circle the five had formed, leaned forward to speak to the taller Danite, who lowered his head only to collide with hers in the pitch black.

Startled but uninjured, they established a safe but close distance between their faces by reaching to touch the sound of one another's voices. In doing so, she had brushed his lips, thin but soft, she noticed. Though the touch was brief, she was surprised to feel a flush come to her face and a warmth in sensitive places.

The young man's reaction to the delicate touch was predictable, and he struggled to suppress its obvious manifestations.

"I am so cramped on this part of the deck," she was able to say in a low voice because of the closeness of their faces, though the wind was unabated.

"The higher part of the deck might be better," Eldad ventured. Through the dense blackness and swirling sand, he crept up hill on the flooring of the tilted deck. A gentle tug at the fringe of his long robe told him Adiva was following. The other three men were huddled miserably beneath layers of robes and took no notice.

The young woman came to a seated position beside, though not touching, Eldad.

"They cannot hear us, nor, for the first time, see us," she said. "What a place and time for me to have the privacy I so need. But I wish I could see you. "

The boat pitched forward and down, then a dizzying yaw to the port side from which it did not right itself. It bore a huge load of sand, which shifted with the momentum of the vessel's tilt in the wind. Odd angles of decks above and below forced mostly uncomfortable changes in where people clung or huddled. The added ballast of sand caused the shallow bottom boat to ride lower in the water, though it continued even without sails to cut smartly through the turbulence of the waves.

In a particularly jarring swell, Adiva fell against Eldad whose restraining arm kept her from being thrown back to the deck when the boat righted itself. Before he could remove his arm, Adiva's hands had felt its wiry strength.

"Thank you, kind Danite," she said straightening her garments, including the veil over her face protecting her from the blowing sand.

They sat in the opaque darkness, not seeing or touching, so close, yet distant. Their words were muffled by the protective layers of cloth.

"There are things I wish to know about you, but do not wish to invade your privacy uninvited. Will you allow me to ask?" Adiva knew she was being forward, but the heightened danger removed some inhibitions. At this moment, she felt as if she could devour any morsel of himself he would reveal.

"Can you hear me over this wind?" Eldad leaned closer, then affecting the gravest of tones, asked, "Which of my darkest secrets does the Babylonian princess yearn to know?"

"You're making fun of me," she said lightly, "but you won't escape into humor."

"Alright," Eldad capitulated, "Where do you want me to be-gin?" He coughed and his voice cleared.

"Why are you so far from home?"

"Like many tribes, we of Dan have a long tradition that our young men undertake a journey as far as their endurance and cu-riosity will take them. A few leave and never return. Those who do train as soldiers to fight in tribal wars, and many more do not come back."

"Will this await you when you return?"

"No, as I am needed by the tribe for what knowledge of herbs and healing I learned from my family. And Saul's honored father taught me what little Arabic medicine he had learned in North Africa during my two years with him. My family is consulted about illnesses and injuries that befall our tribesmen."

"It must be hard to see so many sad things."

"So very hard at first, yes. But what bothers me even more is that I can do so little for many of them. Some are too broken, and others have illnesses that are foreign to our experience."

"There are hospitals, places of healing in many cities of Babylon, and in such places as Sura and Pumbedita, Jews and Christians are permitted in them. But their doctors are ordered to treat Muslims first, then infidels, then animals. The edict really says that."

"I have never heard of a hospital," admitted Eldad. "Tell me of them."

"There is the Great Bumaristan Hospital of Baghdad, in a spot selected by my father's doctor friend, al-Rhazi. To do so, my father says al-Rhazi went everywhere in the round city leaving raw meat in many locations. Checking these locations a few days later, there was a noticeable difference in spoilage, and he selected the place where the meat was least rancid. I am told he is a very great teacher, and a philosopher as well."

"Would that I could shed my ignorance with a teacher such as him," Eldad said wistfully.

All talk suddenly stopped as brutal blast of sand caused an explosive snap of the main mast which crushed its ponderous weight onto the sail covering the huddled men amidship.

Their terrorized screams were whipped away by the wind, but still heard by the huddled group below deck. Eldad stood unsteadily and shouted to the others, "We have to see what we can do! Follow my voice and reach out for me."

Adiva, struggled to her feet, but Eldad did not help her. "Stay here," he shouted.

Eldad untied the rope-like leather sash he wore about his waist and swung it gently around until Yosef caught the loose end.

Yosef already had hold of Saul, and Hillel followed independently in the blackness. He was the first of them to reach the level of the deck, where he could not escape the agonized cries of the crew trapped beneath the mast. Worsening it all, the mast rolled a foot or two back and forth with the port, then starboard with the sway of the ship. He could see nothing, but only hear the agony and the sickening crack of splintering bones enveloping the deck. Stooped over sharply to avoid the howling wind, the men shuffled as a mass of four as the awful sounds guided their steps to the fallen mast. Eldad moved to his right, colliding with a wall that was instead the mighty cedar of Lebanon carpenter. He pulled Eldad and the others toward him, stopping each man at a different section of the thickest part of the shattered mast. Before leaving his side, the carpenter looped a length of sturdy rope beneath the mast and tied it securely around. He guided all hands to grasp the upper loop of the rope.

He shouted, "Heave hard to starboard when you hear me say now."

"Now!", and each man strained at his rope.

The mast did not move. Abruptly, more moving but unseen bodies were struggling across the deck in the direction of the piteous screams. Now muscular seamens' arms hooked through the ropes and readied for a desperate effort to free their trapped comrades. At the last minute, a smaller form slipped beside Eldad, Yosef's hands grasping the rope next to his.

Again they lurched in a mighty effort and the dead weight mast rose a foot allowing the rescuers to swing the beast off the sail and men trapped beneath. Sobs of elation streamed from the bloody carnage under the palm frond sail.

Other crewmen pulled the injured and the dead from under the sail, but no one could see to render much more aid beyond freeing them. Crewmen who could moved from beneath the sand weighted sail. Others writhed on the blood slickened planking of the deck. Two lay very still, one in shock and the other dead.

Eldad dropped to his knees, then to all fours creeping forward in the swirling darkness. His left hand found a sandaled foot and he soon had its owner before him.

Practiced in caring for badly injured persons wounded in war,

Eldad fought off sickening memories, the stuff of his recurrent night-mares which flooded the young man. He methodically probed arms, legs, and trunk of the unconscious man. He could immediately tell the prostrate man's lower right leg jutted at an abnormal angle and it was most worrisome that he did not shriek when Eldad moved the ankle a little.

He now placed his hands on each side of the man's head, his left becoming immediately slick with gritty, iron smelling blood. Quickly sorting his priorities, he shouted for someone to come to his side. Adiva had been just behind him but until he bellowed for help she had lost him.

"I am here. What can I do?"

Eldad turned and grasped her outer garment, tearing a strip of cloth from the hem. Feeling more carefully at the right side of the man's head, he soon found the bleeding point, a jagged wound almost at the crown. He moved the torn cloth between his fingers and the steadily pumping laceration.

"Firm steady pressure, press here. Don't let up. Make folds of the fabric and press beneath my fingers."

Adiva did so, but was beginning to feel nauseated from the sickening stickiness of this man's head and the deck under him. She was thankful there was no light to see this, but her mind's eye correctly visualized the scene, added to by the moans of men who could move on their own. No one could see what help they needed.

Eldad turned his attention to the man lying next to the first, beginning with a search for a pulse on the side of his neck. Even this gentle pressure caused the man's head to loll flaccidly to one side. *Broken neck,* he concluded, and examined the body no further.

His hand found hers still pressing on the gash on the man's head.

"I suspect his lower leg is broken and I have to splint it, but I have nothing to use."

That instant the carpenter crawled up to them and cried, "Captain Mustafa, I cannot find him!" Since the mast fell, he had braved the biting wind to search the length of the deck in the blackness.

Adiva replied in Arabic, "There are two men here, but we cannot see who they are."

The bulky figure moved on his knees to her side and gingerly placed his huge hand on the victim's chest.

"He lives," the carpenter said hoarsely, as he moved his hand about the man's chest, stopping midline. "He wears a pendant inside his robe, and I know there is none other like it." He then choked out, "He is my Master, I his slave since childhood. I am lost without him."

The big man paused as a determined gust of wind and waves gave the boat a mighty gyration, slamming it onto the roiling surface of the Sea.

"And we are lost as well."

Though Eldad could not see the man nor understand his words, there was no mistaking his anguish.

He motioned to Adiva. "Tell him I need four pieces of wood, about two inches wide and two feet long. Maybe he has something. You've stopped the bleeding, but don't let up just yet."

Eldad turned his exploring hands to the captain's legs, first the left, which he hoped was undamaged. Wrapping his long hands wholly around Mustafa's upper thigh, he slid them down to the ankle without encountering unusual swelling or deformity. Even in the dark, though, Eldad could feel the emaciation, so evident in the captain's face.

The break at the midpoint of the lower left leg had not broken the skin, but he felt the crackling sensation from under the skin of both sides. *Two broken bones, more complicated,* he concluded.

More quickly than expected, the carpenter returned with four slats he had torn from the lid of a storage chest. It was well they were of uneven length, as two needed to be longer to position the ankle.

Eldad raised his voice over the pummeling storm, "Tell the carpenter what I say."

Adiva was struggling with the unfamiliar task of stopping blood flow and the gritty stickiness she could feel covering her hands. The lurching of the wind-tossed boat added to her rising queasiness. Sand, blood, cries of the wounded and darkness filled everything. In this agony, she felt reassured by the marked change in Eldad, who was now commanding in his manner.

"Carpenter, hear me," Eldad began. Then he said to her, "Step back after my hand replaces yours." Her hand had begun to tire, so she felt relieved when his long fingers slid beneath hers.

"Tell him to tear strips of cloth arms-length from your robe and give me the first of them." She translated and the carpenter slid his curved edge knife down a seam he had felt. In a moment he had dexterously slit five strips of the coarse cloth and handed them to Adiva. She slung one out in Eldad's direction and he caught it. "Hold this bandage on the wound while I tie the strip."

Contact between them was unavoidable. She felt her much smaller form enveloped by him, though the actual touch was brief and incidental. He worked quickly to secure the bandage, then straightened to his full height, stepping around Adiva and the carpenter, to kneel beside the unconscious captain Mustafa.

He touched the captain's face, then the neck, before saying in a low, but urgent voice, "We have to work fast."

He leaned toward the young woman and said, "Cradle captain in your arms. Hold his arms, in case he arouses from the pain of our splinting."

She moved to the captain's head, reaching gently under him to draw the frail figure to her. Her hands wrapped securely on his upper arms, she said, "Yes!"

Eldad again felt Mustafa's damaged leg, noting more swelling at the break. "Hold this," he told the carpenter, whose massive hands he guided to wooden slats positioned above the angular break.

"Now this is a hard thing. We have to hurt Captain Mustafa to help him." He tied the first of the four remaining strips in a weave around the carpenter's hands. "Stay where you are." Eldad moved his hands to the misaligned lower leg, which had left the foot turned outward. *Do it now! Pull down a little, straighten, brace, now!*

The leg straightened with ease, but as Eldad was tightening the braces below the break, the captain was suddenly awake, screeching in pain.

Though the bracing was finished, the pain of the break itself now overwhelmed the confused Mustafa. When the boat rocked in a sizeable wave, he again cried out but mercifully fainted. Through it, Adiva held him gently. He had thrashed, but not strongly enough to break her firm hold. Now he was limp, a man-sized doll, she thought. Then, *is he dead?* But he was less cold and damp than when she had first touched him.

Released from holding the braces, the carpenter said, "I am moving my beloved captain below deck, out of this hell." With a delicate scoop of one brawny arm, he lifted his master from Adiva's supporting torso. Finding his way in darkness, he soon found the stairs to below deck and the small protection of the captain's cabin.

5

In the murky, wind-whipped darkness, a rogue wave sent the Red Sea water over the deck with such lateral force that it knocked down anyone standing. The broken mast whipped an ark across the deck, then back again in the undertow. No one could see who cried out in agony, but only once, then all that could be heard was the wailing wind of the sandstorm.

Eldad reached for Adiva, but the space around him was empty. Panic seized him for the first time since the storm began. *Did this precious woman get swept overboard?*

The wind dipped for a moment, and he thought he heard Adiva laugh. He cried out, "Where are you?" but then the storm raged again, drowning any response. He thought of Saul, Hillel, and Yosef, who were below deck with the captain and his carpenter when the deluge struck. He crawled across the deck toward where he thought he'd heard Adiva's voice.

He could feel the uncommon speed with which the boat was being driven before the gales of sand. At times, the vessel seemed to jump forward, charging on a battlefield of waves. Debris from the ship mixed with seaweed and sand littered his path along the edge of the deck. With the railing on his right, he crept forward as far mid-ship as he thought would be the opening to below and found it with an outstretched foot. In an instant, his foot was seized by hands from below.

"These long feet...I know them!" exclaimed a loud male voice, whose croak Eldad recognized as Saul's. Eldad was also relieved to hear Yosef and Hillel, both complaining bitterly about the miserable soup inundating below. Now they were all covered with

sand, drenched with seawater, and beginning to get thirsty from
its salinity. Hanging his head over the edge of the opening to be
heard, though they could not see one another, Eldad asked urgently,
"What of Captain Mustafa or his man?"

"The water, still deep, can't see," the Asherite moaned.

Just then, a primal cry of distress was unmistakable from the
aft section of below, the cabins. The water was waist high and
sloshed back and forth with the rocking of the boat. Yosef lunged
toward the captain's door, and though the knob turned, he could
not budge it, as though sealed from the inside. The teak woodwork
of the cabin was so tight as to hold water in.

"Help me!'" Yosef cried out and, in an instant, the bulky
Asherite wedged in next to him. Together they gave a mighty heave
and the door cracked off its upper hinges, falling inward over some
obstruction, and unstopping a torrent of sea water trapped inside.

"I couldn't get out, couldn't get us out, oh, Allah be merciful,"
the loyal carpenter coughed, then vomited swallowed seawater.
"Oh, my master is drowned!" He carried the motionless form of the
captain toward the voices of Yosef and Saul. The lower deck rocked
precariously, causing waves of the yard of water the ship now held.
Yosef tried to support the bigger man carrying the captain, until he
realized the carpenter was carrying him as well.

The mainsail had been carried by the wave to the stairway and
now covered half the opening to below, an accidental, flat tent in a
storm. Eldad pulled dry blankets from the only dry storage cabinet,
another watertight achievement of the ship's carpenter.

He grasped Adiva's hand, causing her to startle momentarily,
then guided her to the bedding, saying, "Make a flat palate on the
stairs, under the sail."

"Bring the captain."

Eldad took Mustafa from trembling arms of the carpenter and
placed him gently on the palate. He didn't like the way the body
felt, nor that he had begun to think of it as the body.

In the two years he attended to the war wounds of the tribes
of Dan and Asher, he'd learned not to let an initial bleak appearance

of a wounded man lead one to give up. He parted the captain's soaking robes and placed his long fingers on the man's left lower chest, noting the ominous sign of the skin temperature being the same as the sloshing sea water.

He remembered that the cold skin from the first time his grandfather took him, age seven, to see and handle a warrior's dead body. But as he tried unsuccessfully to feel the thrust of a heartbeat, he was rewarded with an unmistakable shiver. *Dead men don't shiver!*

"Quickly," he said to Yosef and Adiva, "strip off the wet clothes!"

Saul twittered a nervous laugh, "You mean us, too?"

Eldad didn't laugh, but thought a moment, "We have to warm his body and we have to do it now. He is too feeble to make his own warmth."

No one spoke, but there was an immediate rustle of garments in the dark and Eldad was handed a wet silk blouse and pants. Adiva brushed unseen past him and lay down next to the unconscious captain, enveloping his naked body with all parts of her own she could bring to bear. She scraped the inside of her thigh on the lower leg brace, but her own cold kept her from feeling much.

Eldad was immediately moved by her blessed act but try as he might to focus on the goodness of it, the thought—the flashing imaginary image—of her lying naked and vulnerable on the coarse blanket...she needs my warmth.

He threw the other dry blanket on them, and Adiva said, "My God he's cold."

With the storm's wind partially blocked, now he could hear her more rapid breathing as her body shook to raise its heat, both for her and the captain. When she shifted to a more comfortable position covering the captain's back, her foot brushed against Eldad's ankle, but she did not immediately move it. Rather, he felt the gentle push of her toes, and then gone. He thought he heard, though ever so quiet, the merry laugh that, moments ago, guided him to her.

6

Eldad didn't recognize the small but still audible scraping from the bow of their vessel, felt as a subtle vibration. It didn't matter. Within moments it was followed by the sudden hard and heavy sound of great boards cracking as the ship struck unyielding volcanic rocks. With each successive wave, the lances of stone sawed their way through the keel of the boat. Twice, the lurch of the impaled ship threw its passengers about before a final storm surge spindled the vessel on a spear of basalt rock.

Adiva, clinging protectively around the unresponsive captain, rolled as a bundle in the blanket down two steps, restrained before reaching the water by Eldad's legs, which were promptly swept from beneath him. He flailed into the three feet of sea wash but righted himself and hefted the bundle at his feet up to its original perch.

The other men below deck were in various states of bruised and water-soaked disarray. As always, either Yosef or Hillel bore the goat skin bag. At this moment it was the lanky Hillel who carried it, now half full of what would become more precious than the gold sewn into the bag's lining: drinkable water. But no one thought of that, only of surviving the hellish night. Who has sinned so as to deserve it? Must all pay for them?

And then, an hour before sunrise on the Red Sea, the monstrous wind from the earth turned inside out, died as suddenly as it had overwhelmed them many hours before. The air stayed choked with a fine white powder, the dust that had ridden on the sand. Soon a gentle breeze blew this away and those who could see beheld the breathtaking starburst of the Arabian night.

Every being aboard the ship was suddenly quiet and still, as though no one dared believe it was over. When they did begin moving, most were mechanical and aimless. The faint light from the quarter moon was too little to keep them from running into one another, as they struggled toward the fore deck, where the water caskets were secured. A sailor was kicked away when he tried to use the water to wash his eyes.

Men still down cried out for *ma,* or if Egyptian, begged for *maya,* for life giving water. It was becoming clear, even before blessed dawn broke, that many more were injured than just the captain and a few crew members.

The weary carpenter trudged up the steps to the upper deck to take charge of the crew in the captain's absence. He surveyed the litter strewn deck in the faint light and gathered the able-bodied men who moved quickly to his commands, as though this slave spoke for his master. Four men were down, including one of the Chinese whose head had been bandaged by Eldad during the storm. He sat up, then held his hands to his head and slumped back down.

It was still too dark to see the surroundings, but the carpenter knew they would have to be in the shallow shoals of some Red Sea volcanic island. The boat was still filling with water, though the waves no longer sloshed over the deck. Eldad reopened the dry ceiling cabinet and withdrew three bundles wrapped in oily skins. He handed two of these to Yosef and the third to Saul, who, predictably, grumbled at the new burden. Although the bundles were watertight, Eldad barked at his friend to keep theirs out of the sea water. "The writings, the herbs, the scroll, you know how precious these things are."

Then he quickly knelt beside the captain and turned to Adiva. "Please tell me you're alright. I believe the storm has ended."

Adiva stirred and coughed, sitting up in the dark, reflexively clutching the rough woolen blanket about her torso. With her free hand she tentatively touched her hair. "Nothing wrong a hot bath wouldn't cure. The captain is warmer, and I felt him move just before the wind stopped."

"You're probably bruised from the tumble; I hope not too badly."

"Give me my clothes," Adiva said.

"They're still wet," Eldad replied, handing her the delicate silk garments.

"They'll have to dry on me," she said as she slipped them on. Briefly they felt cold against her skin. Remarkably they were not gritty with sand, as she was, head to toe.

"Yosef," she shouted, "Give me my hijab. It's in the smaller bundle but wait till it's light."

Eldad pulled back the blanket covering Mustafa, and at that instant the captain let out a sustained moan. With tenderness, he touched his face and neck, lingering on the latter.

He wished it was light enough to see the captain's skin color. Instead, he could only feel the skin for its resilience and warmth. He pinched a tent of forearm skin between his fingers and noted its slow return to its original state. He now had no trouble feeling the wiry man's heartbeat, a flutter in an emaciated chest. The captain had still not spoken, but Eldad sensed from his agitation he was in great pain.

He turned to Hillel, now standing on a step below. "Ask the captain if he can speak,"

Hillel did so, and Mustafa managed to rasp. "Ma."

"Bring it, bring the bag," Eldad urged. Hillel knelt and cupped the captain's bony head in one hand, bringing the unstoppered goatskin to his parched lips.

"Drink deeply, brave captain," Hillel said.

At first the water only dribbled on the parched mouth, but in a moment, he was swallowing sips then a mouthful was choked down. His voice became clearer, "The pain in my leg...I want to die."

Hearing Hillel translate this, Eldad shook his head forcefully. "Do not speak of this. I have herbs to lessen your pain. Just drink the water from the Babylonian's wine bag."

But the captain wasn't really listening and his agonized words were becoming less intelligible, though no less expressive. Once more he repeated his plea for death to escape this torture.

Eldad had ascended to the main deck, where the carpenter had directed the injured be assembled on the sprawling mainsail.

As if it were the first morning of creation, the seemingly endless darkness of the night was slowly dissolving as the morning sun fanned out on the golden horizon. Eldad shook what sand he could from himself and began examining the four additional casualties of the wrathful storm. He had not allowed himself to dwell on the fact that their boat had been pitched violently onto a spike of stone which had ripped open the keel. The ship was being racked back and forth over jagged volcanic rocks with the impaling stone acting as a pivot.

At last, the crew and passengers could see one another, and Eldad established that none of the downed crew was as bad off as the captain. One had a misshapen shoulder but no break that Eldad could feel. He lay head to foot with the man and grasped his arm with both hands at the wrist. Slipping off his sandal, he gently placed his foot in the man's arm pit and pulled on the arm quick and hard. An audible pop and eruption of agony were quickly followed by an involuntary kick at the healer's head. But an instant later, an exuberant cry of relief, as the deformity and pain were gone.

Saltwater inhalation and ingestion were the two remaining problems. Both were coughing and vomiting periodically. There was little he could do for near drowning, but he said to the carpenter, "The water, give them as much as they will drink."

Adiva translated, and the man's already grim expression darkened noticeably. "The men," he said, "after the storm, almost all the water, they drank, but no one had enough."

Saul, at the front of the boat kicking empty barrels was the first to cry out at the vista unfolding on their starboard side. The fog of dust had settled, and there, rising six hundred feet above the Red Sea was the three-mile-long conical island of Jubal Zubair. Seeing this, Eldad couldn't help but wonder. Was it their salvation or their doom?

7

Now in full sunshine, the windward coast of the island stretched its ribbon of powder white sand along the base of forbidding black rock faces hundreds of feet high. Near the summit of this cone shaped island, a dense forest of flat-top Acacia trees rimmed the curving ridgeline. Where the beach met the mountain, isolated patches of vegetation hugged the vertical rocks.

The boat moved more predictably in the declining waves, giving those on board their first chance to see what may await them.

Standing on the deck, the sand-choked crew and passengers could tell from its sideways tilt that their vessel was sinking or was going to do so as far as the stone spike would allow. It marooned them hundreds of yards from where the waves crashed onto the pristine beach.

The carpenter left his master's side and emerged on deck, squared his shoulders, and addressed the crew with as much control as he could command,

"Break out the rowboat. You, Ibrihim, tell the others what to do. You two," he said jerking the collars of a pair beside him, "unlash the water barrels and tie the tools I give you to them with long ropes." Others he ordered below to salvage what supplies they could and tie them to the barrels as well.

"Don't leave this boat without your weapons," he added, knowing that many in the crew had small daggers in their possessions and would certainly use them against the injured captain and him if things went badly. In anger they would have to blame someone. It was human nature.

The skiff had been freed of its moorings on the aft deck and was being muscled by six men toward an opening of the ship's railing. The carpenter attached four ropes to metal hooks, two at each end.

He spoke first to his five passengers. "The rowboat will hold only three and the captain is going to be one of these. He paused to make sure they understood. "You," he swept his giant hand in their direction, "decide which one of you joins him and the oarsman for the first try."

They looked at one another. Each had unique assets to offer the situation. Adiva, and, curiously, Saul were the strongest swimmers, should the boat capsize in the surf. When Yosef started to comment on his cousin's ability in the water, Adiva cut him off. "Who is best able to care for the captain is who shall go first, and that is our Danite." No one questioned her judgment.

Hillel moved toward Eldad "Take the water bag, in case, oh, please God, you find some. Here's another little bag with some wine in it. Fill it too."

Eldad, nodded, shouldered the bundle held by Saul, and looked expectantly at the carpenter. Adiva stepped forward and placed her small hand on Eldad's inner forearm and squeezed a little, then withdrew it with a sigh.

Eldad nodded and managed a slight smile. He sensed that she had something to say to him but could not. If they only had privacy. Did she feel, like him, that any moment now could be their last.

Adiva said nothing, but held her gaze steadily, her eyes saying more than words.

The carpenter appeared from below with a bitterly complaining, but more alert captain Mustafa slung over his shoulder. He quickly lay his master in the skiff being eased down the tilted keel by eight men holding four ropes. They had thrown a rope ladder from the deck to the water, and a stout Arab sailor named Sa'id had climbed down it, hopping nimbly aboard as the little boat touched the water.

"Now you, quickly." The carpenter said pointing to Eldad who immediately started down the unsteady rope ladder, made more so by the continuing waves. He got one leg into the rowboat when a swell threw him off balance but he pulled himself back up the

ladder before he could be crushed by the unruly boat whose lurching the attached ropes could not control. The tall African dropped
into the skiff before the next wave could hit and immediately the
oarsman began to row away from the sinking mother ship. Eldad
positioned himself beside the captain who lay miserably across the
stern. It was then it dawned on him that neither man in the boat
spoke Hebrew, and he, no Arabic.

Unable to communicate, Eldad looked back at the ship for
awhile, seeing the sailors throwing the water barrels overboard
where they floated high in the water, tethered by ropes to the sadly
listing ship.

He looked with wonder into the thirty feet or so of startlingly
clear water, revealing for him a never-before-seen riot of color and
shape all the way down to the sandy sea floor. Violet fans waved in
the deepest currents and otherworldly shapes of other corals painted the landscape shades of red, purple, and exuberant chartreuse.
Even more unbelievable were the large fish, some multicolored and
swimming alone, while others swirled in silvery schools, indifferent
to the intrusion of the boat.

Sa'id rowed strongly in the choppy waters, but progress was
slow and the current unpredictable. In an hour, the oarsman was
spent, but their rowboat had reached the point off the beach where
the waves began to break on the island's shore. Now the small boat
began to ride the larger waves ever closer, into the roiling surf,
past a fantastic array of corals reaching for the light just below, but
sometimes breaking the surface of the churning water. Closer in, the
oarsman and Eldad could see an outcropping of green mangroves,
which grew spindly green fingers out of the salt water of the sea.
The murkiness of the water around the low, thick mangroves sheltered a perfusion of sea life, hiding, or lurking, within.

At last, the skiff surged to a halt on a sand bar, a few yards
short of the waterline. Re-energized, Sa'id jumped into the shallow
surf with a rope and threw another to Eldad, whom he motioned to
jump in with him. The undertow caught both men thigh-deep but
they braced against it, then pulled hard to beach the boat. This done,

the Arab sailor crumpled to his knees in the powdery white sand.

Less exhausted, Eldad was able to lift the captain from the boat, now secure upon the sand. Mustafa had lost some of the earlier protest and Eldad worried about the return of stupor. He carried the man to the shade of a clump of acacia trees growing improbably in a small cluster at the face of massive columns of rock. He uncorked the goatskin bag and poured some of the remaining water on the captain's open lips. Mustafa awoke a little and drank a mouthful without much spillage.

Eldad was dreadfully thirsty and tired. The desire to drink the rest of the water nearly overwhelmed his discipline, the deeply ingrained commitment that the sick ones are first to have all things.

He gave the captain another drink, but the man's pain was again becoming unbearable. He clutched at Eldad's robe, pleading for relief.

Eldad spoke in Hebrew, accompanied by whatever gestures conveyed that he was going to make something for the captain to drink, and pointed to his leg with soothing movements. The captain retorted with hand signals which could only be interpreted as *hurry up!*

Eldad began to unroll the carefully wrapped bundle he'd brought ashore. He was looking for a hand sized leather bag. His grandfather had burned a curious design into the leather but did not know its meaning. Sav guessed it may have been in some long dead language, and for reasons he was always vague about, as he was with many of his dream journeys to long ago and far away, he thought it was the name of our most ancient ancestor whose name was written down in the time of Abraham.

The symbol-covered bag tumbled out of the first layer of the bundle and Eldad worked the strings loose and emptied the black, grey brick into his hand. Withdrawing a small cup from his robe. he poured wine from the smaller goatskin bag. The two inch by six inch brick of opium was of unknown potency to Eldad. Saul had purchased it in Aden, "at a bargain price," Saul assured his friend.

Eldad pinched off a walnut sized corner of the sticky

opium cake. He worried how much is too much, how much too little. The captain was frail, but his suffering was great. He shrugged and dropped the whole lump into the cup, noting it began to dissolve in the strong red wine immediately.

He returned to the captain's side and propped him up with his left arm. Mustafa looked at him as he gestured with the cup to drink, but followed with an exaggerated grimace, warning Mustafa this was not the nectar of the gods.

Eldad held the cup to the Arab captain's lips and a tentative sip caused an involuntary gag. Eldad looked sympathetic, but firmly moved the cup back to the stricken man's lips. Mustafa blocked his mouth with a bony hand and gestured, emphatically, to his healer that *he* should drink his brew. Trapped, Eldad raised the cup and sipped. The acrid taste was just what real opium tasted like, so Eldad repeated the awful face and added more wine to the cup, as though its palatability would somehow improve. Mustafa smiled grimly and motioned for the cup, this time taking a deep mouthful of the red grey liquid. Eldad sat down beside him to wait for him to be more comfortable. He could as easy die, Eldad thought as he watched his charge intently.

Sa'id stirred from his exhaustion and was looking anxiously at the skiff, now at low tide riding high above the water. Too high to easily get it back into the water or would be soon.

Eldad picked up the large goat skin, made drinking motions for Sa'id and pointed to the south of the curving shore. Both men were encrusted in salt and sand and depleted by the lack of fresh water. The Arab sailor needed no explanation as to what he was seeking.

After a last look at the captain, who was beginning to nod and be less agitated, Eldad trudged wearily off to the north of their landing spot. His life, and everyone else's depended on what he found.

8

A narrow strip of mangrove forest jutting out into the water blocked Adiva's line of sight from the sinking ship to the spot where the small rowboat had run up on the sand. The atmosphere on deck was thick with urgency. The vessel listing to its starboard side was only being held up from the sea floor by the impaling basalt rock spear in its innards. The option of staying with the boat, and waiting for the rowboat to return was becoming less viable by the minute.

The obvious alternative was to swim the hundreds of yards to shore. Hillel had an idea. They could use the floating water barrels bobbing off the stern for buoyancy as they tried to swim to shore through the rough costal waters.

On the elevated poop deck lay four of the five injured men. The Chinese sailor, his bandaged head still oozing from the laceration, made his way unsteadily around the ship's railing. In halting Arabic, he said to Adiva, "I know what you and the black one did for me. I am sorry...."

"Sorry for what?" Adiva replied.

"I told the pirates you and your kin carried away something from the banker's home. But they already knew from someone who works inside the Netira household." He bowed his bloodied head and said with bitter irony, "*They* didn't pay me. *You* saved me."

Adiva smiled at the repentant sailor, again impressed with the maddening mixture of conflicting opposites residing in every being, the darkness and the light. Neither would have any meaning without the other, as with all other opposite pairs in nature, even life and death.

The carpenter excused himself and entered the captain's cabin. It was filled with over four feet of water as was everywhere below deck. He carried a hooked iron bar with which he began to rip at the exquisite wood paneling covering the walls floor to ceiling. The waterlogged sheets came away from the walls easily and they floated atop the swill with surprising buoyancy. A dozen of these he gathered under his ponderous arm, and began to exit the cabin, but something gave him pause. Above the captain's expansive desk, scrolled up maps filled cubby holes. Each map had been secured by the captain in one of three heavy leather cylinders, each with water-tight caps of brass. He scooped them by their straps over his free shoulder and made his way to the partially submerged stairs. "Ibrahim!" he bellowed.

A lanky Arab, captain Mustafa's other slave, appeared almost immediately at the top of the stairs. "Yes Kasim."

Motioning, Kasim tossed the leather cylinders which Ibrahim caught with ease. Kassim followed him, carrying the 3x4 wood planks onto the deck. With an auger, he gouged holes at the ends of each plank and told the men to thread ropes attaching the dozen thin sheets to each other.

"Tie them to the barrels," Ibrahim ordered three crewmen. They hauled in two barrels and tied an end of the train to each. After securing a tether line, they threw the whole assembly back into the calming sea. The planks were buoyant and some of the crew, the older ones, were beginning to understand Kasim's concept, and none of them liked it a bit.

Kasim next approached Adiva and motioned her to a private conversation.

"I need you to handle this with your brother, cousin and Saul." he said, tilting his head toward her companions, "even if the boat *does* come back…"

"What do you mean? You think it won't?" Adiva couldn't hide the alarm in her voice.

"We hope, but we must plan. The rowboat can transport only a few and two trips would be needed for the injured alone."

"So, what shall we do, Kasim?"

"We must act before nightfall." He looked up at the sun directly overhead. "No, we go in no more than two hours."

"You're expecting us to swim these treacherous waters to the shore?"

No," Kasim smirked, not even concealing his contempt. "Some of these so-called sailors can't swim. They were laborers out of work, able bodied and desperate. My captain hires them at lower wages,and they're worth nothing until they learn the riggings."

Adiva, now focused on the floating train of planks and barrels, said, "So we shall all cling to our Kasim's ark there and kick our way to shore?"

"Moving together is stronger and safer than swimming alone." He lowered his voice to a whisper. "Look over the side but say nothing."

Among the remarkable number of various-sized fish who gathered to peck at the boat's encrusted hull, another larger species glided indifferently, its black dorsal and caudal fin tips visible in twenty feet of sparkling water.

"You see? No say," Kasim rasped. Of course, he was right, but wouldn't the men see for themselves? She knew not to tell the stout Asherite, as she suspected he would rather sink with the ship than swim with the sharks. Adiva wished the water weren't so clear. She needed her brother Hillel whose journeys in the Persian Gulf had taught him the dangers of the waters. She called her brother away from an increasingly agitated Saul.

"He's just nervous because he thinks he needs to know everything that's going on and he doesn't like the look the carpenter's face. Or yours"

Adiva nodded. "We're going to have to swim to shore. I need you to tell me how dangerous our swimming in these waters is."

"You mean currents and the surf?" Hillel asked.

"Look over the side."

Walking up the 30-degree angle of the tilting deck, he peered overboard. Then, unexpectedly, he smiled broadly at his older sister.

"What is to smile about, brother." Adiva said with irritation.

"There are three of them now, yes, I see. I know them from the shores of the Gulf where they're called reef sharks, but these are bigger. The black tips are the same, though."

"Bigger?"

"They don't attack people." Hillel quickly declared, with conviction he likely did not feel. At the same time, he left unsaid the lesson of the old Indian Ocean sailor: Where you see one kind, others will follow.

An osprey, with black masked eyes appearing to stream fiercely to the back of its head, swooped down parallel to the water, seizing a large blue-grey fish in its raptor claws and soaring away on unseen currents. Adiva reflected that every creature is both predator and prey, not a comforting thought with the unknown perils beneath the waves. But even if the ship sank no further, they could not stay aboard. A fierce thirst was now beginning to sap their energy and would soon erode their sanity as well. Adding to the crew's and passenger's raggedness was the fact that no one had slept since the night before the assault of the 12-hour sandstorm. And now, a distant swim in unpredictable waters.

Yosef, carrying two bundles wrapped in watertight skins, approached Adiva and Hillel, handing one to his male cousin. "This has the, uh, things you wanted," he said to Adiva.

Each bundle had two long straps, one for around the waist and the other, over the shoulder. Yosef and Hillel attached the bundles to themselves, tightening the straps at their brass buckles. Saul ambled up to the group with a large cloth bag in hand.

"No, absolutely not!" exclaimed Hillel. "When the bag gets waterlogged, it will sink you."

The Asherite scowled, his jowls becoming even more pronounced. He began rummaging through the hemp bag before concluding he didn't need, really need, any of it. Eldad had taken their treasured objects with him. He selected three items of light weight clothing and rolled them into a tight bundle, with a questioning look at Hillel, who rolled his eyes but said alright.

Saul said to the three of them, "Come translate for me." He moved to Kasim's side and looked up at the head taller man. "I am a strong swimmer. I know what we must do, and I can swim at front." Kasim looked dubious but grunted his assent.

"Do not pull the group along, you will tire and be useless. *Guide,* don't pull," the carpenter admonished. Then he took Saul by the arm to an open spot in the railing and slung him into the water. When he bobbed up and looked up expectantly, Kasim threw him the lead rope, which the Asherite tied about his waist. Now connected by ten feet of rope to the lead water barrel, he began slow strokes in the water, aiming for the mangrove outcrop, the island's outermost fringe. Soon he had unfolded the long train of three barrels and, divided between them, the dozen buoyant rubber wood panels.

The sailors were already starting to jump in on their own, when Kasim yelled, "Everybody in! Grab somewhere and kick. Follow the fat one." He then stood aside and lowered his eyes, as Adiva removed her outer robe and the head covering and jumped feet first into the salty water whose temperature was not warm enough to enjoy, but easy enough to bear, especially if swimming actively. Her rose silk clothes clung to her body and the clear water hid nothing, and her thought was *when I am dead, who will care?*

A few sailors, Arabs mostly, but one Chinese, held back, cowering on the deck with the injured sailors. Each complained loudly and bitterly with some variation of *can't swim!*

Ibrihim was not yet in the water, and the carpenter told him, "Go hold hands with these men, while I shove them the hell off the side. Drag them till they have the boards or barrels." One of the injured men arose and grasped the hand of the Chinese laborer pulling him over the railing into the sea. Kasim told the remaining three to join hands with Ibrahim who would guide them to the floats. Clinging to one another, they descended the stairs and jumped together with Ibrahim. It is well they plunged then, as the steady kick of the able-bodied sailors was already pulling the watery caravan away from the wreckage that had been their home. Had

they the time or comfort, they may have indulged in some soothing nostalgia, so great was their need to humanize what they were
dependent upon. For Kasim, now was time to shed illusions. After
telling the only fully conscious of the injured men the skiff would
be back for them, he dove headfirst after the departing sea snake of
human beings, all paddling like otters and all watched by a single
pair of cold dead eyes swimming thirty feet below.

9

The wiry young African had the sensation of dragging himself through the sand along the base of the almost vertical mountain of volcanic stone. The beach kept curving and the sheer rock faces hid the longer view. Eldad realized he'd have to seek higher ground but so far had seen no crevasses for footholds in the forbidding black stone face of Jabel Zubair Island.

Wearily following the curving beach, Adiva appeared before him. Struck by the clarity of her image, he stopped walking to feel the pleasurable wave breaking through his hunger and urgent thirst. He closed his eyes to hold on, but he couldn't halt the abrupt intrusions of new visions. Now Adiva and the others lay parched and desiccated, dying for lack of water to drink.

He must continue his desperate search for water.

An unusually long semicircle of beach abruptly ended several hundred yards away where the volcano had broken out of its circle and reclaimed the sea. It was as far as he could explore without swimming around the treacherous shoals where the rock erupted from the roiling water.

A curious shock of green and brown broke the otherwise monotonous beachhead near the barrier of stone. The acres of green grew into the water, like the smaller mangrove forest near where they had washed ashore. Its fingers grew along the beach, met by a dense growth of the very different looking acacia trees with their spindly leaves and expansive flat crowns. As he drew closer, he recognized what trees these were and the phrase from the sacred texts came to him: *Make an ark and a table of acacia wood.*

A few acacias looked higher than the others, suggesting the

possibility of steps in the rocks where the trees were growing. It spurred the exhausted Eldad toward the forest.

The brown he had seen at a distance became flecked with white, brown, and grey wings in frantic flutter on the sheer-looking face of the 400 foot mountainside. The closer he got, the greater his astonishment that there were thousands of these sea birds, of a dozen or more species, taking off and landing on unseen ledges and fractures of lava rock. The noise of the surf no longer drowned out their raucous territorial screeches. Tall herons, some grey and others white, shuffled their feet through the water's edge, picking off creatures they stirred up in the sand. Three took off together and landed atop the stubby mangrove trees where nests full of open beaks awaited their parent's regurgitated offering of fish.

Eldad entered the outer edges of the acre-sized acacia forest extending finger like from the base of the rock mountain. He immediately saw that the trees formed an odd canopy beneath the flat-topped trees, as though lower branches had been methodically pruned from below to a height of 15 feet. The sun dappled the grey, rock-studded soil beneath the trees and the cooler air was temporarily soothing, but thirst was becoming unbearable. Where the tree branches parted, he spied gulls and masked obies swooping toward the rock face. This fortress-like wall proved to be more irregular up close than it had appeared from a distance. Except for a smoother ten-foot base, the whole surface, up to its heights, was a jumble of fissures, some with deep ravines, others sprouting hardy shrubs, and all an aviary of the Red Sea. Osprey, white-chested terns, and a host of warblers all joined together in a chorus to resent his intrusion.

The young man paused to study the terrain above the base, then, after securing the goat skin bags to his lower back, he jumped to the lowest ledge and, clinging to the uncertain sharp outcrop, he raised first his chin, then an elbow to boost onto the nearly level shelf. Still lying face down, he allowed himself a sigh of relief.

Too soon, it turned out. When he turned over on the narrow precipice, he was greeted by the screech and claws of a Barbary falcon whose nest his feet were mangling. He leapt to his feet and batted at the assaultive bird, whose two-inch claws barely missed closing on Eldad's forearm. The menacing creature dove again at his head with a loud "rek, rek. rek!" but Eldad ducked and scrambled to a broader ledge four feet higher. The hawk simply alighted on its nest, and began fussing with a corner, having nudged her eggs and found them unharmed.

Hurrying in his climb up the craggy mountain face, and half-way to the crest, he was halted by a weariness he'd never known before. He no longer thought about himself, the aching muscles, or his burning thirst. Now, it was only his friends, and yes, he realized, his loved one that mattered. He pressed on.

Though his path was jagged, the mountain grudgingly gave way to the more disciplined pace of Eldad's climb to the highest elevation of this end of the mountainous island. Until he was near the top, outcroppings of rocks and the necessity of absolute concentration on footholds, most of which had bird nests with thoroughly agitated occupants. Both his hands and sandal-clad feet were smeared with egg yolk and whatever else he did not wish to imagine.

Abruptly the landscape changed from fractured and fissured to the puffy smoothness of not-too-distant lava flows. At first, he thought nothing grew upon it, but then he could see improbable shoots of green and waxy grey in the smooth sheet's imperfections. Turning toward the Red Sea, he could follow the breathtaking white sand beach and its startling companion coral reefs and lagoons till the higher volcanic crater hid the northern end of this mysterious island.

Exhilaration mingled with desperation as he lengthened his stride and moved more quickly over the alien landscape. Even the multiplicity of sea birds had forsaken this barren quarter mile rising to the mountain's southern rim. But at a distance, he could see the summit crowned by a vigorous growth of flat-topped trees which seemed to well up from the inner face of the higher northern rim of the crater. From there, which he realized was nearly as far back on the island as he started, he hoped he could see the whole of it.

Now that the treeless southern flank of the volcanic crater

was only 100 yards distant and a few feet higher, Eldad detected a change in the feeling of the air, not just its cooler temperature but some indefinable freshness, and the young man wondered if his lack of water had finally begun to show him what was not there, a desert mirage of the senses.

He could not know that in the next few moments he would save the lives of everyone washed ashore.

10

At first, even the mass action of the kicking legs of many crewmen and the straining arms of the lead swimmers failed to close the distance to the shore. Two of the injured were dead weight and the Chinese former spy had lost his head bandage in the plunge off the boat. Rivulets of blood-tinged sea water ran down his face, into his clothes and the surrounding waves.

The caravan of floating broad boards and tethered empty water kegs struggled against a strange lateral current which tended to keep them moving parallel to but not toward the shore. Saul, realizing this, shouted to Adiva, "We have to move them at much more of an angle, toward the outer fringes of the mangroves." He could speak no more, trying to catch his breath from the already exhausting swim.

Adiva nodded, "We don't seem to be moving together, however the currents drag us."

She thought for a moment. "Yosef, Hillel, get out front with Saul. Hook the rope you have to the one around his waist, so you're all pulling together."

Satisfied she was understood, she swam back to where the carpenter Kasim held a thick cord attached to the hemp rope spine running front to back of the water train. "The men are listless, some just floating. You see?"

Kasim nodded and spat, "I'm going to tell them something, these gentlemen of the sea, that will surely cause them to kick for their lives."

Adiva shifted uneasily in the salty water. "Which is?"

"The Chinaman's blood is in the water. Others' too! If we attract sharks, they will feed in a frenzy on everything in the water, even each other. Some come only at night and we are soon out of daylight." He squinted up at the sun, estimating it was about four o'clock.

To four or five at a time, Kasim spoke to his crew in a low, rather matter-of-fact voice. He did not change his tone even when some shrieked their alarm. By the time the last was told, all were agitated and disorganized.

"Kick steadily, use a free arm to add push. We can do this. Look where I point…give me all you have, and we'll get us to the safety of the mangrove forest. Now!"

Slowly, then with greater force, the ponderous mass of humans and wood began to defy nature's insistence that whatever was afloat be carried out to sea. Moving against this was cumulatively exhausting, more immediately so for the novice seamen who knew nothing of pacing themselves. Their panicked thrashing added only minimally to the necessary crosscut of deep-water resistance.

When the water stilled between waves, the landscape of the sea's sandy bottom would have been breathtaking, had they breath to take. Hillel could not help but be dazzled by the exuberant explosions of corals, pink, green, purple, and yellow, many waving like a cheering multitude beneath them. He caught a glimpse of an extraordinary size lobster, whose white flecked spines were accented by ebony legs, the tops of which were also painted their length in stripes of white.

But no time now to dwell on what might be a tasty meal, he told himself, when *he* might be the tasty meal.

The currents that waved the clamoring corals were no impediment to a cruising 6 foot reef shark, which was more curious than hungry. When he again paused to peer below, the black tipped shark was gone, but schools of fish from two inches to two feet in length grazed in and out of a multicolored paradise.

The line between them and the outer mangroves was straightening from its previous bow shape, forced by the outgoing tide. Now, having desperately fought their way through the roughest coastal waters, less than a hundred yards separated them from the salvation of dry land. Adiva told herself to temper her usual optimism. The rowboat had not returned. What had happened? Every person was badly worn down by the prolonged sprint through the strong channel of water flowing seaward. The younger men would recover faster than the seasoned crewmen, but would they have the will? Survival so depends on who can will themselves to keep pushing when there seems nothing left.

They were still at the edge of the riptide when Adiva swam entirely around the assemblage, stopping to speak to several of the men, both young and old. Some smiled and nodded with obviously well meaning, but feigned enthusiasm. A few just thought she had a lovely face and relished being spoken to by this exotic and mysterious princess. She stopped, paddling before five of the crewmen, those who had to pass as able bodied. She spoke clearly in their native Arabic and made no effort to hide her refined dialect.

"Listen to me. I speak to you truly, with a truth as best I know it." A few grumbled grudging receptivity. "If we do not move quickly, we shall lose the light, and our direction this moonless night. The current is no guide. At this time, it is an enemy trying to swallow us as surely as Jonah's whale."

"Wait for the tide, wait for it to turn," pleaded one of little seaworthiness.

The older sailors scoffed. One brandished a scar on his leg made up of ghastly red and blue scars in the shape of large, puncturing teeth, and said, "The Portagee next to me in the water didn't have to worry about scars."

"Go, now! Swim like your life depends on it, as it surely does!" She raced with renewed vigor to the front of the column where her brother, cousin and new friend began to tug their arc the final yards, where the surf hammered the sand but danced with the mangrove forest.

11

Finally mounting the rim of the pillow-like lava rock, the Danite immediately turned east toward the sea, and was crestfallen as 300 feet of older mountain rose between him and the line of sight to the shore.

He brushed away flies now gathering in numbers near his hands and feet, and tried to shake off a light-headed feeling which was more menacing than the flies. He knew well the signs of water deprivation.

As he turned to the west, his rational mind rebelled at the sight he beheld, though he could smell this hallucination as well. Eldad fell upon his knees and wept tears his eyes could not produce, and he thanked God for his deliverance.

For, stretched out before him hundreds of yards to its outer rim, was a dazzling crater lake. Sunlight struck the surface of the crystal-clear rainwater in the deep caldera, reflecting a second sun to greet his not yet trusting eyes.

He began to talk to himself out loud, noting with some detachment yet another sign of what his family called desert delirium. It appeared to him that the surface of the water was 20 feet below the rim. He scanned for some way down to the water.

He could see nothing from his vantage point, but again he was led to watch the birds, as some nested on ledges above the water's edge. He made his way cautiously to the edge of the huge stone bowl's western face. He saw nothing trustworthy as footholds, but did circle far enough to find a second, slightly lower ledge. Assessing its narrow width, Eldad guessed he could manage to balance on a rock no wider than his foot was long.

What he hadn't noticed was that the rock outcropping he wished to step on, though 18 feet above the water, was wet. Flowing from unseen artesian wells was the crater lake's life and the lives of all others.

Eldad crawled spider-like on all fours to the outcrop five feet below. One foot came to rest securely on level stone, but his left foot stepped on the green, slimy surface of algae growing atop and beside the spring's flow. Eldad's sandaled foot slid out from under him, and, with nothing to grasp, he could only watch the rock face fly by before his eyes. His mind registered a fleeting image of a hidden opening to a cavern in the basalt stone.

Then the shock, the blessed pain of hitting the water, the real, non-hallucinated water, with a reassuring smack, a rebirth, this time *into* the fluid of life.

When he surfaced, he gasped for that first sweet breath of fresh air but resisted spitting out the excess water filling his mouth from the sudden immersion, as though it was still more precious than gold.

Laughing till he sputtered, Eldad examined the nearby rock face for a crevice high enough out of the water to hold his clothes and aid in what had to be his immediate effort to climb out. As he paddled along the stone face, attention highly focused on its surface irregularities, he rounded a jumble of craggy boulders to a sandy cove. A shaft of light through the otherwise impenetrable rock wall seemed to illuminate a pathway to the rim of the caldera.

Eldad blinked repeatedly and rubbed his eyes with now clean hands. For when his gaze moved from the water to the black spit of sand, he was face to face with a mother and child, both briefly and indifferently interrupting their long drink at the water's edge. Eldad was slack-jawed as two camels, caricatures of homeliness, then turned casually on massive, long legs and disappeared behind the largest of the waterside boulders.

Then he remembered hearing of sultans who hid assets on unoccupied islands, and of camels who could survive on island trees, like Jubel Zubair's abundant acacias.

Glad to be revived, he uncorked both goatskin bags, and

repeatedly rinsed each by filling and emptying it. He rinsed and untangled his medium length straight black hair, uncommon in tribes of pastoral West Africa.

Tempted though he was, he did not overdrink the sparkling water. Though it was an arduous and dangerous descent, he must get back to the beach. He knew he could waste precious time trying to find a shortcut down from the main mountain, but if he didn't, there were sure to be violent fights over the water he could carry. The captain and other wounded would be pushed aside, even murdered to get to the available water.

It was then he resolved to hide the bags before he reentered whatever gathering of survivors he found on return. He would direct them to the water, and when they were off, the injured would drink. But then, he desperately wished he could soothe Adiva's chapped lips, and bathe the lovely face till it again radiated its inner beauty. But Captain Mustafa would surely die if he wasn't already dead, Eldad thought.

He followed the many camel tracks through a disquieting chasm where 20 foot walls closed in, then opened then closed again, like beads on a string, but always a wide enough passage for an adult camel to squeeze through. Each wider space rose a few feet above the last and soon Eldad boosted his tall frame to the caldera's lip. The water bags were burdensome and awkward. He again recalled being told of the inner linings of these bags, and the weight of them suggested many gold coins and other such treasures. He smiled at the grim irony of how worthless they were if the bags were empty of water.

The summit of the old volcano, whose paroxysms had birthed this newest land on earth, was several hundred feet above smooth basalt rock expanse where he stood. The contours of this one-time river of lava were broken looking above the level of the crater lake.

Eldad struggled with the realization that he must continue climbing up to find a way down. An hour left of sunlight, maybe two, he reckoned as he navigated through and over the bolder-strewn south mountain face. Carrying the life-giving water was quickly tiring him and he knew it would take more than water to restore him.

He came upon a well-worn trail only a few yards from the windswept plateau of the mountain top. He could see at least four trails across this thousand-yard expanse and chose the path to the northwest rim. Though curious about what lay to the east, down that face of the dominating mountain, he had no time to explore.

The wind blew strongly from the east with nothing to impede it on this rocky mountain mesa. Where rocks were large enough to protect from the wind, prickly brush claimed a corner here, a crevice there.

Eldad ran the last few yards to the high northern rim of the volcanic mountain, greeted by a stronger wind from the updraft on the sheer north face. Here he found a vantage point from which the whole of the north shore crescent beach appeared, a quarter mile down the mountain side. He saw first the rowboat, where he and Sa-id had beached it, tiny against the vastness of the Red Sea.

Next, he saw the acre of mangroves, partitioning one long stretch of beach from a shorter stub where he had left the captain beneath the canopy of acacias.

Then something that should have been obvious dawned on him. Unlike mangrove trees, acacia grow only where there is a supply of fresh water. He remembered the fall into the caldera, slipping on spring fed algae, and wondered about yet unseen springs on beach side of the mountain.

His attention was suddenly drawn to a long curve of what looked at this distance to be a trail of debris a hundred yards out. Squinting at this apparition, he could make out human forms on the inner edge of the rough semi circle. He felt flooded with a joyous, hopeful feeling.

Then his eyes fell upon a terrifying sight, a vision of impending hell. At the same distance as the flotilla was from the shore, he could see two, then three, triangular fins knifing through the water toward its straggling tail end.

In spite of demoralizing helplessness, he leapt and bellowed and waved, but the brisk and steady wind smothered his cries, and he immediately doubted they could see him. He couldn't help but realize then, that even if they could see and hear him, it would hardly matter. He hoped his prayer to a most merciful God *would*.

He knew he must find a way, no matter how treacherous, down this mountain of unforgiving stone.

12

Their eyes burned unceasingly from the salty Red Sea water and their skins were prunes stewed in brine. Saul, who with his weight might struggle with distance walking on land, was freed of moving his bulk and could concentrate his remaining strength on the final hundred yards to the mangroves. He had already surprised Adiva and her men with his stamina. At the same time, his usual complain-about-everything manner was gone, replaced by a surprisingly strong and determined young man. Necessity had transformed him.

Saul flipped himself on his back and said to Yosef and Hillel, "You guide us, don't take your eyes off the tree line in the water."

Using backstrokes, Saul continued to pull hard, and could now see how the remainder of the caravan was moving. Two of the water barrels were riding lower in the water, weighted down by bags of supplies, tools and clinging crew. Saul could see at least three men with no swimming skills, wide-eyed with fear and moving ineffectually with the last barrel in the train caught in the riptide flowing out to sea.

Adiva was panting and could barely rasp out her words as she swam up to the men pulling the front rope. She managed, "Do you see what I see?"

"Yes, it's obvious, the back water keg." Saul motioned behind him. "Somebody has to pull back there."

"No! Look back, beyond the tail!" She fought for self control, and said more quietly, "We're being followed."

Hillel, Saul, and Yosef scanned the wavy landscape, where glimpses were swallowed by choppy coastal swells.

Suddenly Yosef, buoyed by a three-foot wave, saw the menacing triangles of death sliding relentlessly toward them. Hillel saw them too, and croaked out, "No black tips."

Only Adiva understood this meant these predators are not the curious reef sharks that had circled the disabled vessel. She swam to Kasim's side and spoke quietly to him, who nodded his consent.

Kasim's basso voice boomed over the water, "Stay together. There are unwelcome visitors and we must swim hard for the shore!" A few men cried out in alarm, but the caravan wearily gathered momentum in the direction of the wave tossed beach.

Adiva untied the exhausted Asherite from the front of the rope and led him to the trailing floating barrel still snagged by the out-flowing riptide. He did not speak, as though no strength remained to do so. Adiva saw no use in goading further effort from him, so she simply threw him a rope attached to the barrel and vowed to pull them from harm's way with the last of what she could give. She knew that the sharks would be upon them within minutes and hoped the floating mass of wood and thrashing men would intimidate the merciless predators long enough for them to reach the shallows. They were still in 30 feet of water.

Also riding the trailing barrel was the Chinese sailor who had admitted his spying on the Babylonians in Aden. His unbandaged head laceration had begun to pucker grotesquely in the briny water. The other man contributing to the weighted down water casket was a terror-stricken Ethiopian who also lacked even a rudimentary ability to swim.

Though stuporous from the prolonged swim, Saul was alert enough to realize the near impossibility of Adiva pulling the four of them free of this determined seaward current. His heart pounded and he was flush with intense body heat despite the tepid water. Almost mindlessly he began kicking and pushing at the weighty barrel.

Adiva laughed in startled surprise. Tying around her waist a tether to the ponderous keg, she swam as hard as her energy would allow.

Powered by the two of them, the trailing tail began curling toward the center of floating ensemble. As both began to falter, they passed through an unmarked interface to the calmer waters whose waves broke on mangroves 50 yards away.

Suddenly a fin then the whole head of the shark reared from the water, back arched and jaws open. A primal scream of agony shot horror through everyone in the water. Ibraham's head and shoulders were pulled beneath the waves, silencing his cries. In the clear water those nearby couldn't help but watch helplessly as their brother was being dragged to his death by a merciless killing machine.

They saw him kick furiously with his free foot which landed squarely on the shark's cartilaginous skull. The stunned shark opened its mouth and Ibrahim lurched away, struggling the ten feet to the life-giving air. His assailant, teeth still coated with the Arab sailor's blood, swam in a confused arc away from train of thrashing legs. Ibrahim was able to hold on to a rope thrown him by Kasim, but he was pallid, weakening quickly from blood loss.

Those who risked a look down wished they hadn't, as the 20 feet of clear water enabled all to see the seven-foot sharks that circled near the bottom. As though having trouble rising in the water, they spiraled upward, drawn by copious tentacles of blood from the leg of their first victim. The first attacker drifted uncertainly back through the bloodiest water just as two of the largest sharks closed on the same spot. They both immediately attacked the first, as though *his* blood had drawn them to this feeding frenzy. The ferocious biting and tearing quickly disemboweled the new victim, whose mouth continued to bite grotesquely, as though it could still eat.

Now four grey sharks gnawed at the sinking carcass, soon so torn as to cause them to seek out new flesh, and their feeding frenzy would lead the ravenous predators to ravage anything in the water. Almost anything.

Hillel called out to Adiva, whose attention was solely focused on reaching the mangroves thirty yards away, through the roiling surf. "I saw the sharks eat their own kind."

Adiva shot back, "Stop watching them. We are so close, so close...get Ibrahim and we'll leave the train, the four of us. Hurry!"

She swam up to Yosef, followed by Saul, who, having looked down with Hillel at the carnage below, was now fully energized by unspoken terror. In a rare moment of self-observation, he wondered at his not falling apart, as he had so often over trivial matters, before these hardening days changed him forever.

When Hillel arrived with the bleeding Arab sailor in tow, Saul draped the barely responsive man's arms over his aching shoulders and said, "Tie a harness around his waist and chest." That done with some fumbling, he secured a line between Ibrahim and the band around his own waist, smiled at a worried Adiva, and, without a word, kicked out toward the beckoning shore.

13

Eldad felt trapped in the maze of sharp outcroppings that broke through the steep north face of the lava mountain. There was no trail as there had been up from the crater lake. The angle of the sun-shaded footholds in the jumble of shards. He worried only briefly about a wrong step, with the weight of the water bags snapping his leg like a twig. A more pervasive panic colored his every thought….must find a way down the mountain to the surf…. the sharks…his imagination conjured sickening scenes.

At times he could see the arc of sandy beach below, even as he climbed down to a level terrace 400 feet above the sand. From this cliff, the unexpected sight of trees drew his attention to a widening gash in the mountain face. The few stubby growths at the top gave way to a lush triangle of trees rising in height and girth toward the bottom of the gap where the forest stopped abruptly halfway down to the sandy shore. Eldad began using the thorny acacia tree branches to lower himself down forbidding faces of rock. He wondered at the multiplicity of ways the acacias had of penetrating and surmounting the unyielding stone.

Just before he broke out of a tangled last clump of trees, he thought he heard a steady rustling to his left, but then he heard nothing as he hurried along the ledge of the last barrier to the beach.

Now he saw a commanding panorama of a vast Red Sea beach, its endless surf lapping, then slapping hard on pale golden sand.

With rising alarm, he realized he could see nothing on the water, no flotilla, nor anything else he recognized. Was this the long southern arm of the island? He immediately realized how irrelevant that was, considering the near vertical drop to the rock-strewn sand.

He unslung the goatskin bags, leaving them hidden beneath a jumble of basalt rubble. There was no time to search for ideal footholds, but the stone surface proved more irregular than it first appeared. Lowering himself steadily, he found hand and foot holds almost anywhere he touched. In what seemed to him an eternity of painful clawing down the treacherous slope, he could at last believe he wouldn't die if he fell off the rocks. He discarded the impulsive notion to jump the final 20', but did launch himself from a bit lower, thudding on an unwelcoming hard pack of Red Sea sand.

He sprinted along the waters-edge north toward what he hoped would be the mangrove forest that separated a two-mile crescent of shoreline from the smaller, deep water inlet where they had beached the rowboat.

Waddling seabirds skittered away from his long strides which soon brought him to the edge of impenetrable thicket of mangroves too tall to see over. Without hesitation he dove into the surf, choked on an unexpected wave, and thrashed through the roiling water at the outer edge of the mangrove island. In a moment he was in the deeper, seemingly colder stream of the inlet formed by the collapse of a long silent volcano rim.

Eldad searched the near waters and found what he so desperately wished for and what he most desperately dreaded. The bedraggled flotilla seemed to float aimlessly 50 yards from the mangrove island's sheltering arms. And his. He could see the bobbing heads clustered about barrels and planks of wood. His dear Asherite friend was the first he could identify, but then a fleeting glimpse of blond hair and golden skin sent a bolt of energy to his core.

"I'm here, over here," he shouted. He saw heads turn and heard cries of relief.

"Everyone is spent," Saul managed to gasp hoarsely. It seemed to take all his remaining strength to say it.

"Hold on," Eldad called out as he swam through the briny water toward Adiva. With only a few yards still separating them, he abruptly froze in mid stroke as he saw two pair of fins slicing the water hard upon the caravan's leading edge. The clear water hid nothing of their menacing size and cavernous jaws framed ghastly white by rows of bloodstained teeth.

Now the others saw and most cried out in terror. Eldad was reaching for Adiva's outstretched hand when he was rudely pushed away by a highly agitated bottlenose dolphin sweeping between them toward the oncoming sharks. Aroused from their favored resting place in the sheltering mangroves, a second and third bottlenose joined the charge.

Before open jaws could reach human flesh, the two lead dolphins struck from below, their bony heads bashing the sharks' underbellies, rupturing unshielded internal organs. The swimmers were speechless in wonder at the sight of an 11-foot shark thrown writhing out of the water. As if to finish the job, one bottlenose struck the white belly again, before the dying shark could sink below the waves, as its murderous brother had already done.

First carpenter Kasim's booming laughter, then the rising cheers of all others, were followed quickly by thanks to Allah, repeated over and over. Instead of speeding away, all three breached together in a joyous victory salute. These synchronized bursts from the water were accompanied by whistles and squeaks from their blowholes. The sleek grey and white creatures circled the floating caravan, as though patrolling for further intruders into *their* world.

Then, as suddenly as they had appeared, their rescuers were gone. Soon a happy babble arose of Arabic, Chinese and Hebrew, with no one needing translators to share this joy of survival. Saul, Hillel, and Yosef hugged and gave exhausted hoots of celebration. Saul promised wine, which no one thought he had, until an impish smile was accompanied by a motion with his thumb toward the last of the bedraggled barrels.

Adiva and Eldad floated near one another. There was a quiet moment, as though they were in the eye of a hurricane for an instant, separate from the perilous surroundings—a quiet moment to fill with forever. They looked deeply into each other's eyes and reached wordlessly for the loving touch that would be remembered the rest of their lives.

14

"I can't make it, I can't." an exhausted sailor wailed. He was only yards from the shore of the deep-water cove. Seeing this, Eldad remembered camels at desert oases who, through exhaustion and dehydration, would simply stop moving and die in sight of life-giving water. The stronger men, especially Kasim, pulled stragglers ashore before they could sink beneath the Red Sea waves. He also screamed at the men who looked like they would give up, threatening grievous bodily harm to anyone who drowned! Some of the crew were so intimidated by the giant that they failed to see the unintended humor, but with their last remaining strength lurched onto the white powder sand.

Eldad did not let go of Adiva's hand, which she had grasped firmly in his after their miraculous deliverance by the gallant dolphins. They swam the distance to the water's edge reassuringly tethered, his right hand to her left. Swimming on their sides was awkward and inefficient, except it allowed them to look at each other with a new fascination. They were hungry for food, yet a deeper hunger stirred each of them to the core. It was now involuntary, and though sleepless for two days, there was from some unknown source an energy they felt throughout their bodies.

When their feet hit the sand, it was a few yards from where they left the skiff and nearly every crewman and all the passengers sprawled thankfully on dry land. Eldad felt an urgency to see after Captain Mustafa whom he had left with Sa-id beneath a clump of acacias a short way around a left-turning bend.

He reluctantly released Adiva's hand. "I must see to the captain. But first, we must retrieve the goatskin water bags The Almighty has revealed a place to replenish. Do you have the strength to come with me?"

Her steady gaze startled him. "I don't have the strength *not to* come with you." He felt his breath come shallow and realized he was breathing fast without moving.

"Hurry, then," he urged taking both her hands to lift her from the sand. She felt his strength, like the warmth of a lambs' wool blanket around her shivering torso. The silk garment she wore aboard was torn at the sleeves but otherwise intact. Covered with bits of sea plants and now a coat of sand, she tried to visualize what she looked like. She touched her hair, removing a seaweed stem. She saw him smiling at her in a way that brushed off sand and seaweed.

They half walked, half ran to the northern edge of the mangrove forest and Eldad reluctantly pulled them into the water, the only way to the southern arm of the island. It was low tide, and the surf was gentle, so the swim around the bulge of the mangrove forest was mercifully brief. Around the bend from the edge of the mangroves, they came to the spot where Eldad leapt off the rock face.

"Stay here," he said, rather more imperiously than he intended.

"No," she replied, perfectly mimicking his tone. They both laughed.

"This way, my spirited princess," he shot back with exaggerated deference. When he started to bow, she pushed him forward toward the rock face. Within a few minutes, they had scaled the broken face wall and stood before the pile of rubble covering the goat skins. Kicking the stones aside, he soon held the precious water vessel to her parched lips.

"Don't drink so fast. You'll never hold it down."

They sat briefly on a boulder while she drank more, then recapped the goatskin.

"Take this. Take it to the captain," she urged, pushing the skin away. "Where did you find water?"

He started to explain but stopped suddenly. Again, as he had coming down the mountain, he heard the rustling of a complex sound seemingly made up of many sounds off to their left in the tangle of mountain side acacias. Adiva heard it too and began walking toward the clump of trees where sea birds squawked in territorial disputes. The sound grew louder and, as they moved closer, their recognition grew.

Only a few trees into the thicket they stumbled upon it, confirming that the rustling was a twelve-foot waterfall splashing its goodness into a natural basin in the basalt rock. The basin shimmered with pure spring water and was as deep and wide as the waterfall was high.

"Leave me. Go to the captain," Adiva said, motioning with a wave of her hand.

Confused and a little disappointed, Eldad reluctantly turned and made his way out of the acacia forest, carrying the water bags, which seemed to have gotten heavier. As he cleared the last tree, he could not resist a look back and caught the briefest look of Adiva pulling her silken garments over her head, then disappearing. Turning away, he fell over a rock before his attention had fully returned to the trail, but it did no damage.

15

Kasim watched as Saul ferried the badly bitten, still bleeding Ibrahim through the final approach to shore.

Surprised at how unsteady his legs felt beneath him, he was determined to move ahead, focusing on one foot at a time until he finally came upon the two men still tethered together on the warm sand of the beach, any notion of personal boundaries abandoned in the stupor following the prolonged exertion.

He knew he must take charge in the captain's absence. He first untied the leather harness holding the sailor to the Asherite's back. Saul roused himself but Ibrahim did not move.

His breathing was shallow and skin color ashen. Bleeding onto the sand was minimal. Too much of his life-preserving blood had now been carried away by an indifferent Red Sea.

Saul sat up weakly and the Babylonians knelt by his side.

"You are a mighty man," Yosef said to Saul with genuine admiration.

Hillel coughed an agreement, kneeling beside the stricken sailor. "Skin cold but no shivering. Bad sign. *Where* is the Danite when we need him?"

Saul was alert enough now to say quietly, "I saw this many times in my village when warriors defending the tribal land were brought home with wounds they could not survive. I think my friend can do nothing, but we Asherites always bandage wounds like his. "Tear up his rags and wrap his leg securely."

Hillel wound two strips of fabric over the oozing gashes in the Arab sailor's thigh. He shook his head with sadness. "No pain." Gingerly he lowered the injured leg to the sand.

Cries for water were frequent from reviving men strewn all along the arc-shaped beach. Kasim ignored them for now and proceed to take an inventory. Among the men were scattered the three barrels with their attached tools, and the nautical charts Hillel had saved from the sinking vessel. He wondered what good these charts were without the string device the captain used to determine latitude.

They were lost and soon Ibrahim would not be the only one dying.

Kasim had seen the empty skiff at the north end of the beach but could not find the captain.

"You come with me," he said pointing to a sailor of mixed blood, who snapped in behind the burly carpenter as they followed the beach toward the acacias growing erratically from the near vertical rock face of the mountain. He feared for his master's prolonged suffering and refused to contemplate his beloved captain's death. He was orphaned as a young child, and slave or not, Kasim knew no parent but him. Even before the mast broke Captain Mustafa's leg, the blood-speckled cough and the sagging clothes drenched with sweat at night, made it painfully apparent something was terribly wrong.

At a distance, Kasim could see the recumbent emaciated figure of his precious captain, his legs propped up on a high mound of sand. A lesser pile served as a pillow. Kneeling in the sand beside him was Sa-id who on seeing the approaching men, waved, but his sagging shoulders and bowed head bespoke helplessness.

Witnessing Captain Mustafa lead sailors for thirty years had taught Kasim to rudely silence expressions of hopelessness. Men preoccupied with their own misery were worthless in desperate situations.

Now within earshot, Kasim called out, "The captain! Tell me!"

Sa-id was standing now and looking even more dejected, and croaked out, "No water. I found no water."

The mixed race sailor gasped, but Kasim's icy stare silenced him. "God shall deliver us," Kasim said. He truly believed that.

Then he heard the captain moaning, then a spasm of coughing

Kasim always heard in the mornings. It was obvious that the more conscious Mustafa became, the greater the searing pain from the break, despite the skillful splinting done aboard the ship. Sa-id had followed Eldad's instruction and, while the captain was still heavily under the influence of the opium, further stabilized the lower leg by packing sand on either side of it. The captain would die soon without water, but not before wishing himself dead from the pain.

The carpenter sat next to his master on the sand. He realized he would, if need be, die this way, as devoted slaves often did. Mustafa had been aware of this and he added stern parental admonition to the master's command. He would say, "There is survival value in separateness, as every creature has his own fate. Mine cannot be yours."

The shadows were lengthening in the late afternoon, and Kasim began to think of what they must do before the light faded. Though moaning periodically, his master was still a merciful distance from full consciousness. Kasim knew the men needed orders, as though the captain had spoken them. Though they may be resentful, they are most reassured, sometimes beyond the realities of situations, by a leader in charge.

The carpenter eyed the acacia forest. How well he knew its barbed branches and abundant seed pods. Once when his master had been too ill to sail for five months, leaving him and his two slaves, Kasim and Sa-id, destitute, they all supplemented their meager diets with boiled acacia seeds. In the wild, he had cut and woven the thorny branches, enclosing their party with a nighttime barrier impenetrable to hungry animals. He wondered what animal had stripped the pods from the lower limbs.

As the carpenter turned away from the acacia patch, he caught sight of the tall African striding out of the surf.

Bearing two goat skin bags, Eldad stopped briefly at water's edge where Saul had roused himself and stood unsteadily. After kneeling to touch the unconscious Ibrahim, Eldad said, "Gently pour this water into his parted lips. See if you can get him to drink. Sometimes they swallow even when unconscious. Wash his face and hands with this precious water." He slung the smaller water bag at Hillel.

But where...?

"God has given us abundant water, so drink," Eldad said, "but share, until I can show you its source."

He pulled at Yosef's soaking tunic, "Come, translate for me." They hurried over the sandy terrain toward the captain and his men. Yosef uncorked the goat skin and drank as they left the others who were strewn along the beach. Word of the water had spread and Saul, Hillel and the still unresponsive sailor were being surrounded by half a dozen men demanding their share. This could turn treacherous if they didn't believe what Eldad had said and thought it was all the water they had.

The stricken captain moaned piteously as Eldad reached his side. Kasim was relived by Eldad's presence and he began speaking to Yosef immediately. "Tell him the captain is bad." Eldad appeared to understand and nodded even before Yosef could translate the Arabic. It sounded the same in any language.

Eldad studied the sand configuration. "That is so much better than I could have done. It is what Captain Mustafa needs." Sa-id beamed, and looked to his senior for approval, but Kasim only looked sadly at his frail master, whose moans were sharply punctuated by wet sounding coughs.

Eldad's family of herbalists and healers taught their countless generations to care for the still healthy living as well as the dying, so he sat on the sand and grasped the carpenter's massive shoulder, saying quietly, "I see how dearly you care for this old man." Before the words were translated, the strong, reassuring grip opened a gate of silent tears, which Kasim turned away to hide.

Eldad motioned for Yosef to give Kasim the waterbag and said, "First, you and Sa-id drink freely." Grief temporarily put aside, both men drank quickly. Life and vigor seemed to flow into them. He looked into their brightening eyes and said, "Perhaps it is not yet the captain's time."

Knowing the sand bagging could still the movement only so

long, probably until the opium wore off, Eldad gently examined the braced and bandaged lower leg. The swelling was constrained by the slender wooden slats and the firmly wound linen holding them to the sides of the broken extremity. Eldad had been taught to brace front and back as well, but there had been no time to do this on the sinking ship. Eldad knew from tribal battlegrounds that moving the leg for additional bracing would be agonizing for the poor man, but they would have to hurt him to help him. This unavoidable reality was as punishing for the healer as it was for the healed, though he was trained not to show this. His grandfather had taken the young Eldad into the ghastliest scenes of carnage and made him practice his skills, not only with injured tribesmen, but also on mangled, newly dead enemy warriors.

Eldad thought, *the big man will not be able to stand this thing we have to do.*

"Go!" he said firmly to Kasim. "The men need organizing to bring the water barrels to the spring. Quickly or there will be fighting over the little I brought down from the east face of the mountain."

After a last gaze at the captain, Kasim moved off quickly, retracing his steps to the shore.

Eldad waited until the carpenter was out of earshot. "Sa-id, get your arm beneath your master's shoulders and raise him to almost sitting up. We must get him to drink. He may strike out at you."

Sa-id got behind him, legs to either side and arms wrapped around, cradling his master. Mustafa thrashed weakly until Eldad sprayed him the water under pressure from the goatskin. Indignant screeches replaced cries of pain, but only briefly. Quickly, Eldad held the water bottle to the captain's parched lips for several swallows.

"Let go of me, you mother dog's outcast!" the captain railed. Then he promptly vomited.

Sa-id held on. Yosef took the goatskin and said in Arabic, "Small amounts, keep drinking."

Mustafa again drank deeply of the life-restoring water, then brushed it away. Eyes closed, he slumped weakly, but managed to complain of bad pain and worse treatment. Eldad knew a painful procedure was now necessary, and he said, "Where your leg is broken, half way between your knee and ankle, we need to brace front and back, not just on the sides."

Captain Mustafa's eyes flew open and he bellowed hoarsely, "Don't touch me, witch doctor!"

Eldad laughed. Called many epithets by frustrated, usually pain-wracked patients, he had never been a witch doctor. Had their situation not been so grim, he would have been tempted to accompany what he had to do with incantation and ritual, as he had seen among the Danite tribe's only black African ally. This non-Semitic clan was actually under the protection of the Danites and added Eldad's family of healers to their more traditional shamans.

Leaving Yosef with the unpleasantly reviving captain, Eldad trudged back toward the shore. He'd surely be able to find the right sized pieces of wood, or Kasim would cut them. No more than two hours of sunlight remained and it would darken first on this side of the windswept volcanic island. The air was cooling, and it dawned on the young African that this remote sanctuary might be as cold as the Sahara night. He passed Kasim, who had opened the tool pouches and given specific orders to each sailor handed a precious iron implement.

Eldad called over Hillel, now looking relieved that the thirsty hoard had departed for the climb to the spring. It would soon become a hungry hoard.

"Tell the carpenter I need two short, narrow boards, like we used on the captains leg. And where has the large one gone?"

"Off with the egg and bird hunters. The first thing he noticed when he regained his senses was the swarms of birds on the mountain's slopes and other nests in the mangrove and acacias. I think he went into the mangroves. He said something about finding a dry passage through the dense growth, so he wouldn't get wet going through the mangroves to the long arc of the island."

Though impressed by his explorer spirit, Eldad knew full well it was the prospect of food. Though some birds' eggs were small, they were many, Saul had remarked.

Kasim had sent a stout sailor back alone to rescue the two injured crew who had been unable to swim.

"They may have been lost if the boat has torn away from the rocks and sunk in deeper water," Kasim told the Berber oarsman.

The two Ethiopian men were sent with their nets to a V-shaped rock formation framing a deep-water inlet. As they climbed up the 10 foot monoliths, their sheer faces allowed an unobstructed view of a coral forest, tended by hundreds of fish of a dazzling variety.

For a few moments the rugged Africans were so stunned by what they beheld that they could only gaze in wonder at an Eden of the sea.

Lazy schools of fish followed an unknown leader flitting from violet domes to yellow fans moving mysteriously in undersea currents. A cluster of larger silver-colored fish stopped at a 9 foot tall red chimney-shaped reaching almost to the surface.

Overcoming their initial shock at first seeing this strangely splendid world, they discussed their choices. They were from different tribes, but they got by on what words their dialects had in common added to their limited Arabic.

"Do you see, countryman, these deep pools where the water is unusually still. Maybe the rock faces silence the waves, the few that break over the barrier." He saw the other man nodding, but doubted he understood much. He had an idea he knew he must patiently explain to his fellow fisherman.

"The trees we passed finding our way here, you know the acacias?" said the taller of the two Ethiopians.

"Yes, I know these trees, their pods and their accursed spikes. My people call them winter thorns," the second fisherman replied.

"A tribe my father knows, from the misfortune of being their prisoner, make a clever use of these acacia pods in their fishing. Crushed up and lowered into still water, there is something in the pods that stuns the fish. You see how the fish use the water at the rock face to hover, as though resting."

Seeing the size of some of the near stationary fish was kindling a raging appetite in both men, as it had been two days since they

had eaten anything. They adroitly scaled the rocky terrain to the edge
of the acacia forest and brought handfuls of pods back to the ledge
overhanging the deep-water cove. These they wrapped in a corner
of their netting, then stomped them to a fibrous pulp. A length of
rope one had brought was tied tightly to a stone spike a foot from
the ledge and then around the waist of the taller fisherman, who
then said, "If this works, I'll jump in and net as many as I can."

The shorter African suggested, "Hold the net wide when you
jump...maybe snag one whether he's poisoned or not."

Without showing themselves over the ledge, they slowly lowered the corner of the net with its malevolent cargo down the rock
face into the Red Sea water. Two feet below the surface it stopped,
forcing a cautious look. The pulpy pods had become more of a ball
as the seawater bloated the shreds. It rested atop the red chimney
coral.

"We wait," he whispered, as though the fish could hear him.
Neither he, rope tied securely around him, nor his fellow seaman
knew how long. Again, their hunger, like a stampeding herd of
animals, tore through every fiber of their being.

As the sailor approached the 10 foot drop to the water, he was
greeted by the sight of a pair of two-foot white fish floating helplessly at the surface. Others, some smaller and some larger, swam
listlessly bumping into each other and the red chimney coral. Both
men became even more wide-eyed as they beheld a multicolored
lobster of prodigious size turned belly up a foot below the surface.
The roped sailor jumped off with joyous abandon, arms spreading
the net wide. First, he ensnared the two-foot-long lobster, then he
swam to retrieve the floating white fish which he was able to throw
to his companion above. He dove under the dozen stunned fish
around the red castle and scooped in all but two.

The sailor untied the rope about his waist and secured the fish
net closed with it. Knowing how precious this netted cargo was,
he shouted, "Pull it up, and throw the line back. I can't believe
what has happened here." Just as he said this, there seemed to be
a subtle shift in the water surrounding him. He was now treading

water actively to keep from being pulled out into the lagoon. Perhaps they had been led beside still waters, but having surrendered their bounty, the remaining fish disappeared in the relentless tide of the Red Sea.

16

Thoroughly revived and mercifully cleansed of Red Sea salt and seaweed, Adiva cautiously climbed down the last of the rock ledges to the beach. Eight parched, exhausted, and filthy sailors implored her to share the path to the blessed water.

"You can climb there from here," she said, pointing in the proper direction. "This first wall is hard, but when you get above the ledge, move right through the first clump of trees." She looked them over and decided that they were a sorry group.

"Fill the barrel *before* you wash yourselves. Then, pray to God our good fortune continues." Before she could finish, three men were already scaling the lava wall dragging long lengths of rope.

From above they dangled ropes to those below who attached them to the barrel's iron rings attached near the rim. The empty barrel was a drum, banging against stone outcroppings, till finally hoisted over the 20 foot ledge. Adiva wondered how they thought they could lower a full water keg past the treacherous irregularities of the rock face.

"We found a way through the mangroves where they have made islands of land, a trail to the north beach," offered the last of them to begin the climb, "Follow this wall around the curve."

Adiva was delighted at the prospect of avoiding a swim, any swim, in the thus far hostile waters. She realized for whom, besides herself, she wanted to be so fresh and clean. Images of the handsome African Jew who so arrested her attention began their intrusions into her awareness. A feeling of something warm at her core, an inner radiation of nascent desire. Didn't she know these feelings, didn't most women? Sometimes these were a surprise, welcome or unwelcome, as when directed at someone wholly inappropriate. Conflict over this would leave Adiva tense and irritable. But now she felt free, as if two forces had come together within her in some magical combination had liberated her from lifelong inhibitions. She stopped a moment in the sand by the wall. She was breathing much harder than the exertion of walking along the sand would require. She must do something, touch something...it had been so long. Now dream like pictures were so vivid when she closed her eyes, she could see his long and gentle hands and imagine them touching her. The pressure behind the fantasies would not allow them to stop there, and in rapid succession she felt his lips on hers, then raw images of his buttocks and something hard inside her intruded with shocking disorder.

She knew it was the wrong time and place, but no force on earth could convince her this gentle, beautiful young man was the wrong person. She shook herself from the reverie born of one hunger, and now felt another to be satisfied only by nourishment.

There was perhaps an hour of sunlight left when she found the opening to the path through the thicket of mangroves. It did not look like someone had hacked a passable clearing through the dense growth, but rather something had eaten its way from the south to north beaches. The trail was narrow, curiously arched in the trees and well-trod. Twists and turns remained on dry land across the wide forest until the trail seemed to end abruptly. From stout tree limbs brown mangrove roots dove into the muddy saltwater forming an impenetrable curtain of vertical bars, as tall as eight feet from limb to water. Adiva had noticed in swimming the outer edge of the thicket that the dense overhang of the trees at water's edge hid these strangest of root systems. She knew of no other plants that could grow from such brine as the Red Sea.

From within the trail, she could hear, but not see, the water sloshing into half-formed land at the forest's edge. She got down on hands and knees and studied the leaf and branch strewn forest floor. What she could not see standing was plainly visible beneath overhanging foliage, was a discreet pile of fist-sized animal scat.

Scanning beyond it, she spied two more of these deposits, spaced a few yards apart. To have left these is to have walked through! Adiva laughed aloud at the irony. In the failing light of this strange world, she was being shown the way by piles of dung.

She scrambled along like a fiddler crab she had just seen till the forest floor suddenly gave way to the sands of the north beach.

At the acacia tree line, she could see cheerful fires billowing smoke and flames at the centers of hastily assembled lava rock hearths. Civilization had appeared on this deserted rock thrown carelessly into the southern Red Sea.

17

The sailor Ibrahim died just after sunset. Carpenter Kasim managed all burials, whether at sea and those few times members of the crew had died in port, usually from knife fights with other drunken sailors. Every time this happened, Kasim wondered what evil was in the foul-tasting brew caused otherwise good men to undo themselves under its influence. It was no small wonder that Islam strictly forbade it. Long ago he had concluded that beating his drunken sailors did nothing to alter their behavior the next time the ship docked at a major port. It seemed to him that everything loose in the world skittered into port cities to make trouble and his sailors were experts at finding it.

Much aggrieved, the carpenter had no time for such thoughts now. He held the pale corpse of his friend while one of the Berbers washed the body three times, as ritual required this be done an odd number of times. They had no cloth for a shroud, so he would, like Islam's martyrs, be buried in the clothes he wore at death. Placed on his right side, his grave must be oriented to allow Ibrahim to face his sacred Mecca forever.

Adiva stood with Yosef and Hillel a respectful distance from the burial preparations. Virtually all ancient cultures required women to absent themselves from these activities, the Jews and Muslims being quite similar in this.

Having passed the body to the arms of another shipmate, Kasim approached and said to the three, "We must bury our blessed Ibrahim, according to the way of the Prophet of Allah. But I do not know the direction of Mecca."

Hillel answered immediately and with far more confidence

than he felt, "I can study the navigation charts. I shall be able to tell you."

Adiva's look of doubt was unseen by the anxious carpenter. "Kasim, Can the captain tell us where we are?"

"The Danite, has mercifully made him swallow an incredibly bitter potion." Kasim's tone was clearly appreciative. "First he cursed the healer, but he soon realized his pain was much less and began nodding off to sleep."

"Better not to rouse him until we must," Adiva said, glancing at Eldad as he knelt beside the captain in the acacia grove. Sa-id had rowed back from the stricken vessel with two injured crew, who lay opposite the captain in the enclosure. They all reclined on mats of dark green mangrove leaves. Flames spiraled above a circle of stones in the center.

Adiva marveled at the clever 20-foot enclosure the men had created by weaving the thorny acacia branches around Captain Mustafa and the warming hearth. If there were aggressive wild creatures, or even curious ones, they'd have no way of menacing the injured. Praise God they had retrieved the tools.

She turned to Hillel. "Go. Study your charts." Adiva realized they were utterly lost, the only clue being the delirious captain's moans. But "Zubair Islands" meant nothing to any of them, not even the crew, they soon found out. What was important, she knew, was for Hillel to state authoritatively the direction to the sacred city, whether he was correct or not.

Retrieving the sealed map cases from their moorings on a water barrel, Hillel upended the casket and balanced a dry plank on it. Darkness was deepening and he implored one of the Ethiopian sailors, as bony and tall as he, to hold a torch as he spread out two of the charts. After an adequate time studying the charts, he had already decided, he was going to pronounce his success at locating the proper direction of the Moslem holy city.

Sa-id brought another torch and peered anxiously at the incomprehensible lines and arcs.

Hillel might have understood them if he knew about where to

look on the nautical maps. The second one he spread out seemed to show a hundred island specks along the coast of Himyar, most unnamed and some, hundreds of miles from shore. For the men in earshot, he murmured, "Hmmm." Then a feigned recognition, "Ahh!"

Yosef spoke to his cousin in Hebrew, saying without a smile, "You always had such an unerring sense of direction. So where, oh sage, is their sacred city?" He, too, pretended to study the two maps.

"I'm going to tell you something and you're going to nod and smile like the fool you are," Hillel said without changing his optimistic tone. He straightened from the makeshift table to his impressive height. Extending his wiry arm pointing north and slightly east, he crisply ordered both Yosef and Sa-id, "Tell the carpenter, Mecca is there!"

The full moon lit the island in a luminous glow, added to by four sizeable campfires, one a few feet from the vertical rock of the volcanic mountain. Between it and the rock face, three sailors used flat pieces of wood from the flotilla's remains to gouge sand from a deepening grave.

"Deeper," Kasim ordered. "And move all this sand away. The master has taught me the grave can be no higher than twelve inches above the surface of the earth." As a slave Kasim was not much schooled in Islam, but Mustafa had seen to it that both he and Sa-id were able to read, write, and use numbers. Such skills were needed to build some things from plans, some written on papyrus or animal hides. Many slave owners failed to capitalize on the increased market value of literate slaves, for fear this gave them power over their enslaving world. Captain Mustafa wanted his men to be confident in dealing with merchants, and in acquiring additional sailors from other ships. They could be deceived less easily by false manumission documents presented by runaway slaves. Of course, some still had wrist or neck marks from long term shackles, and one didn't have to be literate to read that.

Kasim appointed the oldest of the sailors to supervise the burial. Captain Mustafa was in no condition to officiate, leaving Kasim to muster what he could remember from past funerals. He prayed that the words over his shipmate would be acceptable to the Almighty. Of the fellow sailors, two were practicing Muslims, but none had any formal knowledge. The six others followed various tribal religions, but only when convenient to do so.

The oldest sailor arrived at the graveside carrying the body of their departed comrade.

All uninjured crewmen, the Babylonians, Saul and Eldad, stood in a semicircle. He handed Ibrahim's remains to the crewman who had dug the five-foot hole in the firmly packed sand.

"On the right side," the old sailor instructed.

As the body was lowered, Kasim stepped forward and said in a full but saddened voice, "We bury according to the way of the Prophet of Allah." He threw a handful of sand into the grave and continued, "From the earth did we create you."

He paused a while, then threw a second handful of sand, intoning, "And into it shall we return you."

"And from it shall we bring you out once again," he added with a note of quiet finality, while sprinkling the third handful of sand.

Another Muslim crewman cleared his throat and added a reverent, "To Allah we belong and to Allah we return." Others mouthed the sentiment silently.

Everyone present helped push the sand into the pit. And then it was over, and the quiet of the volcanic island was broken only by the waves lapping the shore of an emerald lagoon.

18

In the hour after sundown, most of the crewmen stood expectantly, *too expectantly* for the spoils of their foraging. Observing them, Saul had to admit that he too was ravenously hungry. He, and the three other sailors had collected over a hundred unbroken eggs, ranging from palm to thumbnail size. Saul dismissed the scornful guffaws from the others and continued to amass a larger volume of eggs than they, who collected only large eggs. If he could speak their language, he would have told them how nutritious smaller eggs are if roasted or boiled.

In addition to the cloth sacks they cradled like newborn babies, the sailors had each managed to kill large sea birds which had frantically defended their nests.

When Sa-id beached the rowboat for the final time, he proudly displayed items of great necessity he had hauled along with two injured sailors. After others moved them into the captain's enclosure, its fire now fed by the extremely dense wood of dried mangrove branches, Sa-id brandished five items of iron, saving the grandest for last. Before he began handing these treasures to comrades, he tossed a large roll of still dry spices to Rada, the Ethiopian usually in charge of the ship's galley, meager though it was.

Sa-id produced the two-foot diameter iron skillet and, to the even greater delight of the gangly Ethiopian, the ship's twenty gallon black pot. Rada instructed most willing hungry comrades to fill this with sea water and haul it up the beach to the captain's woven acacia branch enclosure.

Captain Mustafa was awake now and issuing more or less incoherent orders to which every crew nodded enthusiastically but did absolutely nothing. In the few moments between outbursts of commands he would forget what he had just ordered. At times he did not seem to realize his ship was gone, as though they happened upon this volcanic rock while exploring interesting islands. His leg hurt less now because, when Mustafa was most deeply drugged by the opium-laced cocktail, Eldad added to the side splints two short wooden slats in the front and back of the broken lower leg.

Eldad had the stocky Yosef stand authoritatively at the opening of the enclosure, allowing in only those Kasim and Eldad said should come in.

The three crewmen brought in their abundant pouches of eggs, and the seabirds, plucked but not gutted. They dare not waste any edible part of the animal, and even the intestines would be used. The Asherite was the next allowed in and Rada chuckled, but also looked in wonder the cache of white, pale blue and brown eggs he bore so carefully. Saul wanted to stay, as close as possible to the food,

"Get the fat one out of here," the cook told Yosef. "He'll be into everything and what we have will disappear beneath his helping hands." Yosef laughed but didn't translate.

"Cook says nobody in here," Yosef said, then, noting Saul's disappointment, added, "Stand close by and I'll signal you, when... you know..." Saul slouched out of enclosure gateway, but immediately sat down where he could easily see Rada silhouetted by the fire against the darkening acacia thicket.

Adiva walked up to Saul, whose abundance was on his back supported by his elbows.

"Look how slowly he works at his task!" whined Saul.

"Silence yourself. You'll make him angry, and he won't feed you." Adiva had considered walking into the circle, and her cousin Yosef would not stop her, no matter what the others said.

Eldad was concerned about the captain. He called Yosef over to translate. Together, they sat him up with the injured leg still elevated.

"You must eat, Captain Mustafa. It does not matter if you are hungry or not. Tell him he will die if he doesn't eat." Yosef tried to copy Eldad's tone of urgency but the captain merely smirked. Yosef's expression was of total confusion, but Eldad suspected that Mustafa was fully aware of his worsening condition that rattled him to his core with bloody coughing spasms. The drug he gave the captain for his pain had temporarily quieted these ominous reminders.

After removing the largest of the prizes, the ship's cook placed the three cinched sacs of eggs directly into the boiling pot, securing them to a slat of wood spanning the rim.

Rana slit into the abdominal cavity of the first of three birds and removed the long intestines. The large iron skillet was balanced on a bed of embers near the boiling pot. The Ethiopian wound the gut around and around his hand until the contents had been fully extruded and threw it immediately into the iron pan where it crackled and sizzled. The bird's liver he carefully lowered in a ladle onto the pan's hot surface, now glistening from the oil of the cooking innards. After turning it once, he scooped it onto a broad leaf, and said to Kasim standing nearby, "The captain, can you get him to eat this?" He sprinkled it with a pinch of ground bitter lemon and placed it in the cupped hand of the carpenter.

Kasim knelt beside the Mustafa. "Master," Kasim began deferentially, "This nourishment has been sent by Allah. It will strengthen you."

Mustafa glared at his loyal slave, but, having caught the aroma of cooking flesh, he abruptly grabbed the bird liver and bit into it, a dribble of uncooked blood flowing from smiling lips down his chin. In two more bites, this first morsel of their salvation was gone.

Rana repeated the emptying process with the other two birds, but now sliced the emptied intestine into many pieces and added all remaining entrails to the frying pan. By this time, all the remaining men stood encircling the thorny barrier and their agitation increased as more complex cooking smells assaulted them.

To expand the volume simmering in the five-inch deep pan, the cook added brown seaweed he had gathered at the shore. Like almost all the sailors who plied the Red Sea, the Ethiopians were raised in the most austere surroundings and were adept at gathering edible plants anywhere they found themselves. Perhaps, Rana told himself, he'd find others beside seaweed on this strange island. He didn't want to think about it, but they all could be here for a very long time.

Two Ethiopian sailors stood inside the enclosure holding their net of still flopping fish and the two-foot lobster, speckled and striped brown and white, whose fist-sized claw grasped an unfortunate fellow captive.

Kasim had seen to the gathering of large rocks which were skillfully piled to waist high with a flat stone on top. Onto this, Rana gingerly lifted the bags of cooked eggs from the boiling pot. His plan was to distribute these and the stew cooking on the pan. This should allow them to maintain self-control until the other food can be cooked.

He opened a bag and took out one of the larger still steaming eggs. He cracked and removed the shell and rolled the hardboiled bird's egg from hand to hand till cool enough to bite into. He gave an involuntary cry of delight, then muted his enthusiasm, lest he cause a mutiny. Kasim took a handful of eggs and Rana scooped chunks of seaweed stew onto leaves for the captain and two injured crew.

"Get the big leaves and line up!" he ordered, but they were already doing so behind the Asherite and Adiva.

Adiva pulled Saul aside and said in a low voice, "Better for us not to look privileged. We need their good will, not their resentment."

Her brother Hillel had walked up, and he nodded his agreement, motioning for Yosef to admit the first crewmen standing behind them. Kasim had taken the slotted spoon and was distributing the stew, while Sa-id oversaw the eggs. No one tried for more than his share. Men with great hands made for labor delicately peeled their hardboiled eggs and didn't worry which tough little bird organ made up their nourishment.

When all had been given their small share of stew the frying pan held only scraggly pieces of seaweed and the oil rendered from the entrails. Rana cut off the heads of the birds, plucking a few remaining feathers from them before tossing them into the bubbling oil. On a wooden block salvaged from the ship's refuse, he expertly chopped the large birds into ten or twelve pieces each and added these to the sizzling heads.

Though still achingly hungry, the men now had hope they would not starve on this most forbidding rock.

The lanky Ethiopian smiled broadly as he took the fish nets from his two countrymen while telling them, "Get new stones and build two supports for the grill. Sa-id is blessed among men for bringing it." This done, he placed the iron grate a foot above the brightly glowing bed of coals.

He now needed help and joked with Yosef about getting the Asherite to do it. Yosef either didn't realize the jest, or, more likely, saw a chance for a good laugh. He blurted out, "The cook wishes the most skillful Asherite Saul to assist him!"

Though he understood none of this Hebrew, Rana read the tone of Yosef's announcement, and his loud groan at the mention of Saul's name had its intended effect of comedic relief. Eldad joined in the others; it seemed an age since any of them had laughed. He noted the remarkable effect it had on the group. His grandfather had taught that laughter had healing properties. Or perhaps the healer amused the patient while God did the healing.

The Asherite was all smiles as Yosef again allowed him into the captain's enclosure.

"Cut off his hand if he steals so much as a bird's butt." Yosef said to the cook in Arabic.

Saul trundled up to the grate covered with crackling fish and began to judiciously turn them. He also acted as though his friends and fellow shipmates weren't watching his every move.

Hillel had found an unexpectedly light plate of rock, large enough for two portions with the desired cup in the middle to catch every nourishing drop of what he might be given. As they entered the inner circle, Hillel said to his sister, "Take this. Take it to our friend. This will hold enough for two." He smiled knowingly at his older sibling. Sometimes she didn't much like the over perceptiveness of her brother, but now it didn't seem to matter what this family-appointed guardian of their Adiva's honor knew or thought he knew.

Saul joyously fished the lobster out of the boiling pot and quickly split the shell of the foot-long tail. The Ethiopian cook was watching him curiously, as he had never eaten, or even seen a lobster, much less one of such prodigious size. He had thought that the markings were so decorative as to make him believe the beast would, like so many brightly colored ocean creatures, be poisonous to eat.

Saul said to Hillel, "Ask him if I can have some oil from his pan."

Rana motioned to the Asherite to help himself which he did by ladling the almost gelatinous remains of golden renderings onto the steaming lobster tail. This he quartered, giving Yosef and Hillel a piece each and placed the remaining two portions on the stone plate held by Adiva. "You and the Danite can share."

"But what about you?" she asked, then realized the predatory Saul had arranged to have *all* the remaining lobster for himself! She laughed as she saw him decisively crack the huge brown claws, extracting and devouring with a slurp the pink pointed flesh.

Adiva moved to the tall Danite's side carrying the stone plate of lobster. He looked down at her and was clearly thrilled she was alone, even ignoring the steaming nourishment she held. She drank in the ecstasy she saw in his eyes. Not taking her eyes off his face, she picked a piece of lobster from the plate and lifted it to his surprised lips. Without protest he bit into the whitish flesh, then guided her hand to her own mouth, gently feeding her as she had him. Adiva became aware how many eyes watching their every movement but decided that conclusions about their attraction were already rampant.

Adiva stepped from facing to beside the tall young man. He moved closer and his right thigh touched her left without this being visible to others. They were paying no attention to the remaining lobster, and continued side-long looks at each other, until Saul had the ill manners to trundle over and look wordlessly, like a dog, at what they had left.

Adiva laughed merrily and, tearing away half the piece, stuffed it in the corpulent man's yawning maw. The rest she raised to Eldad's lips, insisting that he partake. She had a moment's vision of her own mother's nurturing nature. Smiling at Eldad, she very briefly pondered the significance of her thoughts.

Her focus was redirected when she realized her thigh was still pressed tightly to his. The campfire danced its light across Eldad's face and she knew only that she desperately wanted him to kiss her, here in front of everybody.

Struggling to maintain her composure, Adiva chatted amiably with Saul and Yosef, even as she casually caressed Eldad's leg.

Eldad gave his old friend a subtle but unmistakable head jerk to take himself elsewhere, this noted as well by Adiva's cousin and fellow guardian, Yosef.

Yosef was reluctant to leave her. How was she to let him know it was okay without speaking the words? Finally, saying nothing, he followed Saul through the opening in the thorny enclosure.

Eldad was growing increasingly uncomfortable, rearranging his robe to cover the growing response to even this limited physical contact between them.

"I love being this close and touching you makes me yearn for time alone with you," he whispered, gently twisting away from her.

Adiva looked from his radiant blue eyes down his chest and below his waist. Although inexperienced, she knew just enough about the fullness she saw beneath Eldad's rough woven robe. It was the wetness she felt in her own body that took her by surprise

"Oh, please, don't move," she said breathlessly. "A little while longer."

"Our lingering will be noticed," Eldad said, without much conviction and moved closer to her side.

"Our *lingering*?" she chortled louder than she should. Then whispered, "This is so delicious. I want to say things to you."

Eldad nodded. "And I am flooded within by words for you. Some are sweet, but some are raw."

Adiva had never heard such candor from any young man.

And indeed, Eldad seemed to immediately regret his confession. She recognized that it was probably not acceptable back home in Babylon or Eldad's home for that matter. But here, in this very strange place, she didn't care.

She must let him know everything was okay.

She took hold of his hand. "I want to hear it...*all* of it," Adiva managed.

"Not now, not here. If we say any more like this, I'll not be able to attend to the injured."

Adiva accepted that. "I found my way through the mangroves. There is a clearing just inside the overgrown entrance to the path."

Eldad understood. "When others sleep." He looked about, beyond the four campfires, at the moonlit beach between them and the mangrove forest.

Although both were beyond exhausted, the new fire shot so high within them as to hold back the weariness.

Many crewmen, along with Hillel, Yosef and Saul were making preparations for desperately needed sleep. Because of the storm and the ruin of their boat, none had slept in two days. Most simply coved out spots of sand near the protection of the fires. The night was cooling noticeably, like it did on the desert's miles to the north over the featureless Red Sea.

Eldad spoke to a more clear-headed Captain Mustafa, now wide awake as others, one by one, drifted into the absolute stillness of the deepest sleep they'd ever known. A few still had the energy to give the fires fresh fuel, especially the dense wood of mangrove roots, but soon the contagion of blissful snores felled even them.

Adiva lay on a mat of leaves and small branches over which her brother had draped an extra robe belonging to Saul. Her intention was to lie there briefly until all those huddled in the compound slept soundly. Her mind drifted lazily to a fantasy she had begun to elaborate on the trail through the mangroves. She had no trouble taking up where she had to leave off. Now real experience, or *almost* experience, was added to what she previously could only imagine. What her fantasies could not teach her was how sweetly disquieting the real experience of sexual excitement was in the presence of *his* arousal. She tried hard to think of something else as the tension of her unexpressed longings was making rest impossible. She failed, and again the flash of the dim image of what was pressing the inside of his robe. How she would like him to shed his modesty and show her the beauty beneath his robes. A single image intruded too strongly to suppress and she tasted an undeniable saltiness in her mouth. Adiva involuntarily opened her mouth as she saw the dream-like image of parting his robe and placing the firmness she found in her mouth. She could not resist placing two fingers in her mouth to feel some of what that may be like. Had she been alone, she would have held this image of sucking until her other hand had given her release. Would he do that for her? With her? A sudden anxiety overwhelmed her briefly as she very clearly realized that if she were alone with this virile young man, *she wouldn't know what to do!"*

Girls received no instruction or advice, relying instead on girlfriends who didn't know a useful thing about being alone with a man, as none ever had. Some of the stories were obvious fabrications, such as those of organs too stupendous in size to be taken in. And how did "taken in" work, anyway?

Adiva looked around and no one was moving. She lay back, confident in her ability to rouse herself from a brief rest.

When she awoke, the world was flooded with the light of a new day.

19

Eldad arose before dawn and silently entered what they all had begun to think of as the captain's compound. The moon had set, leaving the only light of the campfire embers, He could see Adiva's recumbent form, partly covered by Saul's rough woven robe. For a moment, her face was more brightly illuminated by a flare among the coals and he caught his breath at her loveliness. A smile played on her lips and the young man knew not to arouse her from a dream so pleasant and a sleep so desperately needed.

A cooling breeze caressed him from the sea and he wished he could share this moment of peace with her. He decided he would just watch over her till morning's soft light slowly emerged.

It was the captain himself who broke the peaceful silence. Mustafa's bellowed orders roused anyone still asleep on the beach and in the compound.

"My kamal. Bring my kamal!"

Kasim glanced at a nearby Hillel. His expression was a combination of sadness and confusion. Did Mustafa not know that this simple but effective navigation instrument would have gone down with the ship? Without, it the captain could not determine their latitude.

Mustafa wasn't done. "And bring the box from the secret cranny you built into my cabin wall."

Kasim hesitated. "Master.... the ship was lost in the storm,"

Mustafa propped himself tip and pushed Kasim aside. He seemed unfocused, manic. "Yes, lost you say?" His bony arm pointed toward the shore. "Then what is that?"

All eyes followed, then widened at the sight of their ill-fated ship, awash on its side and firmly grounded on the northern beach head. The ten-foot gash in the hull, its splintered mouth yawning skyward, told the tale of ruination.

Hillel stepped in to try the end the confusion. He walked into the enclosure to the captain's side, "In the night, I think the tide rose three feet or more, enough to lift the boat off the rocks."

Mustafa looked up at him, much more in control again. "I had this ship built by my carpenter, my loyal Kasim. "It is so solid, and the wood so buoyant, it is almost unsinkable."

Kasim gave his captain a grateful nod.

"You mean, even with the hull breached?" Hillel questioned.

"Well, there it is!" Kasim said, clearly self-satisfied.

The crew began trudging at various speeds toward their treasure, their reincarnated vessel. Some of the older sailors just sat down on the sloping sand, having nothing of their own to retrieve from the craft, to await what others saw. A few whispered superstitious nonsense among themselves, mostly about how only a ghost ship floats with a splintered hull.

Wen Ho, the sailor whose scalp had been lacerated in the storm, was now up and fussing with the fire. Eldad watched his movements, both large and small, before concluding this repentant informer was unimpaired. Sometimes, he knew, people with head wounds and blood loss fainted unpredictably. It was the sailor who had given Captain Mustafa the box hidden in the cabin.

Adiva smiled at Eldad and walked into the acacia thicket out of sight. By contrast, the sailors weren't the slightest hesitant to relieve themselves in full sight of all. Eldad was facing the fire when she returned.

She spoke quietly. "Why didn't you awaken me?"

"You were beyond the bounds of exhausted and sleeping so deeply. I could not disturb your peace and you had a sweet smile on your face. Were you dreaming?"

Adiva's golden skin pinked up from her throat to her cheeks. "I saw us together, in Baghdad, I think."

She smiled and Eldad couldn't help but feel there was more. Eldad noticed that her breathing had become more rapid.

"Perhaps later you will tell me."

Eldad could sense that the physical distance between them was permanently altered last night in the firelight. He was sure Adiva knew that too.

Their brief intimate moment was interrupted by the ship's cook who brought them a warm stone plate piled liberally with fluffy scrambled eggs, their yellow shot through with last night's leavings.

At first light, hungry men had again assaulted the heights and the forest for their bounty, so the eggs were plentiful. Captain Mustafa was now sitting atop a broad stone being fed the same yellow orange meal. Eldad smiled as he saw Kasim unconsciously mimic the captain's movements, including licking his lower lip when a piece of egg dribbled there. Every mother Eldad ever saw feed a baby did that and some mothers, most especially his, continued watching their grown children eat.

Adiva said, "There are things of ours still in our cabin. We do not want them lost to thieving hands."

Eldad nodded. "As we know, some of our hardy sailors were paid to have thieving hands. We should move quickly."

They set off at a rapid pace down to the sands. Kasim had already been inside the ship and held a small chest in one massive hand. He now had every available man, those not out in search of food, attaching long ropes to the railing, the splintered boards, and the intact front mast.

Kasim was barking orders. Four men were moving sand with the boards they'd used to dig their comrade's grave. Kasim had kicked a broad outline of where the sand needed removing.

"What are they doing," Adiva asked the carpenter.

"At high tide tonight, our dugout area will fill and, Allah willing, we shall pull our beloved ship to safety."

"Don't move the sand there!" he called out to a Berber digging earnestly. "Outside my mark, load the sand outside. The boat will move in here tonight," he said with loud conviction, striding within the pie-shaped divot he was demanding they dig. With the long boat on its sloping side, the stubby keel was above the level of the

sand and wouldn't impede high tide cradling it into the waiting
arms of a sandy dry dock.

Hillel had come up beside them and spoke to Kasim, translating for Eldad, "It is a miracle the boat floated onto the beach."

Kasim took a small plank in his hand. "The wood is Cedar of
Lebanon, from the wondrous forest called Cedars of God. It is half
the weight of African teak."

Hillel nodded his head in agreement. "It is a blessed wood,
used to build King Solomon's Temple in Jerusalem."

"I know nothing of this king," Kasim said, clearly pleased to
hear of him. "Master Mustafa has said that for us, this boat is our
only home, where we pray and likely die, so it must be of most
special wood."

Eldad studied the yawning hole in the side of the ship, and,
naïve about the ship building, gestured toward the acacia forest and
asked, "Is there some way to repair the hull?"

Adiva translated.

A bitter laugh issued from Kasim, but then he began to eye
the acacia forest up the beach. He grew quiet. "I had the thought
when I first looked at those trees that a very long canoe could be
hewn from their remarkably long and straight trunks."

Hillel's tone turned gloomy, "But of the tools you need I have
seen in cutting and shaping wood, we have none of these."

"But we do have the tools of my trade still in the ship's storage.
I know there are saws, chisels and I think, an iron ax head without
its handle," said Kasim.

They were all quiet in the morning sunshine. They all observed
the tall Ethiopian cook as he earnestly picked up bivalve shells and
dug for crabs that scurried to holes in the sand.

"It would take a long time to shape anything as long as the
gash, and I don't know what I would do for pitch, between the
boards," Kasim finally said, the discouragement clear.

Adiva and Eldad drifted toward the far side of the ship where
the teak railing was reachable from the ground, but only Eldad could

reach it. She felt lighter than air to him as she allowed herself to be wrapped up in his long hands and nearly floated to the level of the deck. After she gained her footing, Eldad pulled himself up with one arm, then scrambled over the railing.

The upper deck angled wildly upward, but they had fortunately come aboard midship near the opening to the lower deck. Easing down the precarious stairs, they picked their way through refuse washed there from all over the ship, still standing in two uninviting feet of sea water.

"This is the sleeping space we had," Adiva, pushed past a swinging cabin door. Stepping over the shambles, she reached for the knob on the tall cabinet door. "I had trouble opening and closing this before the storm."

The door had been so perfectly fitted to its frame by the skillful hands of Kasim that it was a near watertight cabinet. Smelling the cedar wood, with still its sweet, clean pungency, Eldad was momentarily transported away. "The scent reminds me of another world, one I knew as a child."

Adiva looked puzzled and Eldad at first regretted revealing his thoughts. He realized that her eyes were soft and interested.

"May I tell you of it some time," he said softly.

Adiva said nothing but smiled.

The cabinet door opened grudgingly, revealing the entire contents to be clean, dry and still neatly stacked. She handed the Eldad a rough woven sack, saying, "Hold open."

The first item, a six by four-inch brown sea sponge, she did not hand to him, but placed it in the bottom of the bag herself

"What is that?" he asked.

"Never you mind," Adiva replied as one would to a child.

This of course answered his question; the sea sponge was used in menstruation. Eldad always marveled at the subtlety and resourcefulness of women handling this aspect of their nature. On a deeper, less conscious level, this cycle of fertility was mysterious and arousing.

Next into the bag were the clothes of all three Babylonians, mostly of that monotonous honey color Jews were required to wear in their homeland. The last item of clothing was a full-length robe Adiva shook out to unfold. Like a sudden burst of sunlight on a dreary day, peacock feathers, the whole color spectrum from pale violet to ruby red sprang from intricately sewn beads. Button-sized highlights were unmistakably gold.

She sighed. "This was given to me by the banker's family in Aden. That seems so long ago."

Eldad held the robe, playfully and smiling broadly. "Put it on for me."

Adiva, blushed. Wordlessly, she took the garment from him turned and slipped it on. She closed the front of the robe with its four gold buttons and faced him with a grand open arm theatrical gesture.

Now he could see the complete design on the front. Not only feathers, but a whole peacock peered forward from the right side, its feathers cleverly arrayed on the left, The collar and borders of the robe bore two-inch cascades of colored beads.

"I've never seen anything like this," he said, "And never any-one like you."

Both allowed the quiet moment needed to let their beings feast on this. But such delight creates a more urgent hunger.

Hillel's head appeared at the cabin door "Dressing for a part in the book of the Tale of a Thousand Nights?" The miraculous accounts of Sinbad the sailor were so popular in Babylon.

Adiva ignored him, handing him his extra clothes. "Anything else stashed in here?"

Her brother smiled and got on all fours on the sloping cabin floor. At the base of the outer wall, he felt for a fingernail fitting grove in the wooden paneling. Finding it, he pulled outward, and a quiet pop opened a one-foot square hidden door.

"Hmmm. How clever." Adiva said. Eldad was sure from her tone that it was not the first time her brother and cousin hid things from her.

In this compartment they had stored the gold coins and jewels not sewn into the lining of the goatskin bags by the banker at Aden. These assets were to be delivered to the Netira family in Cairo.

"We nearly lost these," Hillel worried.

"They are not ours to lose."

Eldad and Adiva watched him count the gleaming gold coins into a drawstring purse of some soft animal skin. To these he added a four-foot weighty chain of interlocking quarter inch gold links.

"I see why Saul and I were hired as additional guards." They could hear the sailors loudly emptying everything useful from the hull. This included a remarkably preserved bail of dried fish, its oily cloth wrapping floating it above the salty water flooding the hull,

Adiva reached for the bag. "We must find a place to secure this, at least temporarily."

For a instant, Hillel resisted ceding control over this third of the assets they were transporting but yielded to the insistent tug from his older sister. The bag dipped a little on the exchange, impressing Adiva with the weight of this precious cargo. With mock imperiousness, she handed the bag to Eldad and commanded. "Now. Guard!"

20

Eldad and Adiva walked toward the seemingly impenetrable mangrove forest.

"I think I know a place no one will ever find," Eldad said, motioning ahead. "It may be more hiding than we need, though."

Adiva studied the sand as they walked and, seeing a jumble of footprints, stopped at the forests edge to pull aside a luxuriant branch blocking the pathway through the mangroves. Adiva shook her head, unsmiling. "What we carry can never be hidden well enough. And we don't know how long we will be marooned on this rock in the sea."

Eldad tried to sound positive, which he distinctly did not feel. "At least someone has been here, sometime. I'm sure the gamal with her young that I saw didn't swim here."

"You saw what? Camels here?"

"Yes. It's the same word for you? Eldad moved his hand like a wave to represent a hump. "That's what I came upon, or rather they came upon me as I floated around the crater lake. Though I first thought the lake was a delirious vision, nothing was as startling as those long, droopy faces looking at me as I paddled toward them."

He paused, "They seemed entirely unruffled at seeing me."

In an unexpected clearing within the forest, they could see the telltale leavings of an animal that seemed to prefer the young leaves of the mangrove trees, and whose munchings had sculpted a path to the southern beach.

"I wondered who left these presents for us," she said sidestepping a graying pile of dung. Then she laughed, saying, "If we had something to grow, this would be gold!"

"I doubt you've ever grown anything but flowers." Eldad now felt secure enough to poke at her a little. Adiva smiled.

He was aware of nothing now, save for an otherworldly quiet. A rise in the terrain brought Adiva, walking ahead, to Eldad's height, as though she had ascended steps. Hesitatingly, Eldad softly placed his hand on her shoulder and was surprised when she immediately stopped, turning toward him. It was as if she had been waiting for this very moment. They were now only a few inches apart and he could feel the warmth of her skin.

He tenderly touched her forehead, then caressed down her cheek, stopping below her uplifted chin. He marveled again on the exquisite perfection of her face and the neck of a golden swan. He wished the rope wasn't wrapped securely around him, and he'd like to shed the two goat skin bags he carried. He could feel subtle movements from her and allowed his imagination to overwhelm his natural shyness.

Even while marveling at the intoxicating strangeness of it all, he felt bold. He moved his fingers to behind her neck. Their faces were so close they could breathe the same air from deep and rapid breaths.

Eyes closed, Adiva reached for Eldad's face, tracing with a forefinger the high cheekbones and finally his slightly parted lips.

Eldad could see her lick her lips, leaving them a gleaming invitation.

His voice was low and breathless. "I want to kiss you, so deeply and so long we will never forget."

"Oh, my brave and beautiful man, oh, yes!"

The kiss was tentative at first, a sip from a new bottle of wine. Each sucked in the moisture from the other and Adiva's mouth opened enough to welcome his soft tongue that had till now only played upon her lips. More urgently now, his tongue filled her mouth which she eagerly welcomed.

Now, arms entwined, he felt their upper bodies meet and her firm breasts pressed deliciously against his chest. She held him firmly to her and Eldad wanted to stay there, reveling in her closeness.

Then suddenly there came a boisterous cry of joy from the south end of the trail. A parade of sailors shouted excitedly to each other as they carried their precious bounty of jewels from the ship back toward the encampment. Eldad and Adiva, still flushed with excitement, quickly stepped away from each other. Considering their present circumstances, the absurdity of this secretive behavior didn't occur to them.

Stepping away felt to Eldad like being torn away. He looked at Adiva and was quite sure she was feeling the same. She lowered her eyes, hiding her embarrassment.

Each of the four sailors stopped briefly to show what they had found, dug up, or, for one, brought down with a sling.

But the last one, a Chinese seaman, carried only a large bundle of dried tree branches, their leaves different from either the acacia or mangrove. Responding to their quizzical looks, the sailor said, "Lamu. I found lamu trees. This time of year is just before they shed their leaves. But it is strange. There wasn't a leaf of this spicy hot wood tree on the ground. Not one."

"Ha! Our camels," Eldad exclaimed, "Never miss a tasty snack. But what use do we have of the leaves and long seed pods still on the tree?"

The Chinese sailor, buoyant of mood, smiled broadly. "People in my tribe call the tree the mother's friend. It can be a tree of life. I have seen it return starving children to vigor in a few weeks. We grind these leaves to powder and put it on and in everything we eat."

"This is like no other tree I have known," Eldad said, interested as always in plants useful in relieving suffering, wondered if these trees truly had medicinal value. "Where are these trees?"

"A cluster is just over the western rim of the crater, some trees four times a man's height." The old sailor turned and trudged off with his large bundle of browning leaves and seed pods.

"Now we're going to eat the trees?" Adiva joked when the sailor was out of earshot.

Eldad laughed "Either the trees or the camels. Take your pick."

They were now on the long, curving south beach walking

steadily toward the break in the lava wall where they could climb up. Though Eldad remembered it being farther, the jagged split appeared around the first bend. They found their way between and around boulders to the higher plateau of lava rock. The air was cooler, an updraft of salty freshness from the sea.

21

Adiva was as astonished as Eldad had been on first seeing the vast crater. The steeply sloping crater walls gave the landscape the punched-out appearance of fresh cut dough.

"It is a miracle as you have said. But I see nowhere offering even the remotest concealment. I love the water. It is so peaceful here," said Adiva as she gazed into the depths of the blue green caldera.

Eldad uncurled the rope from his waist and peered here and there over the crater rim until he spied a prominent overhang hiding the rock face below.

"What are you doing," asked Adiva.

"Looking for the spot I fell from into the lake. On the way to that life-giving splash, I saw, or thought I saw, an opening in the rock face. For some reason, I couldn't see it from the surface of the lake, but I didn't look very hard."

The Danite found a man-sized boulder near the ledge and secured one end of the rope about its base and the other end around his waist.

"Hold the rope, just in case," He asked without hesitation. He knew he could depend on her physical competence if something went wrong, and this only intensified his attraction to her.

Eldad eased himself over the lip of the crater wall and began to rappel down the steep face. Soon he had a firm foothold on a two-foot hood shaped rock formation that jutted out from the otherwise smooth surface. He leaned over just far enough to see over the hood's edge, and cried out, "We have found it!"

A surprisingly smooth circle of volcanic rock seemed to flow down from its hooded overhang to form the sides of the five-foot opening. As it had from its top, a narrow band of stone jutted out at the bottom of the circle.

The sun was glinting fully off the surface of the water 20' below at such an angle as to illuminate the ceiling of what lay beyond the opening.

The length of fibrous rope stretched as far as the bottom of the oval entrance, and there he tied it tightly to a conveniently jutting shard of basalt stone, lest it drift away while his attention was elsewhere. He glanced only briefly into the chasm's interior and called out, "A cave! This looks like it goes back many cubits." He grasped the rope. "Can you lower yourself down on the rope? If you fall, I'll catch you, or the water will!"

Adiva was already over the ledge and clearing the rock face easily on the taut rope. Eldad reached for her as her sandaled feet came to his eye level. He held her thighs, then her waist, until they both had lowered her to the lower ledge. Eldad had one foot planted within the cave as he finished lowering her to him. For a moment he held her to him before her feet touched down on the security of the stone.

Adiva smiled, then laughed, throwing her head back.

Eldad looked around to see if anything had caught her eye. "What is so amusing?"

"Nothing really," she said. "For a moment I had a feeling like I was a little girl back home, playing in a pond with my grandfather." Eldad accepted that and smiled.

She wound her arms behind his neck to stop the necessary slide down his torso to firm footing. Eldad turned and eased her down to straddling the cave opening as he was. He ducked his head under the hooded overhang and they found themselves in a seven-foot-tall space whose level floor stretched out twenty feet before being lost in blackness. Light reflected from the water's surface gave a golden glow to the arched ceiling, a bulging crack in the mountain of stone.

"This is bigger than rooms in a house," Adiva said as she studied the cavernous space.

"Let's make sure we're alone here. If we leave our valuables, we don't want wild things tearing them apart."

"Or us," she added.

"We'll go in as far as we can feel our way and listen and smell the air for animals like bats."

Passing out of the ambient light, he reached for her hand and eased in half steps along what seemed to be a corridor as wide as his arm span.

"Feel this," he said, moving her hand to the stone wall to his right.

"It's wet," Adiva said with surprise.

A dozen more blind baby steps ended in a wall, which he could feel was taller than his reach.

"Are we in another..." Adiva stopped before finishing the sentence, her voice magically booming in their ears.

"Cave," Eldad's voice being even more amplified, as though near the resonant frequency of the stone. He looked down at her and was surprised he could see a faint outline of her face.

"I must be imagining I can see you, my lovely princess."

Adiva turned to face him "No, maybe not imagine. I think I see the sparkle of your sky-blue eyes."

They both looked up to see the image each thought they saw of each other brighten.

Piercing the otherwise inky darkness was a shaft of light from a mid-day sun through an unseen defect in the high ceiling. Though dim besides the small ball of light on the cavern's floor, they could make out the faint interior of this echo chamber.

The jagged ceiling of the chamber was 14' in places, higher in others, particularly where the shaft of light found its way in. The floor was a oval, as wide as the chamber was tall, and sloped gently upward into the mountain. It was as though this and the antechamber leading outside had been blown like bubbles into the molten rock eons ago.

"Shh," Adiva commanded. "Listen."

Eldad strained in the quiet but finally could hear the quite unmistakable tinkle of dripping water. "Your hearing is so much more sensitive than mine."

"My Zav used to tell me that," Adiva smiling again at the memory of her grandfather. She paused. "Of course, he couldn't hear anything much at all."

"The other side, somewhere over there," Adiva offered, waving an arm in the dark, smacking into Eldad's belly.

"I shouldn't have let go of you," he said, deftly grabbing her errant hand. "You're nothing but trouble," he added while pulling her to him.

This time it was she pulling him with her shuffling steps to the caverns opposite wall. "Ow!" she cried out as her head encountered an unseen outcropping from the wall. "I'm alright," she reassured Eldad. It was from this defect the water issued, in broad steady rivulets that seemed to spring from the stone face and gather at this point. There was a sudden break in the smooth floor. Adiva clutched Eldad's hand, squeezing harder. She knelt in the darkness, pulling him down with her.

"Feel along the edge. Let's see what kind of hole this is before we fall in it!"

What they felt lapping the lip of the basin was *hot* water.

"What is this?" Adiva cried out, clearly delighted. "A bathtub of hot spring water? How on earth?"

They played awhile on the water's mildly steaming surface, invigorating, though it was wetting their robes.

"Perhaps it *is* from the earth. I have heard of hot springs in some restless mountains," Eldad said.

"What do you mean, restless mountains?"

"There are mountains in my homeland that spew gas sometimes, and even blow up themselves and everything in their paths. I think the Sambation River has something to do with one of these."

"More mysteries from you."

"This river is a mystery to me as well, but one firmly believed by the elders of my people. It is commonly known as the Sabbath River because only on our holy day do the roiling rocks and sand calm themselves. But we are, on their Sabbath day, forbidden to cross.

"But it is you who are mysterious. You have told me only of your schooling, and a little about the Goan."

They were sitting in utter darkness, enjoying the steam on their faces. Adiva shed her sandals, hitched up the honey-colored robe and tried an exploratory toe into the surface of the water.

"Not as hot as I thought. I think your story of exploding mountains made it seem warmer than it is."

She let a leg dip in, both to further test the water, but also to feel the basin's depth. The water was delightfully clean to taste, without the hard taste of well water.

"We could make tea in this water." The stone tub was deeper than she could reach with her arm.

"Is it comfortable?" Eldad asked softly. He brought his hand from the warm water to the back of her neck.

Adiva's turned to him part way and nodded. Her eyes did not meet his own but instead looked downward, only occasionally glancing toward his face expectantly. Was she trembling slightly? Eldad wondered if he should say something but remained quiet.

"Even though I am very far from home. I am still of my father's household," she whispered, and looked at Eldad expectantly.

Eldad was uncomfortable, nervous, although he was not quite sure why.

"I....I.., I have never known a man." She breathed a long sigh of relief, as if after holding her breath. "I am a bethulah, a virgin. You will be the first..."

Eldad stopped her with a gentle kiss. He now understood completely. His most profound dream was to be realized.

He stood, looked at Adiva, smiling, then lifted his robe over his head. She in turn raised her own garment, revealing to Eldad the most beautiful thing he had ever seen.

22

Hillel had long considered it his obligation to see to his sister's safety, even though Adiva hated his interference. Besides she could mostly take care of herself. Now, he had begun to worry about her lengthening absence. He looked to his cousin Yosef and to Saul.

"Where do you think...do you think it has been too long?"

Saul did a bad job of suppressing a laugh.

Hillel, even though he was annoyed, understood. What Saul wasn't considering was that as her brother, in their father's absence, he felt responsible to protect Adiva's honor as well. Hillel's admiration and trust of the young Danite had grown in the last few days. Still, Eldad was a young man and didn't Hillel himself understand what that could mean when one was around a beautiful young woman. For a moment, his mind drifted back home to Babylon and to a sharp vision of a particular woman there, and their time alone together.

He forced himself to stop. There was no time for this kind of idle thought. There was another issue, besides Adiva and Eldad's wellbeing. To begin with, none of them knew what unseen dangers might lurk on the leeward side of the dormant volcano. So far, an aggressive bird protesting their egg thievery was the worst they had encountered.

Hillel had also become burdened with something Captain Mustafa had said in one of his agitated rants. If he was right, and how could any of them know, considering his intermittent delirium, that they were marooned on one of the larger of a string of islands. Hillel, though far from a seasoned sailor, was able to read the captain's Arabic Sea charts, but none mentioned or located these volcanic rocks.

Hillel decided he could satisfy all his concerns. He stood decisively. "We will find Adiva. And discover more of what faces us in this place." He motioned for his companions to also rise.

"Yosef. Pack rope and get knives from the cut-throat crewmen. Better yet, bring one of them. Tell Kasim I said to join us."

Yosef didn't find it hard to locate the burly carpenter, who was never far from his master. Kasim, was at the edge of the acacia forest stooped over the 20 foot trunk of a two-foot-thick acacia his men had felled with an ax. Next to it lay an even longer trunk, curved in the middle, that had fallen on its own.

"It is not impossible, if Allah wills it," Kasim said, without even a greeting.

Yosef was puzzled. "Yes, of course. But if Allah wills what?"

"I know of the writings in your sacred book from Captain Mustafa. Some, anyway." Kasim didn't look up from burning a deep crease in the gnarled trunk. "Captain Mustafa also taught me about wood when I was a child. Allah commanded, 'Have them make a chest of acacia wood.' This was the Ark of the Covenant."

"Mmm. You have in mind fixing *our* ark with this wood?" said Yosef who knew that didn't make sense.

He then noticed other iron tools, several long chisels and a three foot saw with handles at each end, which the ship's carpenter had retrieved from the grounded boat. "Oh, I see."

Kasim nodded. "This wood is hard but floats well and the sea worms can't burrow into it."

"Later," said Yosef, "I will come and see what progress you have made. Hillel is taking us to explore the island and find his sister and the Danite. He wants you to come and bring one of your sailors who can throw a knife."

Kasim looked thru the 50 yards of forest between them and his master's thorny enclosure. "No. I cannot leave my captain. He is helpless. Other crewmen may not love him as I do and I believe one of them hates him without reason. Perhaps he is childish enough to blame my captain for what befell us."

Kasim used the hot poker he was holding to point toward a

man alone at one of the campfires. He was squatting, pushing about unburned wood fragments with a stick. He stood up, and he looked sharply in their direction, his expression a forced smile. He started over toward the two.

"My captain hired this Ashot, from some land we do not know but he is as deadly with a knife as he is with a sling. With the captain's infirmity, the other sailors mostly follow my orders, as my master instructed each of them before they came aboard. Some don't remember, but Ashot does, but just doesn't seem to care."

Yosef winced. "Are you sure we want him? We are not warriors, after all."

"He seems to have no anger toward others, only the captain. He says nothing menacing. Truly, he says almost nothing at all. The captain did tell me that he uses a sling like King David."

Ashot was short and wore robes of more color than most. He stopped a few feet from Kasim, and stood silently, looking at no one.

"They," Kasim said, pointing to Yosef, "want you to guard them while they explore the rest of the island, Ashot." Yosef noticed an immediate and seemingly genuine smile flickered across Ashot's otherwise expressionless face. Kasim had learned the captain's lesson well. Don't *tell* him what to do, *ask* him for his help.

Ashot nodded to Yosef and without delay started down the beach where the others had gathered. Yosef hurried after him. They passed the Ethiopian cook, scraping salt from the undersides of mangrove leaves, muttering to himself, "tilik'i, big," then shouted at Ashot, loud enough for everyone else to hear, "Big, *just* big!"

"Big what?" Yosef asked, finally catching up.

"Birds. Kill big birds."

Yosef remembered it was Ashot who carried three large, skillfully plucked sea birds into the encampment. He compared that to the pitiful strangled offerings of other crewmen. With a faint nod towards this husky man, he acknowledged the achievement.

Hillel was unhappy that Kasim was not going along but welcomed an armed guard. Although he and Yosef could both use a knife, they had done so only for fun.

Wordlessly, without being told, Ashot shouldered several coils of rope and a goatskin bag of water and trudged off toward the north, where, half a mile distant, a forbidding wall of rock dove 600 feet into the Red Sea.

The small group fell in behind Hillel who for now was not the leader, but a follower.

Within fifteen minutes, the group reached the end of the beach.

Swimming around the rock face that jutted out far past the shoreline, Yosef, Hillel, Saul, and Ashot saw that the currents looked unpredictable. Only last night they had buried one of their own who'd encountered the much greater risk. "We don't know how far around it is to the other side of this mountain," Hillel said, looking ahead. "It may be a short swim or maybe no beach for 100 yards or more." He stared at Saul, no doubt the strongest swimmer among them.

Saul noticed the expectant look. "Maybe they'll be so busy eating me the rest of you will slip by."

He laughed nervously. "But who's going to be the first of you in the water on the swim back?"

Yosef didn't even hear him. He and Ashot were studying the rock face and had already found several starting footholds but could not immediately tell which led to higher plateaus. Hillel motioned to Ashot, speaking Arabic. "You take those. I'll try here."

The 25 foot climb was slow, but both sets of footholds led to a broad ledge that, unseen from the sandy ground, curved halfway round the stone mountain. It looked as though the volcanic rock had slipped a dozen yards west from its base.

The sun, now overhead in a cloudless sky, warmed air softened by water droplets from waves that pounded the rock below, the relentless against the unyielding.

Ashot secured the two ropes he'd carried and tossed them down to Yosef and Saul and looked around. "There is something special about this place. A smell of the sea." He paused, putting his nose in the air. "But also, the camel yard." He kicked at ossified-looking balls that skittered away.

"Eldad claimed he saw a mother and baby camels at the crater lake. But here?" Hillel motioned, first to a winded Saul and Yosef, then to Ashot, "Pull up the ropes, we may need them."

The ledge began to have jagged intrusions from younger look-ing, less worn rock. The trail also buckled convulsively in places but remained passable around the far northern tip of the quiescent volcano. Before they reached that point, they could see nothing of the island's broad western face.

That changed abruptly when they stepped single file around a dagger-like rock shard that stabbed into the mountain side. The trail widened enough for all the men to stand together. Astonished, they stood in silent wonder.

Stretching down all the way to the sea's restless shore was a sharply, then gently sloping blanket of hardened lava flow, broken at the bottom by hundred-yard triangles of black sand and soil. Even at their quarter mile distance, they could see tall date palm trees in two inviting clusters near the sandy beach.

Ashot shaded his eyes from the sun and cried out, "Allahu Akbar!"

Hillel squinted in the direction Ashot was pointing but saw nothing.

"Allah's mercy has brought us dates to eat camel's milk!"

Hillel translated for Saul, who exclaimed, "I see them! I saw something dark move between clumps of trees." He looked hopefully at Ashot. "Camel's milk, you say?"

The trail was wide enough but its upper leg sloped downward at an uneasy angle. Ashot was many paces ahead of the others and had slipped once but landed on his butt, no doubt thankful for its ample padding. Thereafter he moved more cautiously, till he reached the edge of the smooth lava landscape stretching two hundred yards to the sea. Cracks were more evident up close and stubborn shrubs clung to life in yard long pale green clusters. As he waited for the others, Ashot unfurled his sling and selected thumb-sized stones, as smooth as he could find.

The last to make it down was Saul, whom anyone could see was about to complain. Once out on the flatter surface, they could see most of the northern side of the volcano, the beaches with trees, the black sand, and the colossal wall of rock, the entire northern tip of the island.

The trail soon disappeared but was no longer needed and they moved easily over the mostly unbroken surface toward the first garden-like cluster of palms, some growing close to the lapping surf. As the four entered the tree line, they heard hoof beats and saw a blur of very long legs exiting the other side of almost fifty date palm trees.

"What have we done that made them bolt?" Saul sighed wistfully. Ashot laughed then fell silent.

"Maybe after we get to know them?" Yosef quipped, first in Arabic, then Hebrew.

Ashot looked very thoughtful. "The camels, they were frightened by our intrusion. But not *that* frightened. More like startled. They are not feral. They have known contact with people, probably belong to somebody. Truly, men killed over ownership. I...." Stopping, he said nothing further.

Yosef thought he saw a brief movement of the Ashot's hand toward his knife, involuntary, perhaps unnoticed.

"But what harm in our milking mothers?" Saul said, perhaps with somewhat more excitement than he wished to display.

Ashot grunted at this, uncoiling from around his chest a length of hemp rope, and tying a slip knot at one end. He moved toward Saul, who was last to shoulder the goatskin water bag, and deftly relieved him of it before he could ask or protest. Without offering the others a drink, he took a long pull of the fresh water, and, to the momentary horror of his companions, he squirted the remainder on the sand.

Almost at once, calm returned when they realized that there was much water on the island, owing to its ability to store what fell from the sky in a vast subterranean honeycomb. It was probably just a reaction to their slaking thirst when they came ashore.

Ashot did not seem to care anyway. He took off at great speed through the palm tree grove, whose other side opened onto a long strip of shoreline strewn with man sized boulders. They lost sight of him when the sandy beach lurched to the right.

Saul kicked dejectedly at the long, slender stalks that once held sweet nuggets of fruit. "No dates. The camels know where to eat."

He looked up in the canopy of almost overlapping treetops, then pointed with great fanfare, "We are delivered!" The tall date palms were studded with clusters of their gooey fruit, too high for craning camel necks to reach. Saul beseeched his Babylonian friends. "Can you climb?"

Hillel was already looking at Yosef. "Just a few years ago you climbed like a monkey, *all* the time, on everything. Now, *kohf*, be something besides a menace to your own safety!"

The stocky Yosef drug his hands ape like and waddled toward a particularly promising palm. He picked up a long rope the gypsy had dropped and wrapped one end around the two-foot-thick trunk, allowing the other to dangle free. The bark was spiked every inch by tough frond stubs cleverly pointing upward to catch every drop of rain. Yosef tried his full weight on the first rung of spikes, and they held with only a creaking protest. The rope held him as he ratcheted up the 20 feet to the first and ripest stalk of dates, looking like clusters of yellow-brown grapes.

Yosef grunted and bit into one of the browning dates. He looked down at an expectant Saul, now barely able to contain his salivation, and gagged, "Aaggghha," complete with convincing retching. The hungry one's face fell to somewhere just above his collar bones, until Yosef burst into a mischievous cackle, joined immediately by Hillel, whose prominent Adam's apple bobbed merrily. Never wishing to be left out of a good laugh, Saul gave an appreciative chuckle at this perfectly childish display.

"Throw it down," Saul said, "Or I'll climb up there with you!" Yosef began rocking the tree by repeatedly shifting his weight. "No, no!", Yosef protested from his perch, "That will be the end for the tree and us!" He unsheathed his knife and cut two clusters which he tossed high in the air, making Saul scramble to catch them. The Asherite popped a particularly brown beauty entirely into his yawning maw. He bit carefully to avoid the pit, which he sputtered out between pursed but smiling lips.

"Oh, a garden of Eden, this is," he rhapsodized, as two more morsels filled both sides of his mouth. He was so lost in gustatory ecstasy, the second cluster of dates dropped on his head. Unfazed, the Asherite looked heavenward and, in a voice pious enough to make him a sage, declared, "And the Lord brought down manna from heaven, and 40 years did the Hebrews eat manna, until they came to the promised land."

Hillel was also munching contentedly on their sweet delights, when with no warning the ground beneath them lurched up and down, shaking a terrified Yosef from his perch, landing fully on both his friends. They all sprawled onto the palm forest floor.

"What in God's name?" was all one of them could manage.

"I can't stand up!" yelled Saul. Hillel was equally wobbly but saw Yosef rise more easily. None of them knew of such earth cataclysms, except in their Torah. If this was an earthquake, Hillel believed it was a display of God's power. Always struggling to be a pious man, he could not escape the thought that it could as well be His wrath.

Then, nothing. They brushed themselves off. Nothing but Yosef had fallen on them. Saul spat out two date pits he'd been savoring after the single jolt. Everything had gone eerily silent, notably absent was the background sound of the many sea birds' calls.

As suddenly as it had stopped, the melody of the seashore resumed with a distressed sounding *ark, ark* of an unseen bird. This leeward side of the island sprouted a mangrove forest three times the size of the one where they landed. Joining the first call from that direction was a deep, emphatic bark, *kowoork*. At the closer shoreline, a gentle surf lapped a long silver sand beach, which, even at a distance they could see swarmed with an improbable mixture of diving, fighting birds. The wading birds, the herons, and egrets were missing from their usual posts.

Halfway down the sandy beach, the trio was stopped cold by a screech from what seemed an apparition. A wildly agitated camel raced by with Ashot straddling its back, clinging to its neck. His expression was one of wide-eyed terror, as he reached out beseeching their help. Close behind ran a baby camel, perhaps a few weeks old, with a length of rope tied loosely around its neck.

It was Yosef who acted quickly. Sprinting toward the trailing rope, he managed to trap it beneath his pounding foot. The little camel was jerked off his feet and squealed as Yosef held firmly to the rope and the baby's writhing neck. As with every mother, the sound of her offspring in distress overrode any fear with a primal survival instinct. She stopped and turned so suddenly, Ashot was thrown in a graceful arc landing in a heap on the black sand.

The young camel cried again. Yosef let go of its neck but not the rope. It was well he did, as the charge from the enraged female would have run over him.

The mother sidled up to and carefully sniffed her calf, who searched out a teat and began to nurse, she calmed noticeably.

Ashot approached, clearing sand from his mouth and face. He was ebullient, what one would expect on finding a long-lost family member. "This mother belongs to someone. Until the earth heaved, she was easy, and liked being fed the dates I brought. She's been ridden before and let me get on her back. I was holding the baby's rope and we were walking when..." He took small, slow steps toward the mother camel, and stroked her neck. She turned her head toward him and spit in his face.

As one, the group burst into laughter. Ashot sputtered and screamed as he ran the fifty yards to the water's edge, plunging himself into the roiling surf. He immediately screamed louder as he sprang up and fled the water.

"It's hot! Oh, help me, it's so hot." He stripped his robe off and stood naked a few yards from the water, his skin bright red. The others ran quickly to his side while Hillel continued to the water's edge. A finger quickly into the water was withdrawn, with a disbelieving expression.

Saul offered the now shivering and hurting all over gypsy his own dry robe, and Ashot gratefully accepted. Saul walked down to the water and silently studied the water beyond the close-in wavelets.

"Look at this," he declared, pointing. "Steam rising from the water, and fish belly up everywhere. Nothing grabs them from the water, only the birds snatch up their meal without landing."

"I saw once a red tide that killed like this, in Egypt," Ashot offered. His pain and shaking had diminished.

Saul walked down the beach until he found an uneaten carcass of a small fish. He picked it up and it fell apart in his hand.

"Cooked! These fish are cooked!" Without a moment's hesitation, he raised flakes of whitish flesh to his mouth, and said dejectedly, "Over cooked."

Hillel thought for a moment, "The shake of the ground and the boiled fish, maybe something caused both."

When they turned away from the water, only a noosed rope was left of their camel caravan. Mother had freed her baby and off they went, not a drop of mother's milk left behind.

23

Yosef looked up at the long lava rock slope toward the 600 foot summit of the island. They were only halfway there.

He tried to slow slightly to let the Asherite catch up to them, but he still trailed the group. Saul, breathing with significant effort could not, for once, even speak.

Saul, however, was not the only malcontent. "What are we looking for? Why climb this accursed mountain?" Ashot complained to unsympathetic ears.

Yosef admitted to himself that there may be something to the gypsy's protests. The higher they ascended, the more treacherous the trail became.

Ashot would never make it to the summit. The burns on his feet stopped any further climbing. Grimacing, he sat, head in hands on a shaded rock.

Yosef accepted the reality of the situation. "Rest. When we find the Danite, he will help you."

Ashot nodded in resigned agreement.

Leaving him and moving on, Yosef was beginning to lose confidence in his plan. They were facing something very strange, and the pieces didn't fit together. A sea that suddenly turned boiling hot. The earth jolting under their feet, then the eerie quiet.

Hillel interrupted his thoughts. He pointed toward the lip of the highest rocky table. "Now, quickly. We must see what we can see." Then, taking to himself, he quickly added, "Maybe nothing, maybe there's nothing to see."

They pressed on, but there was no real trail the last 100' to the crater's pouting edge, only a jumble of vertical spears of volcanic rock, like rows of teeth bared against intruders. Waiting for Saul to arrive, the group gathered beside a boulder taller than any of them.

Hillel looked up, shook his head. "No way to climb these faces. We'll have to go back and try from the windward side of the island."

Yosef could not accept this notion. He scampered up to the base of the nearest 20-foot spike and unfurled the length of rope he'd wound around his waist. Wordlessly, he fashioned a slip knot, on an abundant lasso, which he threw over his head toward the rock's pointed tip. It missed and fell on his outstretched arm.

"You can't..." Hillel started, then stopped when the rope, thrown again, slipped neatly over the mountainous spikes. Before another word could be spoken, Yosef had scaled this first barrier, between them and the top.

"It's easy," he said, without conviction. Saul looked pale, but resolute as he tested the rope, then, with surprising agility, used his strong arms to walk himself up to the first crown, which was easily broad enough for the three of them. Steadying themselves, they eyed the next obstacle, a fissure 10' across, between them and next tier of rocks.

"You fall, you'll kill us both," said Yosef as he looped the lasso about the Asherite's waist, then wound the remainder of the rope around his own. "We jump when I say.... now!" Both men leapt over the chasm, but unaccountably Yosef's foot tangled in a twist of rope, and he was far of the other side when jerked to safety by the tether to the Asherite.

"So glad I could help!" Saul chortled, picking himself up from where he had sprawled. Hillel, who looked as though he could simply step across the moat, landed without incident.

"Where do we go..." Saul was interrupted by the knotted end of a rope thrown from who knows where, smacking him on his crown. Confused, he grabbed the rope and was greeting with a burst of laughter, clearly from a man and woman above.

"We've caught one!" Adiva cried, jerking at the rope just hard enough to wrench it from Saul's hands, then let it dangle within reach.

"No, you've caught three!" he retorted, again taking firm hold of the line.

Yosef unceremoniously snatched it from Saul's hand and quickly ascended to the ledge where Eldad and Adiva stood. He wondered if they would have to haul Saul up, a feat which would require all of them to accomplish.

Yosef pulled himself over the slab's angular crest and was level with a fissured but flat plateau 200' across. Eldad and Adiva were smiling, and Yosef hugged his cousin.

"We came looking for you. What is this shaking the earth?" he asked.

Yosef saw their smiles darken, and Eldad said, "The rest, Saul and Hillel, we'll get them up here and look around."

The rope, looped securely around a boulder, tightened and the anchoring rock shifted slightly.

"Our most robust Asherite has begun his ascent is my guess," quipped Adiva, seating herself on the stone to prevent further movement. Before long, Saul's flushed and sweaty face popped up over the stone ledge.

They waited for him to catch his breath. "No more!" he declared, "You better have a way down from here that doesn't need require so many acrobatics."

Hillel clawed his way into view and was soon by their side.

Walking and climbing along the plateau, every mountain face was a disquieting shear drop down to the roiling Red Sea. Other than from the Sea, this whole north of the island could be seen only from this vantage point.

Their attention was abruptly jerked toward the northern most rim of the mountaintop crater, from which they heard a deep, guttural rumble, then a higher pitched, tooth rattling explosion that moved the air around them. Instantly, a dense cloud of black smoke pierced the clear blue sky, as the five of them approached the crater's far edge.

Then all could see a sight never to be forgotten.

Eldad, first to speak, said in wonder, "The Yam Suph, the Sea of Reeds...*is on fire!"* The party gaped at a spot in the sea 500 yards from the north face of the island. White steam rose furiously, only to be engulfed by menacing flame-encrusted black ash. Even as high as they were, they could see the water boil at its edges.

Hillel looked agitated. "Look. We can feel the heat from this thing even at this distance. And there's a smell in the air I don't like."

"I smell it, too," Eldad said, "Like the yellow powder we sprinkle on wounds. Or rather when the powdered bandages burn. Not easy to forget."

Adiva was intently watching the steady steam and ash spewing from the surface of the Sea. She turned to her brother. "This is dangerous to us. I don't know how it makes the shaking, but the shocks from the earth may be the least of our problems."

Even in the short time they had been standing on the precipice, the plume of swirling of the black and white eruption had risen to a third the height of the mountain on which they stood.

Another loud belch from beneath the waves brought up a core of flame infused with fist-sized chunks of molten rock. Each fired jets of steam on reentry.

"We must get as far from this as possible," Eldad said, revealing no panic in his voice. "The way down to our side of the island is past the rim of the crater lake."

"We have to go for Ashot," Yosef said. "His feet were burned in the hot water, and he stopped halfway up."

The tall African nodded, "The way you came, I think I know the lower part. It is on the same level as the crater lake, and a camel trail will lead us back to Ashot more easily than climbing."

He paused. "Who among us has the best sight for things far away?"

They all spoke at once, each believing the gift to be theirs.

Eldad looked satisfied. "We'll all look in every direction." He began leading the group away from the menacing beauty of a fountain of death toward the windward side of the mountain top. From here they could see a wide-angle view of the surrounding waters, not apparent from their beach.

They could also see the dense, now grey fog of ashen steam, drifting almost intact, as though sandwiched between enveloping currents of air.

When the group mounted the highest point of the crater rim, they were transfixed by the vision of the sun playing on the white-caps of an endless sea.

As they scanned the horizon beyond the southern tip of the island, there was no mistaking the single conical peak rising from the briny water a mile distant.

"There, look!" Hillel pointed. "A sister island!"

"It's a distant relative," Saul injected, unable to resist any pun, "Too far away to visit."

Yosef didn't get the humor. He was hardly listening. He was thinking of how hard and dangerous reaching that island would be but kept his pessimism to himself.

24

The shadows were lengthening as they entered the base camp, finding it unsettled, but still functioning under the bear-sized carpenter's control. The windward beaches had absorbed the powerful, single jolt that shook sand in their faces as it knocked them flat. The men were still terrified, until Kasim's growling commands seemed to make them more frightened of *him*. He demanded that each get up immediately and continue their assigned duty. He had some crew shoveling sand from beneath the ships hull. Others were working the on acacia tree trunks with saws, mallets, and wedges. Two crewmen besides Kasim had experience working wood, and together they had an audacious plan to fashion a patch for the 6 foot gash in the boat's hull.

"Allah will provide," was the ship carpenter's reply to such reasonable questions as, "but what will we do for pitch?" Ordinarily, seams in the ship's hull would be firmly sealed with hardened lamb or goat fat, but tar was better.

Eldad looked at Hillel whose expression reflected some acceptance of Kasim's plan.

The aroma of fish being smoked over mounds of embers, stirred sharp appetites and the vigilant gaze of the lanky Ethiopian cook policed this precious food supply. Fortunately, the crew's catch this second day exceeded by threefold their first efforts. The gutted fish were seasoned with pepper and sumac which the Ethiopian had salvaged in abundance from the beached vessel, and they hung in clusters of six, heads tied together with string on tented poles. The cook knew that his popularity would plunge dangerously if he did not soon feed these sometimes-violent crewmen.

Ashot, hobbling badly, appeared in front of the fire and immediately the Ethiopian fed him a crisp skinned white fish. All eyes tuned to stare at them, but before the envious crew could protest, he cut them off. "The nomad is injured, and I need him or your food will not get done." Motioning with a stick, the cook set him to tending the coals under the clusters of fish, offering protection that motivated a new alliance with the shadowy Ashot. And he didn't talk, which made him even more suitable.

After a few minutes, Eldad arrived and pointed to a flat boulder. Yosef translated, "Let me look at your feet. Sit there." Ashot grumbled but followed passively.

Eldad knelt before him and, grasping his left foot, inspected it carefully.

"Hmm.... red, but no blisters." He gently lowered it and picked up the other foot. He smiled. "This is more painful than it is dangerous. I know the water burned you, but on this side of the island, it is cool and will be soothing. Walk in it, sit down in it."

Ashot, saying nothing, walked back to the smoking fires and began adding wood chips to the nearest.

Adiva had lingered behind Hillel and Saul, who had reached the captain's enclosure. Kasim left the woodworking crew and sat on the sand beside the propped up, fully alert Captain Mustafa.

"Get me up!" he hissed at his loyal slave. He was alert enough to require their full attention. The carpenter's upturned hands and raised eyebrows questioned Eldad silently about what to do.

Mustafa bellowed. "Get me out of here! Jahim, hell awaits us in this place." Hillel leaned in close to Eldad and translated. "The captain says we are going to she'ol if we stay here." He paused "Or *wherever* this place is. Should I ask?"

Eldad knew better than to agitate Mustafa further. He bent down to loop his arms beneath the captain's emaciated armpits, gently lifting him to a standing position. His good leg would not support him, so Eldad held him up.

Mustafa groaned loudly at the movement of his splinted leg and Eldad marveled that from the look of the wound he wasn't shrieking. He knew that unexpected loss of pain was not always a good sign. But then, perhaps, the last dose of black opium tar may still be granting its God sent relief.

Eldad felt the captain's skin, and bones frame shiver in a gust of sea breeze, so he carefully lifted him closer to the fire.

"Take him, Kasim." The carpenter slid a furry arm around his master's chest. Eldad knelt before them and placed his face inches from the broken leg, smelling the splinted limb. Captain Mustafa and Kasim were both watching him suspiciously. Eldad looked up smiling and nodding agreeably but said nothing.

For a moment, Eldad was remembering his grandfather and teacher. Was he really only ten when he began training with the incredibly old healer?

"Remember, my grandson," Sav said, after they had examined an old woman who had the look of death about her, "first with the eyes, then with the hands, never with the mouth."

He could hear Sav's voice, "But try to say something good and positive. Keep your anxiety and gloom to yourself."

"Hillel, tell the captain he is a strong and brave man."

Mustafa waved this aside. "You're not here, any of you, to tell me that. What does this delegation of the damned have to say?"

Hillel looked to Eldad for encouragement, then took a deep breath. "We," he said, pointing to Yosef and the Asherite, "were exploring the leeward side of the island when the shake happened."

He recounted Ashot's capture of a mother camel and her young one, only to be thrown like a sack of grain from mother's back. At this, Mustafa smiled.

Before he could continue, a low murmuring was heard, faint at first, then with a jump in volume so intense they could *feel* the sound rising to a gut-punching boom. At the same moment, the ground under them lurched downward, as though some critical support had been kicked from beneath the volcanic island. Everyone on the beach fell in the same direction, and it was as well they were down, as an even mightier shock split the sand with a two-foot ditch that instantly filled with roiling sea water.

Eldad rolled to Adiva's side and placed a reassuring arm beneath her, helping her to a seated position. The captain had fallen atop his devoted slave, and neither was hurt landing on the soft sand.

Kasim lifted his captain off his chest and set him on the sand. He rose on trunk-like legs and staggered drunkenly the first few steps, then stood still, as though waiting for the next insult to his mobility.

Everyone waited in the sudden stillness and an inky darkness fell upon the beach. Eldad heard what sounded like prayers from the crew, but in so many different languages he had a brief thought that this must be what the Tower of Babel sounded like.

They desperately needed light to reorganize themselves, but the quarter moon had yet to rise above the towering mountain. No matter. The smoke and steam from the fountain of molten rock would have buried its light.

In this blackness, they smelled a faint sulfurous odor, easily recognizable by the five of them who, from the heights, had witnessed the geyser spewing from beneath the Red Sea.

No one seemed to know what to do. The captain demanded to be stood up, and held by Kasim, shouted, "Now, my sons of donkeys, rebuild the fires, all of them, then come here!"

His voice was surprisingly strong, and the affectionate insult would be reassuring to them. Eldad could not help but think this was perhaps a brief burst of flame before the candle went out.

Mustafa sagged on Kasim's arm, the effort at command easily overwhelming his meager energy stores. Though weakened, Mustafa seemed alert and fully engaged. No doubt, as with many treacherous situations he'd faced at sea, his shrewd ability to anticipate had often saved the lives of all aboard.

The night chirping and squawks from the mangrove forest dispelled the dense silence after the two shocks. The cook showed up at the captain's side with two clusters of hot smoked fish. Remarkably, the tented poles had not collapsed in the quake, and the fish were untarnished. Onto a mangrove leaf, he stripped easily separable fillets from their bones, and handed it to the captain. The salty underside of the leaf added perfectly to the delicacy, and the captain's bony hands soon dripped with the luxuriant oil of smoked sea bass still warm from the embers.

25

The thorny enclosure would admit only a few more besides the five of them. Kasim told the cook to bring Ashot but barred any others from the inner circle formed around the captain, now seated on a flat rock atop a yard tall pile of stones. He was holding partly unrolled nautical charts in one hand, claw-like.

"Sit down and be quiet!" Mustafa commanded. A few expected grumbles from outside the circle let it be known not everyone welcomed the whip-like crack of this voice. It was utterly dark only a few feet from the reignited fires, so the offenders could not be identified. Unlike the previous night, the quarter moon had failed to appear above the crest of the mountain.

He pointed to Eldad and the group. "They have told me what they saw from the heights above the leeward side of this island.

"Now," he spread his hand, moving in an arc around him, "the air around us smells of the breath of Iblis, the stench of the devil." Adiva whispered the translation to Eldad, who was happy to have her close.

"Listen carefully to me. We are in grave danger, but not from the shaking earth. It is bad, and we don't know when it's coming, but we're all, praise be unto Allah, safe for now."

He waved the nautical charts at the sailors, invisible in the black surround. "These charts of the sea, they tell me we are in a chain of islands, and some are not too distant."

"We—not one of us—has ever faced a peril such as this. A hellish spout of steam and fire—the sea is ablaze off the north coast." Mustafa was seized by a now familiar fit of deep and repeated coughing.

He waved off a concerned Kasim. "I have made a decision and will hear no complaints about it." He paused to let another shorter bout of wheeze-filled coughing end. He straightened as best as he could and motioned for Saul to stand by him.

Eldad, seeing the mystified look on the Asherite's face, rose with him in support.,

"Oh good!" The captain beamed, suddenly less forbidding. "We have both volunteers for our mission!"

Saul's wariness could no longer be restrained. "What mission? Whose mission?"

Hillel continued to translate in quiet, even tones that fooled no one, especially the old captain.

"You and the Danite, you will do this thing." He paused for the translation. "You said you saw a cone of a mountain, perhaps a mile south. If we flee from this island, we must know what awaits us."

Saul blurted, "Row there in the rowboat?"

Before translating, Hillel glared at Saul. "Don't say that." Instead, he just smiled at the captain.

Yosef broke what was becoming an awkward silence. "Why not me too," he blurted.

Hearing the translation, Mustafa shook his head, putting two fingers in the air.

Kasim interjected. "The weight of a third man might very well overwhelm the small craft."

Yosef seemed to accept this. Energy spent, he withdrew from the enclosure. The other three followed.

Kasim waved the crew away, back to their campfires. The cook and Ashot began dividing the bounty of smoked fish.

In the quiet, Eldad wondered what he should say. To his surprise, Saul motioned for Kasim to join them. "Tell Captain Mustafa, the Danite and I are honored to be chosen for this important task."

Taken off guard by Saul's initiative, Eldad could do nothing but nod his agreement. There was no question that he must support his friend, but a quick glance at Adiva's concerned expression made his resolve as firm as the desert sands.

But, of course, he must go, as the men of his tribe and the men of any tribe do.

Kasim delivered the news and returned with an invitation to re-join the captain.

Hillel spoke first. "Where are the islands on the nautical charts?"

Mustafa opened his tired-looking eyes and with a crooked smile, pointed to his head. "In here. I know from stories old captains and crew told me. No place on earth is like it, they said, as they described the mystery of the changing earth. Between islands in the chain, they have seen new stone mountains appear when they return every two or three years, like new earth has formed."

He looked at Saul as though reading his concerns. "Tell the cook to give you two days food. From what you say, it will be at least an all-day journey. I chose you because of your stamina and strength."

Eldad noticed Saul's slight smile at hearing this.

Adiva looked at Eldad. "If this island south of here has no water, will you seek another, still farther?"

Eldad recognized her rising anxiety and dreaded what would happen when he rowed away in the morning. He was beginning to understand what the fighters back home must feel when they left their loved ones behind.

Saul was ready with an answer for Adiva. "When we reach the island's mountain top, we will start a fire if possible. One fire will mean the island is habitable, two will mean it is not, and we are rowing to another island."

This seemed a good idea to all. Captain Mustafa smiled in a self-satisfied manner.

"This is why I chose the large one. He *thinks* of things," Hillel translated.

The Asherite beamed.

"Your father will be proud to see you chosen for such an important mission," Eldad said, then fell silent when he realized that this was a pivotal moment in his own mission with the son of his teacher and close friend. The remarkable resilience Saul had showed in their desperate swim to safety, and his acceptance of a perilous tomorrow, were all the right signposts of manliness.

Eldad was not sure that he, himself, had the same strength.

26

Adiva could not sleep though made deeply tired by a day so soft and lovely in its beginning, so menacing at its end. Finally, she began to drift away, not into a dream really, but a memory. She must have been around ten or eleven, not even beginning to develop womanly attributes though she wished them to come soon. It was a cousin's wedding. Adiva thought how beautiful she was. They were singing a song.

"My beloved is mine, as I am his. He browses among my lilies. Until the day dawns and the shadows fade, turn again to me, swift as a gazelle and strong as a wild goat."

She giggled, not then fully understanding the meaning of the words. Her mother admonished her, later explaining that it was from a holy book written by King Solomon long ago and that it honored the love between the almighty and his chosen people.

My beloved. The words rolled around and around in her head

Fully awake again, the flickering light of the campfire they had made a few yards apart from the camp, allowed her to gaze into Eldad's eyes, seeing they spoke of the same deep love for her that she now had for him.

The crescent moon appeared, but shifting winds snuffed it out with smoke from the boiling sea to the north.

Adiva shifted to move slightly closer, feeling his warmth on her skin. She reached for his hand that immediately enveloped hers reassuringly.

In the quiet she realized that she really knew almost nothing about Eldad. Would her abba and ima approve of this African prince? Yosef and Hillel seemed accepting of both Eldad and Saul, although Yosef's suspicious look after Eldad and Adiva were found earlier in the day was obvious.

"Tell me, my sweet prince," she whispered. "I want to know everything about you. Everything."

Eldad smiled, firmly but softly squeezing her hand. "Shall I begin long ago and far away, oh princess of Babylon? I wager I can trace my family back farther in Jewish history than yours."

"Please. From the beginning."

"There are portions of my family's history that are ancient and others that are very ancient. I was the first to write down the full history of my family."

"You said your grandfather, he set you to this."

"My father, Mahali, and mother Bilhah added what they remembered of Zav's telling of the family's ancient history. My father was the youngest of twelve children Zav sired with three wives." Eldad paused and smiled. "He outlived all three. He intimated to me that his longevity was as much a curse as a blessing, as he had watched so many loved ones grow old and die.

"Zav taught that l'dor v'dor, each generation, was responsible for training the next in the healing arts, our family tribal legacy. I learned of our earliest ancestor from my grandfather, and the story of that ancestor draws me irresistibly to the land of his birth and to the city where our legend says he buried a most precious object. I do not know.... this story has been told by so many, for so many generations...."

"I so want you to tell me anyway.

"My mother has the same name, Bilhah, as the handmaiden of Rachel, who bore Jacob a son named Dan. My family is descended from Hushim, one of the many sons of Dan."

"I know from the sacred texts that Dan was the judge of his people," Adiva said. Eldad paused to consider this.

"Our tribe's fate was tied to wars not of our making. In King Jeroboam's time, ten tribes, under the banner of Israel, fought the forces of Judah, ending the unity of David's and King Solomon's kingdom. My tribe of Dan was unwilling to shed their brethren's blood and left their ancestral lands. The fear of the rising power of the Assyrians made this more urgent.

"As my pastoral tribe wandered through the distant lands of Africa, we intermarried with many tribes and our faces are like a moonless night. That explains the darkness of my skin."

He looked directly into Adiva eyes. "Unlike your lovely skin, my princess, the color of bronze."

Adiva blushed. Could she possibly love Eldad any more than right now?

"Closer to Saul, I think," Eldad said. "His Tribe of Asher joined us many centuries later."

"Are they all as big as Saul?" Adiva smiled.

"Most of the young Asherite men are lean and aggressive. Saul's quite distinguished family are not warriors but learned men. They teach the law of Moses and ensure the literacy of every child of the Tribe.

"Saul's father also taught me from something called the Sefer Yetzirah, the Book of Creation. It is known among the Mohammedans as the Scroll of Abraham. He believed that some mysteries of the Sefer were not meant for us to understand until God determines we are ready."

Adiva rose and threw more driftwood on the fire which soon crackled its appreciation.

Eldad watched the young women intently. As she returned to his side, the closeness of her body, combined with the Red Sea's gentle night breeze, made it almost impossible not to touch, not to linger on the breathless edge of their deepest longings.

The direction of the wind had temporarily rid the air of the sulfurous stench and the earth had not shaken in some hours, so it was almost possible for him to imagine that peace would come to the strife beneath the earth.

He looked around to see if anyone was observing, but he could not really make out anyone. He decided to content himself with holding Adiva's hand and embracing her with his eyes.

"The book you so carefully placed along with my jewels in the cave, why is it precious to you?" Adiva asked. Its bound leather pages, encased in wax, had been cleverly concealed with the Netira family's gold in a crevice of the high ceiling of the cave.

"On those goatskin pages, twenty-two in all, I have copied what I have been able to transcribe from much older fragments of hide and even parchment, together with my great grandfather's stories, as my Zav could remember them. My grandfather possessed two written sources, one old and the other, incredibly old, neither of which he could read.

Eldad chuckled. "When I was little, he would pretend to read stories from these leather pages, but he knew the family stories of our most ancient ancestor word for word by memory.

"I made him read it over and over, until I was six." Eldad smiled at the memory. "One day, I caught the old man reading with his eyes completely closed. Zav had a falling over laugh, telling me nobody was ever able to read those pages.

"Of course, I know the story my family tells, of our most precious ancestor, whom our legend says lived at the time of our patriarch, Abraham."

Even in the dim light, Eldad could see Adiva eyes widen as in disbelief. Did she believe him?

"When I was learning to be a scribe and to absorb their sophisticated healing skills among the Asherites, Saul's father asked me to look at a peculiar document he'd bought from an antique peddler in Ifriqyah. He had traveled there to study at an Islamic university in Kairouan which allowed Jews to enroll."

Eldad recounted the story Saul's father told him. The blurry-eyed peddler was sleeping off his second pipe of hashish. 'This leather roll, where did you get it?' the young Asherite asked. He replied his memory wasn't so good but might improve for a reasonable fee. Saul's father knew a lie would cost the same as the truth, so instead he tried belligerence, and soon found out he bought it from a maidservant who had stolen it from a Hebrew family. When he showed his teachers the finely tanned scroll of leather with two neatly inked columns of script running down is full length, all were mystified. None had ever seen such writing, if indeed the strange wedge shapes, lines and triangles were writing at all.

Eldad rolled on his side, propping up on a crooked elbow. Adiva did the same, facing him an agonizing foot apart. They may have looked closer together, to prying eyes 20 yards away or to her brother's anxious notice.

"In the course of my studies, Saul's father showed me his curious leather scroll and I immediately saw how alike one column was to the pages Zav had pretended to read from his ancient book. Saul's father said he did know one of the symbols. He pointed out a symbol with four intersecting lines. 'God,' Saul's father said simply. 'It stands for God. I don't know whose.'"

Adiva stopped him with a light touch on his arm. "My father's library in Pumbedita has clay tablets covered with the same strange wedges. He said it looked like an inventory."

Eldad sighed. "What is the urgency to know all that I tell you?"

"Tomorrow you must leave me for a time. It shall be a time of aching for me, an empty occasion. I must fill it with more of you."

Her words made Eldad think of something more primal and, when Adiva blushed and averted her eyes, he realized that she did not at first appreciate its alternative meaning.

She laughed nervously. Then without warning she playfully slapped Eldad's face. Yes, he was being punished for his thoughts, but he was guilty of giving offense. As if to reassure him, she reached and gently stroked his face.

"Before you say anything else, tell me you will return to me after tomorrow, Say it again and again." Her voice was unsteady, quavering. As if releasing energy, she punched his chest in gentle protest.

"Beating me will not make me return," Eldad teased. Adiva rewarded him with a less gentle blow.

"Your story, must I beat it out of you?"

He moved closer to her, their faces inches apart and too near for effective hand to hand combat. Maintaining that distance was arousing, like kissing without touching.

"You will not escape my wrath with your tricks," Adiva threatened. " And about returning to me, you were going to say?"

Eldad laughed, then grew somber. "Every moment with you is loving, and your touch I feel throughout my body. I can barely contain my desire for you."

"Another of your tricks," she accused, smiling,

Eldad wisely capitulated, saying, "I shall return to your side, as I leave with you my destiny."

They sat up together and Eldad added more driftwood to the dwindling fire. It sprang back to life, both warming them from the Sea's night air.

"There was a mysterious woman from the nearby Tribe of Gad, and almost everyone except my grandfather thought her bereft of her senses, as she regularly chewed up toxic plants, leaving her in a dream state for hours at a time. She was said to know many languages, but only when she was under the influence of the disorienting herbs she ingested. I showed her the copy I had made of the family's book, but she looked with little interest and no recognition. Then she flatly refused to help me unless I entered her 'dream world' with her. My grandfather warned against this, reminding me the practice of kashaph is against God's law and this old woman could very well be a sorceress. He said he had heard of people who entered her world and were never able to come back."

Eldad paused and took a deep breath. "My intense curiosity about the properties of dream plants, as well as the chance she could, perhaps read the leather pages, led me to smoke from her pipe."

He smiled. "Of course, I never told my grandfather."

"She made a tea from something ground into a powder. The taste was wretched. Soon, a whooshing sound began in my ears, growing louder by the minute. My heart was beating fast and I began floating as if in water, but it was not wet. In the haze, I saw an enchanting chrysanthemum pattern, with many interlocking colors and textures and through it I could see an image of the two of us, still seated. This woman of Gad jerked the leather pages from my hand, and in a voice that sounded like an old man's, she quite astonishingly began to read from the ancient script.

After a time, I fell into a stupor, dreaming, but not asleep. When I was again alert, she was seated before me. I questioned her about what had happened, but she said she could remember nothing of it. Nothing. She carefully handed the faded leather pages back to me, pointing at the text and for the first time, smiled."

Eldad paused, looked at the fire, then back into Adiva's eyes, shining in the flame.

"I understood--I don't know how-- that she was encouraging me. As soon as I thought about it, I could vividly remember each and every word she read."

Adiva's face reflected the skepticism she must feel. Eldad understood, but at this point he knew he must continue. He didn't hesitate.

"These are the words the old woman read from the fading leather pages:

'Since my survival was so improbable, there must have been a reason for it. I write this not knowing if it will ever be read by anyone.

'I am the azu of Ebla, a physician in the ancient city-state of the Syrian plateau. How I came to be a healer is but a small part of my story, pale in importance compared to the sustaining light of belief I was blessed to be given along the way.

As the finite flame of life grows dim, the candle sputters and molds to a different image from its beginning. It spreads in every direction, as my life moved in ever widening circles.

'I arose before dawn today, awakened by a dream. I walked a league in darkness until I reached the western boundary stone of Ebla. Until now, I could not bring myself to part with the Tablet, as it carried the seeds of mankind's awakening. It told of that moment when the greatest man of my age became aware of the one God Though the clay will, like our flesh, crumble to dust, the spark of the Divine is eternal, a light that shall never yield to darkness.

'As I buried the tiny tablet beneath the boundary stone, I was flooded with memories of Ur, my birthplace, and of the intertwined sweetness and sorrow of my life, now nearing its end. '"

Eldad stopped. Each time when he thought of the words that his ancestor had written three millennia ago, he was overcome by a melancholy feeling.

"You look sad, my prince," Adiva said. "Tell me of this, please."

"The words I remembered from the experience, especially these last ones. I cannot escape the haunting feeling that I may have written them. I really don't understand."

Eldad rose to stand. "I mourn the loss of this man," he said without caring how it sounded.

"Perhaps someday it will make sense."

Adiva merely nodded, wordlessly. As she stood beside him, the first rays of dawn swept toward them from the vast expanse of the Red Sea.

27

The earth rumbled again just before Saul and Eldad finished loading water and their meager supply of food into the roughly 15 foot craft. More alarmingly, a fist-sized ball of flaming rock thumped onto the sand a few feet from where they stood at the shore. The sand around it fused in a circular wheel, and the acrid smell again infused the air with urgency.

In Eldad's mind, the mission had changed. Now they had no option. They must succeed in finding shelter from the menacing eruption north of them. Some of the sailors hovered about the little boat, as though struggling with the impulse to escape in it themselves. It was likely that two forces restrained them: First, none of them had volunteered to take the places of the two Africans, and second, the burly carpenter stood watchfully at the water's edge.

Adiva would not leave Eldad's side. She clung tightly to him, her nails cutting into his upper arm. He understood, even welcoming it as a reminder of the ache of separation that they both felt. Silently, he hoped the pain on his arm would linger.

Eldad watch the tears begin to form in her eyes and wondered how many moments it would be before his own eyes would betray him.

Yosef came to the rescue. Standing close behind Adiva. "My friends, it is best that you embark while the tide is going out."

Adiva was now weeping quietly. Yosef took hold of her arms, offering support. Eldad needed a moment of privacy. Yosef stepped back.

"I shall return in two days, at the most three." Eldad looked up at the unsettling blackish smoke visible above the high mountain ledge.

"Saul and I...we must go now." Eldad was beginning to feel a deep foreboding, which he passed off to the uncertainty of the next few days.

He stood even closer, whispering. "Please care well for my heart. I did not know my heart before and now that I can feel its full power within my being, I have given it to you, all of it." His hand touched her cheek, lingered a moment, then he plowed through the lapping surf to the craft bobbing at the end of a rope. Hoisting himself over the side, he soon stood in the middle of the unsteady boat, He was nearly thrown overboard when Saul hefted himself in, over the starboard railing. The sailors were laughing, and soon Adiva and Eldad as well. Standing with her cousin and brother, Adiva mouthed something, but Eldad could not hear her.

Saul was quick to take up the oars, exaggerating a bit his dramatic strokes. The breakwaters were choppy and erratic near the jumble of gigantic rocks, one of which had speared their vessel in the storm.

"What are you doing?" Eldad shouted. The skiff was turning in complete circles, as though spun on a spike through its middle.

"Doing? It is not what I'm doing. It's being done to us!" Saul was pulling hard with both hands on the portside oar, He gave a lunge at it that could have broken the oar, and the little boat slithered out of the grasp of the whirlpool.

"You are a mighty man, Saul of Asher."

The Asherite was breathing so hard he couldn't respond to Eldad's praise. He nodded and gratefully surrendered the oars to the tall African. Eldad, with no experience rowing in open sea waters, had a time at first getting the oars to move in the desired synchrony, needed lest they wander from their course due south from Jebel Zubair Island. Captain Mustafa had finally concluded that was the name of the island on which they were marooned, and now in mounting peril from the sea below and the heavens above.

The current of the Red Sea, shifting in winter to the north with inflow from the Indian Ocean, tugged against the small boat's determined push south.

At times it seemed as though the cone-shaped island they had seen from the mountaintop of Jebel was moving away from them, as they toiled against the current. Each man had taken three turns at the oars and neither had spoken much during many hours of their flight from Jebel Zubair.

Finally, at 200 yards they could see the tiny cone-shaped island and a few clusters of falling rock, catching and magnifying every inhospitable wave, which was waiting to close its jaws on hapless mariners. As they got closer, the exhausted and drooping Asherite said, "I see no inlet in the north face of this island and the water looks rough close in."

"We've got to row all around the island before giving up," an equally spent Eldad declared and he nudged Saul to give up the oars.

Within an hour, they rounded the southern tip of the unwelcoming cone-shaped island. From that vantage point, they could tell it was a quarter the size of Jebel Zubair.

"No trees," Saul said," No green at all."

Saul stood up, rocking the boat perilously side to side. He squinted up and down the eastern shore, and pointed, "I think I see a break in the rock, or at least, the water is sloshing into some kind of opening."

The current was flowing now in the direction they needed to the possible inlet. The sun cast late afternoon shadows when they pulled even with the break in the rock. Eldad's energy was gone and he was certain it was the same for Saul. Would they even make it?

Mercifully, a tiny hook-shaped cove appeared and, in one perfectly timed wave, the skiff was washed several feet up onto a narrow sandy bog. A flock of white-eyed gulls squawked at the intrusion, but soon settled with the other nesting sea birds on the eastern face of the island.

Lashed at the boat's center were their three goatskin bags of fresh water, enough for a few days, in the event they found none. Their only drink till now was after the first five hours and the prolonged exertion since then had drained not only their strength, but their bodily fluids.

Straining to lift the water bag to his lips, Eldad said, "My arms are so weak I cannot do this easy thing. Yet, my legs are still strong."

Saul smiled wearily and tried to wave a dismissive hand at the steep walls of cracked black rock surrounding the tiny inlet but found himself unable to raise his hand above his head.

"The morning, we'll be able to climb out in the morning," Eldad said with tepid optimism. In his life as a tribal healer, he had seen this many times, such as from horseback warriors whose legs became so weak from days on end in the saddle they could not walk. Only days of rest would return their strength.

The ship's cook had given the insistent Saul a smoked lobster, still in its 18-inch multicolored shell, enough to feed the two hungry men.

Saul collected scraps of driftwood, enough to start a tent-shaped stack of kindling ablaze. Their exposure on the open water left them sensitive to the chilling effect of sundown.

They sat propped up by a pair of convenient boulders, their campfire between them.

Saul, unsurprisingly, found the strength the tear the lobster into four pieces. When they had finished their meager, though flavorful meal, Saul got up to scavenge more driftwood strewn here and there over the 100' beach. He returned with a surprisingly bulky armful, as the pieces he could find were light, dry and weathered. Night fell faster than either man had anticipated and no moon illuminated their cove.

"This may be the only way onto this island," Saul said, sitting cross legged on the sand.

Eldad considered this. "It would be a nightmare to get all of our people through this crack in the mountain." He could see that only the largest waves powered around the sharp corner and crashed onto sands of the cove. Such a wave had luckily thrown their skiff onto the hook-shaped beach.

"Yes, a little like threading a needle. Of course, all of them but the Babylonians are sailors who can manage a little boat in the roughest waters," he added, sounding hopeful. He didn't want to say what he was thinking. Bring them to what?

Eldad was not one to dwell. "Save the rest of the driftwood for tomorrow. Remember, two fires if we must move on to another island. We may see such a place from the higher elevations. There might not be any other wood between us and the summit."

Saul nodded his acknowledgment, taking one moment to play-fully pick up a long piece of driftwood and wave it as if in battle.

"Save your strength, oh mighty warrior of the pasture," El-dad admonished. They unloaded the remainder of what they had brought in the skiff and each spread a blanket on the sand, with coils of rope at its head as a knotty pillow.

Before long, their talk was fragmented with lengthening pauses. Soon all Eldad could hear was sonorous snores mixed with the gentle wind that carried him away to his own dreams.

28

The sun had begun its climb before Eldad opened his eyes, but Saul was already busy. How much new had Eldad recently learned about his friend? Saul had quietly found embers still aglow and shaved slivers from his driest driftwood to bring the fire back to life.

When the light touched Eldad's face, he welcomed the warmth that offered relief from his dreams of disaster. He'd keep any dark thoughts to himself, but wished he could keep it *from* himself. His mother, Bilah, wise in so many ways, would tell him of Joseph in God's Torah. "And Joseph dreamed a dream and he told it to his brethren, and they hated him more."

After the light, his first sensation, indicating he was alive, was the aroma of smoked fish toasting safely above the civilizing campfire. He started to make a joke but could only grunt through parched lips.

Saul, alert and in charge, moved about fluidly now, being less dehydrated and spent than Eldad. He brought over the half-full goatskin water bag.

Eldad was reluctant.

Saul was insistent. "You must drink, or you'll fall apart on me. Drink all you can, we'll take our chances." So he did, and they both ate the warm, crisply smoked white fish, and Eldad could not help craving more.

Eldad finally stood stiffly and surveyed what he could see of the eastern face of the cone.

"We've got to get out of this canyon, then it won't be so hard to the top."

"There is an outcropping of jagged rock where the two walls

meet, Saul said. "Below it is where the driftwood collects. I'll throw a rope over it, and maybe we're strong enough to pull ourselves up."

Saul tied a thin leather strap around his chosen bundle of driftwood. He retrieved a two-inch-thick stick from the fire, one end a fresh ember, and stuck it in the bundle, glowing end out. Their signal back to Jebel was to be one fire if a shelter is found, two if not and another island is sought. They didn't know if their small fires would be visible at the distance they were from Jebel, but night signaling seemed the only choice. They could not know the habitability of this strange shaped rock until the whole of it was explored, and they hoped to be at its summit by nightfall.

The rope looped easily over the outcrop of rock, and Eldad planted one foot on each of the two walls forming the small canyon's apex and patiently inched himself up the 14 feet to the broad ledge above. At last able to study this side of the island in detail, he surveyed the rising expanse leading to the rim of the crater 500 feet above them. Deep furrows, like splits in the mountain's stony skin, ran haphazardly to the crest. Pathways up and around the cone would be fractured by them.

Tossing up a coil of rope he had tied round himself, Saul implored, "Your assistance, mighty Danite." Eldad groaned but heaved to until the big man was safely out of the canyon. A third coil of rope the Asherite had tied to his ankle allowed them to hoist up the bundle of firewood.

As they set off toward the island's south face, they scanned the monotonous grey and black landscape, relieved only by shocks of white, the leavings of the island's sea birds nesting in forbidding niches.

Saul frowned, "If we had wings and could live on salt water, we would do well on this lifeless rock. We might as well just climb to the top and signal we're going for another island." He blew on the smoldering end of the ember stick, and it glowed red. Though they had a flint stone, conditions such as wind on the barren mountain top may make building their signal fires most difficult.

Eldad didn't answer, but just stared at a vista to the south of them. Two quite distinct land masses rose a few hundred feet above the Red Sea, the nearest maybe a mile distant, and the companion on its southeast flank. Because the cone island blocked sight of these islands from Jebel, their existence was unknown to those marooned there.

What so arrested Eldad's, then Saul's, attention was that one of the islands bore green patches dipping toward a crescent of white sand.

"How strange they look," Saul said. "One looks as barren as this," he said, kicking loose gravel at his feet. "I doubt the other is a Garden of Eden, but what choices do we have?"

Eldad agreed, "We'll make sure there is nothing here worth coming back to by climbing down the north face, if we can, after the fires are lit."

They followed the furrows upward toward the crest of the cone, one of which split the rim, allowing them easier access to the top.

Eagerly, they raced across the shallow bowl of the crater to its elevated north end.

What they saw of their home island filled them with terror.

"The island, everyone but us is there on the island. The smoke, I can't see most of the island!" Saul's voice shook in fear.

Then they felt a now familiar spasm of the earth beneath their feet. They reflexively grabbed on to each other for support.

"Oh, no!" Saul wailed. "I see streaks of fire in the sky over our island. Oh, God protect our people."

Eldad immediately thought of Adiva. There was no real shelter on the island, no place to run even if you knew what was coming. No doubt the spasms of the earth were stronger there, closer to the new island being thrust onto the world's face.

As if by divine intervention, the black smoke enveloping Jebel island parted in a gust of hot wind, and there, anchored in the turquoise lagoon, was a triple mast ship nearly 150 feet long.

"It is salvation, we and our friends are rescued!" Saul shouted.

The wind died down and smoke again blotted out Jebel and its inlet.

"The way we know down to the inlet and the beach, the way we came up, will take longer than straight down this slope," Eldad said, peering over the crater's east rim.

His eyes swept back to Jebel. The smoke had again cleared.

This time the view made his skin crawl and he shivered in horror.

Rising on the rescue ship's masts, one after the other, were the dirty grey sails of the galleon of pirates and slavers that had pursued them from the Port of Aden.

29

Adiva felt slightly numb when a crewman first caught sight of the triple-sailed vessel slicing through the sea in their direction. Then the apparition disappeared beneath an increasingly dense shroud of gritty smoke surrounding Jebel. Through some curious and life preserving accident of topography, the air on their beach was clear, a temporary envelope around them. The lagoon, a hundred yards from them, was curtained in unnatural grey mist, denser than any fog.

She glanced at Yosef and Hillel who now stood by her side at the water's edge. They were joined by Kasim along with the Chinese sailor, Wen Ho.

"Can it be that someone has come for us?" Adiva asked hopefully. No one spoke, as all eyes were focused on a brief parting in the smoky curtain. It revealed three empty masts floating eerily above the smoke-hidden vessel anchored in the lagoon.

Hillel dampened Adiva's rising anticipation. Leaning over, he whispered in her ear, "Where is the gold?"

Adiva was startled as if awakened from a deep sleep. Was it possible that she had deliberately kept the details from them? She tried to rationalize that so much had happened, it was merely an oversight. But she was too honest, even with herself. All three of them were entrusted to transport the bankers' jewels and gold and she had no desire to conceal anything from her brother and cousin. No, she realized it was the secret of the location itself. A lover's secret. She immediately rectified her lack of candor, telling Hillel and Yosef of the cave and the hidden ceiling crevice.

Hillel stared at Adiva, clearly annoyed with her. After a few moments, his expression softened. "We shall not allow ourselves to die to protect this wealth, but if we are being rescued by righteous people, they will allow us to retrieve it, and the Danite's treasure as well."

Yosef spoke up. "Our friends, the Asherite and Eldad, are the treasure, and we cannot leave them behind."

Adiva smiled at her cousin, giving his arm an affectionate squeeze. It seemed so long ago the three of them boarded a boat on the Bedita River, bound for its confluence with the Tigris at Baghdad. Carrying sacred books and letters from the head Babylonian religious authorities, who issued rulings on Jewish law for the Diaspora communities scattered as far away as Tunisia, and the Red Sea Port of Aden. The three family members had a secret mission as well: one that would earn each of them a lifetime's wealth in commissions. A small part of their rewards had been given them at the Netira family home in Aden, and these coins and jewelry they kept in their possession, separate from the banker's assets hidden in the cave.

Adiva allowed herself to hope, unrealistically she realized, that the two explorers had found the safe haven and were returning early.

Instead, one, then another longboat was oared strongly from the curtain of smoke. All the twenty or so men had turbans draped over nose and mouth against the acrid smoke. When the boats drew near the shore, it was plain these men were not responding to the cheers of the marooned crew. To the contrary, the eyes showing above the masks were wide and fierce with anticipation.

Coming ever closer, two of the men dropped their face covers. Wen Ho screamed in terror and without explanation, fled in desperation toward the mangrove forest. As the two longboats ran up on the sand, a rat-faced Asian sailor leapt from the bow and, machete waving, sprinted after Wen Ho.

One man, evidently the leader, erupted in a laugh that Adiva could only describe as maniacal. Carrying a knife, he was next to spring onto the sand, followed with lightning speed by twelve heavily armed men.

Quickly surrounded, the stranded party, whose crew seemingly prepared for joyous rescue, not mortal combat, offered no resistance. This saved most of their lives, though for what they weren't sure.

After ordering his men to crowd them together to better watch any effort at escape, the captain strutted around them in a circle, pausing silently in front of the Babylonians. Adiva had covered her head, but not her face. There was little point in hiding behind a veil.

Again, the deranged cackle issued from the captain. They had learned he was called Shabazi, who, between peals of laughter, said, "When we catch the thieving spy, the Chinaman's tongue will wag, or he'll be carrying it."

At that dreadful moment, Adiva knew at once their lives had changed forever. Looking around at the crew, she was sure that everybody felt the same way. The faces of Shabazi's crew she could see were filled with senseless malice over the long chase through the storm and would be so happy to slaughter their prey on the spot. The captain may have detected a rising lust for blood even before they laid anchor, but he had an iron grip on his men, reminding them of his past disciplinary actions and severe punishments.

"Kill yourselves if you must, but our unfortunate guests here must remain untouched." He paused, then laughed. "I need them to remain of sound body."

Adiva learned from stories, mostly from her brother, that there were sound business reasons for their current protection. In addition to being the most vicious pirates to ply the Red Sea, they were renowned for their harvests of human beings from all walks of life. Lightning strikes on shipping lanes of the Silk Road had netted many quality people, who then became the chattel of the rich or the opportunistic.

Captain Shabazi stepped toward Adiva, but Hillel and Yosef blocked his way. He said nothing, motioned with his eyes, then waited a moment until his two guards yanked both young men to the ground. He stood over them with a foot in the small of Yosef's back, a spear at the ready.

"Yes," the captain said to no one in particular, "this is the mysterious woman who tries to pass as an Arab." He smiled. "The Chinaman lied about everything but the beauty of this one."

This made Adiva's skin crawl, but she put this sensation aside, realizing the pirate captain was not appraising her for his own lustful use, but evaluating her value for *sale*. With a disheartening clarity, she realized a universal truth that prisoners, no matter their station in life, or grandeur of their past, were almost always sold into human bondage. In an instant, no longer *who* they were, but *what* they had become–less than fully human, commodities for sale or trade like camels.

The repentant spy whose head Eldad skillfully bandaged in the storm had run for his life. Yosef and Hillel were now sitting on the sand with spears in their faces. Adiva weighed their meager options. They did not know what Wen Ho had reported to Shabazi in Aden before the spy's payment demand was laughed off.

The leering captain jerked away the scarf on Adiva's head. It was part of his early strategy with new slaves, which began with making sure they understood they would kill them if they resisted. Adiva prayed no demonstration was required.

Shabazi scratched his scraggly beard, and his beetle nut-stained teeth were barred in a sardonic grin when he said, "You look at me as though you have no fear, but oh, how soon that will change."

With that, he slapped her hard across the face, sending her to her knees, stars flashing in her vision. She knew the boys would no doubt die if they jumped to her defense, she cried out in Arabic, "No!" then switched to barely audible Hebrew, saying, "Lo, he is provoking so he can humiliate us or worse."

"Silence!" Shabazi bellowed. Adiva's cheek burned, and she stood unsteadily, her eyes downcast to avoid gratifying the captain's wish to see fear in them.

"Jews. These are Jews like the banker's family in Aden," Shabazi said to his second in command standing nearby. "They're not worth as much as a good African or Asian. Too sly, and you can't work them as hard. Good Muslims are forbidden to own these so-called people of the book, unless they are captured in battle." He laughed derisively, waving his hand. "Some battle, eh?" The First Mate feigned appreciation of this with a mirthless chuckle.

A half dozen pirates had fanned out over the campsite and one came running back from Captain Mustafa's enclosure.

"The vulture captain of these animals perches grandly at the forest edge," he said triumphantly, pointing both hands up the beach. Kasim sprang up from the sand, and would have run himself onto the pirate's swords, had he not been clubbed from behind into fortuitous oblivion.

"Put the chains on the ape," Shabazi ordered three men who were still in the longboats. "And bring the rest of them while the captain and I have a little talk." With that he strode off with his first mate up the beach toward the enclosure. When they arrived, they found Captain Mustafa sitting on the rocky bench Kasim had fashioned for him. The slightest movement of his leg lanced him with unbearable pain.

"Ah, my good captain," Shabazi began with cordiality. "Such a pity we must meet in these unpleasant circumstances."

Mustafa didn't hesitate, "And I suppose had we met at sea, as you planned, our circumstances would have been so much more pleasant, you bastard pirate!"

Shabazi laughed out loud. "Such fury from a man who looks like a many-days-old corpse already."

"I am Captain Shabazi, and I understand you are Mustafa. How many crew and passengers, captain?" He said this so casually, as though needing numbers to plan the evacuation of those he rescued. Captain Mustafa simply glared at him.

Now Shabazi leaned down, his face coming level with the wheezing skeleton, all that remained of the once robust captain, and growled, "How many?

Captain Mustafa's face reddened and from deep in his badly infected lungs came a cough so violent it covered Shabazi's face with mucus bearing tubercular stands of pus and blood. Enraged, Shabazi drew a curving sword from his waistband and was about to run Mustafa through when he stopped suddenly, the blade a few inches from the emaciated chest. "Bring all our guests," he told the first mate, who shouted his captain's orders. He added, "Chain the bear in the boat."

Experienced slavers, the crew was swift and practiced in applying ankle manacles to the seven crew and the three Babylonian captives, but they had not yet run the chains between them. They were rudely pushed and prodded up the beach, when simply being told to walk to the enclosure would have sufficed. These guards, Africans, Arabs, and Chinese, bore only the thinnest veneer of civilization restraining them from carnage. The presence of this inviting young woman added to the tension already pushing at Captain Shabazi's control over these merciless men. But he knew, after all, they were only mirrors of himself.

When all had gathered round, Shabazi walked out of the enclosure and stood in front of the ten painfully anguished prisoners. Ashot stood in stricken silence just behind the three Babylonians, and a subtle movement of his left hand touched something hidden in the collar of his robe.

Captain Shabazi's beard was still speckled from Mustafa's revenge. In spite of the mortal danger, Mustafa was laughing in long bursts, punctuated by paroxysms of frothy coughing and, as always, specks and sometimes clots of blood.

Pacing before them, he asked, with his bizarre, yellow-stained grin, "Who among you is wise and wishes to save your treasured captain?" Looking from face to face, he parted the guards in front to better search out a face frightened enough to tell him what he needed to know.

"Now we wouldn't want to leave any of our new friends behind, would we?" His tone was soft. "Simply say who is missing from your group, and your pitiful captain will live out his wretched life."

Captain Mustafa shouted out, "Tell this murderer nothing!"

"Let's see, what are we hiding here?" Shabazi asked as he focused on Ashot's now pleading face two feet in front of him.

"This is all we are, these you see and the Chinaman who ran. One was shark bit and is buried next to the wall," Ashot began under his breath.

Shabazi leaned in momentarily to hear. In a blur, Ashot whipped his dagger from the collar and plunged it deep into the chest of the astonished, then vacant Captain Shabazi. The guards aimed their spears and swords at Ashot, who smiled down on the impaled corpse at his feet.

"Stop!" the first mate ordered with shaky authority that stayed the agitated guards. Perhaps they realized that any one of whom could be blamed, then killed for allowing this to happen.

The first mate struggled to contain his own fear. It was likely that the captain's reign of terror would hang over his head. Then, in the moments of silence, he seemed to strengthen.

He raised his knife and shouted. "Allah be praised, the tyrant is dead!"

The captors looked at each other as if waiting for another to make a move. Spontaneously they raised their arms and cheered.

"He's dead, he's really dead!" a brawny pirate with only two teeth left in his grin strode over to his one-time captain and kicked his face.

Adiva was stunned to see in the faces of their minders only smiling relief. Some eyes were not dry, but they wept tears of joy, not grief.

All of this was thoroughly confusing, but temporarily heartening. Free, for now, to look around, she glanced at Yosef and Hillel and thought she saw expressions of optimism.

Might they be able to bargain with whomever assumed command of the ship? Now, with the unexpected jubilation, might be the time to try, even if chances were slim. Clearly, in some way, their fate had been altered by the gypsy's deadly knife.

Then she had a dark realization. With or without their hated captain, these men were still slavers, and their captives, the grandest riches of their lifetimes.

30

The young Danite anguished over what to do, even beyond his concern about how to navigate the jumble of irregular surfaces down to the island's only tiny inlet. It occurred to him they could get smashed by a single unpredictable wave on their way out. Halfway down to the skiff, Saul was holding his own, and Eldad decided he wanted his usually pessimistic appraisal of the situation. When they stopped to rest, Eldad asked, "What do you think we should do?"

Saul bent at the waist and caught his breath. "First we've got to understand our state of mind and how it may affect our judgment."

"I don't like to hear you say that, but maybe you're right. Give me the rest of it."

"Our hearts tell us we must charge headlong back to Jebel, yes? But first, we need to light the two fires at the top of this mountain, signaling that we are still searching for another habitable island. This will deceive the pirates into thinking that we are still looking for a habitable island, but we shall row back to Jebel in darkness."

No matter his panic, Eldad sat and listened to Saul.

"We know who they are. The Chinese spy, Wen Ho, the one whose head you patched, told his story only to the captain. Mustafa was wise enough to keep this to himself until the pirate's sails appeared. After you cared for Wen Ho, he told me who had hired him and that the ship was a slaver."

Saul allowed the unavoidable flood of dread into their awareness.

Eldad sighed heavily and stared at the rock beneath his feet. "I am mad with fear for our friends. This is the terrible dream I had come true, but in it, I am a captive slave as well."

Saul nodded with understanding, "I know what you're thinking, and you must listen to me about this. Joining the Babylonians as merchandise for sale by pirates will not rescue them."

"I promised I'd be at her side," Eldad said sadly.

"Slaves are seldom sold together, and never have I seen them given a choice of remaining with loved ones. Even our own tribes do not indulge such fantasies." Saul rose. "Let's climb all the way down to the boat, then we'll try to decide."

This took longer and was more physically challenging than either man expected, and the sun was high in the sky when they reached the skiff. A rogue wave three times the normal size ricocheted off the outer wall of the canyon cove, ripping their feet from beneath them. Their gloom was momentarily relieved by their thrashing ride on the surf. When they could see, they stared warily at mouth of the cove, now bathed only by gentle wave after wave. Their boat had come to rest ten feet farther up on the beach but was still firmly tethered to a large boulder. Eldad drank deeply from the half empty water bag, handing it to Saul. The punishing saltiness of the Red Sea that had flooded their mouths and noses, left them desperate for fresh water.

"We have to do something," Eldad said without much conviction.

"Like *survive*, my dearest friend?" Saul replied. "If we don't, no one will ever know what happened to any of us."

"I cannot live without this woman, Asherite. Every fiber of my being flows into her soul."

Saul was about to say something, then thought better of it. "Though I have never known such feelings for a woman, I do understand they can lead to wars between tribes, and sometimes thinking that doesn't make much sense. I think I'm already sorry for asking you what you're thinking." His face crunched up as though expecting unpleasantness.

"Then let us think this through together. The island is infested with many heavily armed men," Eldad said.

"Their three-mast boat would have at least twenty five very

hostile pirates with a stomach for being slavers, or, worse yet, relish it," Saul's tone was gloomy. "They will no doubt find out two
of Mustafa's passengers are missing. *He* will not tell them, but we
have no reason to think there is any loyalty from some of the rest
of the crew, except Kasim and, oddly enough, the gypsy Ashot."

"We have to anticipate they will come looking for us, and there
is no place to hide on this God-forsaken lump of stone," Eldad said.

"True." Saul was clearly trying out ideas in his mind, thinking,
then his face lit up. "You know all the crew knows what signal we
would send if we failed to find a shelter on this island and we're
seeking another. Whatever crewman is currying their favor by
telling of us will gladly interpret the two fires they see from this
mountain top."

"But if no one betrays us, the fires will tell them we are here,
and at first light the longboats will cover the distance in a few
hours," Eldad said with a growing indecisiveness.

"But we shall not be here," Saul said. "At sunset, we, or rather
you, will light the piles of wood shavings, sticks and driftwood we
left at the rim of the crown."

"What will..."

Saul interrupted. "I shall ready the skiff. Currents and waves
are different with the tide, and I'll try to learn the pattern. You've
got to get back down while there is enough light to row our way
out of the cove."

"Row *where*?" Eldad asked, then realized what Saul was thinking. "You're right, old friend. The *only* place we can hide is Jebel,
and we must row the skiff there in the dark."

"That's it," Saul said "We need no navigation, just row toward
the fire in the sky." Until that moment, neither man had considered
the peril of placing themselves next to an erupting undersea volcano. They had feared only the human menace, which, no matter
how dreadful, was more yielding than this crushing force of nature.
With no experience, they did not know how total the assault from
beneath the waves could become. Perhaps it was warning them by
shaking the ground.

It was now a few hours till dark and Eldad collected driftwood splinters that poked up from the sand and he and Saul bundled them up, then coaxed their precious fire back to life.

Each time Eldad began to think about what they would do even if they were lucky enough to reach the island undetected, he imagined one improbable course after another.

He recognized his childhood fantasies of heroic rescue of maidens fair had no place in what lay ahead of them.

"I've been thinking, Saul, that there's a hard truth we're not talking about."

Saul stopped fussing with the sticks, and said wearily, "I think I know."

"If we miraculously freed someone from the immediate clutches of the pirates, where would we go? These slavers are far off the sea lanes, blown here by the same storm that wrecked our vessel. I don't know, but it may be a very long time before a ship would sail nearby."

Saul said. "I've had enough of water and its perils. Are you suggesting our choices are to stay marooned on Jebel till our youth is gone, or to submit to the hospitality of the pirate slavers?"

"Well, let's hope not," Eldad said. "We don't have to make that decision yet. If we make it to the island's west shore tonight, we figure where to hide, and see what we need to do."

He was again assailed by the terrible thought that the only way he could be near his deepest love was to be in chains.

31

Captain Mustafa laughed a long wheezy time, before turning to the still slack-jawed First Mate, Tariq.

"Ah, my new captain. Now your troubles begin!"

The dark-skinned Berber snarled. "Shut up, you putrid street bastard!"

Cutlass drawn, he stepped over the dead Shabazi, who was still oozing rivulets of blood onto the sand and moved menacingly toward Mustafa. Something, probably the memory of Captain Shabazi's shower of blood-laced spittle, stopped him cold.

Turning, he studied the faces of the men guarding the captives. Three of them were slaves of the dead Shabazi, and there wasn't a moist eye among them, nor even unhappy expressions from the other seven pirates. They looked at him in curiosity, waiting for some gesture from the man whose commands they usually followed so unquestioningly.

Tariq, at five feet, was squat-bodied, with thick arms and a neck sporting an almost comic waddle, no small subject of behind-the-back derision from two younger men who would squeeze and wiggle the skin on their necks when they spoke of him. His grey beard just grew in the hills and valleys of the undulating folds beneath his chin, disguising none of its topography.

A screech issued from the mangrove forest and the rat-faced Arab pushed the terrorized Wen Ho to the sand. Another pirate grabbed him by the hair and dragged him, heels gouging the sand, over to the enclosure.

No doubt seeing his chance to assert command, Tariq snapped at rat-face. "Tie the son of a pig and bring him to me!"

Thus far, none of the assembled refuse of the sea had questioned his authority, but their sometimes quite mad captain's body was not yet cold. More importantly, this former first mate had not yet issued orders the men always grumbled about, and sometimes outright ignored. Everyone knew well tests of his control were coming, Shabazi always dealt with such stirrings with a murderous rage that could get even bystanders sliced to death. Tariq, by contrast, was cunning, and not given to explosiveness that wasted able bodied sailors. It was he, without the captain being visible at all, who convinced all the non-slave crew to sign on at the Port of Aden. As always, quick and easy fortunes to the daring, he promised. The captain's name, one that struck cold fear in core of seafarers, was withheld until they were well out on the Red Sea.

"I am now *Captain* Tariq. Chinaman. You will answer to me, and you will answer everything." Wen Ho's head was jerked back as though presenting an animal for slaughter, and the newly minted captain knelt, placing his dagger tip at the angle of Wen Ho's trembling jaw, saying, "Now Chinaman, tell me where the rest of this party of the damned are. Every lie you speak will lose you part of your body."

Adiva could feel her hopes of kinder treatment slipping away at the point of a dagger. Such was the culture of cruelty, though Adiva knew little of it. One thing was clear. The Chinese sailor would protect no secrets, including her beloved's mission to find refuge. She decided she must try to gain some advantage, even if it was temporary.

She took a deep breath and spoke clearly for all to hear. "I will tell you what you demand to know. Do not hurt Wen Ho, who does not know much."

Tariq rose to full height and confronted her. For a moment, he did not notice that she had removed her head scarf.

Adiva could still feel her cheek burn and knew that it must still be bright red from the blow that knocked her down. She was determined to hold her head high, and look at Tariq straight in the eyes, neither defiant nor downcast.

Tariq said, "So you will tell me everything, yes?"

It was Tariq that diverted his eyes for a moment, seemingly lost in thought. Looking up again, he pointed to the side of his face, shaking his head. "Such a brutal man, that pig."

She decided it was best to pretend this made her believe he was not a brutal man, "I am relieved at your concern, and I know you have a heavy responsibility."

In the five years since he left his Algerian homeland, the Berber had heard every sort of entreaty from new captives and was long ago inured to their pleading. He had seen the lights go out in many eyes when they realized they no longer would be treated like human beings. The hardiest lasted the longest, but in his experience, all spirits were broken by the chains and the filth of confinement.

Adiva broke his thoughts, "I wish to know what you will do with us."

The captain's eyes lit up with sadistic mirth he could not conceal. He looked around, motioning with a nod for his crew to share his amusement.

"Do with you? Uh, would your highness wish to book passage on the swiftest boat on the Red Sea?"

Adiva ignored the mocking. "Yes."

Now the crew squealed their delight. No doubt, they had never seen a female captive behave like this. Fearing rape and mutilation, they mostly did not speak, but cried and whimpered.

But Adiva was not going to give in to her fear. "I can pay for our passage, and for our freedom as well. What matters it to you if you receive a few hundred gold dinars at some slave market, or you receive the same amount from me." She waited for this to sink in if it was going to, and added, "Now!"

"You have nothing," Tariq quicky retorted.

But Adiva had noticed that he had stopped laughing.

"I will give you two more of our party who are hidden, Africans worth much more at the market than we Jews. Who is going to believe we Babylonians," she said pointing to her brother and cousin, "were captured in battle?"

This caused the Berber to tilt his turbaned head to the side, his copious waddle drooping in a single hairy drape. His rheumy eyes narrowed, and he studied her.

"Where are they, these two?"

Adiva knew if she did not answer this, Wen Ho could not resist revealing it.

"And you will grant the three of us our freedom in exchange?"

Tariq smirked. "Why should I do that?"

He paused, maybe realizing he was ending the little game too soon.

He, pointed to the seven crewmen.

"These two mysterious men, they are like these seaweed-laced barnacles?"

"No captain, they are quality people, both can read and write, and are sturdy of body."

Tariq glanced at Yosef and Hillel, then back to Adiva, obviously calculating their true worth. Surely, he could see that this family wearing his manacles would be worth far more than ordinary slaves and might be ransomed for much greater riches.

"Yes, I think an arrangement is possible."

Tariq's tone turned harsh. "And you will tell me where they are!" Drawing his dagger, Tariq walked back to where Wen Ho was still restrained.

"The Chinaman, I need no *arrangement* with him."

"On the island shaped like a cone, they seek out shelter farther from the spewing rock. They are to signal us tonight," Adiva said. "From the top of the island, one fire if the island is livable, two if not."

Tariq had seen this nearest island as they had approached Jebel Zubair from the south and thought it not worth exploring. What they couldn't see as they neared Jebel was the source of the black smoke belching from the sea north of the island.

"Two, you say, and then what?"

"They try for the next island in the chain, if they can reach it." She worried that she was dooming them to captivity, but nothing would be worse than being permanently marooned on islands known by few mariners and seen up close by no one. Only the freakish sandstorm and the prospect of easy bounty had lured the pirates there.

The acrid sulfur smell suddenly descended on their stretch of beach. A few men coughed and fearful eyes cast about for unseen demons. The ankle manacle chaffed Adiva's skin each time she moved. Seeing how she winces, Tariq again affected a look of sympathy and touched her hair.

"Such a pity to lose your freedom so young."

His saggy face hardened. "Where is the gold you were given by the bankers in Aden?"

"The Nietos are family friends, from my grandfather's time in Baghdad. We brought precious books to them, and, yes, we were rewarded."

Pointing toward Wen Ho, Tariq sneered. "My good Captain Shabazi was told by this piece of horse dung that his spying housemaid claimed great riches had been given you."

Adiva hesitated, considering her options. She had to produce something substantial but doing so guaranteed nothing from this snake. What would her brother want her to do? She quickly concluded that telling him of *all* the fortune they carried made her plan no more likely to succeed than if she surrendered only their personal gold and jewels.

"In a goatskin bag, sewn into the lining, you will find all of our rewards from Aden. She stopped, making a point of sniffing the air.

"We're doomed if we don't get off this rock that has been abandoned by God." Tariq looked skyward where fate arranged another fiery brimstone to crash into the beached vessel lying on its side. It ignited the desiccated boards of the deck into first yellow, then red, black flames.

Kasim tried to bolt toward his precious vessel, but the point of a pirate's sword restrained him.

"Dig it up," Tariq ordered the three Babylonians, now briefly united.

Adiva led them to the still smoldering campfire where she and Eldad had clung to each other through the night. Stepping off two paces north, she stopped and pointed down. Yosef and Hillel dropped to their knees and soon had scooped away the foot of sand covering the leather wine bag. Yosef looked uncertainly at his cousin and Tariq standing behind her and handed the ebony-stained sac to Adiva.

"What worthlessness is this?" Tariq demanded, but his look of consternation changed to a satisfied grin when Adiva handed it to him, and he felt a pull on his arm. Surely, he realized, it wouldn't be that heavy even full of wine.

Slicing through the meticulous stitching that bound the two goatskins together, the greedy pirate was struck dumb by what he found inside. Ingeniously sewn into the bag's inner surfaces were twelve gold pendants too heavy to wear as jewelry. They were arrayed in a field of heavy chain link strands affixed to the outer edges of each leather leaf, and winding in concentric circles toward its center point. The golden chain wound artfully between the pendants.

"Our passage to the nearest port of call, that is all we ask," Adiva interrupted with a hopefulness she didn't feel.

Momentarily recovering from the bedazzlement of his find, the captain, eyes were still ablaze with the fire of greed, said, "Oh, most certainly, passage for you and our missing *guests* as well!"

His use of the word guests recalled the sardonic Captain Shabazi.

"The manacles, can they now be removed?" Adiva dared to ask.

Tariq looked surprised, smiled at such innocence. Indeed, Adiva could only guess that her handling was the start of the time-honored treatment of prisoners where dehumanization must begin immediately. The first step was always the iron bands around ankles or necks, the latter for those who were more likely to resist.

Tariq barked at a seaman standing nearby, "You, bring the tools and strike the anklet from this woman." He next pointed to Hillel and Yosef. "Not these two."

"But...," Adiva began to protest.

"Silence, or I will collar your neck!" the squatty Berber thundered,

Curiously, Adiva noticed, he did not countermand his previous order to strike her shackle.

Tariq's plans had just become that much more difficult to discern.

32

"What can we hope to accomplish by rowing back there tonight?"

Saul, who was rooting about for more driftwood sticks, stopped to look at his friend. "Our water will last two more days at most, and we have no idea whether the other islands are like this one, where nothing lives but birds."

"If we wait for the long boats to capture us, our rescuers may not be kindly disposed toward their new prizes," Eldad said.

"I don't like the sound of this, not a bit of it."

Increasingly, for the first time in his life, Saul had begun to look at himself as a leader. Eldad was looking to him for answers and he would not falter, not now.

"It's like saying that Dan or any tribe treats warriors overpowered in battle differently from those who meekly surrender."

They were now at the heart of what they must decide. Saul's scholarly father had taught both the ancient mystical writings of their ancestors. Man's life presents seven pairs of contrasts–mutually at war–like peace and strife and wisdom and folly.

Now, suffusing this moment was a pair of contrasts they never thought they would face: Lordship and servitude.

The sun had moved to its late afternoon and it began to cast shadows from the west canyon wall.

Saul came to the point. "Are we willing to risk death for freedom, only to be abandoned at the end of the earth?"

Eldad didn't answer directly. "The pods from the edible tree found by the gypsy, along with the fish and the birds, will nourish our bodies and we shall teach each other to nourish our souls."

Saul nodded. He realized what his friend was doing. But food didn't seem that important just then. He hoped, if the time came, that his body and mind would cooperate.

Being marooned and abandoned on the island was the least attractive of their options, but it was one. Ironically, the more fluid possibilities involved accepting the grim fate of captivity. There was no turning back from there. With most new slaves, the delicate blossom of hope for magical rescue would soon be mangled by lengths of chain.

For a moment, Saul had the sensation of feeling himself being pulled under by despair, sagging under the awful choice before them,

"What will become of us?" he said, looking at Eldad through narrowed eyes.

"It may be hard to stay alive, or want to, at first," Eldad replied, his voice showing little emotion..

"At first?" Saul asked quietly.

"We have both seen slaves treated badly. Not by our families, of course. That would violate our sacred traditions, but *some* treat slaves with a particular viciousness until they are sure they have killed the spirit to resist. There are evil men who don't even stop then, preferring to just take pleasure in another's pain.

Saul had heard enough, but Eldad was not quite finished.

"Some in captivity just die, of what seems to be a broken heart. They stop eating, drinking, or caring who beats them or for what."

Saul took this in. "And you have seen this?"

"Enough to know that stories I have heard are true"

Saul smiled to himself. "I don't suppose these slavers will feed us very well, will they?"

They shared a spontaneous laugh.

At sunset, Eldad scaled the craggy eastern slope alone, carrying two bundles of splintered driftwood and fresh ember sticks. He thought only of Adiva, and this filled him with panic at their separateness, then rage at his helplessness. He knew his freedom would be worthless without this woman, but if enslaved, he would loose both her *and* his future.

Reaching the summit, he could see more clearly than before the darkening pall framing Jebel like a picture on a wall of blue-green sea. He immediately noticed flames in the foreground of the distant beach. He could think of nothing on the beach that would burn except the wreckage of their boat at the water's edge. Though it had been a remote possibility, repairing the gaping defect in the bow with precisely cut acacia planks might have restored sea worthiness. He shuddered to think *why* the boat was burning. The pyre could be the pirate's sport, or their spite, but it was the end of that faint hope. The fire seemed able to burn him from a great distance, as did disturbing images of his people at the mercy of the merciless.

In the deepening twilight, he found the driftwood they had left at the north rim of the island's summit. Arranging his shaved kindling wood in two tented shapes, he blew on the ember sticks until small flames appeared and then patiently added larger driftwood logs. There was at first no wind, but soon an updraft from the precipitous north face billowed the fires into blazes that could be seen for miles.

Eldad gave one last despairing look back, then picked his way carefully down a darkening path until he reached the rope ladder down to their cove. Dropping onto the sand, he saw his large friend tying a rope to the starboard side of the boat.

"What about the waves, Saul?"

"There is no pattern for waves the size of the one that bathed us like babies in a tub. I think maybe every seventh or eighth is bigger, but not *that* big. We have to take our chances."

He tossed the rope to Eldad and took up one from the other side of the boat. Their feet dug into the sand as they strained to drag the boat the several yards the rogue wave had thrown it up from the water's edge. When one end bobbed in the waves, Saul scrambled aboard and thudded with such force as to pull the boat the rest of the way into the choppy water. Eldad hopped nimbly into their ark and seized the oars before the Asherite could.

"I'm better at the sprint we need to clear this cove," Eldad declared, and showed this by quickly maneuvering to face the incoming waves. The last rays of light were gone, and the moon had not risen over the conical mountain. In this darkness, a rogue wave would have no trouble launching a stealth attack.

The strong young African leaned forward and pulled back on oars that grudgingly plowed through swirling seawater. A larger wave rocked them side to side as they rounded the outer lip of the cove, but Saul adroitly shifted his considerable weight, steadying them.

"You see! The large one has his usefulness!" he bubbled.

"We shall see when the great mariner takes the oars soon." Eldad was tiring from the fight with chaotic waters near the cove, but they were clear of the worst part. Subtly, at first, then, more urgently, they began to feel the unmistakable pull of deep Red Sea current. That same immutable force they fought against when coming to the the cone-shaped island was now propelling them north in the inky blackness.

33

It was the prerogative of the self-anointed Captain Tariq to do with captives as he wished. Besides the three Babylonians, his attention had focused on the gypsy from some unknown land, or more likely, no land at all. The stocky Romani stood surrounded by three pirates, who, most curiously, held their weapons casually at their sides, more like standing *with* him rather than guarding him.

"Your name, what is it, you who knows not his father?" Tariq demanded.

Ashot glared at the ground in silence. The three guards tensed and moved slightly away from him and readied their weapons.

Tariq pointed at the corpse that was their despised captain. "Why?"

Ashot finally spoke, shouting loud enough for everyone to hear.

"He sold my people to the slavers at Aden. For this, he died." He again fell silent.

Here was a man unlike any of the ragged crew under his yet-to-be entrenched command. Tariq had been awestruck by the gypsy's speed and effectiveness with the knife. He seemed indifferent to allegiance, but Tariq had learned such men could be bought. Perhaps this treacherous gypsy could be bought for the price of his own freedom. Tariq would test the waters.

"The Jewess wishes to buy her freedom with her riches. What have you to offer for yours?"

Ashot raised his eyes, focusing sharply on Tariq. It was a look so fierce that Tariq felt sweat forming on his forehead. Like most seasoned pirates, Tariq feared little from most men, but he was unsettled by the power that seemed coiled within this captive. He calculated that perhaps put to his use, he might establish the level of threat needed to control these men of raw violence and senseless cruelty.

Tariq sensed the acute attention of his crew. He must move the gypsy away from the group, for his proposal to have a chance of success.

He motioned for two of the crew who had been holding chains yet to be threaded through their prisoner's ankle irons, to do so with the gypsy, giving them more secure control. He had no way to know whether Ashot was as deadly without a weapon as with one.

When out of earshot, Tariq pointed to Ashot's leg, "This chain, you would like to be without it?"

"I would like it around your neck, pirate!"

Tariq was pleased. This man was precisely who he needed.

"Will you work for your freedom?"

"Work? For you?" Ashot's voice revealed his surprise.

"Were you not to be paid for manning that wreckage smoldering over there? I, too can pay."

"You have your crew. Why would you need more?"

"These three," he said motioning to the guards, "are loyal and trusted by me." This was a time for candor. "The others, some hate me, as they did the captain. I wanted him dead but couldn't do it. Most of the crew believe *you* have rescued *them*. Already you are not treated like the rest."

Ashot, seemed to consider this, as though calculating his survival odds.

"So, you four, and how many others?"

"His three slaves, now freemen and a few of the older sailors. They were the ones whose bondage to the captain suffered the most. I have noticed that some smile at you."

Ashot laughed, as if being told a bad joke.

"I need a bodyguard. One of these three will be first mate, but none of them can do this."

Ashot nodded, warming to the proposal.

"And I suppose you need an enforcer as well?"

Tariq shook his head vigorously, "I *am* the enforcer."

"Then the price of my freedom is to keep you alive until we reach the port, yes?"

"You will be indentured to me until then and shall not leave my side. You will stand vigil while I sleep and guard my back when I eat."

"I shall have nothing to do with your vile treatment of captives, neither doing, nor preventing it." He paused. "They are not my people and what becomes of them is their fate, not mine."

Tariq drew close, keeping his voice low, but menacing. "Be clear, gypsy, I do not trust you or any of your thieving kind. I almost expect you to try to steal from me and I'll kill you myself if you try."

Ashot merely smiled. "And I shall kill you if I am not free when we reach dry land, my captain."

"Free him," Tariq ordered his men, then addressed Ashot, "You will begin now."

He turned on his heel and walked back toward the enclosure. The shackle struck from him, Ashot moved fluidly to a pace behind his new charge. Questioning looks from his former shipmates were met with blank indifference. No one wondered why.

Tariq strode into Mustafa's enclosure and Ashot lingered at its yard-wide opening. The captives were herded into a semicircle, and Tariq ordered his iron monger to chain them together in threes.

He turned to the cadaverous Captain of the ruined vessel. "Now to you, you snake who has swallowed a lizard." Then he laughed cruelly at his not inaccurate description of Mustafa's skin stretched over bones. He laughed alone.

This sick old man with a splinted leg is of no value at the market, Tariq calculated, but he still may be of some use.

"You are ready to cooperate?" Tariq began, keeping his voice even. He could tell the old man was in great pain.

"What do you want?" the captain said resignedly, affecting submission. Tariq was sure this was a man who knew his fate. "Who are these well-fed passengers of yours?"

"I know only they are al-yahūd from Baghdad. They speak our tongue, unlike the Africans who do not."

Tariq wondered if the old captain was giving him the whole story. Perhaps he was trying to reduce their value as slaves. But to what end?

"And these Africans, they are Hebrews as well?"

"So they claim," Mustafa said dubiously. "Some of their words are Arabic, but not enough to understand us."

"I saw you at the Port of Aden when our ships nearly collided in the harbor. We were returning with many slaves."

Captain Mustafa could not contain his disgust, and spat out, "You sell human flesh like it is slabs of meat."

"And sometimes it needs to be beaten tender, yes?" Tariq sneered. He looked over at the three Jews who were next to be chained together by three-foot links. He looked straight into Adiva's eyes, wishing to catch the look of surprise that her ransom had failed. Instead, defiance and hatred burned back at him. He found this exciting.

He returned his attention to the seated Mustafa. "Where is the ship's coffer? Where are all the gold dinars I know you received to leave at midnight, even before all your drunken, whoring crew could be drug aboard?"

"Lost in the storm that drove us on these rocks," Mustafa looked desolate.

Tariq did not believe this but was more urgently concerned with what Captain Shabazi had been told about the bankers and the Hebrew captives. "Bring the spy," he said.

"Everything, Chinaman. Tell me everything about the Jew bankers and these three." He stooped a little toward the kneeling man.

After a fleeting look at Adiva, Wen Ho lowered his eyes. "The house servant heard whispers about great wealth needing to be moved to the bankers in Fustat. Very bad for Jews in Aden. They must move gold and then themselves to a safer place. They are bankers for the Caliphs in Egypt. Safer there."

Tariq's watery eyes narrowed, and an overflow tear skidded

down his jowl to alight on a whisker. He was unsure what to believe. His dead captain was cruel but knew how to spot a lie. Perhaps it was the fear. He must learn if he hoped to hold on to his newfound power.

"Where is the gold?" he asked, looking from Wen Ho to Adiva, but lingering on her.

He drew his dagger and grasped a handful of the spy's hair. It occurred to Tariq that this might serve as the demonstration of remorseless violence he needed to shove his control down all their throats.

Wen Ho began sputtering, sensing the end might be near. "Gold bars and strings of coins. Some inlaid with precious stones. She...She said one of the slaves sewed jewels into leather pouches. The banker sold many things. Property. Slaves."

Tariq released Wen Ho and turned to Adiva. "You thought you had me fooled?" For a moment, Tariq wondered it he was going too far. If he was wrong, he would have neither gold nor slaves to sell. But it was too late to change course.

"For this, you and yours will pay dearly."

Tariq watched the iron monger finish tethering Yosef and Hillel's ankles with the yard length of chain. He thought a moment, then had the iron anklet switched to Hillel's left ankle, as was Yosef's. Thus configured, they could not move fluidly together without one of them walking backwards. Tariq smiled at this and ordered them on their knees. Dissatisfied with the speed of compliance, he whacked the broadside of his cutlass on the backs of the lanky man's knees, collapsing him.

Tariq carefully placed the tip of his curving sword in the hollow above Israel's collar bone, turning to the woman.

"The jewels?"

She gasped, but words quickly followed "Hidden in a cave, at the crater lake." Tariq remained motionless. The woman would not submit, but she would surrender.

"I shall take you there at daybreak, Captain, but not if you injure my brother."

Lowering his cutlass to his side, Tariq allowed himself a self-satisfied smile.

"Now, that's being the best kind of guest, isn't it!" He threw his head back and laughed.

The young woman pointed to the half inch thick shackle encircling her ankle.

"Will you honor your promise to take this off?"

Tariq jerked at her robe, cutlass at the ready. "Will you take *this* off?"

Out of the corner of his eye, Tariq noticed the rapt excitement of the crew watching carefully. Perhaps he should share *this* precious treasure with them all. That would keep them loyal.

He stood close enough to smell her fear. He took note of his own desire. Perhaps he would first take her for himself.

Tariq stepped back. He was captain now. Very soon he would be able to buy a caliph's harem for himself.

He would wait.

A sickening thought found its way through the flimsy denial of her helplessness. This slathering toad could do whatever he wanted with her, discarding her as damaged goods at a distant slave market. She could smell his dirty sweat when he was near enough to grab her robe.

"Chain her," he told the monger standing behind him, and he strolled back into the enclosure. No one looked surprised, least of all her.

34

Six hours of rowing, aided by a brisk northern flowing current, brought them in the still dark hours to Jebel's west beach, where the scalding water had boiled the fish. The water had cooled, leaving behind rotting fish carcasses they could smell but not see.

They each pulled a rope to beach the boat, but could slide it no more than a few feet from the water's edge. In the dark, they could see nothing to anchor it there.

"Drive the oar into the sand at an angle," an obviously spent Saul suggested. "We'll tie the ropes to it."

There was no time for desperately needed rest. Although their arms, shoulders and backs were rubber from overexertion, their legs were fresh. The pall of acrid smoke shifted westward, allowing the half moon to cast faint illumination on their path up the craggy slope. Near the top of the crater, the path split in two, one leg angling in the direction of the crater lake, and the other, to the plateau at the mountain top. The path around the crater lake was a shorter way to the other side but would leave them with no information about the hell spewing from the sea.

Eldad wasn't sure who was breathing harder when they had to stop along the deep caldera filled with pristine rainwater.

"There is an hour before sunlight, maybe less," Saul observed.

Eldad looked around. "Each time I think of being stranded on this island, even with you, my dear friend, while life passes us by, I think we should take our chances with the rest of the captives."

"We may feel great agony over how our companions are treated, and we will still be helpless, as well as be slaves ourselves."

"I have to tell you, Saul, I feel I shall die without this woman."

"The way you're thinking, Eldad. Listen, I have seen the extremes of this, when young men say they wanted to die *for* a young woman. My father had a special way of talking to these overwrought men, telling them, 'Going to die, are you? Yes, you are. So am I. What is your hurry?'

Eldad didn't want to hear that, no matter how accurate it was. He must accept the realities of surrendering. It will lead to two possible outcomes—slavery or death. "I will not know what has befallen my precious Adiva unless I am on the ship of the pirates. This is my decision, Saul. I cannot say what is best for you to do."

Saul leaned heavily on the boulder separating them from the vertical drop to the shimmering surface of the 100-foot-wide crater lake. Saul was about to respond when they heard loud, agitated male voices, jabbering in Arabic. The new dawn had just begun to sweep aside the darkness, and, by cautiously peering around the base of the boulder, Eldad could make out silhouettes on the heights above the opposite crater wall. One squat, rotund figure shouted orders, which seemed to be urging haste and threatening consequences. The shorter of the other two men had attached a rope and was rappelling down to the concealed entrance of the cave.

The sunlight reached the higher elevation first, and Eldad caught his breath as he beheld his princess, radiant and proud. His throat constricted as he saw the length of chain leading to her sweet ankle, held by the fat man whose attention was on the climber.

Eldad saw her look in his direction, and he was sure for a moment their eyes met. Overwhelmed by a terrible longing, Eldad begin to move from the shelter of the boulder. In an instant, her expression turned to terror. Unseen by Tariq or the tall pirate, she held both hands at her side in a sharply restraining posture doing her best to warn him. Her shaking her head attracted Tariq's attention, but she quickly looked away, pretending sadness and loss over what was going to be found in the cave.

The disembodied voice of the cave climber echoed, demanding that the tall pirate join him. He was unable to reach the crevice where the Jewess claimed the Netira gold was hidden.

Tariq stepped forward to peer farther over the caldera wall. Adiva could feel Eldad's eyes on her, though he had wisely concealed himself even from her. Every minute or so Tariq would look her up and down, as though suspecting at the edge of his awareness that something was going on. Each time, his greed, and anticipation quickly redirected his attention to below.

"We have it!" came a voice booming with resonance from the cave. Now Tariq's attention was fully focused, and Adiva looked hopefully at the other side. For a moment, Eldad again exposed himself at the boulder's opposite side and he was rewarded with Adiva's deep look of love.

Tariq saw this and looked sharply across the water, but only boulders stared back. He was about to launch an inquisition when the tall pirate emerged triumphantly from the cave, a heavy leather bag and Eldad's book. Believing this to be all there was, the pirate had not probed the back of the recess where the Danite had wedged the rest of his valuables. Even if they had found them, the leather scroll and seed pouch would have been thought worthless and been discarded.

The jewel and gold-laden bag had been slung up to Tariq, and he dropped his captive's chain to catch it, nearly toppling over the ledge in the process.

Suddenly, a deafening explosion brought a shock wave that rocked every person standing. For a moment it was hard to breathe, as though blunt force had struck their chests. Immediately, the jolts began to shake the ledge, three in rapid succession, sharper than the previous solitary tremors.

The short pirate was thrown from the rope he was using to climb, and belly-flopped into the water basin. He flailed about in panic until finding indentations in the rock he could use for footholds.

Eldad risked a look around the base of the boulder. He felt something tear deep within him when he saw she was gone.

"They're gone,"

Sadness overwhelmed him. He knew he must banish the dark thoughts that quickly clouded his mind. He could not accept the helplessness of doing *nothing*. He would act.

"We'll follow them to the beach," Eldad said with an uneasy determination.

Saul's response was instant. "No, my old friend, we will *not*."

Momentarily stunned by Saul's response, Eldad began to object, but Saul raised his hand to cut him off.

"You cannot tell me a single good thing that can come of it."

Both men fell silent. Eldad tried to think but couldn't.

Another rumble of the earth grabbed their attention, but nothing like the spectacular sight of the foot-thick missile of molten rock bashing the water's surface into superheated steam. Only the boulder shielded them, but the next fiery jet, though smaller, splattered on the rocks a yards yards away, close enough for them to feel its heat.

The light of the sunrise had turned to yellow and black from the steam, gasses and smoke, but more ominously, now illuminated a rain of pellet-sized droplets of liquid fire. A fateful shift of wind could determine who lived and who died in its choking hell.

35

The pirate ship's longboats had just pulled ashore after delivering water barrels to their anchored vessel, when the first shower of molten pellets spat a starburst on an empty stretch of sand.

"Chain them in the boats!" Tariq ordered the guards, who wanted nothing better than to leave these wretches and race for the mother ship. Many of them gaped skyward, as though believing they could avoid a fireball meant for them. Unhappy with the delay, Tariq drew his newly honed cutlass and shrieked, "You move now or poach in your own blood on this sand!"

He turned his attention to the enclosure where Captain Mustafa slumped in a makeshift stone chair. Tariq could see no fear in the captain's expression.

"Getting a little warm for you here, captain?" Mustafa said.

Tariq could not hide the sweat pouring from his face.

"Shut up, you old fool."

"You will face the authorities the minute you dock at the port of Aden, pirate."

The Berber reflected for a moment on something he'd not yet considered. Since he seized his shaky command, he'd never decided the galleon's next move.

His thoughts were interrupted by a screech of utter agony issued from a pirate while he was climbing into the boat. Clutching his burning shoulder, he fell thrashing and screaming into the surf. More burning pebbles hit the water behind him.

Feigning indifference to this horror, Tariq turned back to Mustafa, smiling, exposing the yellow-black murkiness of his half-toothless mouth.

"I should just split you down the middle and let the birds have a feast. But you tell me what I need to know and I'll leave you to your fate....ha ha...and your own kingdom of Hell." An outer branch of the enclave's wall smoldered from a droplet of molten rock.

"What is to the north and west?" Tariq's urgency was growing.

"From this Gulf of Aden, the Red Sea continues a thousand miles to Cairo."

"And to the south?"

"A great island, I am told, many weeks sailing, where the Eastern Ocean begins. It is as far as Cairo is in the other direction."

Tariq carefully observed Mustafa. He believed the old captain was telling the truth. But the knowing expression on his face gave Tariq pause. Did he know what option he would choose?

The slaver had learned from Wen Ho that the banking family was a power in Cairo. For a fee, not a few among his mob of pirates would find their way to the Netiras, who might like to know what happened to their gold. Mustafa would tell them for nothing. He would not get the chance.

"I should kill you," Tariq spat in front of Mustafa's feet, "but I think I'll let you fry." The specks of liquid rock were joining into plumb sized masses of molten death. Tariq sprinted with surprising agility toward the waiting long boat, Ashot pounding at his heels.

All other crew and captives had piled both boats over full, and even the gentle surf of the lagoon rocked them perilously from side to side. Tariq landed with a squishy thud in the middle of the craft, throwing the rat-faced pirate into the surf. Hauled back in, he sputtered below audible curses at his captain.

Though the distance was only a few hundred yards, the top-heavy long boats were hard to row, especially in the swirl at the outer edge of the lagoon. The pirates and soon-to-be wretched captives' attention was to the sky, but only Hillel saw that a more deadly menace had begun their escort just beneath the surface of the choppy Red Sea swells.

Adiva felt numb, as though she had become a curious observer, not the bound and terrified captive she was. She saw terror in others' eyes, not for loss of whatever freedom they once had, but the steadily increasing rain of fire from blackened skies threatened loss of *self*.

"Khaloss! Stop! What are you doing?" Tariq screeched toward the sailing ship. The great grey sails were being steadily unfurled, and no anchor line tethered the ponderous vessel to Zubair Jebel. The 150' boat was being steered south and gaining momentum in spite of northwestern current. Tariq turned his longboat 60 degrees to intercept his errant kingdom, which seemed intent on leaving all of them to burn.

The sleek long boats, though badly overloaded, soon cut in front of the ship and rope ladders were grudgingly lowered, not that any of them were unwelcome, only the delay, *any* delay, could be their end. Already they had expended valuable drinking water to put out small, but incredibly hot fires aboard the vessel. The ironmonger released the chains and the eight captives struggled aboard the pirate ship. The pirates converged, blades drawn, on the great bear Kasim, double chaining him to iron rings on the deck and railing. The others were immediately chained to rings a few feet apart on the railing. Wen Ho, happy to simply be alive, was seated next to Adiva. He pulled at the yard of chain. "It is safer in the terrible hold below than on this deck."

He muttered under his breath. "If they had paid me, I would have told them what I knew and gone on my way. Now, they owe me and *own* me as well."

Loud commands from Tariq had the ten crew members moving purposefully. One unfurling sail already had a perfectly round fist-sized hole in it, black and smoldering at its edges. The seaworthy ship was triple-masted, with sails of tightly woven grey Egyptian cotton, grimy with soot from the sandstorm.

The three Jews looked back wordlessly at Jebel Island, now receding from view, not in distance, but from a pall of smoke had blown inland. Sparks floated in unruly spires that winked out on the water. From a quarter mile distance, the active volcano was filling the world around it with choking death.

"There is a terrible irony here," Yosef began in a low voice. "The smoke and the rain of hell from the heavens, these things will likely have killed us, as there was no shelter on the island. These evil men who chain us like animals have saved us from an awful death."

"Don't say that, Cousin. The Danite and Asherite are trapped on this accursed rock, as is the captain, if Tariq allowed him to live. I pray the Africans did not follow me to the beach."

"The lagoon, I can't see it through the smoke," Hillel said, "and these pirates are having trouble sailing south against the current. But if the wind shifts, it will blow us away from here."

"Another irony," Yosef added, "it will also burn us to cinders."

Now the curtain of black curled more ominously around the island, leaving only the upper reaches of Jebel visible from the vessel. From its origin 1,000 yards north, the flow of smoke and debris was not coming *over* the 600 foot summit but rather curling around the steep north face, funneled toward the lagoon and beach. This stirred a strong, cooler wind beyond the sharp line demarcating the ghastly smoke; life on one side, death on the other.

And the line was steadily moving out to sea, having ricocheted off Jebel's west face. Cooled by steam from the water beneath it, the pyroclastic flow had lost speed but not buoyancy. The dense black smoke had turned grey at 50 yards from the slow-moving slave ship. The cooler wind gusted, filling all sails to their fullest, but seemed to pull the grey cloud closer, preceded by a now familiar burning sulfur smell.

Ashot appeared out of nowhere, lugging ragged squares of rough woven sail cloth dripping sea water. Without a word, he kicked at the shackled captives to get them to move closer to one another. Yosef noticed the kicks started with vicious speed, but only tapped the intended victim. He thought he saw a twinkle in the gypsy's eyes, but he saw a look that told him to be quiet.

Ashot threw the sopping remnants over each of the four pairs of them, the largest barely covering the great bulk of the dispirited, doubly-shackled Kasim. The countenance of the Ethiopian cook next to Kasim bore the look of the doomed, the unfocused stare of the hopeless.

As though exhaled from diseased lungs, the volcanic cloud streamed above the Red Sea waves toward the unprotected slave ship in full flight. Ashot roamed the long vessel with a nonchalant casualness, poking here and there, into this and that. Yosef realized that Ashot had anticipated what was likely coming and had found the large sail scraps left over from the crew's replacing the foresail. Lest the crew, or worse, his new employer, think him to be aiding the captives, he made great theater of abusing them before throwing the wet and salty sailcloth over them. When the moment came, only the soon-to-be slaves would know what to do. Ashot would make sure of that. The pirates would not understand the peril. The gypsy saw no reason to explain his repeated dipping of scraps in the sea water and pretended to be cleaning something on deck with the ragged piece he had saved for himself.

Captain Tariq had abandoned the order for Ashot to be always behind or in front of him. The danger of the rain of fire had given the fledgling captain the control he needed...for now.

Ashot, on hands and knees, reached for Kasim's shackled ankle. The great bear roared an insult about Ashot's mother and jerked it away.

The squat gypsy said nothing, but subtle movements of his eyes, and slight nods of Ashot's head, arrested the carpenter's attention. Ashot moved closer and was now offered the iron ring clad ankle, by now, grossly irritated. The gypsy drew his knife, as though to defend against this dangerous slave. Nobody really knew how Kasim would act after being forcibly removed from his beloved master.

Ashot used his dagger to cut shreds of seaweed he flung in Kasim's surprised face, whispering, "Weave this around your ankle, beneath the iron. Be very still." Ashot pretended to cut more seaweed, but his knife tip fit squarely into the tight screw holding the two sides of the shackle together. Too tight to be unscrewed without an iron tool, the victim could not undo it. The knife blade slipped once, but Ashot's second try loosened the iron screw, just enough for Kasim's clever, outsized fingers to do the rest, when the rest was to be done.

The Ethiopian cook stared at the gypsy, then offered his ankle, which was half the size of the carpenter's. The gypsy looked about and nearly bent down to turn the anklet screw when he spied Tariq at the last instant.

Standing, Ashot made sure he was neutral, utterly expressionless. "Yes, my captain?"

"Do not speak or respond to these slaves."

"I spoke to no one, my captain. They are goods to be sold, are they not?"

"Do not play games with me. They are goods for me to do with what I want. You will not misunderstand this again, gypsy."

"No, my captain." Ashot kept his eyes downcast, his face impassive, while within him, the primal rage of his Roma people cried out from their enslavement. Ashot was quite amazed that the otherwise shrewd Tariq hadn't remembered that he was seen by Ashot herding a pitiful cluster of gypsy slaves to the market in Aden. Or perhaps he didn't care about the identities of slaves they'd pirated from another slave ship, adding its crew to the spoils.

He should have.

36

In their haste, the pirates had left their thick rope dangling down to the mouth of the cave. Saul was the first to rappel down, quickly followed by Eldad. Luckily, neither had been burned by the gusting showers of sparks which seemed drawn to the surface of the crater lake. They entered the safety of tall anteroom of the cave.

"This is like a tomb," Saul exclaimed.

"Pray it is not ours," Eldad said, unable to hide the gloom in his voice.

"Did you see the cover of gritty dust settling on the lake's surface. I wonder if it will poison the water." He sat down heavily on a jagged outcropping of rock.

"I wonder if it will matter."

Out of the corner of his eye, Eldad noticed wisps of grey gas drifting past the narrow opening of the cave, a few snaking inwards toward the two men.

"Move!" Eldad shouted, jerking his friend after him to the inner cavern. The lively sound of falling water and the mist from its collision with the rocky basin filled their senses. From somewhere in the blackness, a warm and moist breeze contrasted sharply with the noxious fumes at the mouth of the cave.

They stood a moment, hoping their eyes would adjust.

"I've been in here before, and sight does not improve," Eldad said matter of factly.

Saul didn't ask for any details and Eldad was glad for the moment of reminiscence about his time with Adiva before a dagger of sadness stabbed his young heart. And the fear...did this accursed brimstone rain on the beach where she was? There was no protection there, and the only way out to sea, away from the terrible danger, was in a slaver's chains.

"There is a hot spring and its water spills into a basin. It might be very hot now."

Eldad turned back into the low, jagged corridor to the anteroom.

"I want my treasured things if they are still in the crevice. And we must know what our safe zone is in this cave. Keep talking to me as I go to the outer chamber. I've tied a rope around my chest. You hold the other end and pull me back if I stop talking. Don't crawl out to get me. Understand, my brother?"

Grasping the rope, Saul nodded, "Bring back the bag I brought with us. I think we're going to need it."

Eldad sighed. "Always the food!"

He realized that his little joke could just as easily be about himself. He couldn't remember the last time he'd had a satisfying meal.

At the corridor's narrowest width, Eldad felt the breeze toward the anteroom more strongly at his back, and well it was, for when he poked his head into the outer space, he could see a dense cloud, peppered with black specks, hovering only a few inches outside the cave's circular opening, as though held there by an invisible dome.

"It's alright in here, Saul, you can let go of the rope."

Eager to be out of the watery darkness, Saul hunched down to squeeze out of the narrow opening to the anteroom, momentarily blocking most of the flow of air. In a heartbeat, the smoke filled the chamber. Eldad gasped and fell to the floor, coughing in long paroxysms. The Asherite tumbled backward on to the corridor floor, clearing the channel for the air from within. Some minutes passed before the anteroom was emptied of the toxic fumes.

Eldad was sure he was about to die, and in a most hideous way. Resigned, he gave up the struggle to breathe. Everything began closing off, going black. As a last thought, he tried to maintain an image... my love through all time....

"Danite!"

The voice was distant, nearly impenetrable through the fog enveloping his consciousness.

"It's clear in here, it's alright, wake up!"

A smack across his face aroused his anger, but unquestionably his awareness as well. A few more wrenching coughs seemed to ease Eldad's breathing, and he was able to focus on the big man propping him up to a seated position, and a ghastly headache that nauseated him.

"Might I suggest a gentler tap for any further victims you wish to wake up." Eldad rubbed his face and looked anxiously at the toxic gas lurking outside the cave's round entrance. The warmth of the inner chamber air, plus its mysterious airflow, just outweighed the invasive force of gas, soot and steam covering the crater lake.

"We have been passed over by some kind of plague, haven't we?" Saul said without expecting a reply.

The Danite stood, unsteadily at first, to his full height and reached hopefully into the most convoluted recess of the ceiling crevice. He and Saul had seen the pirates remove the banker's gold, but they may not have found Eldad's things, objects he carried that made him *feel* like him. Reaching in, he was relieved that they were just where he'd left them. He gently ran his fingers across the bundle.

He smiled, remembering a phase of his childhood. He was told it started as far back as 18 months. He was always most fretful without the presence of a small leather pouch his grandfather fashioned for him. Inscribed by burning with symbols from an unknown language, he carried the purse string pouch everywhere. Typically, it would remain filled with seeds of various kinds from grandfather's or neighbor's gardens, such as to grow poppies, or other medicinal plants. When he was older, Zav told him, "Keep the seeds to grow our most valuable medicines with you. If you must run, these priceless seeds, from countless generations of our family's healers, must go with you."

Other things were in the pouch now, like a few gold trinkets, but they mingled naturally with travelers from another time: the precious seeds he had carried with him.

Eldad unrolled the long foot-wide strip of leather, rough on the outside but highly tanned and polished on the inside. Pockets of different sizes were sewn to the inner surface. Imprinted on the elegant leather between pouches were three separated columns of tiny symbols, vividly rendered in black ink. A few sentences had been translated, like those he told to his Adiva. The rest, though he had faithfully copied the verbal symbols onto the skin, remained a mystery.

Wrapped inside the seed carrier was the strange leather scroll with two parallel columns of ancient, undecipherable symbols, but his copy of the family book was gone, taken by the pirates.

He needed to sit in a quiet place, a peaceful moment to touch what remained of his treasured possessions. How he now yearned for simpler times, to stroll atop sand dunes or the vast savannahs, where there seemed to be no sense of time.

Eldad peered out the circular opening to the surface of the crater lake. "It's covered, the lake surface. A floating blanket of gray ash."

"Are we finished, Danite? We might be unable to leave here for days."

"We still have the pure water from the hot spring, even if all the surface water is bad." As he said that, he began to wonder why he was now able to see the water's surface twelve feet below the cave with such clarity. "Saul, look."

Saul moved as close to the opening as prudently as he could and shouted, "It's clearing! The air...now only hazy."

No more droplets of liquid stone pelted the frothy surface of the lake, which seemed to harden when the grimy bubbles popped.

Eldad made a decision. "I'm going to leave you here while I go to the encampment. There is no reason for both of us to risk being in the open."

"Why are you going? Wait till we have hours of clearing," Saul said, sounding like he already knew it was a fruitless appeal.

"I cannot stand the thought that our people...my Adiva and the others...are in trouble, injured perhaps. If there's anything I can do... I must try. If I am captured by the slavers, I shall tell them where you're hiding, lest you be left behind. I can't think of another way, old friend.

Saul didn't say a word.

"But you will know in a matter of an hour." With that, Eldad grabbed the rope dangling from the ledge above and scrambled up the crater wall to the rim. Through the soles of his sandals, he could feel the heat of the rocks, so recently awash in hot gas, but the air was clear as he hurried higher toward the rim of Jebel's west slope.

As suddenly and mysteriously as the eruption had turned the island into a netherworld, it was gone. Eldad realized he had been holding his breath off and on, as he descended to lower elevations in sight of the beach and cove. He was both heartened and deeply depressed that he saw no movement, only gray paint on every-thing--the trees, the sand, the surf, a monochrome of ruin. Their ship lay on its side, the gaping hole in the hull in sharp relief against a blanketing shroud of ash.

Making his way toward the smoldering remains of Captain Mustafa's greenstick enclosure, his dread increased. Though the inches of silt covered the stones in the center, Eldad squinted at what looked like craggy rocks but seemed to be a faint outline of a man. He ran to the pile and clawed frantically at the head.

What assaulted his senses was something he would never forget. The face he beheld bore a look of utter agony, and as he turned the dead captain's head, it revealed the vestige of a burned off ear. Eldad prayed this happened after the captain had died. Added to the horror of the apparent suffocation by hot ash, this would have been more than any human could bear.

It is what he did not find that gave him the only hope he could muster. Adiva, Hillel, Yosef, and the rest had not perished or been killed by the pirates. What fate awaited them tore at his heart, but at least it was not to be suffocated and burned to death like the piteous captain. He looked again at the man's face. That the captain had been dying anyway offered no comfort.

His friends were gone. His beloved was gone. He desperately fought an overwhelming sadness, held in check till now by raw survival fears. He felt inside as the landscape looked outside; all color turned gray, lifeless beneath a blanket of despair. He thought of the story of Job, lying on a pile of ashes, tormented and angry at his fate.

Eldad looked out over the expanse of beach, now more uniformly flat from accumulated volcanic debris blown in or rained down. Out of the corner of his eye, he saw Saul trudging along the upper rim of the beach toward him.

"The sand is still warm, hot in some places," Saul said, a bit winded from the climb down the mountain. "It got so quiet, I..."

Without being told, Saul spotted the enclosure. "Oh, the captain."

Eldad wanted to warn him of the gruesome scene, but he was too late.

Saul moved closer, then he stopped suddenly. "Oh, God deliver us."

The late afternoon breeze from the sea was now scented with its usual earthy seaweed and fish, and the sun, blotted out during the cataclysm, shone brightly in the late afternoon.

The two friends stood quietly.

"We cannot let our pain paralyze us," Eldad said. "If we are to be marooned here, we have to find a way to survive, in the manner of our people."

Saul's attention was suddenly riveted on the water north of the cove where the sheer rock plunged into the sea. "Look. Boats!

Ahead, two strange-hulled longboats, rowed by many men, moved very fast into the lagoon.

"The pirates, come back for us?" Eldad said, hope mingled with fear.

"Not their boats." They could not yet see the men rowing, as their backs were toward the shore.

Then, at the front of the two attached boats, two muscular black men stood to full height and let loose inhuman-sounding screeches that traveled piercingly over the lagoon.

"Look at their faces," Saul cried out in horror. "Painted, naked.... savages!"

"Run!" Eldad shouted, though the big Asherite had already

started pounding over the two hundred yards of sand to the scalable crack in the mountain face. The Eldad's long legs easily outdistanced his friend, but as he glanced to his left, Eldad saw the futility of their flight. Flooding out of the path in the mangrove forest were a dozen men and two women who had beached their boat on the eastern side of the island. Half carried spears, half stone knives, and wore only loincloths. Spears were in full ready, arms cocked in throwing position. They wordlessly encircled them both. With no place to turn, they stopped running and stared at the tight ring of drawn weapons.

Eldad followed Saul's terrified eyes back towards the enclosure, still close enough to see the excited tribesmen huddled about the captain's stone chair. One man shrieked, piercing Eldad's soul, before triumphantly holding aloft a charred leg, butchered at the hip joint and still wearing its sandal.

37

Hillel said a prayer under his breath, beseeching the Almighty. He wasn't sure how much longer he could go on. His skin burned and his lips were cracked. He felt listless from dehydration. He reckoned it was toward the end of their second day at sea, and they had been given neither food nor water. What part of him could still reason knew that it was likely a deliberate part of Tariq's handling of new slaves. Weakened of body, minds numbed by relentless deprivation, they would soon be most easy to control.

He looked at his sister. Adiva's head dropped and bobbed as if detached from her neck and any defiance had left her eyes. Her skin, lighter than his, must be causing her too much agony. He shuddered when he contemplated the fate that awaited his sister.

Earlier he had seen Yosef try to get her attention, but she would not even look up.

"This captain has no mercy," Yosef said. "We have begged for food and water, but the crew, the captain, they do not look at us nor speak."

Nodding, Hillel kept his head down to shield his face from the sun as much as he could. They must hold on. Still, he could feel himself weakening, and he tugged listlessly at the chain and its iron ring attached to the railing. At the edge of his awareness, he sensed something different in his surroundings. He pulled more insistently at the ring, confirming his perception that, ever so slightly, it moved. Perhaps the teakwood into which the ring had been hammered, had cracked beneath the surface.

He felt a touch on his right leg. In his desperation, he had almost forgotten about Kasim to his right.

"We are not alone," Kasim mumbled just loudly enough for only Hillel to hear.

He followed Kasim's dark gaze to the aft of the ship, where the stocky gypsy stood at the railing, apart from others.

"Ashot? What value is he, with loyalty only to his clan?"

Hillel paused. It was true that he threw wet sail over us, he thought. Was he protecting us?

Hillel stood, raising himself to his full height, which he knew from his experience in the Persian Gulf allowed him to see quite a way on open water. Beyond a certain distance the horizon always disappeared. No one knew why.

"Prisoner, be seated," Ashot shouted from behind.

Hillel immediately complied.

Tariq took notice. Satisfied that his enforcer had everything under control, he smiled and turned away.

"I see an island dead ahead, and to the left of it the outline of a coast," Hillel whispered. "The way this wretched ark of grief is moving through the water, we shall pass the island in an hour, maybe a little more."

He looked down at the ship's carpenter and was alarmed to see his bloodied thumb and forefinger gouging at the ankle manacle.

"You're hurting yourself," Hillel said with alarm, but Kasim continued.

"Shut up and listen," Kasim hissed. "Ashot is not what he seems. His knife loosened the screw."

Hillel now noticed that the strength and leathery toughness of Kasim's fingers had rotated the head of the screw holding the manacle together two full turns and unscrewing it entirely was but a few easy turns away. Kasim saw his bloody fingers too and quickly sucked them free of the red stain.

The two prisoners chained between Hillel and his cousin and sister were the Ethiopian cook and fisherman. Anything he said loud enough for Adiva and Yosef to hear would be heard across the deck by their tormentors, so he spoke in Hebrew.

Keeping his tone desperate and cadence halting, Hillel felt he could speak freely without fear of being comprehended, though he still confused the content, lest *any* of his words be understood. "The big one, he does not do well, and his mind is wandering. He speaks of himself as Moshe freeing bene Yisroel."

Yosef seemed to not understand. After a moment a glimmer of recognition appeared. "Mitzrayim?"

Yes, cousin. Like Egypt and freedom from bondage.

"And the Almighty commanded his brother to be by his side, his spokesman."

"With an outstretched rod," Yosef finally answered. A noisy rattle of the chain finished his thought.

Captain Tariq suddenly appeared from his cabin atop the poop deck. He stretched and squinted in the sunlight toward the chained, dehydrated, and starving captives slumped against the railing.

"So, the Yahud still talk! With their last breath, they'll be talking!"

Ashot approached him from the rear, so quietly that Tariq jumped when he caught him in the corner of his eye.

"Don't creep up upon me, gypsy. You know I am quick with the dagger."

Ashot lowered his eyes. "Apologies, my Captain."

Tariq smiled with satisfaction. "First, show our guests my generosity and give them water," he said softly. He paused, then said, "Take our new friends and *shackle them in the filth below!*"

The three of Tariq's ten crew, whose loyalty the captain did not question, were the quickest to respond and stood by Tariq at the ready. Ashot grumbled resentfully, but hoisted the water barrel, resting its lower rim on his right hip, a ladle in the other hand. Between two fingers of this hand, Ashot secreted a narrow sliver of iron he had discovered in the iron monger's unguarded toolbox.

He ladled cup after cup of life-giving water from the barrel to the parched lips of one captive after another. The Ethiopian gagged momentarily on something in his cup of water, then, as his tongue felt its shape, his look of confusion was replaced by one of comprehension. He cheeked the metal object, saying nothing. The tall Ethiopian looked down into the face of the fearsome gypsy and saw Ashot's usually impassive eyes soften, then a determined look and slight nod.

As Ashot approached Adiva, he was suddenly joined by Captain Tariq, who stayed his hand as he tried to offer Adiva her cup of water. Ashot tensed, but betrayed no sign of consternation, only obedience.

Tariq took the ladle and dipped it into the water bucket. Holding it in front of her, out of her reach, he poured it on the deck. Adiva closed her eyes and struggled weakly to contain a cry of anguish.

The captives were badly weakened by lack of food, but their being without water would soon be fatal. Hillel and Yosef slumped dejectedly on the deck a few yards from Adiva.

As suddenly as Tariq appeared, he disappeared to the opposite end of the ship, into his cabin. He was replaced by the rat-faced Arab, chosen by Captain Tariq to be his second in command. He was one of three pirate crewmen whose loyalty to Tariq was unquestioned.

Hillel realized, as Ashot must, that Tariq's trust in them fell short of absolute. Otherwise, why hire a murderous gypsy as a bodyguard? The other seven pirates were loyal if rewards were certain. Each had assigned duties they went about unsupervised, which varied with the complexity of the sailing task.

Second in command, the rat-faced Arab, nudged the gypsy to go on watering the prisoners, and he, too, walked away.

Ashot knelt quickly with the water cup to Adiva's lips and then another. She gratefully nodded.

Ashot moved on to Yosef. "The cook has the tool to remove the manacles. The carpenter has already undone his but leaves it in place."

His eyes swept constantly for crew too close. "The beast will move you below deck, and chain you there. It is unspeakable, but in the darkness and confinement no one will see, and only we will know the moment you are all unshackled."

Finally, Hillel received his portion of water. "The carpenter and I will decide when we will strike, and he will tell you," Ashot whispered. "You may know of the great island called Perim that lies in the strait between the Red Sea and the Indian Ocean."

"Yes, I do know of this island from our captain's charts. A channel of five leagues between Perim and Asia, and on the island's flank, a channel only one league wide on the charts."

"I heard the son of a pig tell the Arab they would sail the small strait to save time." The stocky gypsy smiled. "That will be the second and final mistake our noble captain will make."

"Why is the narrow channel a mistake?" Hillel asked, drinking his third cup.

The bellowed voice of Tariq interrupted. "No more water. Chain them below so they may become better acquainted with our rats."

Ashot nodded and Tariq stepped away. He gathered his bucket and ladle. "Tell the others. The small strait has strong, irregular tidal streams, and passing through it will require the full attention of *all* the murderous bastards.

"Because so many ships come to grief there, it is well-named Bab El Mandeb–the Gate of Tears." He growled through gritted teeth. *"Their* tears, not ours."

38

Blindfolded, Eldad strained to hear what was happening around him. Most importantly, he wanted to locate Saul.

Without warning, a hand stripped off Eldad's blindfold and he faced a nearly toothless crone of dirty yellow color, her emaciated breasts hanging like empty sacs nearly to her waist. Brought to his feet, he towered over his stunted captors, each adorned with more bizarre body paint than the other, except the few women who were bare breasted and painted in single colors.

He quickly looked around for his friend, but he was nowhere evident. He did make note that one of the two boats he had first seen was gone.

The old yellow one seemed to wield authority among those making haste to leave in the second boat. Pellets of smoldering ash lay on every foot of sand, and the young man might have been burned if forced to walk sightless to the water's edge. Now he could see the crone had further adornment, around her mouth, down her front, and on the backs of her hands.

He was dragged and dumped, bound at wrists and ankles, into the pontoon boat. The old women approached. Grasping his upper arm in her bony fingers, she shook her head and said something in disparaging tones to the others.

It was not the sight of her, but her smell–the sweet, metallic pungency of blood known all too well by the young healer from mending wounds of war–that made him shudder involuntarily.

He watched the old woman bend over in the boat and retrieve a bundle she had brought aboard, and Eldad recognized it as his, carried slung about his shoulder from the crater cave. She unrolled it and examined the long leather scroll with pockets sewn to its inner surface. These were quickly emptied of the few gold dinars they contained, but she ignored the pouches of seeds in two of the pockets.

Eldad was able to sit up, and the old one threw the unrolled leather at him, which he managed to catch before it was claimed by the sea. Despite his utter misery, he felt comforted touching the beautifully tanned leather with its mysterious writing, and pouches of seeds from the distant past. At the same time, he could not imagine why the old woman had thrown it at him.

With bound wrists, re-rolling it tight enough to repel water was painful, but soon it was done, and it fit into his robe's inner pocket.

They were soon in open seas, with neither land nor the billowing smoke of the volcano in sight. A breeze was blowing at their backs, and Eldad concluded from the movement of the sun that they were moving north. With remarkable stamina, the savages rowed hard through sunset, and on into the night.

Eldad lay in the rough-hewn hollow of the boat, unable to sleep, but more distressingly, tormented by his own thoughts. He struggled to contemplate his own end and his childhood notions about life and death came back to him, including the moment when he realized that as far as he could tell, the one true God neither took life nor spared it. The random death of his contemporaries, or even younger, in endless, pointless territorial wars, some dying in his arms, taught him well this was the handiwork of men, and men alone.

Yet, he was taught to consider that the Almighty judged who should live and who shall die.

When he asked his beloved grandfather to explain, he shrugged, then smiled, admonishing Eldad to not believe a word he says. "You can study with this sage or that, but it will be their ideas about the reason for existence, not yours."

Even at twelve years, Eldad realized how wise Zav was. Eldad smiled to himself. Too wise for a mere boy to understand.

He closed his eyes. He and Zav were studying together. Seemingly out of nowhere, Zav said to him, "The purpose of the soul is service."

Zav had acted a little embarrassed, saying he didn't know why he said that, that perhaps it was the passages they were studying about leaving the corners of the fields for the poor. Eldad remembered how Zav had wrapped his arms around him, saying that he hoped Eldad would find his own way of serving.

Eldad didn't quite understand. Until now. "If this shall be my end," he whispered to himself, "I hope I did."

He took a deep breath, trying to ignore the pain in his wrists and ankles. He thought of Adiva. It was a momentary relief, that soon brought him deeper, more searing distress.

"Yii yeeee!" the lookout screeched from the front of the dugout boat. All eyes strained to see in the predawn light, but before the sun broke the surface of the Red Sea, they heard hearty cries of recognition, the steady beating of a drum, and even from a mile distant, a din of excited voices, of...*celebration.*

The voices became louder as the craft approached the rocky shore. One sound split the rest, rising above. It was a wail, animal-like in its agony. The screams became deafening when Eldad realized that it was not only a man, but it was Saul.

Just as quickly as it began, there was silence. In that moment, Eldad knew that his friend, his brother, was gone.

He closed his eyes tightly to stem the tears that came to him. He did not want to reveal his anguish to his captors. He could not stop the moisture, nor the dread he felt. It was clear that he would soon share Saul's awful fate at the hands of the cannibals.

He looked around to see if there was some way that he could possibly end his own life, but none was obvious. He could see none of what went on at their campsite, hidden from view behind a broad stand of trees. The celebration began again and was even more spirited.

Their boat pulled ashore, Eldad was surrounded by spear-bearing warriors, who dragged him with ankles still bound up the rocky terrain of a small hill. A tidal wave of nausea invaded every fiber of his being the moment he caught the smell of burning flesh. He retched. His captors laughed, one gently prodding him with a spear.

They dropped him roughly on a level plateau of black earth, and the old woman with yellow paint appeared. The fiercely painted men attended to her every stern, insistent word, their eyes riveted on the bloody dagger she dangled casually in her right hand.

The old woman smiled with toothless malevolence. With great effort, Eldad kept his face expressionless, determined to show no fear. She bent over him, red stained dagger in hand. The pendulous sacks of her breasts dangled comically in front of him, and despite seeing the knife coming toward his belly, he began to laugh.

Startled at first, the old yellow one started laughing too, and, with breasts swinging before his disbelieving eyes, she stooped and deftly cut the leather cords from his blood-stained wrists. His legs were still bound at the ankles, and when he pointed to them, the guards became a chorus of negative advisors. She nodded and made a dismissive gesture with her free hand. Without delay the men grabbed his arms and dragged him to the lip of a deep hole in the earth, obviously freshly dug. The mouth of the pit, nearly fourteen feet wide was covered over by a heavy latticework of wood, strong enough to walk on. The center of the lattice had a larger opening, a foot across, but otherwise openings in the weave of wood were less than half a cubit in width. Two of the savages raised the edge of the lid with ropes and a third rolled him into a deep cavern in the earth. Eldad luckily landed feet first, but he fell backwards onto his back with a sickening thud. He looked up. Three men standing on top of one another could barely reach the top. The loose, pungent black earth of the surface gave way to hard red clay at the bottom, dug to make foot holds impossible.

Laboring to breathe from the impact with the unyielding earth, he felt his limbs and chest for obvious damage, but found none.

Eldad was not quite sure why he was still alive. After a while in the pit, he recalled the crone's disappointment at his lean physique, and it dawned on him he was being appraised like an animal soon to be slaughtered.

It should have been no surprise to him when a few hours later, a basket was lowered down through the hole in the cover. It had a long-neck water jug and two boat-shaped pieces of fruit. After he finished the fruit, he drank most of the water, the small amount of nourishment made him even more ravenously hungry than before. It was a paradox he had observed in men returning from the privations of battle.

Eldad looked up at the unreachable lattice and saw the yellow crone crouched over the central opening watching him. She pointed to her mouth and made pleasant looking chewing motions, her eyebrows raised in simulated delight.

Another basket was lowered with something warm wrapped in leaves. She again encouraged Eldad from above. *Eat.*

A burnt aroma from beneath the leaves pushed aside the earthy smell of the pit with a pungent jab at his senses. But he could not resist opening the roll of leaves to see if it was an edible thing. He knew he was weak and must eat. His will to survive had returned.

One layer of leaves was blackened, with the inner sheaf still bearing the green veins of banana leaves. He tore it open, and the contents spilled into his lap. Picking it up and turning it over, he gasped in horror at the sight of a charbroiled human tongue.

39

The gypsy always ate alone when afforded the opportunity and in silence. He barely touched the morsels in front of him, instead using his time to think. This day, he knew, would either be his best, or his last.

He observed two of the pirate crew. They were Berbers who claimed to be brothers, though one was a foot taller and several shades darker.

Ashot doubted they were blood relations, but what did it matter. They had been slave children until late childhood when they successfully escaped the Ethiopian salt mines of Lake Afrera. Like Ashot, they seldom spoke to others, and at daybreak they stood apart at the stern of the ship. One gray sail stood at half mast, an effort to slow the 150 foot vessel in the dangerous riptides known to be ahead in the two-mile-wide channel.

Ashot stood close, hoping his bulk might intimidate them, if needed. He looked ahead to the large island approaching on their port side. He tried to keep his voice even, his tone casual. "The captain takes risks with our lives in his rush to the slave market on Socotra Island."

The two stared at him for a few moments.

"Tariq is a fool," the shorter brother replied, "Asulil and I were tricked by him at Aden."

"You knew they were pirates," Ashot said.

"Yes," answered Isri, "But, not *which* pirates."

"We are sailors, but we do not want to venture beyond the Red Sea. Tariq will take us into the Eastern Ocean, and there we shall likely be lost and perish," Asulil said gloomily.

Ashot made sure the two were looking into his eyes. "We *have* a choice."

The two men listened attentively as Ashot, risking everything by trusting these unlikely allies, unfolded his plan. They needed little convincing after Ashot asked a question. "Why does Tariq own this ship or the gold he has stolen?" It clearly helped that the Berbers already mistrusted and despised Tariq.

Ashot found rat face on the port side. He motioned toward the two Berbers who were completing their sail mending chores. "The captain wanted our captives below fed, but nobody in the crew really wants to go down there. Why don't you order those two sons of pigs? It suits them."

It was even worse than imagined. The first wretched, de-humanizing night spent below deck chained in stalls left the seven captives stunned by the inhumanity. Human waste from previous occupants had never been cleaned, but simply left to dry where it had fallen. That smell competed fiercely with the even more sick-ening and pervasive stench of something unseen in the blackness of the slave hold—something or someone clearly dead.

They could not tell if another day had begun until the hatch opened and light blindingly intruded. Each of them hungered for the fresh air of the sea.

Asulil and Isri descended the stairs carrying an inadequate ration of barely edible fish, and each also bore a sack of dried figs. They treated the captives with indifference, conditioned to not show favoritism lest they bring misfortune upon themselves. They slung the two bags from their shoulders before turning quickly to escape up the ladder.

Kasim heard an audible metallic clang and wordlessly grabbed Asulil by the arm. The Berber pulled away forcefully. "Something to cut open your fruit," he muttered.

The hatch was slammed shut, and without delay Kasim re-moved two curved cutlasses and three daggers of various lengths.

Since they were all chained in a brutally small space, Kasim knew he could distribute the weapons with ease. They had already passed the cook's stubby metal tool, from one of them to another, a process they had begun within an hour of the hatch being slammed shut. Had they been receiving even remotely humane treatment, perhaps a few moments above deck, what they had accomplished through the night may have been discovered. Each of the seven of them had unscrewed the ankle or wrist manacle, but Kasim left them in place.

Killing might be involved in what was coming, and that determined for Kasim who would be armed. Who among them was willing to kill for their freedom, without mercy?

It took a few moments to think through this. Over many years, Captain Mustafa left matters of combat, whether offensive, or, more often, defensive in nature, to Kasim. He always considered the aggressive potential of whomever he hired. None could be soft or fearful. He handed Wen Ho one of the daggers, as he knew him to be quite terrified enough of the pirates to kill without hesitation.

Of course, the cook and his fisherman cousin had been hired on to nourish their now lost ship, but their survival skills were of little value in combat. Nevertheless, the cook was the deftest of all with a knife. If he could bone fish, he could bone pirates, Kasim reasoned, passing the tall black man a knife.

This left the Jews from Babylon. Kasim could see an obvious difference with Yosef, the stronger and more agile.

In the utter darkness, Kasim asked, "Which of you can manage a sword?"

He had learned that for Jews, swords were playthings for children or objects of manufacture, but never, by the oppressive laws of Babylon, could they possess or carry by them. How odd, he thought. In Baghdad, they could not even wear a belt that would hold such weapons.

He had gotten to know the two young men a little, so his surprise was tempered when they both spoke up. "I can!" both volunteered.

Kasim smiled to himself. "Have you slit as many throats as you have broken young women's hearts?" There was no reply.

Yosef spoke in a whisper, "I am known to do what I have to do. No, I have never killed anybody, but yes, I most certainly can. I understand that they will kill all of us without a thought, and we must be the same."

Kasim handed him the cutlass, handle first, in the dark, poking Yosef's chest.

Kasim would arm himself with the other sword, and that left a knife for him to decide upon.

To his astonishment, Adiva spoke up. "At the right moment, I may be less scrutinized than you, allowing me to strike from closer range."

Kasim did not quite know how to respond, and merely grunted.

Hillel interrupted. "Perhaps it would be best if I took the weapon, but it is true that my sister is strong in spirit. In our holy books, there is the story of Ya'el who killed the commander of a great Canaanite army, up close while he slept. So Adiva would not be the first woman among our people to..."

Kasim hesitated but had to admit that she was as tough and determined as any man, and a good bit smarter. He gave her the knife and kept the second sword himself.

Kasim gave everyone a few moments to reflect. Did the group totally realize what awaited them? They might survive the many days the pirate ship would ply the Red Sea waters on to Socotra Island, but what awaited them was even more dehumanizing than the degradation of confinement in the slave hold. At the sprawling slave market of the island's capital, they would become *property*.

Kasim was prepared to die. He always assumed his end would come violently. But the others?

"We have only one chance, and if we fail, the pirates will not chain us again–they will kill us."

Total silence filled the blackened stench of the cargo hold.

"What do you think the gypsy is planning?" Hillel finally asked.

Wen Ho, a voice in the darkness said, "The Berbers and Ashot make only three. Yet only three are owned by Tariq. The other cutthroats are unpredictable, except for their greed."

The Ethiopian fisherman was next. "Two I overhear speaking a tongue like mine, and one of them chained us down here. He gave me and the cook longer chain and more movement."

"If things become chaotic, a familiar tongue could make comrades," Adiva said, trying to sound hopeful.

Ashot opened the hatch, flooding the filthy cavern of human despair with the blinding light of the mid-day sun and watched as the captives quickly shielded their eyes.

He turned to the man behind him, a despicable human they called Safwan, the keeper of chains.

"I hate coming down to these vile creatures. I don't know how you do it."

"My job is easy," Safwan said. "If they give you trouble, I'll make their bracelets a little smaller. Sometimes they beg for relief."

Ashot turned and looked up into Safwan's smiling face. He recognized the expression of one who takes pleasure in giving pain to others, extracting as much fear as possible. For a moment, he saw his own people, captured by Arab slavers at an Egyptian desert oasis, shackled by this very bondage expert. He clenched his teeth in rage, almost choking.

"You know what the captain wants, I don't," Ashot managed to mutter, "How are we to carry out the captain's wishes? He said you knew."

"The woman," Safwan laughed. "Tariq wouldn't be himself if he didn't have sport with a beauty like her!"

"So, I am to bring her to the Amir?"

The keeper of chains responded with the mirthless laugh of the sadist. "And his eminence wishes you to wash her hair, and the rest of her as well. Of course, he insists on caring for certain parts himself."

They climbed below and moved to Adiva directly, ignoring the others.

"The captain doesn't care how she's treated, but she must not be marked in anyway. I will check all the manacles. His interest is unexpectedly keen, and he orders you to hurry this along."

Unscrewing the ring that held the chain to one attached to the wall, he gave a pull on Adiva's ankle causing her to cry out before tossing it to Ashot. "Remember....parts for him! Ha ha."

Ashot led her to the wooden stairs and onto the deck. He busied himself for a moment, allowing Adiva to breathe deeply of the salty, life-giving, spirit-reaffirming air and revive herself.

The sail cutter was at work on a patch for a large defect which had been burned from the volcanic ash. Six-foot squares were hung for further stitching, and Ashot pushed Adiva rudely into the workspace, staring at the sailor so intensely he scurried away to the foredeck.

Ashot uncovered an outsized wooden water barrel and began ladling the precious gift from Jebel Island, the last it would ever give, onto Adiva's slightly bowed head. To his dismay, her robe and silk undergarment were quickly soaked and neatly outlined the knife Adiva carried in her waistband. He wordlessly moved it to the small of her back.

"Do not use this unless you must."

The water had also clearly outlined Adiva's breasts and Ashot was reminded what a beauty she was. He was surprised that Tariq would risk the value of such a prize, but, of course, for some men he knew, this was a reward worth more than gold. Perhaps Tariq reasoned he could have both.

He grabbed for another ladle of water, again drenching her head and spoke softly. "What he wishes from you is no surprise, only his choice of times couldn't be better for us."

"He does not wish only talk from me. I am not unworldly, Ashot." Her words were muffled by water sloshing on her head.

Ashot was insistent. "Then you must gird yourself to endure. Do not risk injury by resisting, but try to buy time, and wait for a signal."

He hesitated. "It is better to lose your honor rather than your life, along with the rest of us. Do you understand?"

Adiva nodded.

Satisfied, he curled the corners of his mouth downward, pursing his lips to produce first a low whistle, rising in crescendo to a high pitch. He knew the men below had heard this before. It was how he had called the mother and baby camel on the west beach of Jebel Island.

He finished dousing the young woman, who stood and casually ran her hands through her previously matted hair as if she didn't have a care in the world. Ashot tried to pay no attention to her, but he stood mesmerized by Adiva's beauty. He knelt and removed the already loosened shackle.

Ashot pulled back the sail curtains before she stepped through and was immediately confronted by four of the crew and surrounded.

One look at their faces and Ashot knew at once their intentions. Apparently, the captain was not the only one overcome with lust.

Tariq had grown impatient and, opening the cabin door, he saw the situation below. He didn't bother to speak or command, but, in one fluid movement unsheathed and threw his curved-blade dagger which met with a pirate's bone and tissue with a sickening crack. In his agony, the wounded pirate struggled to remove the knife, penetrating two of its four inches into his lower back. He could not breathe for the blade pierced his chest cavity.

Ashot did a calculation, as he watched the man dragged away from the captain's wrath by his comrades, a broad trail of blood left on the deck. The man wounded, no doubt fatally, by Tariq's jealous rage was Tariq's ally, as firmly as the rodent-faced Arab.

Now three, Ashot thought.

"I have to deliver you to your most gracious host," Ashot said. To his surprise, instead of fear in Adiva's eyes, he found determination. "Tonight, you must be as a woman of my people: strong, unafraid, and vicious."

Taking Adiva by the arm, he noticed that her clothes and hair were still dripping, and he surprised her by handing her a woven red shawl, which she simply held in her hand, then wrapped it around her waist. As though straightening her new garment in back, she slid the knife to her side, hidden by drying silk and her rough woven robe and proudly stepped in front.

The captain was still agitated at the challenge to his ownership of these captives. On the way to his cabin, he shouted orders rapidly, seeming to relish the chance to remind them of his supremacy, his life and death powers.

Ashot kept his eyes on the teakwood cabin floor, the only clean place on the ship. The ship's sailmaker had just polished the floor with wax left over from calking small leaks in the hull. It smelled faintly of pine tar.

Ashot hoped that he could soon cover it with Tariq's blood.

40

Kasim had been waiting for this moment since Safwan first chained him to the longboat. It was the slimy pleasure the loathsome son-of-pig so obviously relished that slightly altered the carpenter's thinking while he sat in the darkness. Kasim always believed he would have his revenge. Now, he would make sure that this keeper of chains would be the *very first to die.*

The hatch opened and Kasim's eyes slowly adjusted to the light flooding in. Slumped on the curving hull of the leaky ship, the carpenter starred dully at his filthy feet as Safwan approached. His restraints had been expertly attached, to made sure the chains binding the wrist and ankle were too short to allow Kasim the relief of standing up. The pain of immobilization was without relief.

"Let us see our circus bear!" Safwan shouted.

Kasim neither moved, nor looked up.

With a smile that bespoke of the experience of hundreds of captives deprived into meek submission, he leaned close to inspect the iron bracelets he fitted. Knowing of the manacle's punishing abrasion of the skin, whether an ankle, a wrist, or a neck. He jerked hard on attached chains with practiced intent. This he did now with particular zeal, but his captive's leg barely moved.

Safwan raised an eyebrow, slightly puzzled. He leaned in close, but Kasim remained, expressionless.

"Show me your wrist, ape."

Kasim could feel the spittle on his face but didn't care. In a movement too swift to see, he parted the halves of his wrist manacle and his massive arm closed around the astonished pirate's neck.

Before an outcry, or even a gasp, the carpenter's crushing grip closed off Safwan's breath, then, like a lioness with prey, choked off his life.

The body was limp, but Kasim was not satisfied. With a sickening crack, heard by everyone below, he snapped the tormentor's neck.

The hatch cover banged shut, throwing them again into impenetrable darkness. This time there was no terror, but only the exhilaration of a release from helplessness.

Yosef said, "Whoever did this knew their shipmate down here wouldn't be needing the light. Had to be the Berbers or the gypsy."

Kasim had already used the tool to rid himself of the painful ankle shackle and handed the beveled iron screwdriver to Hillel.

"Leave the manacle attached to the chain and carry it. Swing it at their heads." It took little time, even without light, for each of them to finish removing the screws holding the shackles together, and the tool made it easy to unhook the chain where it was tethered to the planking.

Kasim stood full height for the first time in 48 hours and stretched every joint. He enjoyed this almost as much as he had crushing the pirate's windpipe, then his neck.

"Give me your hands, cover mine with them," the carpenter said. When Yosef, Wen Ho, Hillel, and the Ethiopians had done so, he covered the tower they made with his other hand and held it firmly for a few quiet moments. Kasim hoped the five of them felt it: a sensation of something flowing to each from the others. It was an ancient and powerful practice of brotherhood that prepared them for the fight ahead.

But when?

They listened. "We can hear only footsteps above us, and very few of them since our visit from above," the cook decided.

"The pirates will be at their posts for the transit through the Gate of Tears, not wandering around the deck," Hillel answered.

Hillel groped for the stairs and ascended them to the closed hatch door. There was never a need to latch this door, as no one ever freed themselves and came up from the slave hold on their own. Hillel pressed his shoulder against the underside of the heavy planking and raised it an inch above the surrounding deck. A brilliant shaft of light streamed down the staircase, seemingly beyond the illumination from so narrow an opening. He wedged a link of the chain he was carrying into the slit, allowing it to remain open. They could now see each other, energized and ready.

But Kasim knew to be cautious. "We must wait. We cannot yet tell what is happening above."

Everyone had seemed to accept that Kasim was in charge. But he himself had once been a slave and unaccustomed to this type of leadership. For a moment he had a thought: He missed his captain.

He took a deep breath. Knowing that they were probably all going to die anyway gave him resolve. He must make decisions.

"Our young woman is in grave danger, so we may have to act even if there is no signal from the gypsy. Besides, we cannot stay down here indefinitely. We may be free of our chains, but we are trapped.

"Even so, my sister is the smartest of all of us," Hillel said. "Since she was a little girl, she thinks of things. Her wits will keep her safe until we can help."

Kasim wasn't quite sure if Hillel believed what he was saying.

He pointed to the top. "Open it again, Hillel. And one of us is always on the steps to hear what we can."

For an instant, Adiva thought to run from the captain's cabin. She looked at the closed door and knew it to be the first of many obstacles to her freedom and would probably lead to her death. The whereabouts of her brother, cousin and the others or status of Ashot's plan were unknown. How long could she wait before she would have to submit?

She stood defiantly in front of his desk. Refusing Tariq's offer for her to be seated on his bed, she was surprised that he merely smiled and began eating in silence. She was ravenously hungry but shook her head to his offer of food. She wished she'd eaten nothing to interrupt the appetite-killing effects of starvation, and she tried not to look at what he was eating.

Animal rage began to replace the fear that she felt, but that only heightened the tension in her muscles and the pounding in her chest. She fought to betray none of this, and even harder not to imagine a scene in which she was utterly at the mercy of this animal feasting before her, soon to be feasting on her. The prospect of being overpowered by this thing, slathering before her with flecks of food snagged in his beard, was no less revolting than his rancid breath and half-broken yellow teeth.

She tried to form an image of her beloved, Eldad, but the picture she fashioned was so beautiful that it almost caused her to collapse on her unstable legs.

Tariq hadn't noticed. "Take off your robe," he ordered, still seated.

Adiva realized that removing her rough woven outer robe would expose the dagger held by the silk waistband, so she did not move.

"You *will* show me what I have for sale at the market and do whatever else I want! Do you understand?"

She cringed, trying to think of a way to delay, to buy time. But she was alone.

Tariq stood up and started from behind the desk but stopped when Adiva began removing her robe. He grunted and smiled.

She stripped the robe off to her waist, and she could see his attention was riveted on her silk covered breasts.

"Please, the food you offered, I will show my gratitude," she asked plaintively. She bowed her head and continued to remove the robe, grasping the unsheathed knife in a wad of robe she held as though for modesty in her left hand.

Tariq's lecherous stare was revolting. She worried at that moment that he would rush her and take what he wanted.

She interrupted. "The food, good captain?" The pleasantry, of course, could not possibly be believed, but Adiva's only goal was to disarm him a little and delay. It was clear now that Tariq meant to have her.

The portly Arab reached beneath the zebra wood desk and produced an array of dried fruits and a lump of hard cheese. He tossed these on the narrow bunk bed which took up a third of the cabin and was covered by an entirely out of place brocade quilt with floral motifs, one of several ill-gotten prizes visible in the quarters.

She hoped he would not assault her while she was eating, another delay, and that she might as well sit on the bed as be thrown there. She meekly sat on the edge, clutching her robe, and began slowly eating the dried fruit.

"You are a hard man, but can be most generous," Adiva managed. "Water, might I have some?"

He gestured at the brass pitcher an arm's reach from the bunk, another stolen artifact from those who stole it from others. The two-pound rounded bottom prevented its tipping over, even in rough waters.

Adiva had to let go of the robe with its secret passenger, which she let fall to the bed, for both hands to handle the pitcher. She felt what a devastating bludgeon this water vessel could be.

The hard cheese seemed the best she'd ever tasted, which of course it wasn't, this being another manifestation of prolonged hunger. For the moment, Tariq was content to watch his prize become more grateful to his most generous self. A quick glance from Adiva noted his more rapid breathing and sweat-beaded, oily brow.

A thought occurred to her. Perhaps it may well be *she* who will signal her companions that their fight for freedom has begun. If they were alive that is. If not, she would join them in death, and trust in the judgment of the almighty God. Her determination grew. A proud daughter of Israel should not allow herself to be enslaved and dishonored.

The pirate ship lurched slightly, and Tariq had to clutch at the rim of the desk to steady himself. Ordinarily, a captain would be concerned enough about this unexpected shift beneath him, but Tariq, looking very much like an animal in rut, was fixated on Adiva.

She remained seated, eyes downcast, on his bed.

As he moved toward her, it was clear the time for thinking was over. She tried to imagine how the prostitutes of Babylon must act after coins changed hands, but of course she had no idea.

"What do you want me to do, Captain Tariq?"

He stopped close enough for her to see an obvious erection beneath his robe. Adiva shifted over on the edge of the cot, as though inviting her captor to sit beside her. As she did this, she was sitting on her robe, and could feel the bone handle of her dagger under her thigh.

Tariq had other ideas. He moved in front of her, and she was nearly sickened by the closeness of the tented robe.

"Perhaps the captain would like to savor his prize?" Clutching her robe wrapped around the knife, she rose and glided past him, draping part of the robe over her shoulder. She began moving as she had seen an Arab belly dancer do in Baghdad.

Tariq sat, without once taking his eyes from her. Hips swaying, her lips gave the illusion of desire.

She had a sudden inspiration. "Part your robe, my Captain." Perhaps a little more theater would slow the pace.

She immediately regretted it. Adiva tried not to look at what he uncovered, but his face betrayed nothing but hunger–for all of her.

There was no turning back. She continued to sway, reaching the tie on the waistband of her silk pants, and slowly pulled, undoing the bow. She fully expected this vile man, so accustomed to bestial treatment of human beings, to halt this abruptly, and then she would *have* to act. But for a few moments, she had captured his full attention.

Adiva moved the front of her garment down far enough to expose her navel. Her other hand closed over the dagger handle beneath the draped robe.

She could hear his heavy, rapid breathing growing louder. She turned her back to him, as gracefully as she could, letting the silk pants fall to her ankles. Nimbly stepping out of them, Adiva moved toward the transfixed Arab, who reached a rough hand to grasp her naked left buttock and pull her closer.

Adiva felt ashamed to be totally exposed to this man, but it would be over very soon, one way or another. With a force of will she didn't know she possessed, she allowed herself to be drawn toward Tariq. She could feel the touch of his thigh against hers.

Adiva looked directly into his eyes. He was completely defense-
less, overcome with an expectation of the immediate pleasure that
was to come. She touched his face with her left hand to make sure
he didn't see that she had freed the right from her robe and without
delay dug the dagger deep into Tariq's hairy neck. It happened so
quickly that, for a moment, Tariq still wore a smile of pleasure. But
with the knife's tip impaled in the back of his tongue, he could not
even speak, only growl agonal protests, and flail his stubby arms at
his assailant. Adiva savagely twisted the dagger, shoving until Tariq
tumbled back on the bed with her on top of him. Blood spurted
volcanically in neatly timed geysers from a whiskered forest. She
was soaked in it and wanted to cry out for help, but there was no
telling who would come. His thrashing weakened, and before long
there were no more rasping, blood-filled breaths.

41

It had been seven days, Eldad calculated, since the cannibals, who called their tribe *Romrom,* had thrown off the bamboo lattice covering the pit and lowered themselves into the cavern. Now they had come again and Eldad, weakened to the point of being unable to stand, offered no resistance as they trussed him up in ropes and hauled him to the surface. The savages were less vividly painted now, as they were no longer on a raid, but were stained and had a putrid smell that made Eldad gag despite his stupor.

His emaciation was plainly evident from the deep coves of his temples to the sagging skin over shrunken muscle. Rudely jerked to a seated position, he was again confronted with the yellow-painted crone he'd seen peering at him for long periods through the triangular opening in the lid. This was especially true after he received his food, cooked meat from various animals the cannibals hunted besides humans.

Eldad knew why she watched. Being a rare catch; young, tall and muscular, she seemed to attach a greater value to him. Hers was no maternal instinct, watching the nurtured one eat, but rather feeding him as one would fatten a calf.

She wrapped her bony fingers around his bicep and shook her head with grave concern. He was thinner, no doubt about it. She gripped his thigh with both hands and shouted some command to one of her men still down in the pit. Fear rose in Eldad, about the only emotion he had left. He had made sure she had seen him eat the fatty meat and highly sweet melon that was lowered to him twice a day. Sooner or later, she was bound to get increasingly suspicious of his continued loss of bulk.

Through the past seven days, his hunger was gnawing and relentless, which made his deception even more agonizing. The taste of the warm food lowered down in a basket to him was remarkably savory, and he yearned for the next feeding, with his mouth watering the moment the basket appeared.

But rather than self-preservation, it was self-torture. Each time he brought the meat to his mouth, he would lower his head and his other hand would catch an uneaten bite, dropping it to the mud floor. Appreciative, even gluttonous sounds added to the impression he was eating, and at times, he felt a near overpowering urge to chew the greasy, salty meat. Instead, he would mash it into the soil he had clawed loose. When the old yellow one left her perch, he buried the still warm food deeper.

Apparently, it was not deep enough to hide from the probing hands of the savage still in the pit. His shout above needed no translation. He had uncovered not the expected buried feces, but the maggot ridden remains of every meal the cannibals had fed him. If Eldad had the strength, he might have offered a smile that he had been able to trick his captors this long.

The crone's jaundiced eyes were alive with rage above her bitter, two-toothed smile. None of her staccato words were comprehensible, but Eldad was beginning to learn that tones of angry recrimination were the same in every language. It occurred to Eldad that the savages might simply kill and eat him now, emaciated as he was becoming. He discarded this panic when it appeared that they had not given up efforts to feed him. The old women fished out a tender leg from small bird of some sort, still warm from the campfire, and put it to his lips. Eldad felt so frantically hungry that the aroma of roasted flesh was nearly too much to bear. He closed his eyes in a desperate attempt to keep from seeing the morsel he was being offered. The old woman drew a sickle-shaped obsidian blade from her loin cloth and pressed it to the angle of his jaw. The food held at his closed mouth and the knife at his throat were a clear message: eat or die. The irony almost made him smile. He was starving and would die if he did not eat. He could end it sooner, he knew, if he did not drink. Either way, death would be agonizing. He forced himself to think about this, and the dreadful possibility he would have to *choose* the manner of his death.

He hated himself that he decided to make the immediate choice. He knew it would take more than a few feedings for them to have what they want, so he would eat now. If they put him back in the pit, he could make himself vomit the food he'd consumed. He recognized he may be unable to do this, as it was contrary to a basic survival instinct.

They made him eat more, with the crone passing the blade to a subordinate, the one who dug up the evidence of Eldad's subterfuge. This cannibal was most determined that their prize eat more than he wanted. As he chewed without even tasting, an awful thought occurred to Eldad that, like many animals slaughtered and cooked with full stomachs, he was being readied for an abrupt end.

But it did not come. He thought that if he continued to eat it would itself make him vomit, but abruptly, the savages stopped forcing food down him. They untied one arm and handed him a gourd of surprisingly fresh water. When he had drunk his fill, they rebound his arm to his side and tied him securely to a tree near the pit. He still could not see their main encampment, and really didn't want to. Even the wooded hill between him and camp could not abate the putrefaction from unburied remains from their slaughter. He knew *that* would make vomiting easier, but watchful, menacing eyes never left this face.

Because of the attention to Eldad, the guards never saw what hit them. Long arrows lanced their chests, and both fell immediately, one dead, one soon to be. It was only then that Eldad saw the dark-skinned native people with short, cropped hair and woven tunics pouring out of the tree line, one phalanx of painted warriors descending furiously onto the terrified cannibals, while the others surrounded Eldad. Expecting death the moment they reached him, he was momentarily relieved when the invaders lowered their spears as they came near.

One of the cannibals moved slightly, moaning. The attacker, who

Eldad had already identified as the likely leader, drew his sword and without a sound, hacked the back of the fallen man's neck, nearly severing his head. He wasn't finished. Raising the sword once more, he swung it in a wide arc toward Eldad, but at the last instant, aimed the blade at the ropes wrapped around him. Cut off with great force, the ropes popped away from him and he timidly stepped away from the tree, his wrists still bound together. To his dismay, instead of freedom, a raider with red, flame-shaped blotches on his cheeks, threw a stout noose over his head and tightened the slipknot around his neck. They jerked him forward, willing to strangle him if he did not keep pace, storming around the hill to rejoin their tribesmen.

Eldad could hear the desperate, pleading cries even before they reached the clearing, now littered with the dead. A hot burning fire he could not yet see filled the air with the sickly-sweet stench of burning flesh. Suddenly Eldad was yanked into a cluster of kneeling warriors, each with a noose around his neck, this rope being attached to a 20-foot pole in front of them. These were the survivors of the overwhelming force brought to bear by the invaders, who immediately killed even more cannibals after they resisted. Terror, combined with choking ropes, established absolute control over the remaining fifteen cannibals. What was in store for these new captives?

A blow to the backs of his knees forced Eldad down on the ground. He could feel the fire growing in intensity and realized why. The invaders were making repeated trips around the campsite, gathering up the carelessly strewn human and animal remains and throwing them into the blaze of fat and bones.

Once the length of rope securely tied Eldad's neck to the common pole, he felt safe enough to see who was bound next to him. He gasped at the apparition.

There was the toothless yellow one. Flat on her back, one pendulous breast was thrown towards her right shoulder, while the other dangled down her left side. The slipknot around her neck had a few coils smaller than the versions tight around the necks of the others.

She looked up at him, her eyes yellow either from disease

or reflection from her yellow painted skin, and cackled a hearty greeting, incomprehensible of word, but, bizarrely cheerful, like he was long-lost family. Her grin, he noticed, now had only one tooth, its companion probably lost in the tussle of confining her, not that she resisted. Eldad looked in her eyes, wondering if he had misinterpreted her greeting, but saw no guile.

Was it possible that she was showing empathy for this turn his life had taken? He smiled to himself. As though his fate in her hands would have been somehow better.

But what, he was forced to ask himself, *was* their fate? Were these also cannibals, saving their captives for feasts of triumph? They were clearly not as primitive as the cannibals, as they were cleaner, only sparingly painted, and were not celebrating their possession of the corpses of the recently dead. Rather, they dumped the bodies unceremoniously into the pit where Eldad had languished for seven days. They left the cavern open to whatever animals might venture in.

Eldad could see signs of contact with civilization among these people, such as odd articles of well-sewn clothing, and even finely tanned leather sandals, both seemingly well beyond this tribe's sophistication to produce themselves.

They were traders, he concluded, bartering for the trappings of civilization. But *what* does this raiding tribe trade?

The fire at the center of the camp was now towering above the men throwing the last of the camp refuse into it. Dusk was only moments away and all the nearly forty tribesmen gathered in a circle around the sickening, though cleansing bonfire to the cannibal's bestiality, and, quite astonishingly, *bowed down* reverently.

They are fire worshipers, Eldad realized. He knew of tribes like this in his homeland. True, they did not consume their fellow human beings, but they were just as savage.

Finally, Eldad's attention drifted from the roaring fire, while he studied the long pole to which all were attached. He noted the holes drilled in even spaces, through which their restraining ropes were looped and securely tied. The holes were worn, from years of use, he could see. The ropes, too, were worn and stained by human contact.

Then he knew.

The fire worshipers chanted and began circling the fire, which had grown so large that four men could be laid across the middle. Charred bones, some human, but most unrecognizable, began to show. He could not escape the thought that the roaring blaze was a funeral pyre for his childhood companion and dear friend. Jews did not practice cremation, but this was surely better than the continued desecration of his body.

Slumping on the ground, as though his bony skeleton had already departed his flesh, Eldad searched for some thread to weave a tapestry that would give meaning to the recent events of his life.

As he often did in times of turmoil or danger, he turned to the lessons of his precious grandfather, particularly what the old man often taught him from The Book of Creation. Zav called it the oldest book of mysticism in their faith. He usually used its name in the Qur'an, *The Scrolls of Abraham.*

Of course, Eldad the adolescent was bored and distracted by Zav's intense discussions of what the young man could expect in a life fully lived. He spoke of pairs of contrasts in nature, to be experienced in the lives of every being. Some of the seven were easy to understand, like *fertility* and *sterility,* and *beauty* and *ugliness.* He could imagine these things in his lifetime, though seeing himself as old was beyond him then. Until an hour ago, the only pair of contrasts that preoccupied him was the eternal struggle between *life* and *death.* He could not think of himself as *not being,* though annihilation had seemed certain.

There was now a different certainty, a different pair of inescapable contrasts, a reality he never thought would be his: *lordship* and *servitude.*

Eldad ha-Dani, a proud prince of Israel had lost everything: his family, his freedom, and his future.

He was now certain to be sold into slavery, or worse yet, remain chattel for the fire worshipers. He was envious that Saul had escaped this fate, and fervently wished to join him.

He knew of herbs that took away pain, and then life itself. Perhaps he could find a similar plant.

As he thought about self-destruction, he began to feel a sense of relief. *That* made him realize he was in a most dangerous frame of mind.

Suddenly, he had a vision of Adiva. How long had it been since they were together? He was overcome with the warmth of her love, lifting any remnants of despair.

Though he could not know *what* agony his reality would now bestow, nor for how long, he knew *why* he must endure.

42

The grim slave ship listed to starboard, a course that would surely run them aground if not immediately corrected. Ashot stood directly behind the second in command.

"All hands, man the sails," Rafik shouted. He looked towards the captain's cabin.

Ashot knew what he must be thinking. The ship's movements should have brought the captain on deck immediately. They had both heard a scuffle minutes earlier emanating from the cabin and rat face smiled, probably imagining himself in the captain's place.

Now there was silence and Ashot hoped that the young Jewess had taken his advice and traded her honor for her life. He realized that he had grown quite fond of the woman, admiring her determination as well as her beauty. If she lives, he thought, she may have a chance for revenge. It not, Ashot would gladly avenge her.

"Shall I retrieve the keeper of chains from below?"

Rat face nodded, then turned toward the captain's quarters.

Ashot acted quickly. Throwing the heavy hatch open, he realized that rat face was not even paying attention. He called out Safwan's name, then followed the first mate. Those below knew what to do.

Kasim and the others had been ready.

A quick look back showed Ashot that Kasim and his band had burst onto the deck, their scanty armaments at the ready. Their allies, the mismatched Berber brothers, Asulil and Isri, had joined the six other crew in a frantic effort to turn the ship back into Bab El Mandeb. They had stationed themselves next to the pair of pirates most loyal to Tariq and the Arab first mate. They needed no command, only a signal, to act.

The diminutive first mate noticed the increased activity, combined with ghastly sounds of mortal combat. He stood frozen for a moment, unsure what to do next.

Ashot prepared to act. Rat face must not be allowed to warn the captain. But he was too late. The mate, clearly panicked, scrambled up the stairs to the captain's cabin door and burst in. It was an impulsive act that would likely get him killed.

Instead of issuing the captain a warning, the mate began to bellow with rage.

Ashot reached the door and saw the reason. Tariq's motionless body lay across the young woman, nearly smothering her. Adiva continued to clutch the knife, deeply embedded beneath Tariq's hairy jaw. His head waggled, as though on a stick, when her hand moved. Looking like it was thrown on the two from a bucket, the blood made Adiva's hand slip when she shoved him off her.

Cutlass drawn, the rat charged through the doorway, intent on vengeful slaughter. Adiva sprang to her feet on the opposite side of the bed. Tariq's head still held the dagger.

Ashot knew he had to act. The captain had been eliminated, thanks to Adiva and this was now their best chance for success. He looked at the door. Nobody was coming. The sounds from the main deck made that obvious.

The rat grinned demonically, eyes wide and enflamed with sadistic excitement. He raised his sword, pausing to savor the moment as Adiva moved away to his left. Ashot made his presence known. A little confused, rat face whirled around and was immediately struck in the chest by Ashot's heavy fist which sent him sprawling atop his dead captain.

Barely able to breathe, he looked at Ashot's hands, to see which one held the instrument of his death. But Ashot's hands were empty of any weapon. "Drop your sword and live," Ashot said calmly, hands open and at his side. Adiva stood dumbfounded, then exhaled loudly when first mate unclenched the handle of his cutlass and let it drop to the bed.

"You join us now, pirate, and you both live and prosper."

Sitting up, the first mate nodded. "What will you have me do, gypsy?"

"Shout to your men to lay down their arms."

"They will not, and they will kill me."

"Pick up your sword and go out on the deck. At the same time, I'll order my people to stop fighting. If we don't act now, many more will die!"

Ashot knew this was the moment of the greatest danger. He turned toward the door and the Arab rose, sword in hand, stepping nimbly past Ashot onto the poop deck.

The scene below unfolded on the four quadrants of the deck. Surprise had been complete, temporarily to the advantage of the captives and their two Berber allies. Yosef, carrying a dagger, sprang on an equally stocky pirate who was drawing his cutlass. Arms pinned to his side by Yosef's bear hug, the pirate was lifted like a child and tossed in a high arc over the railing into the Red Sea.

At the same time, the Berber pirate brothers fought their former ship mates with swords that clanged the resonance of violent clashes. Of all mortal struggles on the deck, this was the most evenly matched.

On the starboard foredeck, the intimidating bulk of a sword-wielding Kasim stood below two unarmed pirates who clung precariously to sails they had been mending.

And it was only moments before Wen Ho, armed with a knife as was the Ethiopian cook, would confront the last two pirates, now lunging for their weapons. The captives' daggers against boarding axe and sword in the hands of seasoned pirates made the outcome of this encounter predictable. But before the double-edged axe could rise above their heads to strike, the lanky Ethiopian swung the heavy chain that had bound him, its iron manacle still attached. The leading edge of the ring of torture crushed the pirate's temple.

Seeing his comrade plummet to the deck momentarily distracted the other pirate, a lapse that let Wen Ho lunge, his shoulder slamming into the pirate's chin. The two crashed to the deck like embracing lovers, one stunned by a blow, the other surprised to be alive.

Still clutching his cutlass, the desperate pirate tried to free his arm from an equally desperate grip. Their free hands grappled, then settled into fingers locked together, neither stronger than the other. Wen Ho could not reach for the knife in his belt. He was about to take the chance that, in close quarters, his knife hand would be faster than the pirate's sword.

A kick that came with a warning stunned his adversary.

"Stop your fighting or we die!"

Mostly, though, the clang of metal on metal amid grunts of hand-to-hand combat paid heed only to their inner voices demanding survival.

Ashot did what he could to end the fighting, but without lethal force it was difficult.

At midship, the larger Berber brother bled from two quick knife cuts to his upper arm but was still able to wield a pike with a three-foot handle. Shouting derisive curses and thinking he could finish the bleeding man, one of the pirates raised his sword but Isri struck first, ramming the four-inch tip of his pike into the pirate's chest. His cursing silenced, replaced by spasms of coughing frothy blood, the pirate slumped to one, then both knees on the deck.

Growing weary of battle and seeing that the odds had begun to shift away from them, some of the crew began to heed the calls of surrender from the first mate.

On the port side deck, Hillel had subdued the non-pirate cook, who had burst from the galley with a three-pronged grappling hook held somewhat comically above his wispy gray head.

Then the two pirates, treed on the sails by Kasim, seeing the pools of blood below them, pleaded to come down.

"Lie on the deck and be silent," the carpenter growled at them, waving his cutlass toward his feet. Though they were unarmed, he eyed the two warily as they scrambled down, heads lowered submissively.

The only unaccounted for pirate suddenly sprang from behind barrels, flattening Yosef on the foredeck. The pirate pinned down Yosef's hand still clutching the dagger and closed a bone-crushing grip on his wrist. This weakened his hold on the knife's handle, and the powerful pirate tore it away. With his arm released, Yosef bucked desperately and rolled from under his heavier assailant.

The pirate raised his arm high for a killing stab, but his hand froze, stopped in mid air by a dagger thrown so hard it impaled his wrist. The embedded knife and the now useless hand still clutching its own lethal weapon collapsed in a grotesque assembly at his side.

The lanky Ethiopian cook, whose skill at throwing a knife rivaled the gypsy's, grunted triumphantly and wrapped a chain around the pirate's neck, forcing him to his knees. To screams of pain, the cook yanked out the knife he had thrown so precisely. The other knife fell out of his grasp on its own and Yosef scooped it up.

Ashot, observing this, was unsure if Yosef and the cook intended to kill this man. Their indecisiveness gave him an opportunity.

"Stop. It is finished. Hold, but do no further harm to these men, unless they do not yield."

Ashot looked around and realized that they were waiting for him to tell them what to do next. He was in charge.

"Throw a rope to the bastard in the water. He'll be shark food in a few minutes if you don't." The Arab, following close behind Ashot, uncoiled a long hemp rope and threw it toward the seaman who was trying unsuccessfully to stay above the 4 foot waves of the choppy sea.

The Arab shouted over at him, "The gypsy is now our captain. He throws you this and saves your life. Take this line only if you agree to serve as he orders."

Besides showing *his* acceptance of Ashot's authority, the first mate obviously wanted to continue his previous duties. Though Ashot liked none of these thieving slavers, he knew of no role the Arab played in the enslavement of his Roma people. The two dead captains made the bad mistake of abusing, then selling the wrong people.

Yosef and the Ethiopian lowered their knives, and relaxed the chain, but not their watchfulness over their spared captive.

Then, it was absolutely quiet aboard the ship. No one moved, as though stillness was needed for a new reality to settle on them.

Kasim shattered this silence with a cry, "We're headed for the shallows!" With the deadly combat on deck, no one was sailing the great vessel, now drifting with the treacherous eddies of the small channel, straight toward the ship-foundering rocks of the Gate of Tears.

43

Adiva still felt a little numb. She had cleaned herself as best as she could, but the dried blood of the man she had killed burned against her skin.

The man she killed. The thought kept running through her mind. Yes, Tariq was dangerous and despicable, but he was still a human being. Even with the hidden knife she had possessed, she never imagined what would happen. Could she ever forget?

With Ashot's help, she had gathered a few articles of coarse clothing, rags, truly, and with her hair under a cap, she could almost pass for a young boy. She was grateful that she no longer was the object of everyone's attention.

She watched as the rudder of the ship, an ungainly boom attached to a broad paddle, strained against the current, while Kasim struggled to hold it starboard. The two pirates he had subdued looked at each other and without a word jumped to their feet. Kasim saw this and seemed alarmed but could not let go of the rudder to defend himself, lest the ship loose the arc it was cutting in the water away from the massive shoreline boulders. They sprang toward him, but landed not *on* him but *beside* him, each lending a strong shoulder to the rudder pole.

Kasim took this opportunity to extend this sudden brotherhood of survival.

"Tell your mates to join us. We'll not save the ship without them. Now!"

They shouted in the direction of the four other uninjured pirates held at bay on both sides of the deck, "Help us save our boat and ourselves."

For a moment, Yosef, the cook, and Wen Ho stood, weapons at the ready, though a coordinated charge from the pirates might well be their end, but Hillel came between them.

"Tack the sail," he shouted. This maneuver would pull the stern of the ship into a tailing wind, but the heavy boom of the mainsail needed all hands to swing and secure it to the port side.

Without noticing, the slavers and their former chattel had become *one* crew, hatred forgotten, all now equal so that all might survive.

The Red Sea current pulled harder as they were drawn into the shallows of the Asian shore. All available hands struggled to secure the ponderous booms of the largest sails to rope harnesses on the port side deck. Angled sails and steady shoulders on the rudder began a serious challenge to the powerful rip tide dragging them to ruin. They were now close enough to boulders breaking the water's surface by 10 to 30 feet to hear nesting seabirds shriek at the oncoming intrusion. Hundreds flew in startled clusters away from their boulders, as though remembering other wreckages at this Gate of Tears.

Adiva sprinted up to the foredeck railing, scanning the depths ahead of the bow for the dangers hidden beneath the choppy sea.

And then she saw it, looming straight ahead of them, a broad shelf of stone barely breaking the water's surface, but enough to disturb the waves around it. Looking at least 20 yards wide, the full extent of the shelf could not be appreciated from what was above the water.

"Ahead! she cried out, "A wide band of rocks below the surface." Then she realized that *no one* was listening. They were all intent with their tasks.

From what only she could see, the arc of the ship, though taking them away from the shore, was dooming them to wreck the keel on the stone barrier.

She spotted her cousin. "Yosef, look! Yosef, ahead! She pointed frantically.

All at once everybody understood.

Hillel acted first. "Hard to starboard!" he commanded. This would take them into the treacherous shallows, and the stone shelf could well be wider than was visible, but they must risk getting marooned to avoid drowning.

Kasim heaved with the other two men to move the boom of the rudder to its opposite position.

The gypsy elbowed the former first mate in an unmistakable command but remarkably, the six uninjured pirates were already beginning to swing the heavy mainsail boom, changing the tack. The steady landward breeze mysteriously gusted toward the sea, ballooning the sails into the faces of the sailors and knocking Hillel down. Adiva could see the submerged rock clearly now, 40 yards away and closing. Though this sudden reverse gust of wind, followed by another longer one, gave them no control over the boat, it miraculously slowed the vessel to a vague drift in the wreck-hungry current.

At ten yards, there seemed no hope of avoiding collision, but the current suddenly slackened, dampened by the underwater mass of stone. Having lost all momentum, the weighty pirate ship with its grey sails, bumped almost imperceptibly into the continent of Asia. The boat swiveled in a gentle but persistent arc about the point where the bow met the stone. Soon they were drifting to the stern, all aboard silent with wonder at their good fortune.

But the pirates, all products of a Muslim world, though none much a believer in anything, had to acknowledge that they had been saved by this woman.

The short and very tall Berber men, who had risked their lives to free the captives, crossed the deck to her side. Of the original eleven pirates who landed on the Zubair Island, Captain Shabazi, Tariq, the keeper of chains, and the pirate Isri killed with the pike, had met violent ends, leaving seven crew, including the Berbers. No one considered the wisp of a cook cowering in the galley to be a pirate, and the old man was too slight to be of use on deck. As there were other submerged sand bars and rocks waiting to snatch an unwary vessel, strong arms and keen eyes were needed to navigate back into the narrow Red Sea channel. An uncooperative riptide pulled them relentlessly shoreward, though they were still a mile from land.

The men all stared at her, this time not with lust, but awe. They had seen Tariq's bloody corpse, eyes bulging, now dumped on the stern of the ship.

Adiva considered that they were now fearful of her.

"Who is loyal to me will be richly rewarded at journey's end." She paused. "Who is not, will be chained as you did me."

She looked at Yosef and Hillel and then to Ashot. She saw approval in their eyes.

"You will take orders from Kasim." Rat face grunted his displeasure but said nothing. Adiva was sure Kasim knew how to establish control over a crew, and he now took over immediately.

"Assign your unholy beasts to the sails and as lookouts," he bellowed at rat face, who seemed to understand that he had regained a small element of control over the others. He flashed a toothy grin. He now spoke for Kasim.

"Easy to starboard," Kasim ordered the two pirates on the rudder boom. He shouted to Hillel standing midship, louder than he needed.

"You, Babylonian, show us your navigation skills by manning the rudder."

The two men already doing so were having no trouble, but it was obvious to Adiva that Kasim wanted it clear that every man aboard took orders from him. She hoped he would speak privately to Ashot, before ordering *him* to do anything. He had to earn respect from everyone.

The Red Sea water beneath the vessel changed suddenly from the murky swirls of the shallows to crystalline green depths in the narrow channel of the Bar El Mandeb. In perhaps an hour's time they would round the tip of Perim Island into the Gulf of Aden. They could then choose to sail through the broad channel, plying the steady northward current, or tack southwest into the vastness of the Gulf.

The bear-like carpenter called his gypsy ally to his side, as he walked from stern to bow watching the work of each man. Adiva joined them and they spoke so no one else could hear.

"You are always in danger from these thieves." Ashot began.

"But the strange Berbers, can we not trust them?" Adiva said.

Kasim shifted uneasily, "They could have died fighting the other cutthroats. They are able swordsmen and seem capable of loyalty."

Ashot sighed. "Loyalty to themselves alone, I suspect." He looked away. "I know what that is like."

"We must decide now what we are to do with the six, or perhaps the four," Kasim said. He waved Rafik over. "Tell the ship's cook to attend to his injured comrade."

He scurried away to the forward deck before Kasim turned to Adiva. "We may have one more pair of able hands if we treat him kindly."

Yosef and Hillel joined the circle around Adiva, but rather than facing her, they watched the pirates warily. They, including the large and small Berbers, seemed to be going about their duties.

"We do not know if we can trust the Berbers, but certainly they more than the others," Kasim said.

The sea breeze powered their vessel away from the clutches of the Perim Island shoals, and they were within half a mile from clearing the narrow strait. Kasim spoke up, admitting what they all suspected. "The eight of us cannot sail this ship."

Hillel could navigate the three-mast boat, if the pirates had charts of the Sea and a kamal, the clever latitude sailing invention of the Arabs. The knotted string and wooden block used the polar star Polaris to sail a steady course along the parallels of the earth.

"It is either make them into a crew or make them into slaves," Yosef said. "We could very well lose our lives trying to do the latter. Even unarmed, they are highly combative."

"They will follow their self-interest," Ashot replied. "The Arab can, if paid well, keep the cutthroats at bay, but, except for the Berbers, they will never be *our* crew. And they could easily turn on our friends, the Berbers."

"Though we are not fighters, by training or by trade, we are ten pairs of eyes watching four pairs of hands," Yosef added.

Adiva spoke in a firm, steady voice, "This is a risk we must take. Bring the Arab."

"Rafik, come to us." Everyone was surprised that Kasim knew the Arab's first name. "It means friend," he whispered.

Looking frightened, Rafik hurried back from the fore deck.

"I understand your name means *friend,* and that is what we offer to be for you," Adiva said softly.

Rafik's eyes narrowed, as if searching for some deception.

"We will bury your dead at sea in the manner of your people. As we know it."

Rafik smiled faintly, unable to hide the contempt in his voice. "The keeper of chains and Tariq had no religious beliefs. There would be little caring among the men if you fed them to the sharks."

Adiva shuddered at this perfectly serious suggestion. She shook her head. "We will wrap them in sail cloth and send them to the sea."

Kasim and Rafik spoke at the same time. "But Tariq..."

"Yes, even him."

Adiva quickly realized that she had not convinced them that it was the right thing to do.

"I trust he will reside in Gehinom for his deeds. And the keeper as well." She looked around. Only her brother and cousin had any idea what she was talking about.

Yosef came to her rescue. "My cousin speaks of Jahannan, Hell. We all know they will dwell there; our task is to make sure that they arrive properly without interruption."

This was accepted by all. The not yet death-stiffened bodies were wrapped in cloth, and brought to the railing.

The crew gathered around Adiva, protectively ringed by Rafik, Ashot, Hillel and Yosef.

"My people have a prayer for the dead, but.."

Rafik shrugged. "Indeed, to God we belong, and to God we shall return," he said hurriedly. And with that he waved the bodies to the sea.

Having no weights to sink them, the bodies soon floated into the wake of the ship, and then the current carried them away.

The crew returned to their duties with no one telling them to do so. All the burdens of sailing and survival began to feel lighter. Adiva took a moment to thank God for her freedom, and her life.

Before long, the ship rounded the western tip of Perim Island and headed into the deeper, and today calmer, waters of the shimmering Red Sea.

44

With Yosef and Hillel by her side, Adiva peered into the captain's cabin. Satisfied that it was relatively clean of blood and anything else of Tariq's or the previous despicable captain, she was ready to occupy it.

"Find some cloth to create a separation for me. We will share this together for the time being." She thought it best that they stick together

"I am hungry," she announced. Yosef and Hillel nodded in agreement. "Does everyone on board intend to starve?"

Yosef noticed the cook near the galley and called him over.

"Do not fear, cook," Yosef said as he approached. "Have you joined us?"

"I serve the master of the ship, and do not care who it is."

"What is your name?"

"They call me Greek, but I don't know why. I am not Greek."

"Then what shall I call you?"

"I know no other name. I did not know my father, so just Greek."

"What food stuffs do we have on this vile craft?" Adiva asked.

"The pirates," he answered, clearly separating himself from the ranks of his former employers, "had me purchase large barrels of dried beef and lamb at the port of Aden. Also, a few weeks before I was so foolish as to sign on, they had raided a small merchant vessel, taking its only cargo, which was dried vegetables, fruit, and exotic spices. I have been a ship's cook for two decades, but never tasted such flavors as these."

"I want you to break out these stores, and accept the help

from our ship's cook, the Ethiopian," Adiva said, "I want the food slow-cooked, so the aromas fill every corner of the ship. Then we can eat." Greek seemed relieved at his good treatment, backed away and walked back to the stern, where the two Ethiopians were securing the trailing fishing nets. This complete, the black cook looked down at Greek, listening to him with growing delight, and they both moved quickly toward the forward galley.

A single billowy cloud appeared near the four o'clock sun, then was joined lazily by another. The prevailing breeze shifted, and Hillel emerged from the captain's cabin and descended the stairs. "No need to strike the sails. The wind comes from port side and moves us gently with the current."

There was a happy rattle of pans from the galley, and the two cooks were laughing. It was the first time laughter had been heard on this vessel, possibly ever. By the time Rafik reported back to his new captain, the irresistible aroma of cooking meat drifted with the gentle breeze over the deck. Carried with it were citrus and garlic essences, causing even the driest mouth to water copiously.

"Bring all the men," she told Rafik. This was quickly done, and Adiva mounted the steps, halfway to the elevated captain's cabin.

"It will be dark in two hours, the time it will take our cooks to prepare double portions of food for every man," Adiva said with a smile lighting up her face. Then she said, more sternly than intended, "But no one will eat until we have emptied the hold of its filth this crew has allowed to collect." Paying particular attention to her crew, she said pointedly, "*We all* will work, hate this task though we do." No one said anything for a moment, then Kasim's bellow called them to arms. The men trudged down the steps to the slave hold, each with an implement or a bailing pail, and bucket passing brigade, a frequent necessity on sea-going ships, formed to empty the bowels of the vessel. The first buckets were only slightly less vile than the final loads of refuse, with the floating dead rats.

The clouds darkened and multiplied and Rafik had the sail maker prepare small torches, which not only illuminated the darkening hold, but the smoke was a relief to assaulted senses. He told them, "The faster we work, the sooner we shall be freed of this hell." The wily Arab chose to labor alongside the others, using his dagger on his portion of a now almost dry hull. Kasim came down with a larger torch to inspect the work, grunted his approval, and went back on deck.

Adiva chose that moment to explore the captain's quarters and to wash herself more thoroughly. She could wait no longer.

She saw Ashot standing a few feet away, "Come with me, please." They ascended the stairs to the captain's cabin, where she stationed him at the door, saying, "Let no one in," and she closed the heavy teakwood door behind her. Though the blood had been wiped from the floor and walls, and the coverlet was gone, she noticed that the sickly iron smell persisted. The cabin had covered portals at eye level on opposite walls, and Adiva opened one, then the other.

Now the beautifully crafted quarters filled with light and a gentle breeze caressed her face, filling the cabin with the sea air. The exquisite detail of the room, like the herringbone patterned floor of three different African hardwoods, spoke of extraordinary artfulness, she thought. Below the open starboard portal, cabinetry of teakwood reached all the way to the floor with drawers at the bottom. A chart table was a yard wide slab of wood, laced with whorls and polished to a high shine. On it were a half dozen rolled up maps, and Adiva fervently hoped the Jebel Island was on them. Hillel, whose experience in the Persian Gulf had taught him navigation, might be able to retrace their eight days sailing since their capture. The irony that it was also their rescue did not escape her. No matter how hard she tried, she could not keep her mind from opening a flood of longing, enough to stop her movement around the cabin. Then she felt the lancinating fear of what could have happened to him and the dear Saul on an island afire from volcanic ash.

Adiva scanned the room, seeing that some of the cabinet doors were inlaid with Arabesque scrolls of lighter wood. She unlatched and opened the first of these, revealing an 18-inch-deep wooden crypt. A chest of leather stretched over bent wood rested beside a loose woven bag cinched at the top.

The aroma of the cook's productions made its way through the cabin from the starboard portal. The blood stench was mostly gone. Adiva realized the men would restrain their hungry bodies only so long in the presence of the grilled fresh-caught fish and a soon to be perfectly seasoned lamb stew.

She lifted the dusty foot long chest to the chart table and undid the sickle shaped latch that held the dark leather lid on tightly. Prying open the chest, she was greeted by a most surprising floral scent even before she unwrapped the contents. These were wrapped in the softest lamb's wool blanket the young woman ever felt, and the scent of vast fields of wildflowers bathed its fabric. Adiva wondered if the things wrapped up in this chest had belonged to passengers, or even owners, victims of pirate treachery.

On the table before her lay a flute-like whistle of grimy bamboo, and an eight-inch tall, quite human-looking doll. The dolls face, carved of balsa wood and painted with astonishing clarity of features, gazed with delight at whomever looked upon it. Densely woven fabric was skillfully fashioned into perfectly proportioned torso and limbs packed tightly with down.

Sweet tears, the first she had known since lying contentedly beside Eldad, came unbidden with a flood of her earliest memories. It was, she realized, this precious doll with her beaded silken garments and arresting expression was so like her own most favored companion, who always soothed and never disappointed, given her by doting grandparents on her third birthday. Then she felt sad, as this doll, and maybe the well-used bamboo whistle, had been treasures of some child, whose fate was unknown but unlikely it was pleasant. Slavers sold everyone, sometimes fetching the highest prices for the young.

Beneath the blanket, she found what had made the chest seem so heavy for its size. Carefully layered between sheets of tanned leather were every gold coin, each piece of precious jewelry, and, at the bottom, the several feet of dense gold chain that had been concealed in the wine bags. She thought she'd never again see this Netira family fortune she had been entrusted to move to safer banks of theirs in Egypt. She laughed involuntarily when she recalled dinner that fateful last night in Aden at the Netira family's mansion, when the family patriarch told Yosef, Hillel and her, "If this goes well, there will be many other, most enriching opportunities for you. Why, my friends in the Christian banking community, two families in this port, have desperate need for trusted couriers." "*Some business!*" she told herself.

She carefully but quickly wiped herself clean and put the rags back on. Her mind emptied. She drifted away, forgetting herself.

Adiva jumped when someone banged on the door, and she heard argumentative voices through it. She quickly closed the lid and replaced the chest in the crypt. Opening the door, she saw Rafik standing toe to toe with the much stouter gypsy, both clenching fists, but not holding weapons.

Seeing her, his tone became imperious. "The men are hungry and surly, and maddened by a feast just out of their reach."

"And what is preventing them from partaking?"

"The cook. He *insists* that you must join them and be afforded the respect you deserve." Adiva stepped out of the cabin and from that elevation, she could see the Greek looking expectantly at her. She smiled and nodded towards him.

"Ashot, go with Rafik and explain that I am honored and will join them shortly. Eat your fill and rest easy tonight," she nodded, "for tomorrow we sail again into the Red Sea." She nodded at the cooks, who were obviously relieved to no longer be standing between the men and the life-sustaining food awaiting them.

The trawling fishing nets had snared half a dozen two-foot fish with startling blue fins, a large coral grouper and a single fish that looked like a crocodile. The pirate ship's stolen spices delighted the tall Ethiopian, who, unlike Greek, was eager to try each, first tasting and smelling them cautiously. Some went well with both the lamb and the fish, and some with neither. Greek said he thought some were medicines. Most of the fish was grilled over hardwood coals in a large square iron pan. Their livers were simmered in a small pan set beside the fish on the grill, and with these the Ethiopian delighted in experimenting, a few at a time. The galley had a few crude wooden plates, and twenty or so cups, which were simply half coconut shells that could not sit upright unaided. On the plate he ladled the lamb stew he had created with the rehydrated meat and dried fruit. The aroma of this cooking is what drove reluctant, grumbling men to finish a loathsome task so they could have their share, and each burned his fingers with too eager intrusions for pieces of spicy meat.

The Ethiopian carried a steaming platter of smoky citrus fish, skin golden brown and flesh falling off the bone, along with a clay bowl of the aromatic stew, and knocked on the cabin door.

Bade to enter, the tall black man set wide plate and bowl on the chart table, which Adiva had cleared of its rolled-up maps.

"You are so kind, and I'll not forget that when it's time for you to have your portion." She knew generous payment for loyal service creates dependable bonds, and he smiled as he ducked his head to leave the room.

Adiva paused as she picked up the single wooden spoon the cook had brought. She thanked God for her sustenance and her freedom.

Adiva marveled at the feast in the bowl and the wooden plate. She could not remember ever knowing such hunger as her captors had inflicted upon them, a cruelty that easily justified vengeance. But such thoughts detracted from the sheer joy of a meal that filled the senses even before it could be tasted. The Ethiopian fisherman had told her he thought *their* ship's cook could make something edible out of *anything*. The stew issued its maddening allure in the steam rising from the bowl but was still too hot to eat.

She could not remember her last hot meal and had to force herself not to eat the way she felt, like the hungry animal she was. One of these smoky delights she allowed to rest a moment on her unmoving tongue, until the salivation of her mouth made it necessary to chew and swallow the thin slice of blue fin. Dried figs littered the plate beneath the squares of fish as wide as her hand and some had absorbed the juice with the exotic spices. She ate the skin and thought of trying to chew up the brittle fish bones but discarded this starvation-coping strategy as unnecessary in the face of temporary plenty. The fillets were moist, and the blessed relief of satiety began before she had finished the last of them. She knew it was wasteful to eat beyond this point, as eating too much when too hungry has unintended effects, like vomiting the nourishment.

She opened the door wide enough to tell Ashot, "Tell Hillel and Yosef to come." She was hit by rapidly cooling gust of air and stepped out of the cabin to see a sky billowing with black and grey clouds and feel large droplets on her arms and face. Soon the rarest of all Red Sea weathers bore down upon them from mainland Asia, but the rain was at first so light, no one was alarmed, and Rafik ordered two of the men to uncover all the water barrels clustered to catch the runoff from the captain's roof. Adiva breathed deeply and let the gentle drops of life-giving rain bathe her face and arms.

Ashot returned with Hillel and Yosef, now thoroughly wet and not seeming to mind it. Seeing them, their hands and faces still smeared with the residue of their labor below deck, Adiva had an inspiration, and said to them, "Stand in the rain. Let it rain on you till you are clean." Ignoring their looks of dismay, she told the gypsy, who was laughing at the two, "You, also, gypsy. The cook has soap in his galley. Bring it and tell Kasim and the Arab I need them now."

When they ascended the steps to her, she asked Rafik, "The rain is coming harder now, but the wind favors us to the north. Should we strike the sails, or sale through this rainstorm?" The Arab beamed at being asked his opinion, and said without hesitation, "It is the storms of sand we fear, not of rain. Sail on, and we shall be out of this by morning."

The wind was rising, driving rain into concave sails that caused it to pour in sheets from beneath the booms.

Some of the men began to strip and wash themselves. Adiva said to Kasim, "Tell the men I have ordered them to wash the filth from themselves and their clothes in this rain. They will laugh, but this is safest for all. Adiva turned away in modesty.

Laughter billowed from the deck, and everyone joined in. Even Hillel and Yosef could be heard.

Adiva reentered the cabin alone. She had closed both portals when she felt the first gust of rain-laden air, and now it was cool and dark in the cabin. Since the rain was coming from the port side, she could reopen the circular cover on the starboard wall, but little light penetrated the rain. She opened the shiny cabinets opposite the treasure cove and found a surprising stack of elegant clothes. From the pile she pulled a folded robe of some soft weave and shook it out in the dim light. She longed to slip it on, but realized it was wiser to wait. The clothes might be needed later.

Through the partly opened portal she could hear the pounding rain, and then, a crack of thunder so loud it seemed the sky above them exploded.

"Sister. May we enter?"

She opened the door and hustled them in, pale and shivering, but not unhappy.

The rain pounded much harder on the cabin roof and port side wall but did not leak through the well-made portal. Below them, the rain had overfilled all the open barrels and had pelted the deck clean of salty grime and the sand from the storm weeks ago.

Then, as suddenly as the ship had blundered into the blanket of Red Sea squalls, it broke out, lunging into a sunlight made more brilliant by the darkness it dispelled. The fearsome rain was not lessened, it was utterly gone, as though this God-sent fountain of life had blessed them and moved on.

The three of them were quiet a moment, not quite believing the abrupt departure of the roaring downpour. None of the men on the deck could be heard either, startled by the sudden flash of afternoon sun. The air, still heavy with moisture, made them feel like they were standing beside a waterfall, wrapped in its soothing freshness.

"Open the portals," Adiva said, walking over to close the door left ajar for light. Now the brilliant late afternoon sun aligned portside, flooding the captain's quarters through the open portal, which also invited in the magic after-storm breeze.

Hillel picked up a hand-sized clay lamp. "The light will not last long, and these things will be about as bright as the moon light," he said with some urgency. "Did you find sea charts?"

Adiva motioned to the neat pillar of rolled maps in the corner and Hillel was quick to hand her the wooden plate, clearing the elegant chart table. The first of the six maps would not stay unrolled for Hillel to study, so Yosef pinned one corner and Adiva the other.

"What is this?" Hillel said, trying to get the best light in. Instead of drawings of coastlines and representations of rivers, islands and ports of call, the document stretched before them, striking for its bright rust and deep blue colors, depicted a rectangle of land in the middle of a body of water, complete with waves.

"Oo kee aan os," Hillel sounded out the Greek letters beneath several waves. "This must mean ocean and the map is signed below by its maker, Cosmas. I think this says it is his *world map*."

Hillel's long finger tapped one of the three perfectly circular bodies of water opening into Okeanos from the south of the russet-colored land mass, and said, "See here, our Euphrates and Tigris Rivers join and the Red Sea must be this, though he calls it the Arabian Gulf."

A smile of recognition spread over his face. "This mighty river flows from the distant sea," he said. "It refers to what our holy books call the great sea. However, it seems to hollow out most of the left half of the world, all the way to this beautifully painted band of generous fruit-bearing trees and profusions of flowers. It is the magic river that flows through what the ancients called Dilmun, and in Bereshit, Gan Edan."

"This world map must be very old, Yosef said. "We know the world is much bigger now, and that inland sea does not take up half of it."

Hillel nodded in agreement. "Not only very old, but utterly useless except being something pretty to look at. Let's look at the others and hope they tell us more than the way to Paradise."

The second scroll was of some stiff animal hide and lay flat on its own. Attached by a leather thong to the right upper corner was an insignificant looking square of wood, not even one finger long, easily ignored but for the telltale string of woven silk knotted in five irregular intervals from its attachment.

Adiva was puzzled about the object until Hillel said, "This was the lifeline of seafarers, allowing courses to be plotted and destinations reached," Hillel said. "It's called a kamal. I believe on a clear night we could establish our place on earth by sighting the top of the stretched-out string on the polar star and knotting where the string met the distant horizon. Then we could compare their position night after night to what he had recorded, correcting our course to align with the first night.

"Why is where you tie the knot significant?" Adiva asked, observing her brother, handling the instrument like it was a delicate flower.

"I don't know," Hillel confessed. "Captain Mustafa showed it to me early in our journey, and I asked him the same question. He said there was an imaginary line going from where you are to where you want to be. Somehow you have to follow it, or wander aimlessly at sea till you are lost. He told me nobody knows how kamal guides work."

The map spread before them had none of the fanciful land masses and unified oceans, and the highly tanned leather bore Arabic writing without embellishment. A deeply incised ink line, breaking the surface sheen of the leather, traced an unmistakable shoreline of the Asian continent, a boot with the Port of Aden at its heel, and the Gulf of Aden along its sole.

"This is where we are!" Hillel said, pointing excitedly to the Perim Island, overlarge on the map relative to how much of the strait of Bab El-Mandeb it actually blocked. "From this, it looks like we could barely squeeze through the wide channel."

He paused, as if waiting for Adiva to say something

"Sister, what it shows of the Red Sea has no Zubair Island chain that we know is there. We have no way of knowing where the sandstorm drove us after we left Aden."

Adiva realized the implications of what Hillel was saying but let silence hang in the air.

Hillel hurriedly unrolled the other maps, all but one showing disconnected segments of the eastern Red Sea coastline, each with a single port at its center. "Look at the drawings at the left edge of each map. They look like the string of the kamal," Hillel observed, stretching out the navigation device that was attached to the second map. "The first knots match exactly, but there are two in addition on each of the other charts. Wherever we are now, we will need to steer a course keeping us aligned with the sixth knot of the kamal to find these ports."

Yosef spoke up, "But, cousin, you can only guide us at night, isn't that so?"

"But a sighting after sunset and again just before dawn will tell us the direction for our rudder and sails, which we will follow till next twilight."

He paused. "There's something else I just remembered Captain Mustafa telling me. His kamal had eight knots, and from Jebel Zubair, the horizon aligned with the *fifth* knot, placing it much closer to the western coast than the welcoming harbors of the east. Perhaps Mustafa's longer cord with its extra knots may have shown him the ancient sea lanes in the vastness of the Eastern Ocean.

Adiva wasn't quite sure she understood, "These ports, how can you tell which we shall reach first? And when?"

"Why not ask Rafik what he knows," Hillel suggested. "That they had these charts in their murderous pirate hands may have meant they used these ports-of-call, and he'd know how to fit this jumble of charts together."

Yosef didn't need to be asked. He left and soon returned with the Arab in tow.

But he wasn't much help, "Where on the coast of the Sea are these places?" Hillel asked.

He looked utterly blank. Yosef saw the problem. The first mate could not read, not a word. "Adulis, it says," he said, pointing.

Rafik nodded vigorously "I know it! It is a very old, deep-water port and a bay with many moorings. Much trading there."

"What is traded most?" Yosef asked? "Ivory? Hides?"

"Slaves," Rafik interjected.

Adiva felt a chill. "It is why you were there?"

"There and others, but Adulis is the southernmost port. I cannot read the charts, but I know it is the first port we will reach on this sea."

Rafik acted even gloomier than usual. "If something does not reach us first. There were ships we raided in the waters outside these ports, as others would overpower us if they could. We sold their slaves and crews as well in Adulis, and the Egyptian port of Berenice."

He spoke of selling enslaved human beings as casually as one might sheep, but Adiva let this pass for now. She had learned from growing up with her brother and his friends that civilizing men takes time. She smiled to herself, remembering her mother's sister fondly calling all men, young and old, *poached apes*. She couldn't help thinking the little man in front of her was more like a monkey: nimble, grasping and opportunistic.

"How many days sailing to Adulis?" Hillel asked the Arab. Then he added quickly, "If our captain decides it will be our port of call."

"The current is with us, but we are still at the mercy of the winds. Now it blows us steadily northwest, but it will become un-predictable if we stay in sight of land. Also, the curves of the coast would add many days to Adulis."

Rafik paused a moment, then, with wholly surprising candor said, "People like us, we prowled these rough coastal waters for ships in distress and smaller vessels which could seldom outrun our triple sails."

"If that be so," Adiva said, "we can sail as swiftly away from harm as you did to cause it."

"This ship....*your* ship, there are not enough fighting sailors to repel boarding from as few as a dozen determined pirates," Rafik admitted.

"So, if that be our fate, it is best to run."

"And in open water, miles offshore?" Hillel asked.

"We can be followed but not overtaken if our seamanship is clever. When night falls, we slip away, as I saw Captain Shabazi, cursed be his memory, do twice. Silence on board is critical."

His eyes darted to Adiva and then to the others and back. "Uhm, where are we going?"

"Tell Kasim to stay the present course, and we," she said, gesturing to Yosef and Hillel, "shall decide in a few hours."

Adiva couldn't quite tell if her brother was smiling or grimacing.

"Yes, my dear sister–where *are* we going?"

45

As there were Silk Roads upon land, from Cairo to China, there were well-traveled sea lanes, one of these rounding the horn of Africa and hugging the eastern shore, to halfway down the continent to the great trading center at Rhapta. This port city was the first African stop for ships sailing the Clove and Cinnamon routes across the Indian Ocean from southeast Asia, China, and India. The sprawling waterfront market sold everything from carpets to the slaves who wove them. Buyers came there for human goods from as far away as Persia and were willing to pay the much higher prices for exotic merchandise from the east.

Orel, a Persian Jew of forty who traded at the market, was irritated at his friend, a man his same age, with whom he traded daily. Both were merchants in Rhapta, specializing in whatever their opportunistic spy network said was in oversupply at a given moment, but especially from desperate sellers. They avoided dealing with eager slavers docking with barges full of the half-dead.

Nearly a half a head taller than most, Orel could see over almost all heads in the slow-moving press of humanity in narrow corridors between stalls, usually lean-to tents of tightly woven goat hair, open at one end. No sign of the wiry explosion of unkempt black hair that topped his friend Dov's boat-shaped head.

Orel smiled to himself in anticipation of what he would see today. In the middle of negotiations with Muslim and Christian traders, Dov's wounded-at-such-a-meager-offer face would appear, more theatric depending on how much money was involved.

Orel loved the show.

The clamor of endless bargaining, from dozens of stalls, quieted as Orel walked on to the broad expanse of caked mud leading down to the Rufiji River banks. Boats as small as a man's height bobbed precariously next to tri-level junks, with their Chinese crews. One imposing vessel drew everyone's awestruck attention. Flying a long ribbon flag of resplendent silk adorned with pictograph symbols of men and war, the 30 foot mast had no riggings for sails, only climbing rungs up to its spear-pointed tip. Rather, the 110 feet long, 30 feet wide vessel's hull bore two broad paddlewheels on each side. The top halves of these wheels disappeared beneath a two-story oblong structure with ornate ironwork of peacocks and dragons, concealing and protecting the men whose legs powered the ship. Despite its size, it was fast, maneuverable, and independent of wind and wave.

Orel scanned the waterfront and was relieved, though he quickly denied this to himself, to see the black-frizzed head of his friend talking to a robed figure who was vigorously shaking his head, looking skyward as though to beseech the Almighty to deliver him from this conniving Jew. This was, Orel knew immediately, the second phase, and the robed man was indignant.

"For years, since you first came to Rhapta, have I not been good to you, taking you under my wing, like a son?"

At this, Dov laughed so hard he snorted. "I think you want me under your foot, not your wing. Nobody in the history of the world has ever paid this many gold dinars for a slave." The Arab trader smirked, but quickly returned to business as Orel walked up.

"Mehdi, do you know my friend, Orel?" Dov asked the trader.

"No. What does he want?"

Mehdi's aggravation, Orel knew, was from seeing too many precious deals sour when a third party intruded. Still, it was a mild insult, one that should at least be challenged. Orel was about to respond when Dov spoke first.

"He may want to help me shoulder this terrible burden you're placing on me."

Orel maintained a pleasant expression, pointing to Dov. "My friend here has told you what we require, why we have come to this wretched place?"

"An important family needs a house slave who might teach and protect their children. This is what the black-headed one says you need."

This was the third time Dov had dragged Orel down to this dock where slaves were traded freely. Nearby was the long plank walkway holding clusters of human beings roped or chained to one another. Most had just been unloaded and were being herded into crudely fenced holding pens. Here the merchants had their first view of the goods for sale. Orel did not come here because the sight and sound of this suffering was unbearable to him.

"Alright, you understand what I need. What is it...I mean *who* is it you bring me here to see?"

Dov nodded to the slave trader to begin. "He is an African, a slave like no other, sold twice by tribes who pay dearly for him, then suddenly rid themselves of him." Mehdi smiled benignly, adding, "Always at a substantial profit."

"How strange," Orel said, "What more of this slave can you tell me?"

"He is poorly nourished but aren't they all. He is whole otherwise. He does not speak our language but seems to understand much. No one knows who he was before slavery, but he was not born to it."

"And you know this how?" Orel wondered.

"He looks me in the eye as though he were my equal. He is too sure of himself, and I do not want to own him."

"But the price you ask, only caliphs can pay," Dov said, reentering the negotiations.

"Now you too, Arab, want away from him," Orel observed.

Pretending not to hear this, Mehdi continued his defense of the outlandish asking price saying, "The family who wants a house slave would do well with this African. I have watched him, and even when his hunger is extreme, he eats in a refined way, unlike the usual savages I sell."

"Yes, the eating habits of those you sell are known," Dov said. "Both what they eat, and whom." Orel thought that perhaps the Arab would burst in rage, at the insinuation he sold cannibals, even if it was true. This degradation of Mehdi's merchandise was the next ploy in determining the final price, whether for cotton or the slaves to pick it.

The slaver sighed, "Others are interested in this man. I care little who pays my price."

Orel shot back, "Come now, friend, if these others are on their way to the docks to buy this slave, why are you here with us?"

"Delayed, they are, uh, up the river," Mehdi stammered. He shouldn't have. Nobody told anybody the truth at the Rhapta market, but all pretended to. Twenty years had taught Orel to pick people to whom he could lie *less*, thus weaving a fabric of trust that could bear the weight of ordinary transactions. This preliminary negotiation was already non ordinary.

"Where is this captive prince?" asked Dov.

"We will *not* go among this pitiful refuse," Orel interjected pointedly. "Bring this victim of your evil trade to us." Even as he so labeled the sale of human beings, Orel understood that slavery was accepted without question everywhere. His tribe of Issachar, who lived high in the Caucus Mountains of Persia, owned slaves. Orel's family owned other families who had been with them so many generations, no one could remember how they came to be together, only that it was some time after their ancient tribe of Israel was expelled by the Assyrians from the Holy land. The three slave families, like the Tribe of Issachar, were practicing Jews who read and spoke Hebrew. The people of Issachar were scholars and religious teachers, thus the insistence that slaves be literate. The tribe's most important occupation was teaching the children of their neighboring allied tribe of Zebulon. This arrangement had evolved because the men of Zebulon were almost all merchants. Many were gone long periods of time on caravans plying the overland Silk Roads, so they paid the tribe of Issachar to teach their children the words of Moshe Rabbenu and nourish Zebulon's spiritual longings. They were aware of the Book of Chronicles, "...from Issachar, men who understood the times, and knew what Israel ought to do."

But teaching or studying religious matters had failed fire Orel's imagination as a youth and nothing had happened in the decades since he left the tribe in the mountains to make him regret his life as an itinerant merchant.

His success had been notable. At forty, this son of Issachar had acquired well-hidden wealth by trading all manner of goods, from gold to grain, without touching them. This was safer for a Jew in a port city marketplace where no one oversaw maintaining order. Clans protected their own kind, but not others, and the Jews, few in number, were no different.

Dov was from the lands of the Tribe of Zebulon which extended from Armenia to the Euphrates River valley, his village being near the river. Or rather it was near the Euphrates River, until all the Jews were driven out by edict of the caliph in Baghdad. Al-Mu'tamid claimed the higher elevation of the village was needed to fortify the river and for observation towers. Dov's family managed through friends in the Zebulon tribe, to book passage on a ship from the Persian Gulf port at Basra at the southern end of the Euphrates. The ship would sail over the weeks out of the Gulf and down the coast of India to the ancient southern seaport at Murziris. Dov's family knew this was the home of the Cochin Jews, who had lived near the port city of Cochin since they arrived as traders in the service of King Solomon. Once among them, Dov's family learned of the Hindu majority's absolute acceptance of the Jews, like nowhere else in their world.

And there on the south Indian coast his family stayed, but the restless teenager yearned for the wider world promised by ships of every sort that left from Murziris to cross the vast expanse of the Indian Ocean.

The almost weekly docking of ships from India at the port of Rhapta afforded Dov access to mail from his family, but they would never make the perilous voyage to Africa, and, at his last visit, forbade him to do so again in order to see them.

The three men pushed their way through the grudgingly yielding mass of humanity of the upper marketplace where smells of fresh

slaughtered meat mingled with acrid garlic and sweet oranges. A
ten-minute walk over twisting cobblestone paths between haphazardly placed mud huts led the trio to the high ridge overlooking
the mouth of the Rufiji River. Structures built into the sides of the
mountain showed small openings into their cave-like interiors.

Orel and his family had been living for eight years in what
appeared to be a small space carved out of the stony mountain, and
that is what they had begun with. Since then, Orel and his Persian
wife had added two children to the household, the boy now eight
and the girl six.

Orel had, in his wanderings, passed through the astonishing
stone cities of Cappadocia in central Turkey. Carved into solid rock
by seemingly superhuman effort, these subterranean cities, hous-
ing thousands of people, plunged as many as 19 stories beneath
conical towers of stone. Orel had marveled at their engineering of
ventilation, secure water access, and even light far underground.
He was told people had been living in these caverns for eight
thousand years.

The circular opening to his cave initially led to a 12 foot arched
vault, fractured at the peak by an open fissure in the core of the
mountain. The fissure admitted light from above, and, in the cold
of winter, was a natural flue for cooking and warming fires. As
Orel's trading ventures succeeded, he was able to hire many stone
cutters to enlarge this.

The present structure had three levels, one added as each child
was born. It was not likely to get bigger as Devorah threatened
both suicide and murder of Orel if another pregnancy occurred.
Orel got smacked for commenting on her diminished availability
when he said he might as well dig another hole in the mountain.
Although, each time they did make love, she reminded him afterwards that she didn't want him to think she was *not* still hungry
for this joy.

Each of the three levels of stone rooms was carved around a
central 6' across shaft which opened near the mountain top. His ma-
sons had used the natural break in the stone to bore 25' down to a

freshwater spring. A few feet above the water level, a narrow escape tunnel led to a rock-covered opening on the mountain's east face.

Rhapta's port city mixture of races and cultures, and the titanic forces of religion, had rendered this community volatile and unpredictable. For this reason, the entrance to his cave could be closed from the inside by rolling an exquisitely balanced circular stone into grooves in the rounded door frame.

This, Orel had learned, is how the stone cities of Cappadocia closed out a threatening world, though he and his family had never needed to. The eight-year-old boy had already taught his sister to insert the square post with its crank handle into the matching well chiseled into the center of the door stone. Rolled into place, it could not be opened from the outside, as the door fused seamlessly with the face of the stone mountain.

When the three men arrived, Devorah was outside on the landing, attending to a cone-shaped oven, its waist high opening radiating far more heat than the noonday sun. The maddening aroma of baking bread caused its expected visceral reaction, and Dov was quick to say how his usually most giving wife had fed him nothing today.

"Is that the same nothing she was cooking when I took the sewing to her this morning?" the tall Persian woman replied to his entreaty. "Or maybe she was cooking that for your stray dogs."

Unfazed, as usual when caught in bald face untruth, Dov smiled, then changed tactics with a theatrical, "I come to share a bounty, not receive one."

"Never mind, you beggar."

"No, no, Mehdi has brought the answer to your mystery family's need."

"And *that* is this one's name?" she asked.

She didn't expect an answer, nor wait for one. "Well, peace be with you, Mehdi. Please accept this fresh bread," handing him a still-warm bun bigger than his fist.

Oren looked on hopefully, knowing full well some promise or other would be extracted before he and Dov got theirs.

"The wonderful silk you two were so certain you would acquire, some of it promised in blood to me, what has happened? Where are my bolts of elegance from the east?"

Devorah drew pictures of clothes for the very wealthy of the city, and Dov's wife sewed the garments. Both made substantial profits in this endeavor, even more when they agreed to always say they were "too busy" to do a special order, while being known to move it up in line for a small extra fee. These rich people, who waited for nothing, evidently *loved* being told to wait!

She gave Orel a practiced look which conveyed she smelled something fishy here. As usual, she could interpret his expressions, or even failures to change his expression, with uncanny accuracy.

"You sold it, didn't you?"

"Well," Dove began, but Orel immediately confessed.

"Yes, we did," he said, ignoring the stare from Dov.

"No silk, no design of gowns and robes. And for your wife, Dov, no sewing. No garments, no profits. Your wife and I suspected this after grand allusions to fabrics that shimmered and had an inner light of their own, were followed by deafening silence on the matter. We want a share of the profits on this sale of our silk!"

As she said this, Dov's wife appeared from the stone staircase below.

"What have they done?" she asked Devorah.

Devorah had scooped four loaves from her oven and pushed them off her wooden paddle into a basket lined with red cloth. She handed one to Chanina, she said, "Our men have a little secret they want to discuss."

"We made the best profit of any commodity this year!" Dov blurted, "The Egyptian seemed to be drunk or something, and offered twice what we had paid!"

"Oh! That's so pleasant to know!" Devorah shot back. "Now we can see what wonders the drunken Egyptian hath delivered to us from the land of the pharoahs."

The slave trader clearly was uncomfortable with the domestic squabble. He looked at Devorah almost pitifully, pointing to the fresh warm bread.

Devorah toyed with him, at first refusing and then relenting before also offering a piece to Orel and Dov.

"You will get our fabric from somewhere, or we shall buy it ourselves with the proceeds you gained."

Medhi spoke up, his face animated. "I know a man; his ship is due in here soon. He always carries the finest silk, all the way from China." He self-consciously clasped his hands together but wound up rubbing one on another when he proposed, "For a modest fee, of course," he added, still chewing the irresistible bread.

"Yes," Devorah said sweetly. "Exactly my fee for the royal feast you will have at my table tonight when you bring this slave to be seen by us. No doubt he, too, will welcome being fed food meant for humans, even if he cannot thank us in a language we can understand. You will bring him clean and properly clothed."

46

Adiva bat Zemah missed her home. Still, she had to admit that after nearly a year of living with the Netira family in Fustat, she had grown quite comfortable.

She had become much like a big sister to Nura, the youngest of the clan. Regaling Nura with stories of her adventures on the seas, as well as her love of the black prince from Africa, she was careful to leave out any intimate details. Nura, not quite sixteen, had yet to be betrothed although she knew that her father had begun to search for a suitable candidate for marriage. She peppered Adiva with questions about what men were like behind closed doors and how to make them happy or at least prevent them from being unhappy.

Adiva mostly stuck to the advice that she had been given at Nura's age. But she acknowledged to herself that she had learned a great deal about the nature of men, both their kindness and courage, but also the evil they sometimes held in their hearts. She had also learned that while never matching men in strength, women had their own unique power.

The Netira family's banking skills were in great demand in this city of 120,000, a dusty half-day's camel ride from the sphinx and the pyramids. Nura's father had been overcome with relief and gratitude that Adiva, along with her brother and cousin, had managed to deliver a major part of their family's fortune from the tumult now seizing the Port of Aden. Through his Jewish mercantile contacts at the Red Sea Port of Suez, Chiam Netira had quickly added to Adiva's and her family's wealth by selling the three-masted sailing vessel to a group desperate for safe transit of their goods down the coast of Africa.

Adiva never ceased to wonder at the stately palms shading broad cobblestone streets, dotted with markets selling iridescent pottery so delicate it was transparent. Domes of mosques with tile so polished it always looked wet, seemed to grow in many sizes from city squares ringed by luxuriant gardens.

It was unlike anything she had ever seen, even in the larger Baghdad. Fustat housed many of its people in buildings up to seven stories tall. More remarkably, families of Jews lived in buildings with both Muslims and Christians. The Netiras shared a four-story building with a Nestorian Christian family, the Bukhtishus who were the private physicians for the sultans and caliphs. Each family could easily have their own separate spacious quarters, but preferred the security of sharing walls with trusted neighbors in a modest building

Each family had its own rooftop garden endlessly fussed over by family members. Competition for the finest fruit and most inviting vegetables had made each garden so abundant it supplied all their needs for produce.

Respectful of each other's religious traditions, they sometimes even shared an occasional meal like Pesach.

In the year Adiva had lived with the Netiras, she had come to believe that the secret to wealth of this great city was its long history of tolerance. She had heard people say that the great ruler of Egypt, Ibn Tuulun, who had died earlier in the year was responsible for maintaining the people's great fortune. His son and successor, Khumarawayh, thankfully showed no signs of disturbing the commerce of his greatest city although he did seem impulsive.

There were rumors that al-Muwaffaq, the Caliph in Baghdad was determined to retake control of Egypt. Adiva bitterly remembered how he had re-instituted the humiliating restrictions and harassment of Jews and Christians throughout the lands he ruled, but Ibn Tuulun would not be told how to treat his people. Neither did he pay the tribute demanded from Baghdad. Rather, Adiva learned, he used the gold to build his royal compound, fully fortified by walls so thick, two horsemen can ride abreast on them. Enclosing half a square mile, the central courtyard was large enough to parade 10,000 soldiers entering through its seven arched gates. A few miles north of the thriving Fustat, Ibn Tuulun had made Cairo the new capital of Egypt.

The neighbor's daughter said her father went to the royal compound three times a week, and perhaps could slip Adiva past the guards for a tour of the palace. Taking up a fifth of the entire enclosure, the palace was said to have 400 chambers, including the Emerald Hall with pillars of marble, and another incredible hall, the Golden Hall, where Caliphs sit upon a golden throne. But the death of Ibn Tuulun had postponed Adiva's trip to Cairo, as these were unsettled times.

"*Adiva?*" Nura gave Adiva a little push on her arm. She must have been lost in thought. "Were you even listening?"

Adiva nodded and smiled, not quite acknowledging her inattentiveness.

"You must cover your head when you meet the rabbi today."

They stood in front of their destination, a large building which had become the latest bet ha-kneset for the Jews of Fustat.

"My brother, Avram, is inside at prayer. Afterwards he will introduce you."

They sat on a stone bench in front.

"And you will not be allowed on the first floor. Only men pray and study there.

Adiva nodded. But she was already thinking back to the events that brought her to Fustat.

Through the treacherous winds and tides, they had finally been delivered into the Port of Suez.

On the vessel, she had begun to understand the stories of men who went to sea or to battle and the affection they often felt for those who were by their side. Adiva most keenly felt a responsibility to reward them as she had promised,

Still dressing in the clothes of a lowly sailor, she also had an empathy born in the life and death struggle that had all endured together.

They had already sold enough of the slave ship's ill-gotten

treasures to reward each of her crew with enough gold dinars to live modestly for a number of years.

Most, she knew, had no homes awaiting them, and life at sea was all they knew. Some would take their money and spend it on drink; others on the multitude of women that swarmed around the port. A man without a destination might, with ease, lose his money and his life.

Ashot, the gypsy to whom she owed her life, was the exception and she felt a special trust and loyalty towards him.

"What will you do now?" she asked Ashot, who was again the more withdrawn, mysterious character she had first met. In the month it had taken them to sail the full length of the Red Sea, it was obvious that his protection of her went quite beyond his assigned duty as bodyguard.

"I do not like the sea, nor trust most of these men. The pirates and our crew from Captain Mustafa's boat want to stay with the ship, but not if it transports human cargo."

"What about you?" Adiva asked.

The stocky gypsy smiled and sighed. "Even if I could find my brethren, the gold you have given me will be found out and, being thieves, even blood kin will wish to relieve me of it."

"Is there a woman for you among your people?"

Ashot laughed without mirth, "Oh, yes. But that is also a reason I choose the sea." He cast his eyes down.

Adiva smiled but said nothing.

Before they left the Port of Suez, she said to Ashot, "You know I, with my brother and cousin, are transporting assets for a family at Aden to their safe haven in Fustat. They are alert, and Yosef can handle a sword, but neither is a match for what we might encounter on the trail to Fustat"

"I know what you carry. Wen Ho told me what he had learned from the disloyal servant woman of the rich family."

"And the other crewmen?" Adiva asked warily.

"The Chinaman was too afraid of the slavers, even after you killed the son of a pig, Tariq, the only one he had told."

"Why did he tell *you?*"

"He knew Mustafa's crew blamed him for bringing the pirate-slavers upon us, and they're right. He particularly feared Kasim, not only because of his size, but more the angry grief over losing his beloved Captain."

"And he thought you could protect him?" Adiva asked.

"I *did* protect him, though no one saw how. He was right about Kasim, who only growled through gritted teeth when I warned him away from Wen Ho. He ignored me until he saw me gut Captain Shabazi. The carpenter warned away the others, one by one."

"Alright, but can we trust Wen Ho? Knowing what he does, how do we know he will not form his own venture, perhaps for others to find us somewhere in the three-day journey through the mountains, or even on the Nile?"

"There are two choices," Ashot offered.

"And they are?"

"You could pay him for his pledge of silence, though you have already been so generous it shouldn't be necessary."

"What is the other choice?"

Ashot touched his knife, answering in a low monotone, "You'd let me handle it in my own way."

Adiva had seen enough blood. Ashot must have sensed her resistance.

"Perhaps a little talk with him is all that's needed."

It occurred to Adiva that if Wen Ho had told others, killing him was of no value, save revenge. A third possibility dawned on her. "We shall take this spy with us, to Fustat. That way, what happens to us happens to him. Bring him to me."

Ashot looked at her curiously. *"We?"*

"Oh, yes. *We,* I hope, includes *you.* I shall pay you a gold dinar every seven days. You may buy and sell anything our camels can carry." Her plan was to acquire a cargo immediately, perhaps silks and nutmeg, as a pretense for the small caravan crossing the 70 miles from the sea to Fustat.

Ashot beamed with rare warmth. "You trust me, though you

know my gypsy nature. He nodded resolutely. "I shall be vigilant," he laughed and went on, "and unlike my previous plan, I will not steal from you." His candor was disarming, but also revealed his honor. Adiva was relieved he did not linger for her reaction, immediately leaving to find Wen Ho.

It was dangerous in the Port of Suez, and she made it a point to dress in modest, colorless robes, and then sheathed her head in Muslim black. If she were discovered dressed as boy, it would be reasoned that she had secrets to hide. She walked about the ancient port city accompanied by Hillel and Yosef, who for the first time in his life wore a leather belt, which was forbidden to Jews and Christians in Babylon, and it was easy to see why. Worn beneath his robes, the two-inch-wide belt secured the sheathed cutlass he was never without.

Now, they must secure transport overland and there was no end to the camel drivers promising the easiest ride on the swiftest camels. Ashot had come along with them, shadowing the three from a short distance away. It was about as far as he could accurately throw his dagger. His presence made the camel drivers uncomfortable. Whether it was because he was a gypsy or just looked dangerous, Adiva did not know. Ashot himself found an old Egyptian who no longer feared anyone. He was as insulting to Ashot as the gypsy was to the parchment-skinned camel driver. After mutual accusations of the other being fathered by a donkey or a goat, they started laughing and the old man was hired.

Back at the ship, Adiva addressed the burly carpenter, Kasim, who had been hired by a very large merchant vessel which had been damaged navigating the silted and rock-strewn estuary. His huge head was bowed, eyebrows knit with sadness, Kasim spoke softly, "Where will you go now?"

She would miss the strength of his massive presence. He feared no man, yet no righteous man need fear him.

"My mission takes me to Fustat, but after that I cannot say. As you know, I am a Jew, and I don't know how my people are treated there."

Then he jolted the young woman with, "Your young African, don't give up hope that he survived. Just because *we* did not find him doesn't mean *no one* will."

Adiva felt her eyes filled with tears at the mention of Eldad. She thought she had hidden her despair well.

Kasim reached a huge paw to the top of her head and left it there for a moment. She felt a warmth and tenderness flow from the calloused hand into her head, then her whole being and began to sob.

Kasim stood still, unsure of what to do next. Then he said, "I know he lives in your heart." Now she stood and wrapped her arms as far around his ponderous trunk as they could reach and released a grief that had been coiled within her. It came out as a cry, only one, but of such sorrowful depth, Kasim felt physically struck by it.

Then she regained her composure as quickly as she had lost it. Stepping back, she looked up at him, his silhouette blocking the sunlight streaming in from behind him, giving his head a haloed appearance. She suddenly laughed at the apparition, and said, "You look like a saint in Christian paintings." Joining the fun, he held out his arms, munificent to all, and said, "No one ever accused me of being a saint, but if I must!"

Adiva could not remember the last time she had laughed. It was as though the outcry released something, allowing in the light of laughter.

Adiva regained her composure as quickly as she had lost it.

"Where are you from, noble carpenter?"

"I am from the sea. I was so young when my dear Captain Mustafa bought me, I remember nothing before him. I worshipped him and could never imagine being without him." He fell silent now.

"We've asked about the ship you signed on with and it is said to have a fair and just captain."

Kasim nodded in agreement. "The ship goes places I do not know, picking up cargo from Adulis Bay, at the southern end of the Sea. When they leave the Red Sea, they say they hug the coast of Africa to the south, but I do not care where they go. I never thought

I'd have a choice as to what to do with myself. But now that I do, I do not wish to choose." He was quiet for a few moments, then said, "I didn't know how much to ask for wages, since what you gave me was the only pay I ever got. Rafik was telling me how to negotiate with the ships' owners, when he decided to talk to them for me. He tried to get them to believe I had magical carpentry skills, and seamanship as well.

Kasim chuckled. "It was the Arab they hired right away, and he told me this was a rich, but deteriorating vessel that needed me more than I needed it. The rest of the pirates have signed on and our Ethiopian fishermen as well."

The carpenter said, "There are ten more crew on this new ship who I do not know, and wonder if I can trust. These gold dinars you have given me could be a menace to my safety."

Adiva had an idea as she remembered what the banking family patriarch in Aden had described to her early on their last evening, when he said, "The bankers in major cities, like Aden, Baghdad and especially the Jews of Fustat, have signed agreements with one another to honor with gold any 'letter of credit' from another member of the alliance. Number codes prevent forgeries. Christian banking families honor them as well."

"Letter of credit? What if the letter is ruined or lost?" Kasim wondered.

"Then I shall keep a copy for you," she reassured him.

"But how can the Netira family give me the letter? As soon as I buy the wood, pitch and other supplies, my new ship will sail."

"I am empowered to give it for them, both the Netiras of Aden and of Fustat."

Without a moment's hesitation, he popped a purse string bag from some unknown place beneath his tent sized tunic and handed it to her. She moved to the desk and opened it for parchment, ink and quill.

"I can't read," the big bear of a man admitted with a quiet sadness. "You could write any nonsense you wanted on it, and I wouldn't know."

"But me you do know." She counted the 40 gold pieces, some misshapen as their purity made them easily bent and she penned two identical statements in Aramaic.

One she rolled tightly in a thin leather scroll, sealing the seam with wax from the cabin candle. The second she attached to the draw string purse, adding it to the banker's gold and precious stones.

She lifted the heavy bag when something caught her eye. She was puzzled why we hadn't noticed it before. About six inches on a side and an inch thick, it was leather covered in a thin layer of dense brown wax. She recognized it with a cry that caught in her throat.

"What's wrong?"

"It..." Adiva took a deep breath. "It is the Danite's special book. The pirates must have thrown it in with the gold, believing it was valuable to somebody."

Adiva examined the object, its burnt brown casing smooth and strangely warm to touch. On end, many thin, precisely cut leather edges could be seen beneath the wax. Tears fell upon the precious book, quickly rolling off the polished surface, and the realization that this small object may be all she will ever have to remember him by made it difficult to even stand.

A feeling of finality struck her with overwhelming strength. Even if he lives, her beloved Eldad was lost to her forever.

Handing the mysterious book to Kasim, she tried to recall what Eldad had told her of its contents. "The Danite told me this book was the reason he journeyed from his homeland. It is a copy he made of scraps of leather bound in one of the family's books that no one can read."

"Why would he care about such a thing?"

"Eldad told me his grandfather, who was the guardian of the book, said it had been passed down for so many generations nobody knew when it came to the family. They believe the images are some unknown form of writing, and every few generations, another copy of the symbols is penned on new leather. It took him a year to make two copies of it. From a strange experience with an even stranger healer, he knows only the beginning of this story of an ancestor who may have lived 3,000 years ago. To know this story, to find someone in the world who can read it, *this* is why my young man left his people. He left them to *find* them."

"But found you, instead," the carpenter said softly.

"I thank you for your acts of bravery and, most especially, your loyalty to me. I shall miss you." She grasped his massive forearm and watched as tears welled up in his eyes. She couldn't help but observe one drop as it rolled over his high cheekbone into his ragged black beard. She was sure he wouldn't want her to notice.

He sniffed. "In time, the owners of my new ship say, we shall return to Suez with the cargo from far down the coast of Africa. Rafik had me make my mark on a paper that says I am crew until that time. I don't know how long that will be."

He turned slowly to leave. Adiva called after, "Remember that your letter will introduce you to the Netiras and their friends, who are in most port cities. They have ways of communicating with distant places." The big man nodded and, without looking back, ducked under the door frame to leave the cabin, passing the ever-present gypsy standing guard. Kasim towered over Ashot and Rafik. "You will guard her well, especially from the both of *you!*" Both men laughed, and without further word, Kasim thundered down the gangplank to the massive wooden dock glistening from the caress of high tide on the Red Sea.

47

Eldad could no longer depend on his memories to sustain his spirit. Adiva could not be summoned in his mind to comfort him, nor could Zav's teachings offer him any meaning.

His fear of the unknown had grown with each passing month. Now the entire purpose of his life was to avoid further pain. Even the brief pleasure he was offered by the chieftain's concubines was not relief. Instead, ordered to service them, he had been ashamed.

But now, even shame eluded him. In the early morning sunshine, he considered the four women being held in Mehdi's separate enclosure with him. He understood enough to realize that together they were being prepared for an auction. They would fetch a high price for Mehdi, the current master.

The youngest, a girl of maybe thirteen or fourteen, smiled at him. Eldad just blankly stared back at her.

As for himself, he did not know his fate. He had cried out to God so many times without answers that he was certain he had been abandoned.

A small basin of mostly clean water had been placed in front of him with a small pile of ash. "Strip," the guard ordered, motioning for him to clean himself.

He stepped out of his robe, to the tittering of the slave women and also, he now noticed, from above the high earthen walls where they were being observed.

He heard the unmistakable rasp of the head slaver, Mehdi.

"That is unfortunate, your funds being limited. Those who will see him this noon, theirs are not so limited."

A half dozen men and two women were paying close attention.

"Any of the women below will make an excellent domestic servant for you. And at a reasonable price. An excellent value. They are both young and healthy."

He paused, letting his words sink in. "The African? I'll keep him if I can't get the price he is worth."

With that, the slave master ordered a heavy noose to be tightened around Eldad's neck. He could scarcely breathe, let alone try to run. It didn't really matter. Eldad had no will to escape. A rough woven tunic replaced the rags that clothed him for the month on the barge, and who knew how much longer.

He became anxious when he realized that he was not going to be auctioned but taken somewhere. His mind raced. Could he escape? With each pull on the rope, he realized the impossibility.

Forcing Eldad to keep to their pace, the slaver's guard led him through the crowded paths to the stone mountain dwelling above the harbor. Two men were standing on the semicircular landing as the slaver and his guard mounted the steps, with Eldad the slave securely in tow.

Greeting Mehdi, Orel carefully observed his unfortunate human chattel. He appeared much as Mehdi described, although it was hard the tell the brilliance of his eyes since they were mostly kept downcast.

"You may all enter," motioning Dov to be last so he could take a closer look at the man being led about like a dog on a rope.

Devorah was just inside, flanked by the two children, who were peering out from behind their mother. They seemed just as fascinated by Mehdi's large guard as by the black man and were disappointed when Mehdi told him to wait outside.

Orel had Mehdi sit at their polished granite table and produced a small wood stool and motioned to the slave to sit.

Mehdi looked at Dov. "Is he not as I have told you?"

Dov nodded. "Yes, my friend but I am not the purchaser."

Devorah spoke for Orel, "We must know more than he was just sold to you by some nameless tribe, for unknown reasons.

Mehdi agreed. "I understand. Before long, the mu'azzin will call us to prayer. I will return afterwards. Will that be sufficient time to gain the understanding you wish?"

Orel was non-committal. "We shall see. Yes, return before we begin our Shabbat. I'm sure that we will find mutually agreeable terms."

"Well then," Dov said, standing up. "Did I not tell you that?"

Orel could see that his friend was distracted by the same thing as he. At the mention of Shabbat, the slave had become agitated and was mumbling. For a moment, he thought he recognized the words, but it couldn't be possible. It was Hebrew.

"What did you say? I couldn't hear you"

The slave was silent.

Medhi stood. "Speak up, slave. This man who would be your master commands it." He raised his hand to strike.

Devorah stepped in front. "No. Not in here, slaver!"

Medhi thought better of any conflict. "My apologies, mistress."

Orel looked carefully at the young dark-skinned man and was startled by the sensation of being scrutinized by him. They stared at each other intently.

Orel waved his hand across the room. "You are in no danger here. Tell us of what you speak?"

"Vay ku lu hash sha may-im v' haAretz. And the heavens and the earth were completed and all of the totality. And on the seventh day, Elohim finished his work which He had made; and he rested on all of His work which He had made..."

Orel was not a learned man but recognized the verse from the book of Bereshit of the Torah. As a child he heard it every Shabbat.

"How..."

"What does he say?" Mehdi interrupted.

"He mimics words he's heard but does not understand. Clever but deceitful. I see why you want to rid yourself of him."

"However, he does have value. At the *right* price," Dov interjected. Medhi just grunted.

Orel was the first to regain his composure and he said in the

Aramaic dialect of the Persian Jews, "How do you know this, slave? Did you belong to Jews?"

"No, my kinsman, I *am* a Jew."

Orel turned to Medhi. "Return to us after your prayers and we will continue."

"Allah be with you," Mehdi said.

As soon as they were alone, Devorah rushed to remove the rope from the slave's neck, who seem to relish the softness of her touch. She handed him water and a small piece of fresh bread.

The man smiled gratefully.

"How do you come to recite from our holy book, the Torah? Did you live with Jews?"

"No. My name is Eldad ben Mahli from the tribe of Dan."

"As soon as I heard that you celebrate the Shabbat, I knew we are kinsmen."

"From the tribe of Dan, you say?" Orel looked at Dov whose face revealed his own confusion.

The children took the first step. They slowly moved closer to the strange guest, wide-eyed with fascination. Orel, perceiving no threat, let them be.

Eldad got down on one knee, eye level with the eight-year-old. "I am Eldad. What is your name?"

"Yacub. This is my sister, Chava."

Chava said nothing, frozen wide-eyed in place.

Orel picked her up and held her. "Now that you have been introduced to my children, I am Orel and this is my wife, Devorah. Over there is my friend Dov, who was to help me purchase you.

He immediately regretted his words. "I mean. We didn't know who you were." Eldad smiled. "It is good to be reminded."

Orel changed the subject. "How do you come to be the property of the slaver Mehdi?

"Many months ago, even more, the tribe who had enslaved me was going to kill me. A very clever cannibal woman, a fire worshipper's slave like me, persuaded the vengeful chieftain that I could be sold for much gold."

Orel remained expressionless, not wanting to reveal that he already knew something of that.

Devorah interrupted with, "The Shabbat candles must be lit now." She covered her head and gathered her children beside her at the table. As the candle flame brightened, she said the blessing that welcomed the Sabbath. Eldad was flooded with sweet memories. Yacub blessed the bread and Devorah placed large plates of stew with vegetables and the bread they had blessed in front of them. While ravenous, Eldad ate slowly, deliberately.

"How do you come to be a slave in the first place?"

"My story may seem a fanciful creation to you, but it is true. My people have lived in the lands beyond the River Kush for five hundred generations." Eldad told of a midnight flight from the Port of Aden, of a pursuit by pirates, the storm, and the shipwreck.

"I shall never recover from the loss of my friend, Saul. As with all this journey, there was a terrible irony: One of the cannibals who killed him was she who *saved* me." He told them also of the three Jews from Babylon and of the young woman who had captured his heart.

Orel was positive that there was much more that he had not told them. Perhaps in time.

"I am sure she was sold into slavery. A mighty slave ship with grey sails took her from the island inferno." With that, he became quiet, starring dejectedly at the plate before him.

Devorah rose from the table, brushing a tear from her eye. It was obvious that they all had been touched by Eldad's tale.

Dov seemed to be lost in thought, "Maybe I don't know much about dealing in slaves, but our Muslim rulers tell everyone that Jews may not be bought or sold unless they were taken in battle. They say they are protecting us."

The contempt in Dov's voice was not lost on Orel. But the idea, he decided, was brilliant. He turned to Eldad. "I am sure you don't quite understand. You, my new friend, are not a slave, you are a *captive*."

48

"Rabbi, I wish to introduce Adiva bat Zemah, ha'Almah," Avram said, smiling.

Adiva hated to be described as an unmarried woman, but knew it was necessary.

"As you may know, my father considers her a part of our family and appreciates the courtesy of extending this invitation to visit.

"Of course," Rabbi Natan ben Yosef said, offering Adiva a place to sit.

"Nura, come over here child and sit. I haven't seen you in some time. The way you have grown, maybe it's been longer than I thought. I understand your father is looking for a suitable partner for you. I hope that I will be honored to wed you before long."

Nura blushed. "Thank you, Rabbi."

Adiva realized that the Rabbi's small talk had put her somewhat at ease. She wasn't quite sure of his age, but some gray had begun to invade his beard.

Adiva looked around the beautiful building, until recently a Coptic Church. Besides the rabbi's private study, the second floor had been converted to a gallery where the women prayed.

Adiva gazed at the marble pillars supporting a soaring arch of maroon alternating with white stone blocks, which framed the ornate Ark of the Torah. From her vantage point, she could see the semicircle of stalactites above the Ark, and the luxuriant inlays of lotus flowers and palmettos on its doors. An octagon of ivory-colored marble rose above the center point of the ground floor, the bimah with a lectern from which the rabbi read the Torah and spoke to his flock.

"The legend is that once the Nile flowed through here." Rabbi Natan said. "And it was on this spot that Bat Pharoah, Pharaoh's daughter, rescued the baby Moshe, naming him so because she drew him out of the water. It was revered by Jews long before the Christians built their first church here five hundred years ago.

The Rabbi smiled warmly. "I am rambling. My apologies."

"No, it's a unique story and a special place." Nura's father told her how the Muslim governors had imposed a tax on Christian houses of worship, one the Coptic El-Shamieen Church could not pay, thus the sale to the Jews for 20,000 dinars.

"It would not have been possible without the Geonim of Baghdad, including, I believe, your esteemed grandfather."

"Thank you, Rabbi. You have been very generous with your time. I will come to my purpose in visiting you. I have come to ask your help understanding this book."

Rabbi Natan narrowed his eyes wearing an expression of deep curiosity. He reached over and accepted the leather pages bound with tight silk stitching.

"My friend, whose book this is, said this is written in a language more ancient than anyone knows today, perhaps it is even from the time of Avraham, our patriarch."

Adiva began to feel tears forming and lowered her eyes in the hope that the rabbi would not notice. She was relieved that she didn't need to say more.

"When I studied near my home in Tunis, there was a mystic, a teacher of Kabbalah who read and wrote eight languages, and collected scrolls written in tongues no one could decipher. He wanted to find man's oldest written record of God."

He paused. "Perhaps, a futile search."

Adiva remembered something her Eldad had pointed out. She pointed to the first page of the leather leaves and located the symbol.

"This starburst of four intersecting lines. He told me this is the symbol of God, and it was so in the time of our prophet Abraham."

"If this be so," the rabbi said, "it must be saved in a special place. Such was the first interior addition to the synagogue, an airless vault ten feet long and half again as high. We call this a geniza, and I have received fragments and manuscripts in Arabic, Aramaic and Hebrew, along with business documents which evoke the name of God in their solemn promises–an unwise endeavor if you ask me.

"Your volume here reminds me of what I'm told is our most precious object. It is a book, centuries old, of Kabbalah called the Sefer Yetzirah, the Book of Creation. It is a copy of what is said to have been given to Adam and passed through Noah to Avraham. The Qur'an, of which I am somewhat familiar, calls it The Scroll of Abraham. When I first saw it, shortly after I arrived, I opened the badly deteriorated cover, and the first page had clearer, more recent writing of a single sentence: *God cannot be understood by any feat of intellect.*"

Adiva found this very interesting, but really couldn't focus.

"What's wrong. You look agitated," Rabbi Natan asked.

"I'm alright, Rabbi. It's just that I have a recurrent dream that has left me dreadfully afraid of losing *this* precious book," Adiva said, tracing her hand absent-mindedly over the regular rows of complex, wedge-shaped imprints of black ink. "Perhaps a learned scholar, like your teacher in Tunisia, could tell us what these strange markings in this book mean."

Natan sighed. "I don't know if he is still alive. I accept what you have said about the starburst being a sign for God, but I burn with curiosity to know whose God."

Adiva pondered that for a moment. "I wish I could take it safely to my homeland in Babylon. My father, as the Goan of Pumbedita, has secret friendships with the notable scholars at Baghdad's House of Wisdom.

"One of these men taught me some science and mathematics, in secret I thought." She smiled. "I think he just enjoyed teaching someone that would sit quietly."

Rabbi Natan nodded in agreement. "You speak a truth. I have three sons at home and they would much rather play–or get into trouble–than learn." They shared a laugh.

"Surely your family did not forget to educate you in the proper skills and behaviors needed to be a praiseworthy Jewish wife and partner."

"Oh yes, Rabbi. My mother saw to that." *But it's complicated, Rabbi,* she said to herself.

She changed the subject. "In any case, I shall not return to my homeland, and cannot entrust this book to any traveler."

"Why will you not return to Babylon?" the rabbi asked.

"I miss my beloved family every day, Rabbi, but since I've lived in the freedom of Fustat, I do not wish to return to the oppression of our people that I saw growing up. It becomes worse everywhere Baghdad rules. Here, we mingle freely with Muslims and Christians, and the Netira family even has partnerships with both."

"Yes, isn't it an irony, that, Jews can flee *back* to the land of the Pharoahs."

Adiva closed her eyes, thinking about her decision to stay, conveyed with profound sadness in a letter delivered by Aaron and Hillel to her family in Pumbedita. Though she knew it would do no good, she pleaded with them to escape the tyranny of al-Muwaffaq and join her in a land where they could live without fear.

The rabbi interrupted her thoughts. "Did you know that Fustat is said to be the richest city in the world? I think this is because our three peoples practice all trades side by side, enriching one another."

He took a deep slow breath, exhaling deliberately.

"I'm afraid, however, that ultimately Jews will never be completely safe no matter where they are living. Something will befall us, not now, perhaps not in my lifetime or even yours. But history has taught us the danger. Not even in Eretz Yisrael are we without fear. The Mohammedans detail the hate for us in their holy works, the Christians blame us for killing their savior, even though he was one of us. At least the Romans, back when they ruled, treated us like all the other subjugated peoples–badly."

"But Rabbi, Fustat..."

"Yes. I'm sorry. Fustat is a wonderful place. Muslim, Christian, and Jewish children play together. Most everyone is treated with respect."

"But you can see what can happen back in your homeland. Or mine."

"That is why for Jews, ultimately, there is Torah, family and Am Yisroel, the people of Israel. And of course, faith in Adonai, the giver of all our blessings."

It was Adiva's turn to change the subject. She opened the book to the final leaf.

"Take a look at this," she said. This page has two parallel columns and the markings in each look very different from one another. See this curious line through the first row of markings across all both divided columns. This was a new addition to the book copied from his double-columned scroll of the unknown languages."

"I see. It is somewhat like a manuscript we have here of the Ten Commandments, divided in the middle with one side Biblical Hebrew, the other, Greek."

"Perhaps you might like to study it," Adiva said, "while we look for someone to point our translation in the right direction."

Natan cleared his throat. "I shall write a letter to the Gaon in Tunis. In it, I'll reproduce the top row of this last page. We lose nothing by trying. If my teacher still lives, he may know how we can proceed."

Adiva agreed that it was a good plan.

"This book belongs to my friend, named Eldad ha-Dani. I do not know if he survived the misfortunes that befell us."

"The Danite? That's an odd description."

"He traveled with my brother, cousin and me. Someday in the future perhaps I will tell you the story of our harrowing journey."

"I look forward to it. We shall keep this in a special place, much more secure than the geniza, where treasured things are kept."

"I trust you, Rabbi."

"Only I and the Zoroastrian mason who fashioned it know of the secret crypt. Oh, and my wife knows since our personal valuables are kept there as well."

It was time to leave. "I would like to contribute something to your congregation, Rabbi." With that she handed him the two gold dinars she had thought to bring but hadn't thought to ask Nura if such would be customary. In Babylon, religious and scholarly authorities were all too happy with contributions.

He accepted the coins without surprise. "Your kindness will be remembered by the widows and orphans who will receive this support."

As she left, he called after her. "And Adiva, please consider letting us find you a suitable match. If you are not going to travel home, I think our entire community would be pleased to help. There are many fine candidates to choose from. They in turn would be fortunate to have you as wife."

Adiva smiled faintly. "I'll consider that. Thank you for your kindness."

Outside, the late afternoon sun bathed the sanctuary in golden light, the momentary illusion of floating upward, as the sun was setting.

She turned to her young friend. "Nura, you go ahead. I'll be along shortly."

Finding a quiet place, she felt tranquility and sat awhile. She thought about what the rabbi was saying. Perhaps it *was* time to find a life partner among these wonderful people.

She longed to experience such moments of peace with Eldad. But she knew with each completed day that the promise was fading. She was comforted by a single thought; if she had the choice, her wish would be to spend her last moments on earth with him.

49

Orel was becoming increasingly annoyed. Where was the slaver Mehdi? Each passing moment seemed to remind him of his distaste for the buying and selling of human beings.

He wanted to just call the entire thing off, but looked at Eldad and, for a short time anyway, had a renewed purpose.

"Where is he, Dov?"

His partner just shrugged.

The table had been long cleared, and the children put to bed. Devorah had also retired, although Orel was sure she was still listening for any possible activity.

Eldad sat in the corner on the floor, noose replaced around his neck. His very nature seemed to brighten as the hours passed, but now with the approaching presence of his current master, Mehdi, his demeanor had changed yet again. He was again a slave and his posture and downcast eyes spoke of his status.

"I think I hear something, Dov said, going outside to check. Within moments he had returned with the slaver.

Acknowledging Orel, Mehdi whispered in Dov's ear, causing him to smile.

"Yes, my friend, I still have some of that honey wine from the South."

Orel prepared three goblets, while Mehdi starred hard at Eldad, inspecting his property. The slave appeared not to notice.

Satisfied, he sat on the offered chair.

Orel raised his glass, anxious to get on with the negotiation. It would have to conclude tonight as the slave auction was tomorrow. One of Orel's informants had learned of a bidding war developing between three of the port city's richest merchants. Apparently, Mehdi had convinced them–or maybe their wives–that the presence of the African slave in their household would increase their status.

Orel smiled. "To our success tonight," he said trying not to sound forced.

"Mehdi, do you remember the first time we drank together?" Dov asked.

"It is a day I pray Allah will help me forget! My punishment for ignoring the Prophet, peace be upon him. Why do you remind me?"

"Look, we've done good business since our awkward beginning." Dov smiled pleasantly. "And it's been profitable for both of us. Another bit of this excellent wine?"

"Yes, of course."

Orel could tell that the awkward silence that followed was making Mehdi uncomfortable. His darting eyes searched for some immediate resolution.

Orel and Dov had a plan. His friend was to play the conciliator, while Orel the aggressor. But it was quickly falling apart.

Orel decided not to wait any longer, "This man you bring us, we don't believe you *own* him," he blurted out.

"What Jewish trickery is this? Do you think I stole him? I paid much gold and silver for him, and other slaves and guards saw me do it. For him I paid as much as ten of the other savages."

Probably that was a wild exaggeration, Orel decided.

"And did they tell you how he came to be their slave?"

"I do not care how, but I was told the fire worshipers enslaved a tribe of cannibals, who were about to eat him. I don't speak the African's language to see if this is true. Slavers lie all the time, anyway."

"All *but* you, our dear Mehdi!"

The Arab smiled but didn't laugh.

"Do you know he is a Jew?" Orel asked.

"Yahud? No," Medhi said, looking over at Eldad, whose eyes never raised from the floor. "I can spot a Jew easily. No offense meant."

As far as insults went, Orel and Dov had heard worse. Neither spoke.

"I know nothing of this," Mehdi went on, "and am not concerned with the stories of the slaves I sell,"

"Well," Dov said, nearly jesting, "how many Jews have you sold at Rhapta?"

"What do I care? Whoever saw a *black* Jew, anyway."

Orel looked at Eldad. "He is not like your other slaves, and you know it. Besides, Islamic law forbids the buying and selling of Dhimmis, be they Christian or Jew unless they are captured in war."

Mehdi spread his arms wide. "And who is going to enforce this?"

Whatever hope Orel had for a quick, easy negotiation had dissipated. In fact, their strategy had failed.

Mehdi stood, looking at Dov. "Look, I came here out of friendship and respect, but now..."

"Guard!" he shouted, "Come in here."

He paused, looked towards Eldad. "Take the slave. We must prepare for the morning's auction."

"Wait!"

Orel looked up. Devorah had entered the room. What was she doing?

She stood in front of Eldad, stopping Mehdi's guard.

Orel tensed, poised to protect his wife.

Devorah's voice softened. "Please, Sayid Mehdi. Why don't you send your man back outside?"

With a wave, Mehdi complied.

"I know it is against custom to negotiate with a female, but sometimes you men get twisted around with all this talk of war and slaves and gold, especially gold."

She lowered her eyes in an expression of deference.

She was having an effect. Mehdi was holding onto her every word. Orel was reminded how much he cherished this woman.

"Though you may not own or sell this man, as my husband has made clear," Devorah said sweetly, "you do *hold* him hostage by force of arms."

"Continue, please." Mehdi had shifted anxiously in his seat but remained calm.

"I am saying to you, honored master, that my family is willing to pay a ransom for this Jew's release."

"Ah, perhaps." Medhi slowly nodded his head up and down.

Orel again looked at Eldad. He remained motionless. He wondered, was he following the discussion of his fate?

Devorah moved closer to Mehdi. "We understand you wish to recoup the gold you paid for this black *Jew.*"

"Yes, of course," Mehdi agreed, rubbing his meaty hands together. "As I have said, I paid with my blood for this slave, uh, captive, and another party has an interest, and has offered 38 gold dinars."

Orel took note that in his wine-soaked state Mehdi had forgotten the 'more than 40 dinars' he'd previously quoted.

Devorah moved closer to the slaver. "I'll leave it to you experienced merchants to arrive at an equitable price. I must withdraw to sleep. The children require my attention quite early. Good night."

"Thirty-eight dinars?" Dov said, watching Devorah disappear. "At the auction, this man may bring as many as five gold pieces. Oh, he may go for more than that when those people come down the river."

"Of course, if this cloud hangs over his ownership, a couple dinars are all you'll get." Orel interjected.

"No one worries about this but you. Do not waste my time with childish games, Jews."

Clearly, Devorah's spell had worn off. Orel was on his own.

"For tonight, twenty-five dinars," he said.

"Thirty-five," Mehdi countered.

After significant back and forth, a final ransom of 32 gold dinars was settled upon. This was an unheard-of amount to pay for a slave, Orel knew, but the freedom of royalty might be bought for such a price.

"I want the gold tonight, or I'm not leaving him," Mehdi insisted.

Orel and Dov were sure he was bluffing but decided not to take a chance. Dov would go and retrieve the sum, hidden at a secret location. It was a short but dangerous expedition in the moonless African night, but Mehdi offered his loyal guard to accompany him.

Orel noticed that Eldad had fallen soundly asleep on the floor, rope necklace, sign of slave status, still around his neck. Orel thought about removing it but didn't want to wake him. He wondered if perhaps he was already having the dreams of a free man.

Finally, an hour before dawn, Dov returned. The sparkling gold coins were spread across the table, counted, then put back into a pouch.

"One more thing," Mehdi said, before he put the enormous sum away. "You must not speak of this transaction, neither the amount or the circumstances."

He smiled broadly, shaking his head. "To be outsmarted by Jews. After all, I must protect my reputation."

"Of course, my friend," Dov replied. "We understand. It is between us. Your reputation is intact."

And with that, they watched him head out into the early morning gray.

50

The noonday sun had forced itself into Orel's eyes and he reluctantly awoke still sitting in his chair.

Clearing the clouds in his mind, he saw Eldad continuing to sleep on the floor.

Devorah was hovering nearby as Chava and Yacub looked on. His wife's expression conveyed an unspoken question. Orel nodded in assent.

She reached down to remove the rope from his neck. Eldad stirred, then eyes wide, fearfully tried to pull away. Devorah placed her hand gently upon his shoulder which seemed to calm him immediately, allowing her to complete her task.

She leaned in close.

"You are free," she whispered.

Eldad looked at Orel, as if seeking confirmation.

"My wife speaks the truth."

Tears began to form in Eldad's eyes. He closed them to stem the flow. After few moments, he seemed to gather strength.

"The Lord has delivered me from bondage," he said largely to himself.

He picked up the discarded rope, observing it as one would look at a precious jewel, then tossed it aside.

"It does not matter what you require in repayment, I shall do it."

"To see the joy," Orel said, "of a kinsman freed from oppression is our reward and repayment, Eldad ha-Dani.

"Besides," Orel said, we are not the..."

Devorah cut him off.

"First you must wash yourself. We will provide fresh garments."

She smiled. "For a free man."

She touched his head. "I think I will have to help you wash your hair. It must be a nest for many things. Chava and Yacub, fetch some water and a basin."

Devorah placed the basin on a small stool, then forced Eldad's head above it. She poured water and some soap and began rubbing with her fingertips.

"Come, Chava," she called out, "you may help."

The little one began imitating her mother. Devorah handed the five-year-old the water-softened bar of soap, and put her hand, nails bared, on Chava's scalp, digging in slightly, saying, "Use your nails like this. Ignore complaints and scrub away." Chava and Yacub positioned themselves around the recumbent young man's head, their scouring hands lost from view beneath luxuriant suds. Soon the soap bubbles were all over them, a communal bath and laugh. The women brought pans of heated water from the hearth and made surprise dumps on soapy heads squealing in delight. The children were not alone in this, Eldad's first hours as a free man were spent as a joyful child. Shivering like wet dogs, the children and Eldad were thrown towels and herded over to the warmth of a dancing fire in the hearth. A dry robe allowed the young man to remove his sopping rags and feel the wonder of downy-soft cloth on his skin.

Devorah helped him to sit up. "I'm afraid some of your hair cannot be saved. It is too badly knotted. Yacub, bring the combs and scissors."

Devorah observed Eldad carefully, "Or are you like the great Samson," she joked, "whose hair was never to be cut?"

"I am no Nazirite." He looked at Yacub who wore a puzzled expression.

"Do you know what that is?"

"I'm afraid that none here have the education we desire," Orel said, "But we do our best to be faithful Jews."

Eldad nodded his head, smiling. "A Nazirite like Shimshon ben Manoah ha Dani is dedicated to the Lord's service from birth. Leaving his hair uncut was the foundation of his power. In a tribe of warriors, my tribe, he was the fiercest. And strongest. He once killed a lion with his bare hands."

Yacub gasped. Eldad motioned for him to come closer.

"He was a Judge over all Israel for twenty years and protected us from the Philistines, our great enemy.

Orel noticed that his son's eyes had grown ever wider in wonder. He had to admit that he also was fascinated by the depth of this young man's knowledge.

"Then, he fell in love with a woman, Delilah, who betrayed him."

"What happened?"

"She discovered the source of his strength, and while he slept, cut off his hair."

Eldad gave a quick demonstration with his fingers.

"The Philistines were then able to easily capture him. They put him in chains and made Samson a slave."

"Like you," Yacub said.

Orel marveled at how his son had begun to mature.

Eldad nodded, "But worse. They gouged out his eyes and humiliated him.

"Then, the Philistines gathered by the thousands to celebrate and brought Samson to dance for them. But they didn't realize that, over time, his hair had grown back. Placed between two pillars, he called out to the Almighty to restore his strength one last time. He pressed against the pillars, and they came crashing down, killing everyone, including himself.

"Are you a warrior. . . like Samson? Yacub said.

"No. Although we are a tribe of warriors, I come from a tradition of healers. Somebody must care for those returning from battle. And many others, of course."

"When you told us your story, you called something the seeds of Canaan, and said they were for illness and injury. Is that how you know of these things?"

"The art of using herbs in healing has been known in my family for more generations than we have written records."

"We should let you have your bath, and maybe afterwards

to rest." Devorah said. As usual, she already had guessed what Orel was thinking.

"Yacub," Orel called out. "Enough stories for now. Run and fetch Dov and bring him back to us."

Eldad emerged, freshly scrubbed, and wearing new garments. Looking at him, Orel could not help feeling a sense of self-satisfaction at their efforts to free him and was sure that God would grant him merit for himself and his descendants.

Eldad read his mind. "I must repay you for everything you have done."

Orel smiled, looking over at the recently arrived Dov, "The Almighty has arranged all this, I'm sure. But when we first went to the slave market, the effort was on behalf of Dov, not me.

"He needed a servant to help care for his family, and it was becoming impossible to find someone suitable. That is when he turned to the slaver Mehdi. It was becoming somewhat too expensive, so I offered to help."

Eldad looked more than a little puzzled

"I assure you," Dov said, "that we would have treated any servant as a valued member of our household and according to God's sacred word. And furthermore, I promised Orel that I would never again sell this person."

Orel added, "I also point out that it was Dov here who created the formula for your freedom."

"Do not be troubled," Eldad said. "Your intentions were plainly honorable. And after all, was not Billah, mother of Yakov's son Dan, handmaid to Rachel? Surely, we can see God's outstretched arm in all of this"

Dov was physically relieved. Orel continued to be astonished at the insightfulness of this young man.

"In any case, now you are free and can choose your own path. Orel tells me you have knowledge of the healing arts. That is quite uncommon around here."

"Yes," Eldad replied. "Do you have someone who suffers?"

"My wife's mother. She lives with us and was the reason we sought help from the slave market.

"She is old, probably nearly sixty. But my wife loves her and cares for her and my children adore her. I admit that I, at one time, appreciated her."

"But now?" Eldad said.

"She is in great pain with every movement."

Dov paused. "And she makes everyone know how unhappy she is."

"How long has this been going on?"

"It started out with stiffness, like my wife has sometimes, but then it got worse, much worse."

"There may be plants or herbs that can help. I will see her and then you can help me find what I need at the docks, perhaps amongst the spice traders.

"She also might be the affected by the foods that she eats."

"I will pay any price you ask," Dov exclaimed, smiling. "Especially if it offers my household more peace."

"No need for payment, my friend," Eldad said. "God has granted me a way to repay you for your overwhelming kindness."

"Enough," Devorah announced. "Healer or not, this young man needs some rest."

As if he had been put under a spell, Eldad eyes began to close.

Eldad stretched and ran his hands down his neck and torso, as though to reassure himself this was not a dream. Was he now, full of stomach for the first time in many weeks, going to sleep on something soft? What a lifetime ago he'd taken for granted was a miracle to him now. Dare he hope for another?

And he would sleep with no dreams he could remember, for this was a dream he could not forget.

51

A gentle breeze seemed to blow the morning light through the cave's entranceway, easing Eldad awake from the deepest sleep a free man could possibly know.

His first thoughts upon wakening were of Saul. Dear unfortunate Saul, may God bless him forever.

He closed his eyes in a moment of prayer, but also to avoid revealing the tears that were forming. A feeling of hopelessness overcame him. He had lost his sole possession, the book of strange writings and with it his search for its meaning had ended.

His dearest friend was gone. Saul's soul was surely in the embrace of Almighty God, but Eldad couldn't help wondering if the pain and loneliness would ever end for him and the Israelite Saul left behind.

Now the anguish that he had kept buried, hidden even from his own thoughts, came at him furiously, like shards of broken glass cutting into him all at once. It was the pain of losing his future, the life he was once certain was his destiny. Adiva. He whispered her name in the hopes of summoning her face. But there was nothing.

Sitting up, he focused. Orel and Devorah and their children were looking at him.

He smiled "My friends, good morning. Your kindness has made me feel reborn."

Devorah removed a loaf of bread from a warming shelf in the stone hearth and placed it in front of the family with sizzling beef cut in ribbons on wooden skewers.

Orel took a large chunk of bread. "What will you do now Eldad, now that you are again able to choose you own path?"

He looked at his wife for confirmation. "Of course, you are welcome to stay here as our honored guest, for as long as you wish."

"Thank you for all your kindness."

Eldad sighed. "Perhaps I will attempt to return to my homeland. If that is even possible. Tell them of my friend's horrible fate."

"I understand. If I can help in some way..."

"I must first satisfy my current, great indebtedness to you and your partner, Dov, before I could possibly incur another. I wish to start by examining Dov's mother, the old woman, who is in such distress. I have some ideas how to ease her pain."

"If it be God's will, that would be wonderful, Devorah said. "When shall we do this?"

"Now, if possible," Eldad answered. "While the day is still fresh."

Orel stood. "I will take you there at once."

Orel handed Eldad buffalo hide sandals, the first shoes he had worn in a year and the two of them followed the cobblestone path toward Dov's home.

"He's gone already," Sara said, "but I should tell you he will be at the wharf until midday, then return."

"He's here to see mother," Orel said.

Eldad could hear the old women before they were close. Her repetitive moaning was relentless. A faint odor of old urine permeated the room's air.

Sara ignored her mother. "She won't walk to the pot, most times, and it's not even far," she said, clearly exasperated. "She says she doesn't smell anything."

She pushed Eldad closer, "Mother, this young man is a healer, He might help your pain."

"Who is going to help *me?*" Puah spit out in disgust, "Besides, he doesn't look like a healer to me."

Eldad smiled, then gently took the old woman's hand, turning it over. "Despite the difference in the color of our skin, I am your kinsman. And I very much want to ease your suffering."

Puah looked at her daughter, who nodded, confirming what Eldad said.

He pulled back her covers and removed the knitted socks from her feet.

"You see," he said to Sara, "the purple discoloration, peeling skin and severe swelling of her big toes, and her ankles have the malady as well."

Puah winced as Eldad closed his hand over her right foot and gently moved the ankle.

"This hurts you very much when you walk, but you must not stop doing so." He again held her hand. "Are you willing to let me help you, Safta?" She nodded a silent assent while tears began to roll down her cheeks.

"There are herbs I shall try to find for you for the pain and swelling, but they will not be enough. *You* must join us in the effort to help you."

The old woman sighed, saying, "You are kind, black man."

"You had better wait with that until you know what I demand," he replied, sitting on the bed next to her.

Eldad asked her what she liked to eat and was unsurprised to hear of her love of organ meats and beer.

"Will you hate me for taking these things away? No one knows why these foods make what you have worse. Why do you not drink water? Is it not fresh from wells and springs?"

"It makes me have to pass water. Walking to the pot is agony."

"I know you will not like it if I make you drink and walk, but you must do much of both."

Eldad stood and reached out both his hand to hers. "Let's get up now."

She slowly rose with an exaggerated wince, but little complaint. Eldad closed his hand about her elbow and immediately felt the heat of an inflamed joint.

"Any others?"

"Not now, but sometimes."

Together, they walked about the room. Eldad wanted to know how she spent her days. Puah admitted she almost never left her bed and had lost contact with her few friends, who lived too far away.

"You *must* move more, walk. Then you could visit them."

"I'll try," Puah said.

Eldad thought he detected a little hopefulness in her voice.

"I am going to leave for a while, honored mother. To look for plants that I know will help you."

"We should be off to the market," Orel announced.

"Do you or Dov know traders who might have what I seek?"

"I'm not sure. The Jews of Rhapta are a mingling of Israelites from many places. North Africa, India, even Palestina, the name they now give the land of our patriarchs. Some of us have maintained some connection with our tribal past, but with each passing generation, it diminishes. My family is Persian, from the tribe of Issachar, and Dov's people, the Tribe of Zebulon, live mostly in the Euphrates Valley."

Eldad didn't know any of these places but was fascinated to hear of the existence of the other tribes.

"Are there more?" he said.

"I have heard about some. In the land of the Khazars, on the shores of the Caspian Sea, are descendants of Simeon and Manasseh. East of the Sea, they are joined by the Tribe of Ephraim, in the area of Margiana."

"And the children of Moses the Levites?"

"They are still scattered among us, as ever." Orel answered.

Eldad nodded, knowing this was true even back in his homeland.

Orel placed his arm on Eldad's shoulder.

"My brother, we are really all just Jews now, I think."

'Yes, I have heard this elsewhere. Perhaps you are right."

As soon as they arrived at the south perimeter of the sprawling Rhapta market place, they immediately saw Dov.

"Good morning friends. I wasn't sure you would make it."

"We saw Puah," Orel said.

Dov raised an eyebrow. "Oh. How did that go? The old woman can be difficult."

"She is in much pain," Eldad said. "I think I can help her,

though. Many changes must be made in her diet, her activity. There are plants that can also be of help. I will endeavor to identify what is readily available in this city."

"We have just started," Orel interjected, "Did you have any success with your venture?" Orel asked.

Dov shook his head.

Orel looked at Eldad directly. "Regardless of what you achieve with Puah, she will still need day-by-day help. After all, that search is how we made your, uh, acquaintance."

"Don't you agree?" Dov asked.

Yes, Eldad thought. The conclusion was inescapable.

"I could not find anyone suitable," Dov said. "So now we are back to the beginning. I must visit the slaver. We hoped to keep you away from it. Out of respect."

"I am quite sure he will not be pleased to see me," Eldad allowed, "but perhaps I can help find a candidate."

Dov didn't hesitate. "Mehdi is this way."

Circles of permanent fences pounded into the hard earth-formed corridors to the auctioneer's platform. Eldad was stunned at how different everything looked from the outside–and free.

In only one day, he had thrown off the vestiges of captivity and the feeling that he was somehow less than human. He now understood, in a way that few of his people would ever know, the feeling of exhilaration at the exodus from Mizraim and the removal of the yoke of pharaoh. He quietly thanked God for this gift of understanding.

Some slaves were offered as a group, these usually having more of the sick and frail than the more highly sought-after youth.

And now a new marvel at the hand of God. Barely visible, leaning against a wall, ignored by everyone, was an old woman, a skeleton who like in death had shed her skin.

Eldad's own recognition started him. It was Subi.

Orel and Dov noticed. "What is it?"

Eldad pointed. "It's the old woman who was sold with me. The one who saved my life."

"The cannibal?"

"Like all of us, what she *was,* she is no longer. I owe her my life and now I must save hers."

"It pains me to say then," Dov said, "it looks that she is beyond saving."

"Perhaps, but, I... *We* must try."

The three spotted the oily slaver, not realizing at first that Medhi was already eyeing them with suspicion.

Dov sighed. "Stay back."

Mehdi called for his guards, so Orel and Eldad moved closer, just in case. A fleeting look of fear passed over his face when he realized who accompanied Orel and Dov.

"And what do *you* want?" Mehdi snarled.

"You have an old woman," Dov began, "one you bought from the fire worshipers at the same time as our friend here."

'It was an additional burden forced upon me. Two dinars." Mehdi said.

"You barely feed her, obviously. And you won't be able to sell her at any price. We've heard how you operate, Mehdi. Before long she will just disappear."

Eldad could not understand but saw that a negotiation was underway. But to what end, he wondered.

"I think you have taken enough gold from us," Dov continued.

Hearing the tone, but not the words of this tense exchange, Mehdi's henchmen sidled up to their master, hands on sword hilts.

Mehdi raised his hand and immediately they relaxed. He placed his palm over his chest. "This is what the goodness of my heart tells me to do for you."

Orel translated, which made Eldad laugh out loud.

Mehdi ignored this gesture. "Because of your splendid generosity paying for this so-called Jew of yours, I shall *give* this old one to you."

With a shout, he had the guards bring the emaciated skeleton to her new masters. Within moments she landed in a heap, eyes downcast.

Eldad knelt, took a wet rag and wiped her face. "I thought you were dead, Subi."

She looked up, her eyes growing wide in surprise. A thin smile formed on her face.

"Not quite yet," she said, grabbing her boney wrist.

They moved her out of sight of the slave enclosure–and Mehdi.

Subi seemed stunned, not quite sure what was happening to her.

Eldad pointed. "These are the men who rescued me. And now you."

Subi understood.

"Now what?" Dov said, somewhat sarcastically.

Eldad thought for a moment. He really hadn't considered what to do beyond freeing Subi.

But all at once he knew.

"Dov, this old woman will help Puah and your family."

Dove laughed. "Are you sure this is not backwards?"

"This woman was my helper during our captivity. She has a special ability to learn languages, knows many medicinal plants by sight, smell, and taste, as we were required to forage together for healing herbs."

"It makes sense, Dov." Orel interjected. "After all, this young man can't stay with us forever."

With a nod, Dov agreed.

Eldad turned to Subi. "You shall be the slave of this one's family."

Eldad noted her apprehensive expression. "They are kinsmen."

Subi pointed to Eldad's arm, noting his dark skin.

Eldad gently smiled, then shrugged. He knew Subi had no concept of religion, only the worship of survival, but had always seemed insatiably curious about *his* beliefs. Her vocabulary had been limited at first, so Eldad started simply, with what his people believe is *right* and what they know to be *wrong*. His pupil's intuitive grasp leapt ahead of her acquisition of words.

Subi looked up into Dov's eyes. "How many other slaves?"

For the first time Dov spoke to her directly. "None. Our helpers work for pay as you will. My wife's mother will need your help. You will live with us and we will feed you and clothe you."

"Shouldn't cost much on either count," Dov joked.

"How old do you think she is?"

"She's told me no one knows her age, nor did anyone in their tribe keep track of theirs."

"Well" Orel announced, looking towards the sky. "Perhaps you should introduce one old woman to the other. We will start our search for the herbs that Eldad seeks."

It was a mostly fruitless exploration. Eldad had been able to pick up the odd flower or plant, but although they could be useful, it was not really the right treatment.

"Naked Lady," Eldad announced in front of one merchant.

Orel laughed.

"It is the name of the plant. I know other names for it."

The merchant had never heard of it.

"Meadow Saffron?" The merchant shook his head.

The pair was running out of options.

He suggested they try a Christian Arab, a spice dealer who was sometimes known to have more exotic items.

The pair figured that he at least would know what they were talking about. Besides what did they have to lose?

Most importantly, one could ask him for something without being taken to endless cousins, who didn't have it either, but could offer them "silk so alive with beauty."

They were told to walk away from the water, and let their noses tell them the exact spot. The man they sought had a tent near a baker who had long since departed. Nobody knew why.

The last fire in the baker's tent had been months before, but the musty smell of singed goat hair warned them when they were near the spice merchant, who could now be heard harking his merchandise over the din of voices. Whatever was the spice of the day, was "just off the boat from India!" and surrounding merchants resented the fact that this was invariably true. Today the aroma of his fresh clove dispelled the sour ash of the baker's fire.

Orel nearly shouted over the throng to be heard, "This African is an herbalist from far away and is trying to help our family. The Jewish merchants sent us to you," he lied. "They said if anyone had the healing herbs we needed, it was you."

"Sometimes, the Christians have an affinity with Jews, sometimes not," he explained to Eldad.

The Arab appeared middle-aged, with a prematurely grey beard.

"Come into the tent," he said brusquely. His stall was divided by well tanned leather drapes, and behind them was a ring of chest-high tables with all manner of dried plants, nuts, roots, and pungent cinnamon.

Eldad hunched over one bundle of fern like leaves with bright yellow flowers and inhaled its scent deeply,

"Sweet wormwood, I know this plant. We use it for the relapsing fever."

The spice merchant nodded with approval. "And you wish to buy what today?"

"Meadow Saffron."

The language barrier was becoming a bit of a problem. The merchant went on a bit about the 'jewel-like quality' of his many saffron cooking spices.

Orel blurted out the Arabic. "Naked Lady."

The spice merchant laughed. "I know of this flower, and this is the time of year when it blooms. I do not have this," he paused, "but I do have a cousin!"

52

Kasim, now deeply immersed in a rescue mission for the aging, but still elegant, merchant ship, was surprisingly happy in his first year as ship's carpenter. The owners were wealthy Egyptians, whom no one aboard could ever remember seeing. Their agents would hold private meetings with the captain, leave with written reports and return with the gold to finance the journey. Left up to the Indian-born Captain Tushar to decide, they would begin excursions with Red Sea ports dotting its western shore, then follow the African coastline as far down as the Zanzibar Archipelago and the riches of the Rufiji River Delta.

At every port, Kasim had complete responsibility to purchase any sort of wood, tools, and iron bars with which he was greatly strengthening the creaky vessel's hull.

In a few hours, they would land at Mafia Island. As had become his custom, Captain Tushar invited his bear-sized carpenter to dine with him in the elegantly restored captain's cabin. Because he was often in the cabin, Kasim had fashioned a oversized chair from black and creamy white streaked zebra wood. Tushar noticed with amusement that other crewmen were uneasy sitting in this chair which made them children again, their feet dangling above the floor.

"Tomorrow we'll make landfall at Rhapta where most of our cargo will be sold," the captain began. "Two years ago, in this very place, I had to deal with men who could only be described as slippery eels." Kasim nodded his agreement that indeed he knew this type of man.

"Only the highly unusual goods I offered forced the merchants to deal fairly."

The mostly silent Ethiopian cook placed a lidded iron pot on the captain's table, handing a ladle to Captain Tushar, then leaving as quietly as he had arrived. Curry aroma filled the cabin as Tushar served the steaming fish stew, first to his guest, then himself. Tasting an enchanting first bite, Tushar laughed.

"Our Ethiopian now cooks like my mother! At any moment I expect to be reminded to finish my food, to grow strong."

Kasim chuckled. "I saw this when the fisherman and cook signed on with Captain Mustafa, Allah bless his memory. They are resourceful and adaptable. When we were stranded, their skills allowed us to survive."

"Speaking of survival, I have no reason to believe our safety at Rhapta is any better than we ourselves can manage," Tushar said uneasily. "Even though there are many from my home in Bharat, be it Hindu like me or followers of Jainism or Buddhists. We all mostly get along. Or did in my youth. The Mohammedans see things differently and only want us to follow their prophet. Now, they eye all strangers with suspicion."

"Remember, Captain, we have our secret weapon, the gypsy."

The captain nodded. "He has proved his worth to me. I hope it will continue. But the answer to our success here will be in gaining the trust of someone on the inside of the hundreds of traders at the port. Some who approach you on the wharfs engage strangers so effortlessly that an almost believable illusion of trust develops. They often tell you one of their alluring secrets, sure to excite the greedy and further ingratiate themselves. Our problem is we carry a dozen different types of merchandise, requiring as many connections as possible."

Kasim grunted. "There is no choice but to start with one or another of these dockside rats. If they ask us to follow them somewhere, Ashot will be at arm's length, and Rafik has a natural eye for murderous thieves, as he was one himself. He will remain out of sight and watch behind us."

"When my father traded with ships at the Indian Ocean Port of Murziris, he often heard captains from Babylon, or even China, ask first, 'Are there Jews among your merchants?' If we ask, 'Are there bankers here?' we are sure to attract unwanted attention, but, as is true everywhere Islam rules, only the people of the book ply this trade. Have you ever been around these people, Kasim?"

"Indeed I have, Captain."

"Christians *and* Jews are safer to ask for. What valuables we carry with us will be in Rafik's hands, distant from our party,"

Tushar seem pleased with the suggestion. With an ordinary captain, such direct statements would have to be dressed up with vague suggestions, but Tushar cared little for such stiffness. In so far as it was practical, he sought to make his crew *partners*, with a genuine stake in the success of the endeavor, encouraging their portside initiative to find a bargain here or a buyer there.

Kasim was soon to learn that this is how Tushar came to acquire the most valuable cargo he would seek to sell as soon as he could after docking. No one would kill for the bolts of the finest silk they carried, but they might for what the gypsy had called *sea gold*.

While taking on supplies and a hundred bales of cotton at the Port of Aqaba, Tushar sent men ashore with the assignment of finding a list of the ship's needs, but also to seek goods in high demand at Red Sea and African ports. If the captain bought what they found, they would get an extra share of the profit when it was sold at journey's end. As in every port, Ashot had no trouble finding his own kind, though sometimes they were rival Roma clans.

In Aqaba, it was one of these, and caginess dominated the interchange, after the universal, "I have something of value that will interest you." The colorfully-robed young gypsy was practiced in the art of snaring customers for the 'market without walls', run by his itinerant tribe wherever they went. Seeing nothing to lose, Ashot followed the man to his wagon, covered over by a blood red tent, and inhabited by his extended family, which scurried out when he barked. Even with the flap thrown back, the tent was suffused with a sweet, earthy scent, so unmistakable, Ashot would know it anywhere. It emanated from a rough-woven hopsack wrapped around a foot-square object.

"Where did you get this?" Ashot asked, fully expecting a lie in response. The younger gypsy studied his face, and said, impassively, "From our usual suppliers." Ashot understood this to mean *stolen*, the source of most gypsy prizes. He was having trouble concentrating because of intrusive memories sparked by scent from the bag. He picked it up and removed the thick waxy gray slab almost six fingers thick and held it to his face.

"A rare thing, is it not, kinsman?" began the young gypsy.

Ashot tried to seem only marginally interested. "This ambergris is everywhere to be had in the marketplaces of every port." Of course, never in his life and travels had Ashot seen or even heard of a lump of whale vomit this size. Through the pungent casing of gray wax, Ashot could see the faint outline of a six-inch curved object, and he said, "I've seen better, and without half its weight being from a squid beak." He could not have known how eager the man was to rid himself of this piece of ill-gotten booty. One of his daughters had stolen a pinch, and a perfume she made from it had the other women angry and demanding. Another sibling had gone so far as to eat a blob of it melted over eggs. Even thus pecked at, the lump was stupendous in size and its magnetic aroma spoke of years of seasoning as it floated in the sea.

"I have to return to my ship," Ashot told the anxious salesman, and turned to climb out of the long cart.

"What? No offer for a prize of this rarity?"

"This thing would be a millstone about my neck, hard to sell and troublesome to keep." Then he hurriedly said, "Ten gold dinars, take it now or I go."

"Twelve," responded the young man. At that moment, Ashot realized the gypsy had no idea how much the ambergris was worth, and how rare a piece of this size survived years in the pounding seas. He counted out eleven of the coins and without a word relieved him of the sack. Ashot knew only that, by weight, the worthless-looking gray mass he carried was worth more than the purest gold.

Now, this many months later, Captain Tushar would try to fill the ship's coffers, as well as give Ashot his share from his remarkable find. He told the cook who was clearing the plates, "Bring the first mate."

Moments after the cook ducked out the cabin door, Rafik appeared from the darkness, his eyes darting about, taking in everything. "Sit," said Tushar, and the wily Arab pulled up another of the carpenter's artworks in wood.

"I apologize for not revealing this little secret. It is not a matter of trust I assure you. I thought it better that nobody knew until the proper time."

He pulled out a cedar box that Kasim recognized as something he had fashioned some time ago.

"You know of all the cargo on board, except for one small bundle our gypsy has given us. You crafted this, Kasim, without asking what it was for. It contains a precious block of ambergris."

Tushar opened the cedar box, and the arresting earthiness caused each of them to breathe deeply. "I have decided not to break up this remarkable treasure, though there would be more to earn selling off small pieces."

He smiled at Kasim. "Maybe we *do* need to ask for bankers, after all, since they're the only ones with enough gold to buy this!"

They were still planning who was to do what in disposing of their goods when the Ethiopian fisherman, who was manning the rudder, shouted out that he could see the lights of Rhapta. Their intent had been to stop first at Mafia Island, but the swift-flowing Mafia channel, between the Island and the Rufiji River delta, barred easy entry to the deep-water port. It was easily apparent why Rhapta had been a favored port for a thousand years since the Greeks used the prevailing current to guide them effortlessly from the Indian Ocean to the deep moorings at the mouth of the Rufiji River.

Rafik ordered the sails struck and took over control of the stout pole connected to the rudder, as the floating dock approached. This was the most perilous time of any voyage, when even small misjudgments could spell disastrous collisions with docks or other boats. Captain Tushar and Kasim stood at the starboard railing as the swells from ocean-fighting river lurched them toward the 200 foot floating islands of cedar anchored to bedrock. Leading to dry land, they were so massive they could easily bash the hulls of anchored boats, so Rafik used two anchors to moor the ship a dozen feet from it.

"Well done, first mate," Tushar said, looking on with admiration.

The boat secure, Kasim noticed Captain Tushar's uneasiness when his first mate was first to hop on the planks to the dock. It was nearly midnight in this entirely strange land, where the solitary become prey, but Rafik brushed off the captain's suggestion that Ashot might join him.

Just before dawn, the barely audible creek of gangplanks awoke Kasim and his lightly sleeping captain. The first mate joined them in the bright candlelight of the captain's cabin.

"The lateness of the hour hindered me, as those still awake, quite beyond the time when respectable drunkards are finished, are not inclined to idle chat," Rafik began. "They are suspicious, and tell nothing that does not benefit them directly."

"So, you found out nothing tonight?" Tushar asked wearily.

"One mentioned–hoping for a commission, I'm sure–a Christian Arab, a spice dealer, who might help."

"We must go at once then, while the day is young," the Indian captain said.

The warmth of the morning sun stirred a breeze from the earthen riverbanks, at once seashore fresh and pungent with the decay of rotting kelp. Kasim was last as Tushar, his first mate, and bodyguard alighted before him on the swaying cedar planking of the dock, Rafik ordered the remaining men to pull back the gangplanks. The crew left behind, though they had been told they would be ashore tomorrow, grumbled, as even civilized men would, after months with no women and little fresh food. Of the two, there was always time to *eat* later.

53

A heavy rain had fallen on Rhapta over night, and the cobblestone path leading to the market still conducted rivulets of runoff. The heavy cloud cover was split by a corridor of brilliant sunlight, which seemed a golden path to the jumble of stalls and tents that wove together the commerce of near and far away lands. The air was filled with the after-rain feeling, soothing and invigorating, like standing near a waterfall.

"Subi is everything you said she was," Orel said. "And more. I know Dov is very relieved with how things have gone."

Eldad nodded but said nothing.

"So quiet, my friend. What troubles you?"

"I am lost in my own thoughts. It is a world that I do not understand."

"Is it possible for me to help?"

Eldad looked at Orel and realized that he was serious, no matter the challenge.

"I have observed you and Dov and your families, and children and wonder if it is now my time to find such a life."

Orel chuckled. "Ah, it is a feeling that overtakes most young men sooner of later. A family and a woman to create it with is what truly makes one blessed by God." Orel smiled. "A good woman will keep you warm, nourish your spirit and sometimes, if they are feeling generous, offer you other pleasures."

"I thought that I had found such a woman, but she, like everything else, was taken from me." Eldad felt tears forming.

"I understand your sadness," Orel said, "but life must be lived, no matter what."

"Devorah and I could help you find a wife. I will pay the bride price on your behalf."

"Your continued generosity is overwhelming," Eldad said. "I am hungry for the touch of a loving woman, but I do not know if I have the love to give back."

Entering the market was like falling into a funnel with a thousand other beings, swept into a narrowing pathway. Mud sucked at every slogging footstep, and Eldad again wished the spice merchant had his tent elsewhere besides the exact center of a grid of dozens of irregular rows.

He noticed, but no longer needed, the wet ash smell of the charred baker's tent to tell him he was near. He felt disquiet at the absence of the Christian Arab merchant's steady hawking, but more so, that the huge front awning had been lowered to shut the tent entirely.

A turbaned man stood outside the tent, a cutlass at the ready. He blocked their way.

"What goes on here?" Orel demanded.

The man would not yield. "Step back," he shouted.

The flap was raised, and the merchant appeared. Eldad got a whiff of a powerful, but pleasant smell that he did not recognize.

To the guard he said, "Stand easy, Fatehbir. These two are trusted by me."

"My friends, hello! I'm glad to see you are back. You must wait until I have concluded my business with another." He glanced back toward his tent. "It won't be long, I'm afraid it does not go very well, but we shall see."

Orel nodded his agreement and the two of them moved away.

"Ambergris," Orel said.

Eldad was puzzled.

"That's what we smelled. Comes from the vomit of whales. It's very valuable."

"I have heard of this."

"Judging by the strength of the smell it must be a very substantial quantity. No wonder they are so protective."

They sat for nearly an hour. The sun was now high in the sky.

"Perhaps we should come back another time." Eldad suggested.

"Wait," Orel said. He walked back to the tent, talked to the guard, who opened the flap slightly. Within a few moments, the merchant appeared.

Eldad watched as the two came toward him. They were in an animated conversation.

"It is as I suspected," Orel explained. "The visitors are from a ship docked here for only one day and night. The captain is inside. He is a Hindu."

Eldad didn't really attach any importance to all this.

Orel signaled him to be patient.

"I am assured by our friend here that they are honorable men. They want to quickly offload their small but precious cargo and be off."

Orel paused with a deep breath. "Our friend has not quite gotten around to telling the good captain that he cannot possibly afford such a prize. Most of the discussion to this point was whether they would be willing to apportion it. Apparently, the answer is no."

Orel looked to the merchant for confirmation.

"I will take over the purchase and then split it as our friend and I agree."

Eldad was only beginning to understand the mysterious ways of mercantile trade.

"I will go inside—it is best I am alone—and negotiate."

Eldad patiently waited, listening to the sounds of the market being carried to him by gentle breeze. It did not seem long before the guard motioned them to enter. He raised the flap.

The candlelight within was no match for the outside sun and Eldad's eyes were slow to adjust. Before he could see a face, he heard a familiar voice.

"Is it even possible what I behold? A mirage straight from the sea."

Recognition and sight came to Eldad simultaneously. It was Kasim!

"*What...How?*" Eldad was stunned.

"Kasim, I'm sure you and your black friend have an interesting story to tell. But for now we must conclude our business."

He turned to Captain Tushar and Kasim, saying with resignation, "Your unwillingness to divide your treasure has put it far beyond my reach." Orel spoke immediately, a skillful trader's gleam in his eye.

"Eldad, go to Dov. Tell him we will need to replenish our reserves, and we have to do it now. He'll know. Then return here." Tushar translated for Kasim, who said with rising delight, "I'll accompany him." Hurriedly leaving the tent, the carpenter broke a long silence. Gesturing to breach the language barrier between them, Kasim declared, "You must sail with us!"

"Where?" Eldad gestured, his hands sweeping out.

"Fustat. Egypt."

Mitzrayim? Why would he go there, Eldad thought to himself?

"I may stay here. Or return to my home. Saul is dead."

Kasim seemed to comprehend. Or did he?

"No. No. No. You must come with us!"

"I do not understand."

Kasim stopped walking and faced Eldad.

"Adiva!"

Immediately upon hearing her name, Eldad felt his knees begin to buckle under him. He was grateful that Kasim noticed and would not let him fall.

He composed himself, silently said a prayer of thanks and began to formulate a plan. He had not allowed himself to even dream he would see her again. Adiva was alive!

Arriving at Dov's house, Eldad relayed Orel's instructions. Knowing a most substantial success was dependent on his immediate action, Dov hurried away before Eldad could ask the questions bursting from his mind. He said his goodbyes to Dov and Orel's families, and gathered his few possessions; a single set of clothes, a woven vest holding his medicinal seeds and the leather scroll with double columns of unknown languages.

Dov had already arrived at the spice merchant's tent. Eldad could detect no tension in the air so he was pleased that it appeared that Orel had been successful.

"We must return to our ship," the Indian captain said, smiling.

Orel nodded. "As we discussed, we will deliver your passenger to you shortly. We wish a few private moments to say our goodbyes."

Eldad could not understand and had a momentary fear that his beloved was slipping away, but no, he knew that was not possible.

Orel read his mind. "I made all the arrangements for your passage and have paid the captain handsomely. He will treat you well."

"He who once lived as a slave will now travel like a king," Dov added.

Arriving at the dock, tears of joy and gratitude streamed freely down Eldad's face.

"Shalom, my brothers. I shall never forget your kindness."

He turned and nimbly sprang from the plank to the rocking deck, feeling like Moses rescued from the bulrushes.

54

Nura Netira was growing ever more inquisitive–and aggressive. Each day she pestered Adiva with questions.

"What do you plan to do about these men who stop me at the market to ask about you?"

Adiva knew of her prospective suitors in Fustat. How many were there? Two? Three? Nura was sure to let her know the status of each new prospect. One more impressive than the other.

"My brother is growing weary of being asked as well. Although he says you are dear to him, he will happily arrange a meeting."

"Thank him for me," Adiva said. "I will let him know when I am ready."

Nura frowned.

Adiva could sense Nura's frustration. She understood, at least she thought so. She had become, in Nura's eyes anyway, her older sister, as close as if by blood. The tradition was for the oldest to be married first.

In fact, some of Adiva's potential mates could also be suitors for Nura.

So, Adiva had to admit to herself, why was she waiting? And truly, she was flattered by the attention. She had observed these young men near the market. They were handsome, well-dressed and seemingly excellent prospects. And Adiva could likely have her pick.

She remembered her mother's words, that you must live in the world as you find it, not as you wish it would be. But the problem was, *she* didn't know the world, even now. Perhaps she was just fearful of the future. How long could memories, no matter how compelling, sustain hope and comfort her?

With thoughts of her mother came contemplation of her home. Her real home. She imagined her brother Hillel had put weight on his scarecrow bones, and perhaps had returned with cousin Yosef to trading in the Persian Gulf. She often asked herself if she wanted once again to live under her parents' roof in Pumbedita, forty miles by river from Baghdad. She had been so anxious for the opportunity to leave her father's protection. She vastly underestimated the peril of her journey on the jagged road of adventure, leading her near death, but also to a vision of life to the full and sweet.

It was with these things on her mind when, a little while later, she sought out the Netira family patriarch. "I've been thinking of getting a home of my own," Adiva said, knowing a hail of protests, some quite logical, would follow.

Saba didn't disappoint. "What is the meaning of this, then?"

Adiva was relieved that there was no anger. No matter how much the Netiras gave to her, they never seemed to tire of expressing their appreciation for her delivering the fortune in gold and jewels from their family in Aden.

After 200 years in the port city, the family would soon return to their homeland of Babylon, still a financial stronghold for Jewish bankers.

In the silence that followed, Adiva shifted uncomfortably.

"Who is putting these thoughts in your head?" Saba finally said.

"Nobody, sweet Saba. The ideas are my own."

She always addressed him with some term of endearment, even when he was in the middle of one rant or another. "Your family is now my family, but I told everyone when I accepted your shelter it was only for a time, and a year is much longer than I intended."

"So, you like it here and here likes you. The letter I received from your father two months ago said the same thing as his missive to you. He was very pleased you were under our roof, and most pointed in his insistence you abide by our customs."

"But have I not, Grandfather?" she asked, as innocently as she could manage. Until now, she had deftly avoided the *appearance*, of caring little about their pronouncements.

"Have you written to your honorable father about this dangerous idea?"

"No, Saba. When I left Babylon, even though I had my dear brother and cousin with me, I made it understood that I alone decided what course my life would take. I don't know if my father has ever accepted this."

The old man began a litany of objections. "Who will protect you? You own no slaves and may attract unwanted attention."

Adiva knew she could choose to respond to the content of this, or the fear behind it. In 884 C.E., Fustat was in a state of disquiet, owing to declarations of jihad against al-Muwaffaq, Regent of Baghdad, echoing off the pyramids, and from the mosques throughout Egypt. Caliph Khumarawayh now had a force of 10,000 garrisoned at the fortress of Cairo, a few miles to the east, but the 120,000-person grand capital of Egypt, was nearly undefended. Rumor had it that the Regent of Baghdad, having put down the Zanj Slave Rebellion in the marshes of Babylon, could now turn his attention to their rebellious province of Egypt.

"Who can protect *any* of us if the trouble comes from Babylon?" She had already converted, with the Netiras help, nearly all her assets—her portion of the pirate ship's hoard, the sale of the vessel and her reward—into letters of credit from Fustat's Christian and Jewish banking families who were established in nations as far away as France and Cordova, Spain. Plus, she had ample funds, hundreds of gold and silver dinars remaining.

"Perhaps, instead we should direct our efforts to finding you a suitable husband," Saba said, scrutinizing Adiva carefully.

"Oh, Saba, you are really quite hopeless. You will have more objections than I have *things* to do!"

She suspected Saba would write her father immediately at the yeshiva in Pumbedita, perhaps in the guise of some Talmudic question, but append a casual *I'm sure you have been informed,* or a more subtle, we so miss your gracious daughter's presence in the Netira household.

A breathless Nura swung around the last turn in the staircase, her eyes aglow. She took a moment to calm her breathing, and doused the flame in her eyes, managing a nonchalant, "A visitor is here for you."

"Visitor? Who is it?"

Saba spoke up. "Perhaps it is a very bold suitor for you."

Adiva was relieved when she saw his witty smile.

Nura just shook her head. "No there are three."

The bottom tier of steps reached the ground floor facing away from the ponderous teak front door, now slightly ajar, admitting a crack of bright afternoon sunlight, crisp with the scent of many gardens and the dust of the eternal pyramids.

Surprised neither of the two servants were at the heavy door to open it, Adiva grasped its circular iron knob with both hands and pulled. The angle of the sun cast a giant shadow on the doorstep and her eyes followed it to its source.

"Kasim!"

Standing beside Kasim was the gypsy, Ashot to whom she owed so much. They both looked good and happy.

As if they had choreographed it, they stepped aside to reveal to Adiva, a surprise, an apparition, a mirage in the sunlight.

She blinked repeatedly to clear the tears involuntarily forming in her eyes. The image remained. It was not illusion. It was her beloved Eldad, from the Tribe of Dan.

55

"My princess...oh, my princess," was all an overwhelmed Eldad could mutter. She felt weightless in his embrace, her face inches from his, her emotions changing in an instant from startled to joyous. She wondered how this extraordinary man could be even more handsome than on their first meeting. The contour of his jaw so perfectly matched his high cheekbones. She was breathless feeling his strong body holding hers, and lost any perception of their immediate surroundings, which no longer seemed to matter.

She whispered fragments of sentences, none requiring all the words to be understood, "I feared you were....where, how...could not stop longing for....closer...oh, I don't care."

"Soon, every doubt, every fear, every longing we shall..." Eldad replied so only she could hear.

The bright and flushed countenance of Nura appeared in the doorway. She had been watching in the shadows and now her curiosity could not be restrained.

"Might we be introduced to your friend?" she said.

"Yes, it would be proper." Nura's grandfather along with his manservant had also appeared.

"My young friend is Nura Netira, and this is her...our grand-father." Adiva could see that Saba was pleased by her words. "And this...this is King Solomon!"

They all were laughing as she broke away to embrace both Ashot and Kasim. She motioned to Eldad. "Once again you have saved my life."

"It is the least we can do for you who has done so much for us."

Struggling with his composure, Eldad bowed slightly to the

old man and manservant, and said, "I would be honored to know your names."

"Ah, Ivrit. The sacred tongue," Saba answered. "So, is it true what Adiva says. Though your skin is dark like an African, you *are* a Jew? Please call me grandfather."

"He is from the tribe of Dan, as I told you Saba."

Saba nodded. "Like the Judge, the mighty Samson."

"Yes. Honored grandfather. I don't know what I should be called, but I hope you will accept me as your kinsmen."

Adiva took note that Eldad immediately realized the need to charm the elder.

"Why yes, of course" Saba said. He cleared his throat, hiding his surprise at Eldad's forwardness. "We will need to learn more about you and your people. For Adiva's sake."

Adiva could imagine the letter to her father, already being sent right off to Babylon.

"I'm sure you will find that our beliefs are the same," Eldad said. "That is faith in Adonai, the one God. Only our traditions may differ."

"We'll see," Saba replied.

Adiva rushed up, and wrapped Saba's arm in her own. "That's enough for now, Saba, there will be plenty of time for that. Besides, I'm sure you will learn much from each other."

Saba smiled agreeably.

Eldad continued to charm the old man. "I would be grateful if you could teach me in the ways of which I am ignorant," he said. "I was taught by a great scholar from the tribe of Asher. I can see that you are also held in esteem."

"Asher, you say."

Adiva could see the wheels turning in Saba's head. The prospect of a new pupil, an adult who could occupy his time with endless discussions of faith.

But now delayed, like the thunder that follows the lightning bolt, the name Asher exploded in Adiva's mind. Saul! Where was the Asherite?

She turned to Kasim and Ashot for any clue, but they continued to stand smiling, saying nothing at all.

Capturing Eldad's attention, she mouthed Saul's name but immediately regretted it. The Danite shook his head, almost imperceptibly and his eyes began to moisten.

As if noticing Adiva's growing discomfort, Kasim interrupted. "Perhaps you should show Eldad a little of your new city. I'm sure he will no longer be traveling with us."

Adiva smiled at Eldad. "Yes, good. Let us go, my prince."

"I'll go too," Nura said, excitedly.

"I think not," said an ever-wise Saba.

Ashot and Kasim quickly said their goodbyes after extracting a promise from Adiva to visit the ship and meet its captain. Watching them walk away, the couple strolled off in a different direction.

"Perhaps tomorrow, we will visit," Adiva said. "I wonder how much longer they will live on the sea. They can afford to put their feet permanently on the earth."

Eldad smiled. "Yes. Even more so now. If they wish."

Adiva didn't understand. And really didn't care now.

"I thought you were dead," she blurted out.

"And I was sure you were enslaved. Yet I was the one who was made to be a slave."

Adiva had so many questions. "And Saul?"

Once more she saw the pain appear on Eldad face.

"My brother," he whispered to himself.

"We were both captured by a tribe that eats human flesh. Then Saul's bulk betrayed him."

Eldad closed his eyes. It occurred to Adiva that he was not trying to remember but to block the vision.

"They set upon him. Even from a distance his screams pierced my soul. I was glad when they ended, even though I knew what that meant."

"Oh, poor Saul," was all Adiva could manage.

"I was to be next. I tried to starve myself and resisted all attempts at giving me nourishment."

Adiva squeezed his arm.

Eldad smiled. "I had given up all hope. But the Lord had not abandoned me after all. The tribe of cannibals was set upon by followers of Moloch. I was enslaved, along with a strange woman, a leader of the flesh eaters. Later, I found disfavor with the chieftain of the fire worshippers, and he wanted to kill me."

"Why?"

Eldad smiled. "I guess I was not a very good slave."

They shared a laugh.

"Of course not. You're a prince. My prince."

Adiva was sure there was more to Eldad's story but didn't press.

"So, what happened?"

"The leader of the flesh eaters, an old woman named Subi, convinced the chieftain that I was worth more alive than as a corpse. And so it was that we both were sold to a slave trader and brought to Rhapta, where two Jews, Orel and Dov, realizing that I was a brother, redeemed me and set me free."

"That's an extraordinary tale," Adiva pronounced.

"Not nearly as amazing as the story Kasim and Ashot told about you, my warrior princess."

Adiva could feel herself begin to blush.

"We should probably head back," she said.

"Wait. While we are alone, I must speak."

Eldad had wrapped his arms around her waist. Oh, how much she missed the feeling of him close.

"I can't bear to be apart from you again," he said. "We should be married. At once."

Adiva felt exactly the same way, but it was still jarring to hear the words, now, so soon after their reunion. Did her surprise sound like hesitancy?

Eldad noticed. "I *have* money. My rescuers were also generous with me. Especially after I told them of my love for you."

She held him tight and buried her head in his chest. "Oh, my prince. I'll explain later, but I assure you we will never want for money."

"What then?"

Adiva looked around and found a suitable place. "Let's rest here for a few minutes."

They settled under a lush tree.

"Until a few hours ago, I was making plans to reside here in Fustat. You do not yet understand fully, but Jews need to be careful about where they live."

"I see. In my observation, nowhere in the world is truly safe."

"Perhaps you're right. Where do you want to live?"

"My quest for the answers I sought is certainly over. I think I would like to return home and inform Saul's family of his fate."

"After what we have both been through, we will again travel through the unknown? It's too dangerous!"

Eldad was silent, which made Adiva's head spin in confusion even more. She was thrilled to be with her beloved, but there was no denying that, despite their physical closeness, they were arguing. And she was unhappy.

How silly she felt. She had made it clear to everyone that she was going to be her own woman, yet here she was, acting with no more maturity than Nura.

Reminding herself to be strong she quickly formulated a plan.

"My prince, there is a man I would like you to meet. A rabbi at the synagogue, here in Fustat."

"Synagogue?"

"Bet Knesset. It's a magnificent place, unlike anything you have ever seen."

"Would he marry us?" Eldad said, his mood obviously improving.

"We will ask him. But there is more. He has something to give you, I entrusted him with it when I thought you...Well, I didn't know what to do."

"Yes?"

"It's your book. It's in a place called the geniza. The rabbi has taken an interest in it and has written letters about it."

Recognition began to reach Eldad's face. "How did...?"

"When we were captured, I was forced to reveal our hiding space."

"In the cave?"

Adiva nodded. "The pirate captain kept it." She wanted to spit on the ground. "He probably thought it had value."

"God has blessed me in so many ways," Eldad said.

Yes, Adiva thought, looking deeply into Eldad's blue eyes. Both of us.

Smiling, Eldad rose to his feet, offering his hand of support to Adiva. She felt as light as the wind.

56

"I have your family's book," Adiva told him. "It's in the geniza at Temple ben Ezra. The rabbi has taken an interest in it and has written letters to the university in Tunisia, and The House of Wisdom in Baghdad."

"One little miracle after another follows that book," he replied. "I had the scroll with two languages with me when the cannibals set upon me. She who is called Subi planned to use it, and some other objects she thought precious to me, to induce me to eat. During the weeks in the pit, I was going mad from the isolation and agreed to eat a few meals in exchange for having the scroll. The fire worshippers left it slung around my shoulder when they overran the Romrom, and I have it still."

"You said if you could translate one of the columns, you could learn the mysteries of the book."

"I have studied it until my vision blurs but can make no sense of the strange wedge-shaped marks, except that they do not seem to be like our Hebrew alphabet. The shapes of the symbols in the left column may be letters I cannot yet recognize, since they are so unlike our block letters of Hebrew and Aramaic."

"The rabbi wants very much to meet you and talk about your family's intriguing history. He is particularly fascinated by stories that began three thousand years ago. So is the rest of the world."

"I also wish to see the rabbi about another personal matter." When Adiva last stood in front of the grand synagogue, she was looking for answers—and a solution.

Until now she had wondered what would she do with the mysterious writings that she inherited. She felt responsible for their safekeeping, but even more, they represented the embodiment of her memory of Eldad and, as such it had been difficult, no, almost impossible, to give them into the care of another.

Yet, she had done just that. Her mother and God, both out of reach, had let her know that she must live. Her mother had taught her to accept the life she was given, but God had allowed her to hold on to her dreams. She smiled. Perhaps they had been working together.

Here, at this great building, they would retrieve the book and with it Eldad's quest for his ancestors which would now become her pursuit as well. The stories they would tell their unborn descendants!

"It is as magnificent as you said, my princess." Eldad's eyes were wide with wonder.

"Wait until you see the inside," Adiva replied.

Finally, they were led to the rabbi's study.

"This is a wonderful place for worship," Eldad announced.

"Yes, for study too," the Rabbi replied.

The rabbi already understood why they had come. "Your arrival, young man, has caused quite a stir here in Fustat."

Eldad smiled. "I have noticed the looks."

"I have requested someone to retrieve your book from the geniza where it is being kept safe."

Eldad nodded. He fidgeted awkwardly until he finally said, "I have something else I wish to discuss with you."

"Of course."

"I would like Adiva and I to be married. Could you perform the ceremony?"

Adiva was thrilled to hear the words.

But the rabbi did not look happy. His pained expression was obvious.

"First comes erusin, the betrothal, where the terms of the union are spelled out. Then after a suitable time, we..."

"*How long* is that?" Adiva spoke a little too loud.

"Maybe a year. But even without that hindrance, I can't possibly sanction such a marriage." The Ben Ezra rabbi was immediate with his answer. "I would be stripped of my rabbinate by our authorities in Babylon. I realize your father, the Gaon, cannot be expected to travel here and that he may never forgive me for joining you with a man he has never met, no matter the goodness of him."

The rabbi's smile was ironic. "Why couldn't you have been somebody else's daughter besides the head rabbi of the yeshiva at Pumbedita? Even if he weren't, Jewish women do not marry without their father's blessing."

Adiva's resolve to go her own way was weakening. This was not just from deeply held respect for her father's authority, but rather the image of her mother's face. Though she could convey the depth of love she now felt to her mother, whose heart would understand, she still wondered if her mother would accept not sharing her daughter's dreams? While it would not be a report of her death, it would be the end of *her* cherished place in their life.

Her confusion was interrupted by a soft knock at the door. The assistant had arrived with Eldad's manuscript.

The rabbi reluctantly handed it to Eldad. Somewhat abruptly, a relieved rabbi returned to his previous inquiry of the African's mysterious book. He had received an unusually rapid response from the university in Tunisia. They mourned the loss of their honored scholar, their mentor in the study of ancient languages.

"My teacher has died. The wedge-shaped symbols I copied for them are most certainly much older than any known language. In my teacher's letters, they found recent ones from a renowned linguist in Baghdad. He is a scholar in residence in the largest library in the world, the home to inventors, philosophers, mathematicians, and remarkable translators of ancient languages. Established half a century ago, it is called the House of Wisdom."

"I know this place," Adiva said. "I was secretly taught in a shed behind it. Our teachers from there risked much, educating not only girls, but Jews. Teaching girls was hard enough for them, but teaching Jews was punished harshly."

"Yes," the rabbi added, "the letter from the university suggested that if this inquiry were to be pursued at the House of Wisdom, it would not be by Christians or Jews. The rulers of Babylon have laws forbidding admission of *dhimmi*, we so called infidels."

"I must not only learn the way of Jews, it seems," Eldad admitted.

"Do we dare the journey to my homeland?" Adiva whispered like she was nearly afraid to speak the words.

Things were happening quickly. This possibility had barely been mentioned. Until this moment she never wanted to travel anywhere beyond their glorious Nile valley, pungent with fertility and freedom.

"It is perilous," Eldad said, "but I am certain it is what we must do."

Tears began to form in her eyes, then rolled down her face. Her dear brother Hillel, whom she so hoped had put on weight, her younger sisters, whom she hoped had not, and cousins like fellow adventurer Yosef she would wrap them all in welcoming arms. She did not ask herself what she would do if *some* arms failed to open.

The young rabbi smiled at them. "I hope you find a way of understanding. I know of a man from a town named Sura, on the Euphrates River south of Baghdad, a linguist who teaches at the large yeshiva there. Rabbi Isaac ben Mar will be known to your father in Pumbedita. If there is anyone in Babylon who can interpret the ancient symbols, Ben Mar will know."

"I have visited Sura on many occasions, when my father would take our family with him during his visits to their yeshiva," Adiva said. "The Gaon of Sura would invite him each year to join in learned discussions."

"How will you travel home?" the rabbi asked.

Adiva laughed. "I hadn't thought about it until now, but the elder Netira told me his merchants use what he called the Syrian Trunk of the Silk Roads, from Fustat to Baghdad."

"Yes, I know of this. Couriers bring us letters from Baghdad. From here, it is a hundred difficult miles northwest to the Port of Alexandria, but they say large numbers of merchant ships sail from there up the Mediterranean coast to Tyre."

"Netira has friends, and, he says, a few enemies in that ancient Roman city. Several of their caravans leave each week for Palmyra in Syria."

It almost made the journey home sound simple and easy, but she knew complex and arduous was closer to reality. There were mountainous regions that could freeze a person at night and deserts that could bake by day.

"Will you stay for a few days? Purim begins in two nights."

"No Rabbi, we should begin our journey by then."

"What is this Purim? I have not heard of it," said Eldad.

"We commemorate our rescue from certain death. Queen Esther was a Jewess married to the King of Persia who saved us from the evil Haman. A long time ago. We read her story out loud and celebrate."

"I know nothing of this."

"Yes, well. I'm sure you will learn this and many other things. If I could delay you for a little while longer, I would like to give you a warning. And a blessing."

Eldad looked at Adiva, who said nothing. "Of course," he finally replied.

"The Jews who you will encounter on your journey owe their existence to the men who wrote the Mishnah and Gemara–the Talmud–and those, like Adiva's father, who study it today. Being a Jew is tough and they have established a way of living that helps us to survive in a world that is not always friendly to us. Understand?"

"I'm not sure, rabbi."

"Those sages established a framework that you do not yet grasp. Their followers may not accept your common roots. This is especially true for the scholars among us like Adiva's honored father, who may feel an extra obligation to protect our people's spirit. Still, they are deserving of great respect."

"They may make you angry, or frustrated, since clearly you are a man of wisdom in your own right. But offer them sweet wine whenever possible."

The rabbi stared deeply at Eldad's face, saying nothing.

"And now," he finally said, "a blessing for you both."

"Yevarechecha Adonai Ve'yishmerecha. May the Lord bless you and keep you. . ."

"We are so appreciative of your time and thoughtfulness, Rabbi. Chiam Netira will bring you something I wish to contribute," Adiva said.

The rabbi nodded. He walked them to the stone stairs leading down to the main sanctuary, where Eldad and Adiva paused to take in the beauty of the great marble bemah and the soaring arches that rose above the very place on earth where the baby Moshe was rescued from the bulrushes.

57

When Caliph al Mansur selected the site on the Tigris River to build his capital city, to be called Baghdad in 762, his major consideration was not only its strategic location on the Royal Route coming all the way from China, but the fact that it had no mosquitoes. Hundreds of years before al-Mansur, it had acquired the name of *The Market Held at Sarat Point*, legendary for its monthly encounters of buyers from the west and sellers from the east, as well as its glorious black grapes from its vineyards. The water at this bend of the Tigris had been irrigating fields and sustaining Jewish and Persian Christian villages for many hundreds of years. The word Baghdad meant *founded by God* in Persian.

Engaging the services of two visionary city designers, a Zoroastrian and a Persian Jew, the Caliph told them he wanted to be equidistant from all his subjects. Thus they decided the city shall be round, with the Great Palace of the Golden Gate and the Mosque of Mansur at its center. A work force of 100,000 came from everywhere in Babylon and Syria, and they began by surrounding their new creation with a moat 4 miles in circumference, lining it with kiln-dried bricks.

Ingenious covered conduits brought the gushing waters of the Tigris through an elaborate series of canals to the Palace and the four quadrants of the city. The innermost circular wall enclosed a space over a mile across, the palace at its center. Environs beyond Syria, Basra and Kufa gates were laid out, those quarters west of the circle being irrigated by the Dujayl Canal that coursed forty miles from the Euphrates to Baghdad.

Rabbi Isaac ben Mar had crossed over this canal from the Anbar

Road he had taken from Sura in his reluctant journey to Baghdad. Nearing the city's outer wall, he could not help but again be awe-struck by the immense double iron gates, richer in their history than the sprawling metropolis they enclosed. Weighing many tons apiece, they originally adorned a temple built by King Solomon at Zandaward, later recovered for the building of Baghdad from the ruined city of Wasit. They were said to be 'such as no living man could have made' and required a dozen soldiers to close them.

Just outside the Syria Gate was the Bab Abu Kabisah, the Gate of the Sweepings, so called because in the open space were great rubbish heaps amid all manner of livestock and beasts of burden that languished, awaiting their owners's return from marketing, or selling *them*.

Ben Mar hated having to pass through this revolting place and was sure the Turkish Guards who controlled Baghdad through intimidation and even murder, did not by chance locate it on the only path to the Qantarat al-Yahud, the Jews Bridge. This rose higher above the canal than most nearby bridges, as though trying to rise above its origins at the Gate of Sweepings, and descended into Dar al-Yahud, the Domain of the Jews. The sun was high in the sky, but he knew his business must be completed before sundown, when the Shabbat began in the Jewish Quarter.

The rabbi's primary mission, necessitating the two day's boat trip up the Euphrates and then enduring the 40 miles on camelback along the Dujayl Canal, was to acquire books. The growing enrollment in the yeshiva at Sura had gone beyond their supply of religious texts. Copies of the Tanakh in book form were the hardest to come by, as their production required Masoretes, and their exquisite ability to copy the Holy works exactly. Rabbi Isaac was especially keen to purchase copies of a book compiled by Amram Ben Rav Sheshna of Sura who had first set down the order for daily prayers known as a siddur. Isaac remembered meeting him many years earlier.

There were eighteen booksellers in the half square mile Domain of the Jews, maybe twenty percent of Baghdad's total. All were known, but all not trusted, by Rabbi Isaac ben Mar. His partner in teaching, Rabbi Simhah, had preceded him to the city by a week and Rabbi ben Mar was eager to learn what he had already found.

They had pre-arranged to meet at one of the bookseller's homes on the banks of the great loop canal around Baghdad. As a linguist and collector of books, the bookseller had acquired rare volumes, not all of a religious nature, like one published in Baghdad in 879 called Kitab Alf Layla, the book of the tale of the Thousand Nights, a well-known story rarely seen on paper. Joseph ben Aaron had also found for him a wood block-printed Sanskrit scroll of the Diamond Sutra, the enlightenment dialogues with Siddhartha Gautama, known throughout the East as the Buddha. It carried an inscription which ben Aaron had translated for him: "Reverently made for free distribution by Wang Jie on behalf of his two parents; dated '15th of the 4th moon of the 9th year of Xian tong…11 May, 868."

He opened the door to bookseller Joseph ben Aaron's one-story home and was surprised to be greeted by a broadly smiling Benei Netira.

"Greetings my old friend, what a wonderful surprise," Isaac said, probably revealing more curiosity than pleasure.

Netira smiled, embracing Isaac warmly. "I have received letters from my brother Chaim in Fustat, one of which is addressed to you."

Before he could explain, Rabbi Simhah quietly entered the room.

"Ah, there you are. Safely here," Rav ben Mar said, turning back to Netira. "You might as well read it for both of us."

Through cleverly placed windows, the broad, brick lined Karkhaya Canal could be seen flowing abundantly to its many branches. Often named for the predominant businesses lining the branch waterways, they included the Fowl's Canal, leading to a quarter of the city called the Market of the Poulterers, next to the Butcher's Quarter.

"Esteemed Rabbi ben Mar, I am honored to introduce in advance, Adiva bet Zemah, eldest daughter of Zemah ben Paltoi, yes, the Gaon in Pumbedita. She has been our house guest here in Fustat, and we have come to consider her a member of our own family. We hope to welcome her back. This letter is likely to reach you before she has completed the long journey home. She will be traveling with a gypsy bodyguard, as well as with a young Hebrew man with an extraordinary story. They told us they would stop in Sura. The young man has an endless curiosity about other Jewish communities around the world and how they live. He says it is because they are so different than his own people in Africa."

"Africa?" Isaac interrupted.

Netira nodded.

"He says he is from the Tribe of Dan."

"HaDani?" Rabbi Simhah said, clearly skeptical. "After what, a thousand years?"

Netira ignored him and continued.

"In his possession he has a book—a duplicate of one in his family's possession for so many generations no one can understand its words. It is said to be a story of the earliest Hebrews, from whom his family believes they descend, long before the sons of our Patriarch, Jacob, became the *tribes* of Israel and before their descent into Egypt. A rabbi here wrote to his teacher about this book and the double column scroll the young man also carries with him, but their scholars knew nothing, except they believed the book's language was quite ancient. The rabbi was aware of your reputation as a translator of ancient languages, and thus did he send them to you."

Ben Mar smiled. He could not help but be pleased that his reputation had traveled so far.

Ben Aaron's wife entered the courtyard followed by two female slaves bearing plates of fruit, three-cornered poppy seed-filled pastries, and a steaming pot of tea.

Rabbi Simhah gently picked a pastry up. "I've been waiting the entire journey to again taste these delights."

Ben Aaron's wife nodded pleasantly and quickly left for the kitchen with the slaves in tow.

The three men enjoyed the pastries and fruit as they gazed at a square-sailed boat drifting lazily down the broad canal toward the Tigris. They spoke for a while of other things, like the unpredictable assaults on Jews and their property in Pumbedita, which the Muslim rulers now demanded be called by its Arabic name–Fallujah. Benei Netira was still highly influential in the Royal Palace of Baghdad, because many of the older Turkish Guards, completely in charge there, were investors in all manner of his enterprises. He and his partners were trusted advisors, and often lenders to the Royal Court. These loans were secret, as the Messenger of Allah had condemned both the collector of interest and the payer as well.

"I would appreciate one, or both, of you writing me a letter about your impressions of this rather mysterious man who now travels with the Gaon's daughter," Netira said, "to pass along to my brother, as well as sharing what you observe with your Gaon, Zemah ben-Hayyim. This may help you decide what to say to Rabbi ben-Paltoi. They know each other well."

Shabbat was falling on the Jewish quarter and none of the other 17 booksellers would breathe a word of business after sundown. Netira rang a tiny bell left on the tray, the tinkle as faint as a whisper, and suddenly both slave women appeared.

"Summon Master Joseph," Benei asked them. When the young man appeared, Netira said, "Joseph, the Rabbis would like to use your gracious home for a meeting with travelers who may stop here in the next few days. Your Uncle Chiam and I would like you to offer them lodging for their days in Baghdad." Everyone knew they were not related. The elder Netira was 'Uncle Chiam' to many.

Joseph seemed pleased by the prospect and nodded with delight at the prospect of meeting exotic travelers.

"And one other thing," Benei announced. "According to my brother, Eldad ha-Dani is dark as an African. He does not look like any Jew we've ever seen."

58

The three weary travelers rested for a brief time on the west bank of Tigris River.

Eldad marveled at the great scene before him, unlike anything he had even imagined. A swarm of many thousands of boats ferried people and all manner of living, squealing, braying animals across the 250 watery yards to the old city.

He had been told when they started up the Euphrates about the place of the dhimmi in this Moslem society, and how it was ruthlessly enforced. Now he could see with his own eyes that their dress was conspicuously different from most of the thousands of people surrounding them.

A four-inch square of yellow cloth had been sewn to his robe, front and back, the sign he was the slave of Jews. His belt was cloth, not leather, which could carry a dagger, and his 'owner' was dressed head to toe in bland, yellow cloth. No other color was allowed, nor could it show from under the infidel's robes. They passed an occasional Christian's slave, bearing the four-inch square of blue. Ashot had simply laughed, shaking his head when invited to sew on the yellow patch. His clothes were clearly gypsy, and under the outer flash of his rough woven red blouse, he was wearing a leather belt.

"I cannot imagine how such walls could be built", Eldad said, as they waited for an available boat. "How do they stand? The outer wall must be 60 feet high or more, but I can also see another rampart in the distance that towers over it and must be 100 feet."

Adiva smiled. "I remember them. They were built well over two hundred years ago. As a girl, I used to get annoyed that the only way we could enter was at certain gates, spread almost a mile apart."

Adiva pointed to the shore at a string of barges spanning the river. "We could have gotten in the line of miserable humanity waiting to cross on the Main Bridge of Boats, but that would take us many hours. The upper and lower Bridges of Boats are even worse. We'll have to pay whatever pieces of silver the boatman demands. "

They found a saucer-shaped reed vessel that rocked perilously in the brisk Tigris current. The price was three pieces of silver for crossing the Tigris in it. The wind off the river caught the triangular sail and they were soon crossing the wake of the vast flotilla that united Baghdad's eastern and western shores.

"Ferry us to the tip of the Bent," Adiva told the boatman, using the local term for the spit of land where the Tigris *bent* sharply south.

"That's another piece of silver. It's harder and takes too much effort to return upstream," the leather-skinned boatman grumbled. Ashot tensed and his hand moved almost imperceptibly toward the opening of his robe. But of course, as usual, Adiva was in control.

"For that much silver, you will take us up the Great Sarat Canal, to its juncture with the Little Sarat."

"To the Patrician Mill?" the boatman asked. This hundred millstone grain mill was known as the remarkable feat of an ambassador from Greece, whose engineering and hydrology skills he used to please the Caliph. Highly educated and refined, the ambassador was called *the patrician*.

"Yes, there," she replied, handing him the additional silver dirham.

As Eldad sat quietly, cross-legged in the saucer-shaped reed boat, a strange thing began to happen. The pouch he had strapped to his side, carrying the mysterious book, felt noticeably warmer, and an odd vision flooded his awareness, as though an overlay on his surroundings.

He closed his eyes in the bright sunlight and a vivid scene appeared. Two men were with him, one young, tall, and strong, the other, small, old and frail. He could see the old one's face, but seemed to be doing so through the eyes of the youth. Dressed in ragged togas with one shoulder bare, both men are securely roped around one ankle to the reed boat, which is, itself, tied to a floating caravan of other such lowly reed vessels.

Without hearing words, he knows what each is saying. *"I am called Sumanu, a scribe in the Royal Temple at Ur. Or what was once Ur."*

"And I am Adu, the healer they call the Akkadian."

The vision is unaffected by the occasional jolt of a larger boat's wake. The old one said, *"When they next tie us up on the riverbanks, gather all the clay you can, and on tablets made from it, you shall tell our story."*

And then, as abruptly as it had intruded, the vision ended, as did the feeling of warmth from the leather pouch.

Eldad noticed Adiva's puzzled expression. "I saw a vision of long ago, two men tethered to a boat like this, captives being towed upriver. It was here at this spot." He touched the pouch strapped to his side. "And I believe they are people of this book."

"Like your dream in Palmyra. You told me you saw an old man digging with his hands at the base of granite obelisk. Is it the same old man?"

Eldad thought back to what he could remember of that restless night, the voice in his head repeating, *"Go north, to Ebla."* They had asked among Palmyra's Jews what this might mean, but no one knew, earning them only odd looks.

"No, not the old Akkadian, but there was a likeness of features with the young scribe, though many decades older. I wonder..."

Another round boat on a perpendicular course crossed too close in front, hooking their craft long enough to set them spinning in the current. On the second turn, their boatman threw rotten vegetables and curses of one's father, mother, or the lowly animal who bore them, at the receding offender.

Their course righted, they soon stepped ashore on the Sarat canal, where the High Road of Anbar led to the great Syria Gate. The boatman claimed he could get them no closer than this north-west mooring and Adiva agreed. "It's faster and safer anyway," she whispered, "to reach the Syria Gate by entering through the

Kufah Gate and crossing the inner city to the Jewish Quarter in the northwest."

Even at a hundred yards, the pair of outer walls looked insurmountable, as they were meant to.

"You see the defects in the outer wall?" Adiva asked, pointing to poorly repaired gouges in the outer rampart. "Two caliphs fought in a siege of Baghdad more than thirty years ago. This is their work." She laughed mirthlessly. "I'm told the winner was soon assassinated by the Turkish guards, who replaced him with his son, Mu'tamid. Our glorious caliph now hides from them at Samarra, 100 miles north on the river. The governor of Baghdad is the Caliph's brother, al Muwaffaq. He makes all the decisions of state. But even he has little control of the Palace of Mansur's cadre of guards."

They approached the stone bridge over Baghdad's outer moat. "To see the Palace and great Mosque of al-Mansur, we will pass through five gates..."

She stopped abruptly, staring speechless at the bridge. Eldad and Ashot followed her eyes to a pike, taller than two men, with its handle driven firmly in the ground. The point of the spear bore a bald head, deeply embedded with brown resin, its mouth showing snarling teeth. At eye level, Ashot read the Arabic sign to Eldad. "See Wasif the Eunuch, a Zanj slave who rebelled and died in Matbak prison."

"This is the notorious main prison of western Baghdad, between the Basrah and Kufah Gates," Adiva added. The head had evidently been there so long none of the other passers-by took notice.

Safely across the 40-yard wide, rapidly flowing moat, they now approached the great southern highway, the Pilgrim Road, which started at the Kufah Gate and ran the length of Babylon to Mecca and Medina. Before the first of Baghdad's two outer walls, they smelled the pungent barnyard surrounding the Dromedary House. Next to this squat building was the larger rough stone Istabl al-Mawai, the Freedman's Stable.

"If we need horses, we can buy them there," Adiva said, "although it is forbidden for Jews to ride horses." Passing through the first defensive wall, she remarked, "This is not the original circular wall, and was built after the siege. This entrance to the city is called The Gate of the Horse Market."

They could now appreciate the massive second wall, 50 yards distant, and nearly twice the height of the first. On its summit, wide enough for two war chariots to pass, were eight-foot turrets at 60-yard intervals for the entire circumference of the old city, nearly two and a half miles. Not only could sentries see many miles in every direction, but they could also rain grief down on intruders who breached the outermost rampart. Defenders could easily see the forty-foot-wide road along the inner side of the first wall, and the paved square between the ramparts, offering no place for an enemy to hide.

Though Adiva barely glanced at the familiar sight, Eldad was awestruck at seeing the domed-shaped cupola of the towering gate-house flanked on all sides by four story porticos. Clad in gleaming green tile and topped with a black iron weathervane, its vaulted inner ceiling was 75 feet above the floor. From the hall beneath the cupola, they could see the glint of gold leaf swirls painted on the inner dome. Colossal teakwood doors on foot-thick hinges guarded the inner archway of the Kufah gatehouse.

Passing through the arch, the Jewess and her slave were accosted by two Turkish Guards. As had become their custom, Ashot walked a few paces behind them and did not come under scrutiny. Hearing nothing of what the guards said, Ashot continued to brace for trouble, but he perceived there was no immediate threat. Standing with his back to them, as though waiting for someone yet to emerge from the cavernous gatehouse, he shifted his weight impatiently while edging closer.

The heavier of the two guards, whose wrists were as thick as his meaty hands, looked up at the taller Eldad and addressed him in Arabic.

"This infidel's property doesn't look like a slave. Tell me of your duties, slave." Eldad knew well by this point the word for slave but wasn't quite sure what was being asked of him. He looked uncomprehendingly at the guard, then glanced towards Adiva.

"He does not speak Arabic, only his African tongue."

Eldad understood his role. He was not to speak. As a slave from a strange land, his role was clear. Remembering his experience, he lowered his head and slumped his body.

The smaller guard brandished his curve-bladed sword. "He won't have a tongue for long anyway if he's hiding a knife."

Adiva had already warned them about what comes next. First the search of their persons, and then the automatic discovery of coins and jewelry that would soon disappear.

Adiva had observed this secret form of low-level bribery but had never actually experienced it. Women did not usually carry anything of value to avoid trouble.

Ashot seemed incapable of understanding their orders for strict restraint, but reluctantly agreed to let them be victims.

"We carry no weapons," Adiva said emphatically. She was ignored. She carried a modest number of inch-sized silver dirhams, and Eldad the slave's drawstring bag held lesser value copper coins, making it much heavier than it was valuable. What other assets they brought with them from Egypt were beneath Ashot's robe, securely fastened to his illegal leather belt. He would not have minded gutting these two paragons of law and order, should they presume to search an itinerant gypsy. The crowd in the 30-yard square flagstone courtyard, surrounded by walls 60' tall, was easily observed from the porticoes. People gave wide berth around the guards and the objects of their attention, looking the other way to neither see nor be seen. All except the unnoticed gypsy, six feet away, his short, thick body barely disguising its combative tension.

The guard with the thick wrists quickly found both pouches, but in removing Adiva's, he trailed his sausage fingers over her breast. Smirking at her revulsion, he was jolted as her shrill voice split the air.

"Stop!"

They laughed at her outburst at them, but Eldad could see indignation was not her purpose. From the corner of his eye, she could see Ashot withdraw his hand from the opening of his robe.

He was breathing hard and perspiring, but quickly obeyed, resuming his act of looking for someone in the plaza.

Adiva must have seen Eldad's rising anger.

"Do not fight if they touch me again," she said in Hebrew. "Act scolded and contrite."

Turning back to Arabic, she feigned desperation for the guards, who were dividing the coins.

"You leave us with nothing," she pleaded.

They laughed at this all too frequent plea of destitution, and, turning toward the upper story of the white marble portico, raised an open hand which then became a grasping fist indicating a successful robbery. In case they were still being watched, Ashot walked ahead ten paces. Now they were moving freely down the broad avenue, beneath a barrel-vaulted arcade from the Kufah Gate all the way to the gates of the central palatial and governing section. Dozens of permanent stalls lined both sides of the avenue, with many streets that seemed to flow with branches of the great canal. Merchants clamored from densely-packed spaces, and the flowing throng of shoppers would deposit customers at their desired destination.

"Before we get to the inner-city gate, I should explain something," Adiva said. "We'll pass the streets of the Water Carriers, the Horse Guards, and even the Criers to Prayer. There is the strange custom here of each type of merchandise having a street of its own, each run by merchants who will have nothing to do with those who peddle other kinds of goods. Neither will a merchant sell anything other than *his* kind of merchandise, on *its* particular street."

Now another sight caused Eldad to stop where they were on the bustling avenue. They stared in awe at a triple life-sized, charging horseman, his spear menacingly pointed forward. Mounted atop the tall, green marble and tile dome of the central palace, the warrior could be seen even though they were a half mile distant. It reminded Eldad of the first time he had seen the pyramids.

"His javelin is said to point in the direction from which enemies come." Adiva said. "It should really be pointed downward toward the Palace where Caliph Muwaffaq, the real menace, resides."

In the final few yards before the inner-city barrier, it became apparent it was no rampart, but rather just a tall stone wall meant to promote privacy within its mile-diameter circle.

Adiva said to Ashot now walking beside them, "Your coming close to the Turkish Guards barracks is unsafe for you as they prey on anyone who looks different."

"And for them!" the gypsy shot back

Adiva sighed. "This is what you must do, my faithful friend," she whispered. "Give the Danite and me the second pouches of valuables we prepared. For the next few days, you will fade into the surroundings of the city, but in three days, begin coming each sundown to the Gate of Sweepings."

Eldad noted Ashot's confusion.

"Find your people, as they are no doubt nearby a metropolis like this, perhaps several clans, and even women who might be fascinated by your travels. Although I doubt they will, I don't care if the gold dinars you carry for us disappear, but I hope some will do so in the service of your pleasure."

Adiva blushed. "If you know what I mean."

"Indeed, I do," Ashot said. "I will see you in a few days."

With a nod to Eldad, the laughing Romani disappeared down the wide road that circled the inner city.

Now it was just the two of them. Adiva had little more than a vague notion of how to get to the Jewish Quarter, but she knew for their own safety they should arrive by nightfall. Eldad was not that much help, stunned by the city's overwhelming complexity, but was willing to put his faith in Adiva.

She did not disappoint. They had, as yet, no way of knowing if the letter of introduction written by Chiam Netira had even reached his younger brother, but they had his instructions given to them in Fustat. They included directions to the home of the bookseller.

They carefully maintained public guise of slave and master, and she reminded Eldad to be sure to walk a step behind her, forcing him to follow her lead. It made even simple communication difficult.

Emerging from the ornate stone gate to a broad brick paved

roadway lined with elegant buildings with soaring Arabesque arches, their doorways shuttered by tile-encrusted gates. Adiva stopped in front of one with tall wrought iron fencing. "This is the Bayt al-Hikmah, the House of Wisdom."

Eldad nodded. He recognized the name of the place where, he was told, his book might find a translator, as the scholars assembled therein were known to study manuscripts from all over the known world.

"When I was taught mathematics and science as an adolescent by two of their teachers, they were quite revealing about what went on behind this marble façade. Their bitterness stemmed from their alliance with the former superintendent of the House, an ingenious code breaker, named al-Kindi. My teachers were working at the observatory in this building when al-Kindi was brought encrypted texts written in a substitution code. He soon determined that certain letters in a text occur with predictable frequency He called his breakthrough *frequency analysis.* The reason I mention this is...."

Eldad interrupted "Yes, I see. It may be a way to start understanding the ancient symbols in my book. It may help if the writing is some sort of alphabet. Tell me why the scholars were embittered."

"They said al-Kindi was a wise director, a philosopher, mathematician and physician to the Caliph, until three brothers, called the Banu Musa, caused his ruin. They were renowned for their invention of automatic machines, like a flute player using hot steam, and a hundred others, described in their Book of Ingenious Devices. My teachers said the brothers coveted al-Kindi's personal library, filled with priceless manuscripts. The scholars taught us illegally to spit in the faces of the Banu Musa who forbade it."

"Without a contact person, it doesn't sound like they would talk to a Jewish woman and her black slave at all, much less help translate some very ancient text," Eldad said ruefully.

"Perhaps my father will know one of their resident scholars. They translate Greek, Aramaic and Persian into Arabic, and the man he knew many years ago translated Hebrew documents. He was notable for having devised a system for organizing the House of Wisdom's vast number of books by *type*, the first library to have done so, my father says. There are thirty other libraries in Baghdad now."

Eldad gazed down the arrow-straight road that led through many blocks of homes, small shops, food vendors and clothes merchants to an open space free of buildings, a quarter-mile ring about the great Palace of al-Mansur. He was again struck with the awesome power of the spear-bearing horseman charging enemies from atop the highest dome in the absolute center of the largest city in the world.

"Except for that horseman, there are no animals since we came through the stone gate," Eldad observed.

"And you will see none. Only the Caliph was allowed to ride in the inner city. Since the Caliph is exiled from Baghdad, only the horse soldiers who guard the Palace complex have mounts."

They had now entered the open space and the spectacular Palace, 200 yards on a side, came into view. The afternoon sun flashed on the highly polished green tile dome of the central Palace building, ten stories above the ground, from which not only the giant iron horseman but also sentries stationed at portals watched many miles of the Tigris River. Nestled next to the grand Palace, about half its size, was the Mosque of al-Mansur, the first built in the round city. Its highly polished teakwood roof contrasted softly with the dominant green dome of the Palace.

"You see the great Mosque?" Adiva said. "Perhaps because the city's architects were a Zoroastrian and a Jew rather than Muslim explains why it does not face the Kiblah, the Mecca point, as every mosque should. I wonder what al Muwaffaq did about *that* a few years ago when he seized all the synagogues in Baghdad and turned those that were big enough into mosques."

Eldad took her word for it. "The Tribe of Dan has no synagogues, no buildings of worship–or buildings at all. We are in the thousands, so there are many tents where we worship. The Torah binds us together, *not a place*, because the Tribe moves in its vast lands with the change of seasons."

"Do you miss your life with the tribe, and with your family?"

"My heart hungers for the warmth of my family's love, and daily I think of things I wish I could ask them."

Eldad walked along the road following the inner wall in silence. He knew he must say something. Abruptly, he stopped, and dropped the servile guise long enough to turn her toward him. "I'm not going back, not ever. My beloved family knew and accepted that. No, they *wanted* that, wanted me to be away from wars they fought year-round with bordering tribes. But if it were *paradise*, I would not leave your side for it."

Adiva's eyes told that him that his words made not stepping into his arms nearly irresistible. What was passing between them, even at arms length, would be obvious to a casual observer, but at that moment, neither cared.

59

The two rabbis had returned to the home of the bookseller. Fueled by steaming coffee and twists of fresh-baked bread sprinkled with cinnamon, their conversation seemed full of anticipation.

"Have you thought about what you might ask this young man," Rabbi ben Mar asked his fellow teacher.

Simhah shrugged. "First, do we even know that he is truly Jewish?"

Ben Mar nodded. "If the people of this strange visitor were isolated from mainstream Judaism for a thousand years, what religious law would they follow?"

"Perhaps he is a follower of the doctrines of Anan ben David, Simhah said. "You must admit it would make some sense."

"A Karaite?" ben Mar shook his head. "How then, my friend do we account for his dark skin? We know Karaites living right here in Baghdad."

Adiva, entered the room along with the mistress of the house, interrupting what had promised to be an enlightening exchange for her.

Both men stood, bowed their heads.

Adiva smiled. "Good morning, learned teachers."

"Good morning to you, my child." Ben Mar was embarrassed as the word left his mouth. He cleared his throat.

"No rabbi, I am no longer the little young girl you remember," Aviva said. "Although I sometimes feel like it still.

"Let's go to the courtyard by the shade beneath the tree. It's such a wonderful spring morning."

And soon it would be well into the oppressive summer she

hated so much, Adiva realized at that moment that her mind had not fully followed her body back to the land of her birth.

Adiva sensed his presence before she noticed him. He was standing with their host, the bookseller.

It had only been a few hours, but she missed him.

"Honored rabbis," Joseph ben Aaron said. "I would like to introduce you to our other guest. This is Eldad ben Mahli ha-Dani."

Adiva thought the silence that followed uncomfortably long while the two rabbis looked Eldad over. Seeming not to notice, he just took a seat and smiled pleasantly.

Adiva knew it was time for the three men to speak in private. Her presence would make the two rabbis uncomfortable. She had not forgotten that this was her father's world.

"I shall return when it is time for a meal." And with that she left.

Finally, Simhah spoke up. "We have heard a little about you, but we are anxious to learn more."

"And I from you," Eldad replied.

"I don't know what Adiva has explained to you," Rabbi ben Mar said. "We and our contemporaries are inheritors of a tradition going back to the time of the last temple and most importantly, after its destruction, by the Romans. What the sages began all these centuries ago, we teachers continue to study and pass on to another generation.

"Adiva's father, the Gaon, is a leader in this great effort."

More silence. Surprisingly, it made Eldad nervous.

Rabbi ben Mar sighed loudly, then exhaled in an exaggerated manner. "Chaim Netira has told us about the document that you have written. He calls it the Talmud of the Four Tribes."

Eldad nodded. "He asked me to write it before we left. It concerns our laws about the proper way to slaughter animals and what we are permitted to eat."

"May I interrupt?" Simhah said. "We can get back to that. But some...many of our colleagues insist that you are Karaite, coming to deceive us, especially our youth."

Eldad expressed no emotion. "I know nothing of this."

"There are people living among us who reject the rabbinic

teachings. They will only accept what is written in the Torah and reject the validity of our laws of Jewish life and everything else."

"I can't reject what I don't know," Eldad said. "On the contrary, I want to learn about your teachings. I hope that we will come to realize that we are one nation of Israel."

This seemed to move both rabbis and their faces softened.

"But how do you explain your dark skin? Simhah said.

"Yes, it does not help that I look African, if by nothing more than the color of my skin makes me less of a child of Jacob. Over the generations, we have won many battles over our neighbors and slain many great warriors. Their wives and daughters became one with us. It is that way since the days of Joshua ben Nun and his defeat of the Amorites."

He paused as if remembering something. "When I was a child, my father used to read me passages from something, I think, was called the Book of Jasher."

"*Sefer ha-yashar?*" ben Mar exclaimed. "We only know a *tiny* fragment of this."

"I will write down what I remember. We are a simple people trying to live as best as we are able honoring the Almighty's commandments. We have no great civilization nor impressive buildings, but live off the land and sustain ourselves with his word."

Our King is Adiel ben-Malkiel, and there is a prince Elizaphan of the House of Elihab. We have no bloodline rulers, so the title of king cannot be inherited."

"And this royalty," Simhah asked, "are they absolute rulers with the power of life and death?"

"No, this rests with a judge named Abdan ben-Mishael, who has the power to inflict the punishment of death as prescribed by tribal law. I learned in Egypt from Chiam Netira that your Talmud forbids it. I could not agree more, but our opinion on this, and practically everything else, is never asked.

"As a people, we believe we are descended from Hushim, the son of Dan."

"After the death of King Solomon, his son Jeroboam began

warring with the Kingdom of Judah, and he demanded his ten tribes of the Nation of Israel bear arms against fellow Israelites. The Tribe of Dan refused and gathered its people to leave the Holy Land, en masse, and forever. The Tribe also feared subjugation, if not enslavement, by the Assyrians whose rising power they could not ignore."

"First, the Tribe moved across the trackless desert to Egypt, then south to the safety of the vast expanse of West Africa, as my people say, beyond the River Kush. The Tribe of Dan sheltered and joined forces with the Tribes of Naphtali, Gad and Asher as they fled the Assyrian siege of Jerusalem. They are in close alliance today with Tribe of Dan, sharing the burden of border wars with other tribes, each being in the field there."

"This Talmud of the four tribes," Simhah said. Tell us more about your ritual of slaughter?"

"My people believe there are 18 Terefot, conditions that render an animal unfit to eat." Eldad removed leather pages from his satchel, said, "I have written these for your keeping and study. I hope you can read my writing; my letters are quite different than yours."

The rabbis pointed, exchanging quizzical glances at some unfamiliar point in the document. "I thank you for this gracious gift to our yeshiva," Rabbi Simhah said, holding the papers tightly. "I can see why Chiam thought this would be fascinating to us."

"He was sure you would be." Eldad smiled. "When we spoke at length in Fustat, the rabbi said the tehorot, the purities, made no mention of the conditions I described."

"Such as what?" Simhah took out a quill pen with a small bottle of ink and began making notes on pages of paper he always had with him.

"We inspect the animals before slaughter, watching especially the way they move. If the goat, or sheep, or cow is seen persistently turning to one side, we suspect a condition we call 'gid'. After slaughter, you must examine the fluid from its meninges. If it has the appearance of meat cooked in water, and, upon adding salt to it, gas bubbles appear, the animal may not be eaten."

"We do not know of this, isn't that right ben Mar?"

"No, but it sounds like we should," the senior rabbi replied, "Did you often slaughter animals?"

"No, I did not, but was frequently called to look at odd things found on opening the animal's body cavities. I am from a family of herbalists, who are the tribal healers. My grandfather taught me the insides of every type of animal we slaughtered for food, and a good many we did not eat."

"I would be called to view such anomalies as a gallbladder leaking fluid on the caudate lobe of the liver."

"And this single defect, this would render the animal impure?" Simhah asked.

"That is so, along with other conditions I describe in the pages you are holding."

"What birds will you eat?"

"Only pigeons," Eldad replied. "We are taught that the only fowl acceptable as tribute in Solomon's Temple were turtle doves and pigeons. We have never seen doves, but we raise many pigeons. Some are used as messenger birds carrying tiny scrolls of information over battlefields."

"What other books do you have besides the five books of Moshe?" ben Mar asked.

"We have many books that tell the stories of our people. Some like the book of Jasher I mentioned. I remember also one called the Book of the Wars of the Lord."

Simhah gave ben Mar a quick glance, but neither spoke.

"But how could you know of things hundreds of years after you departed Eretz Yisrael?"

"There must have been some communication. My Zav thought so. It was so long ago; it had been lost to us."

"My son, if you are to be believed," Simhah said, "and I believe that you should be, all this has important implications for Jews everywhere."

Eldad chose this moment of good will.

"Forgive me for changing the subject, Rabbi ben Mar, but you are one of the main reasons we have traveled here."

Ben Mar raised an eyebrow.

"You're renowned as for your study of the earliest origins of the written word."

" I guess that's true. I don't know how renowned."

"Come, my friend." Rabbi Simhah interjected. "You know he speaks the truth."

Without another word, Eldad loosened the strap holding the pouch and opened it, removing the leather-bound book, and handing it to the rabbi.

"This is an exact copy of a many-page document passed down for generations in my family. We believe it tells the story of our family's origins, but that may be a myth, as no one in the many generations who have faithfully copied and recopied it could read a word."

Ben Mar carefully opened the parchment pages and looked puzzled. Then the older rabbi seemed to withdraw in intense concentration. After long minutes of silence, his tightened features relaxed into a pleasant glow of satisfaction.

"I know of this wedge-shaped writing, but this is unlike any I have ever seen. It seems to be as old as the hieroglyphics of Egypt, and like them, no one knows what it says. I'm afraid you may have come an ever so long way without finding what you want."

Eldad heard the delicate rustle of clothes, saw the rabbis' eyes focus behind him and knew that his beloved Adiva had returned. His disappointment in ben Mar's words was tempered, maybe even canceled by the joy he felt.

He could see that her presence had an effect on both Simhah, in his '40s and ben Mar, in his '60s.

"Ah, you have returned," ben Mar said, taking the small plate of food offered. "I meant to tell you earlier. Though I know your esteemed father only from attending rabbinic debates, I am old enough to have to have been a yeshiva student four decades ago when your grandfather, Paltoi ben Abbaye, was the Gaon of Pumbedita. I recall your father Zemah climbing trees at Sura to dangerous heights, horrifying the poor Gaon."

Adiva smiled. "He died before I was born. I know how influential he was, even as far away as Spain and North Africa."

"I'm sure you know that most of the Jews in the world look to your father for guidance," ben Mar said. "Some follow other teachers, like those remaining in Eretz Israel. Still others. sadly, no one at all."

He looked to Eldad. "And what rabbis guide your people, young man?"

"The tribes of Dan, Asher, Gad, and Naphtali have no rabbis, but our spiritual education is passed on from generation to generation by our elders."

"My grandfather was called an *elder* and met with their council for decades, until he outlived all his friends. He admitted to me that he had begun to question some of what they were teaching."

"He struggled with demons of doubt?" ben Mar asked. "It is a learned man's fate that the more he learns, the less he understands."

Eldad nodded. "He began to believe that true understanding of God cannot be achieved by any feat of intellect. Perhaps, he said, we should spend our limited mental energy on trying to fathom how God wants us to live, to treat one another and the world we live in."

"I, too, have wondered if we do some things that may have been useful for the ancients, but are now only quaint reminders of ages past," ben Mar admitted. "For example, despite Torah's teachings, few men are willing to marry their brother's widow."

Adiva now spoke up, "Don't you think it was an effort to prevent her from marrying someone else, thus losing the family name and influence over the brother's descendents. Many times, it is not marrying, but *possessing*."

Simhah audibly gasped, looking at Adiva with disapproval. "Surely your esteemed father does not speak of our revered customs in such a way."

Adiva did not back down. "He is determined, through reason and life experience, to understand the deeper meanings of our rituals and holy laws. His judgments in matters of observance are much sought after by the Jews of Babylon and from distant lands, as well. To arrive at these decisions, he will start arguments among the Pumbedita yeshiva's inner circle of thoughtful scholars. I have witnessed times where the motive for this marriage of brothers to widows has been vigorously discussed."

"I am surprised a woman concerns herself with such things," ben Mar said, without rancor.

"My father has his own vision for the role of women in *everything,* and literacy is the cornerstone in the struggle against the ignorance of the ages. My mother began teaching me to read at age two, she says, and I could read Torah when I was six."

"I still struggle to understand the imperfections in mankind it portrays. So did my father, who taught us the same paradox of man's nobility and brutality plagues us to this day. He made me understand that belief could change behavior, but not change man."

"Is it your father's notion about educating the women in his family different from other rabbis?" Rabbi Simhah asked. "Should all women be taught to read, even in the poorest families?"

"Though he makes no proclamations about it, neither is it a secret that he believes we squander the productivity and creativity of our women by keeping them illiterate. He does not fear the power women acquire if they can read and write."

"Do you know how a man like your father, so steeped in our tradition, came to this unorthodox view?"

Adiva laughed and said, "He married my mother!"

60

The evening meal was a welcome respite from the day. The two rabbis had been relentless in their scrutiny of Eldad and he was both physically and mentally exhausted from it.

To his surprise, the night turned jovial, perhaps aided by delicious wine that was served. Ben Mar and Simhah regaled Eldad with stories from the Talmud beyond just discussions of the law. Aggadah, they called it.

He was fascinated by the thousand years of Jewish history of which he knew so little. It was not lost on him that increasingly he was thinking of himself as a Jew. He wondered if Adiva had noticed.

He was told of the Roman conquest of Judea, of the Temple destroyed, of the Roman's carting off its most sacred artifacts and of how Roman soldiers laid siege to a place called Masada, a mountain stronghold where hundreds turned swords on themselves rather than be taken as slaves.

Ben Aaron stood up and returned with a book, written in a language unknown to Eldad.

He turned its pages carefully. "What is this?", Eldad asked.

"It is an account by a man named Yosef ben Matityahu," Joseph ben Aaron answered.

"We know him today as Josephus," ben Mar added. "It was because of his writings about this history that we know so much about what happened during that tragic time."

This led to a discussion about Christians. Eldad had certainly met a number of them but never well enough to know what they believed. He was surprised to learn that Christians worshiped a man who was born a Jew and that they considered him the son of God.

Eldad didn't quite understand but accepted the premise.

"Here, though, Christians are also considered infidels by the Mohammedans, just like we are," ben Mar explained, "We have often incurred their wrath."

"Why is that?"

"The man they revere as their Messiah was executed by the Romans in Jerusalem, but some Christians blame us. Plus, we cannot accept their beliefs," Simhah said.

Ben Mar nodded in agreement. "Ironically the early Christians started out as Jews. The Romans detested us because we resisted their yoke. But they came to hate the Christians even more because they subverted their empire from the inside."

The two rabbis looked at each other and stood.

"It is time for us to leave," ben Mar said. We are staying with one of my former students who lives nearby."

He hesitated, taking a deep breath.

"I am sorry, young man, that I wasn't able to help you with your ancient writings."

Eldad smiled. "I understand."

"I regret that I have no contacts, no fellow scholars, at the House of Wisdom, but I did have a thought. Bien Netira has many business dealings with the scholars who manage the institution. I believe you have met his brother."

"Indeed," Eldad said.

"Netira tells me how impossible dealing with them is, that they are worse even than the Sura Yeshiva. But almost everyone who does business with Netira owes him something, and likely the House of Wisdom is no different. Simhah and I will see him briefly tomorrow and will prevail on him to help if he can. He surely knows of the great debt owed to Adiva bet Zemah in saving the family assets in Aden."

Eldad looked at Adiva and they shared a silent moment.

"You are so very kind to try, though I realize it may be futile," he said.

Darkness had fallen and the fresh scent of spring's luxuriant flowers blooming in the courtyard drifted through the open portals. The table dispersed.

"Good night then," Adiva said, dropping her hand to touch Eldad on the arm ever so slightly before the servant led her away.

Eldad couldn't take his eyes off her for one moment as she left the room.

61

The floor was cool and the mat that lay on it comfortable enough, but Eldad's mind would not let him rest. There was so much he had absorbed throughout the day and yet so much more was left to be learned. Questions only led to new thoughts and queries. Was he in the Rabbi's eyes a Keraite or worse a pretender to the mantle of Judaism?

As a diversion, he made a conscious decision to focus instead on his beloved Adiva. He easily conjured her beautiful face and form and should not have been at all surprised when he became aroused.

At some point, however, he fell into a sleep too deep for dreaming, yet again a vivid intruder from an unknown time filled his awareness.

He and Addu are running toward a patchy-bearded man named Eliezer, whose sickle-shaped sword slashes the face of a camp defender. He points with the dripping blade to the southeast where a contingent of his comrades tells us to keep running and not stop for anything. Lot and nine other prisoners are just ahead in their flight toward a cluster of boulders at the base of a hill.

The clash of swords and cries of the dying fill the Elamite campsite behind them. The main body of Chedorloamer's army is rapidly closing the distance between the camps, ready for pitched battle.

Seeing this, Eliezer commands his troops to withdraw, leading them down the road to the south, at a sharp angle from the direction we are running. As soon as the Elamites commit to that path, he shouts another command and his warriors suddenly disperse, each in a different direction, some into the darkness of the wooded mountainside, while others disappear behind huge black rocks strewn across the landscape. Clouds blotting out

*the moonlight make it impossible for the Elamites to follow or even see
the disappearing raiders.*

Though still asleep, when his physical sensations should not
trouble him, Eldad felt a weariness, as though it had been he running from captors. This dream—is it his history, or the irrepressible
illuminations of sleeping consciousness—was then more real to
him than the waking world, its colors more vivid than life and a
darkness that could be felt. He stirred, but did not awaken, and
another scene lit up his inner landscape.

*Sumanu walks through the tents of those who follow the only holy
man he's ever known. He finds Adu seated before him with Sumanu's seeds
he had brought to Adu early in their captivity from his grandfather's vast
store of healing plants, which he calls seeds of Canaan. Sumanu knows
it is time to say goodbye, and the thought tears the fabric of his being.
Seated on the huge black tent's brightly colored, woven blankets, he listens
intently to the old Adu's explanations of the healing properties of herbs
grown from the seeds in the small leather pouches before them.*

*Tears form in his eyes. "Today I must begin my journey to find my
people, if God has made his face to shine upon them."*

The two old men search for the proper words.

*Adu spoke first, saying, "You have learned much, noble Sumanu. Your
hands are steady and your mind clear." He bows slightly and continues,
"I am honored to have taught you the sacred art of the azu, as you will
in turn teach it to others. The seeds of your wisdom, like those of your
healing plants, will be carried by your descendants to all earth's people."*

*The chieftain now stood, placing his long, graceful hands on
Sumanu's head, filling his body with a sustaining warmth that stilled its
trembling. "Blessed is God the Creator, by whose eternal light we live.
May he bring you peaceful days in your youth and beyond. If tears fill
your nights, He will bring joy to your mornings. May you dwell in the
house of the Lord forever."*

*A quiet falls like silent thunder. There is no need to speak. Bathed
in light, he prays to God to lead him home.*

Eldad awakened with a start. Fully alert, he could not tell how
long he had been asleep, though he thought only a short while.

He quickly determined to write down this lucid vision before the cloud of deeper sleep could erase it. He knew that he had heard the voice in the dream once before, during the strange experience he had crossing the Tigris in the reed boat.

He wrote quickly, recalling the words as though they had just been spoken. He thought it unusual that any dream could be remembered with such clarity, since he recalled only fragments of other dreams, even sensual delights he only wished he could remember in detail.

Eldad wondered why he was dreaming of characters from the Torah, one of whose names he hadn't thought about for a decade, and another whom he barely knew from somewhere in Genesis. Eldad again felt the unexpected sense of familiarity with the young man, Sumanu, and began to suspect these dreams were from a coherent story of another life he had lived in the distant corridors of time. He had only his intuition to tell him that the mysterious book he carried told the rest of it.

Finally, after writing everything he could remember, he lay his head down and was again asleep as abruptly as he had awakened.

No more dreams awaited him. Nothing until the sensation of being shaken woke him once more. But this was no dream. Standing over him was Rabbi ben Mar, vigorously rocking Eldad's frame, first by his shoulder, then his whole body.

He opened his unready eyes and saw that the sun was out, but not too high yet. "Rabbi, what are you doing here?"

"Rabbi Simhah and I have been given the honor of introducing you to people you should meet."

Ben Mar looked around at Eldad's papers tossed about in some disarray. "Gather your things and then meet us in the main room."

He pointed to his face, moving in a circle. "I will send the bookseller's servant with a basin. A little water would be in order."

Eldad nodded meekly, then watched the rabbi walk out. He rolled up the parchment he had written, adding it to scrolls which contained what he could recall from the other worldly, herb-induced experience with the mysterious woman of the Tribe of Gad. He recalled his dream in Palmyra during which a gently commanding voice pointed him north to this unknown place of Ebla. He hoped these fragments of a story would prove of value, should Netira secure the cooperation of the House of Wisdom. In his most honest moments, he allowed himself to doubt anyone alive could read the text. After all every generation of his family believed it was from their earliest roots. No one knew exactly how deep into history these roots reached, but there was a certainty that the family's healing arts had been passed down from the early times of the Tribe of Dan. But the writings he carried were from long before then. Upon entering, he surveyed the room. Standing next to Adiva was a slightly older woman with the same lovely face, her eyes wide with surprise. An identical look, mingled with barely hidden alarm, crossed the face of a tall man behind her.

Eldad knew at once he stood in the presence of his beloved's mother, and standing behind her, struggling with his composure, was the most influential rabbi in the world.

62

For a painful minute, no one spoke or moved. Perhaps sensing a delicate family scene unfolding, the visiting rabbis quietly excused themselves. As they said their goodbyes, they both glanced at Eldad. Each wore a faint smile. Were they offering support or sympathy? Eldad couldn't be sure.

He stepped forward and bowed slightly to the woman, looking to Adiva for reassurance.

"I am pleased to meet you, honored Rebbe and Rabbanit."

Aviva's mother smiled. Her expression was warm and friendly. The Rabbi's face on the other hand, remained tense and stern.

Eldad decided to get straight to the point. "I know I am not likely to be exactly what you expected your daughter to bring home, but..."

Rabbi ben Paltoi cut him off with a wave of his hand. "Our son Hillel has told us about you, although we never expected to meet you, especially not traveling in the company of our daughter. He said you were as dark as an African and spoke like an ancient Israelite. I can see both those things are true."

Eldad remained silent.

"Well," the Rabbi said. "Perhaps we could continue our discussion a bit later." He looked toward his wife, then to Adiva. "We are thrilled to see you, my daughter. The news of your well-being is scarce these days."

"I am sorry, Abba." Adiva shifted nervously. "I am well, but I have found a life far away from the oppression of our homeland."

The Rabbi frowned. "So I understand. I have been asked to send a young scholar from here for consideration as suitable mate for you or at least help choose from among candidates in Fustat. There are a number I'm told. And yet you have refused to even consider such a match."

This sort of talk was making both Eldad and Adiva very uncomfortable.

"Later, Zimah," Adiva's mother said, placing her arm gently on her husband's.

The effect was immediate. His face seemed to soften, and he nodded his head.

A maidservant appeared from an unknown direction. "My master has told me to serve you anything you need." She pointed to chairs in the next room. "Would the Gaon and the other guests like hot tea?"

She poured and ben Paltoi dismissed her.

Adiva reached over and took her mother's hand in her own but looked directly at her father. "I didn't expect to see you here in Baghdad. Why have you come?"

Dinah answered for them, "Although your letter told us you were coming, it said nothing of when, so it is not why we came. The governor of Fallujah, as they insist we call our beloved city, has begun to survey our Yeshiva's land near the Bedita River, including all buildings of learning and dormitories for many of the poorest scholars."

"He is claiming them as houses of infidel worship so as to confiscate them if and when he wishes," the Rabbi added. "Our yeshiva has been there six centuries., before the Mohammedans even existed."

Adiva's mother continued, "When al-Muwaffaq reissued the tight restrictions four years ago, he converted Pumbedita's two synagogues into mosques, leaving us nowhere to worship, except the homes of prominent Jewish merchants. Now, they too have been threatened."

Adiva's father shook his head, "We cannot continue to attract the brightest Jewish minds, neither students nor teachers, when this whole center of learning could be lost overnight. We have now taken the first steps to move our 600-year-old yeshiva here to the domain of the Jews. It's painful."

"I shall miss my childhood home in Pumbedita," Adiva said wistfully. "It houses generations of family memories."

"Eight," her father clarified. "Going back 200 years. It just reminds us that Jews must always be ready to carry their culture with them to find a better world."

Adiva said, "Fustat is a better world, Father, where Jews find peace and prosperity."

"Yes, it is said to be a better world. But it is not *our* world. Our people's roots in Babylon are ancient, from the time of the exile and the destruction of the first Temple where Ezra returned to Jerusalem and restored Torah to the land. It was at the Academy where our sacred writings were woven into the fabric of Jewish history."

"But, dear father," Adiva answered sweetly, "The word of God came to the Israelites in *Egypt*."

Ben Paltoi smiled in silence but was clearly proud of his daughter.

The Gaon sighed. "It is our eternal struggle, it seems, to maintain our faith. And our way of life no matter where we reside. Even in Eretz Yisrael."

"If we didn't have trouble enough from outside forces, there are those from amongst our own people that would deny the authority of Mishnah and Gemara to establish the guidelines for Jews to practice our faith. And live properly."

The Gaon looked directly into Eldad's eyes.

"So, tell me young man, what is any of this to you? Are you even a Jew?"

"*Zemah!*"

Dinah looked at her daughter apologetically.

"Forgive my husband, Eldad. He is a great man with great responsibilities. But he sometimes forgets that he has two families. The flock out there and the one he shares with me."

Ben Paltoi touched his wife's restraining hand and nodded. "I have always to be reminded that I am not the chief rabbi here. My father, Paltoi ben Abbaye, thinking himself the Gaon of his own family, was rigid and authoritarian at home. But Adiva's mother showed me a much better path to contentment."

Eldad realized that he had been given an opportunity to change the subject but chose not to. "Respected Rabbi. I have been brought up to think of myself as a Danite. Every time I am referred to as from the tribe of Dan, it honors my parents and theirs before them."

He had the Gaon's attention. "Go on," he said.

"I traveled with my friend who was an Asherite. His father was my teacher."

Eldad paused and quickly wiped a tear from his eye. "He was murdered by cannibals."

"Later, when I was enslaved..."

Dinah interrupted. "You were a slave?"

Eldad nodded. "Yes," he said softly. "I was without hope and believed the Almighty had abandoned me. I was redeemed by two Jewish merchants, Orel and Dov, who paid handsomely for my freedom. Orel's family is Persian, from the tribe of Issachar and Dov, the Tribe of Zebulon. Both call themselves Jews, and I have come to understand that their tribe is little more than a family designation for them."

"Very interesting," the Rabbi said, "but what are you trying to say?"

"At first, to hear myself called a Jew was confusing. *Yehudah?* I am not from the tribe of Judah.

"Now I see we are one nation, one people. Like in the time of King David."

"In Fustat, Chaim Netira told me of a great sage of the past named Hillel the Elder."

"He was born here in Babylon," Zemah said.

Eldad paused to consider this. "I am told Hillel said, 'If I am not for myself, who will be for me? And being only for myself, what am 'I'?'"

Ben Paltoi smiled and added, "And if not now, when?"

The storm among them was for now just over the horizon.

Muttering and scurrying of servants drew their attention to a dining area, where the long table for as many as twelve was being set with covered platters, the curved lids releasing lines of steam, pungent with the spices of Babylon. This aroma had already attracted Rabbis Simhah and ben Mar, who were shooed out of the dining room by the lady of the house, pending the readiness of all guests.

Dinah gave her husband a raised eyebrow and a look of impatience, as all were waiting for him.

Rising and needing no second gesture, Rabbi ben Paltoi led them to the alluring table where each stood in front of a high-backed chair while hot loaves of twisted bread were placed before them.

Eldad waited to be shown where to sit. The rabbi came close behind him. "Young man," he whispered. "You seem very wise. Know that Hillel studied forty years before he became known as a great voice of our people."

Eldad turned to address him, but the rabbi was no longer at his side. He wasn't sure why ben Paltoi had said that to him.

Ben Aaron, as he usually did, brought up the subject of rare manuscripts. It gave Rabbi ben Mar an opportunity to bring up Eldad's book

"Zemah, the young man has a curious relic from his family he has shown to me. It is an exact copy of pages, written in a language too ancient for me to recognize. It has been handed down for many generations. Isn't that right Eldad?"

Eldad nodded. "It is my family's tradition that these pages tell a story from long before Yaakov, his sons, and the descent into Egypt."

He placed the bound leather pages on the table. "This is all I have brought with me from my world. It is agonizing to me that the words of him who wrote this may never be revealed."

Ben Paltoi picked up the book and gazed intently at tightly organized rows of wedge-shaped symbols. He looked at Eldad, seated across from him. "Perhaps my daughter told you of how my, how would you say, little gifts to the House of Wisdom allowed us to penetrate their walls of learning."

He smiled. "Two scholars risked everything to teach infidel

children, and right under the noses of their masters too. They both died a few years ago. Each was a brilliant teacher of science, mathematics, and astronomy.

Though they left no traces of even knowing me, I know the name of their younger colleague, whom they said had grown suspicious of the little extra of everything they seemed to have. He *wanted*, but never got, a little extra, too."

"And perhaps he might know someone?" Eldad asked.

"No, this arrogant puppy *is* someone," ben Paltoi said. "I was told as long as ten years ago that his facility with ancient languages was beyond what anyone in the House of Wisdom had seen in its six-decade history. And as is too often the case with younger generations, he knows it."

Adiva spoke up. "Boys, boys, always adding contests to ordinary business dealings. Perhaps gold's gentle touch would engage our scholar's attention outside his usual translating duties."

"He may just take your dinars and push you aside, ben Mar said, "they have that reputation. We would be powerless to stop them."

Adiva looked into Eldad's eyes and smiled. "We have a friend, one who returns to the Gate of Sweepings nightly. He enjoys taking care of situations like that. No, this scholar can refuse our offer, but he will not simply steal our gold."

"I am always cautious in dealings with the Mohammedans," ben Aaron said. "Though they are often honorable in commerce with me. I do not wish to be *too* untrusting, but perhaps this translator would see this as a rare and valuable book and try to profit handsomely in its sale to some vulture."

The bookseller paused.

"Like me!"

He waited for the hearty laughter he had caused to abate.

"Suppose we kept eyes on our scholar by inviting him here, to *ben Aaron's* House of Wisdom, if, indeed, he can even do this translation."

"This may take him *some* time," Adiva cautioned.

"That's alright," Eldad said, "it's been waiting three thousand years."

63

From Rabbi Isaac ben Mar to Gaon Rabbi Zemah ben Hayyim, most honored and esteemed in our eyes:

Greetings of peace. May Heaven show compassion to you, your children and all the scholars, their students and our Israelite brethren who live there. As you and our yeshiva's benefactor requested, Rabbi Simhah and I met with the traveler who calls himself Eldad haDani. I shall mention Simhah's report in this letter, but a much more detailed rendering of his observations of the traveler's dietary halakah will accompany it. The courier is a gypsy in the employ of Adiva bet Zemah ben Paltoi, who shall wait in Sura for your response to questions he has handed you. These involve prices being demanded for books since there are no more Jewish houses of worship in Baghdad. We have had to resort to buying overused works, in particular Nevi'im, the book of the Prophets and the Writings contained in Ketuvim stored in genizas.

Our meetings with the young African held many surprises, not the least of which was the young man's language. I do not believe he is an Ethiopian Jew from Beta Israel as he does not speak their Ge'ez. He says he is from beyond the rivers of Kush, by which he may mean what we know as the Nile. I was fascinated by documents he wrote for us, which are much like our Talmud's Tehorot, especially the laws of food purity. Simhah believes Eldad's 18 Terefot bear more resemblance to the Talmud Yerushalmi than our own Talmud Bavli. But some, Simhah has said, resemble neither.

Neither has anyone known to me ever heard a dialect of

Hebrew such as he speaks. Some of his words are from an older form of Aramaic, like the language of significant chapters in the Books of Daniel and Ezra. Other words which I have read but never before heard spoken are Phoenician, likely older than Hebrew.

Finally, his written and spoken, language has Arabic constructions in grammar and syntax. Unlike *our* Hebrew, he places demonstrative pronouns–like these and those—*before* their nouns, and not a few of his words are Arabic, as well. But having analyzed his elegantly written and spoken language, I do not believe he could have *made up* a dialect of Hebrew. Adding to our impressions of authenticity is Simhah's conclusion that Eldad ha Dani has brought us the laws of purity from a *real* nation of Jews, 'till now lost in the mists of time.

My heart soars at his tale of other lost Tribes of our brethren—Gad, Naphtali and Asher—united in Judaism and fighting together under a banner that proudly declares, *Hear O Israel, the Lord is our God, The Lord alone.* Beyond these four tribes, he has direct knowledge of the Tribes of Issachar and Reuben, whose lands stretch from the mountains of Persia to the Euphrates Valley. If this is so, where else have our people been hidden for a thousand years? Could the Jewish Khazars around the Caspian Sea, as both they and the Roman historian Ptolemy claim, be descended from the Tribes of Manasseh and Simeon?

I believe this information is rich teaching material for our Academy at Sura. As you are aware, there are gaps in the history of our people, especially after violent conquests of our lands, and I am hopeful my meetings with a traveler from half a world away will illuminate these darkened corridors.

I should say that Rabbi Simhah and I found our most esteemed Gaon of the Academy at Pumbedita to be preoccupied with reestablishing their yeshiva in Baghdad. Though our situation in Sura is slightly different, he asked that you begin to consider the safety in numbers in this city's Dar al Yahud. You and our staff have discussed moving certain assets of the yeshiva from Sura to the care of Benei Netira, who again yesterday urged we act upon this. Netira has sent ten gold pieces with this letter to aid you in this effort. Ashot, the courier who brings this to you, is a safer alternative than an armed caravan, and a great deal more trustworthy.

Rabbi Issac ben Mar

Wordlessly, the two teachers watched Adiva's trusted man Ashot, carry off the letters to Gaon Rabbi ben Hayyim.

"Well, my friend," ben Mar said smiling. "Should we resume our search?" "Yes," Simhah replied. "We haven't even scratched the surface of Baghdad's more than 100 book sellers, not to mention the libraries. There are over thirty, you know."

Ben Mar nodded. "We desperately need those books. Many are counting on us."

"It's funny. The Prophet Mohammed declared us to be the People of the Book. Now it seems we Jews are the people *without* the book."

The most prominent of the Muslim booksellers was also a scholar at the House of Wisdom, and it was there they had agreed to meet him this morning. The two rabbis were instructed to use this contact to secure an introduction to the masterful translator, Musa ibn Ishaq, who had somehow escaped Caliph al-Mulawakkil's purge of those who denied the status of the Qur'an as 'uncreated and co-eternal with God'.

These crushed Mu'tazilites, whose branch of Islam was based on reason and rational thought, included some of the House of Wisdom's brightest minds. Now disgraced and harassed like so many infidels, they disappeared in the choking fog of orthodox Islam. Revelation had triumphed over reason.

Disdainful of *all* manner of religious belief, Musa would not have escaped persecution by al-Mulawakkil's soldiers but for his singular ability to read military codes in exotic languages. Shrewdly, he had taught no one else his method of doing so. Being the son of the House of Wisdom's most famous translator, Ishaq ibn Hunayn, young Musa had been tutored by the master code breaker, al-Kindi, whose system of frequency analysis ended the secrecy of substitution codes. Musa's particular genius was to apply this code-breaking technique to unraveling the most arcane and ancient languages.

"I *told* you I'm not to be disturbed!" Musa thundered at the cringing adolescent copyist who managed his office in the House of Wisdom.

Recovering his composure, the young man condescended, "Just some Jews here to buy books from our library. They bought enough to overload a camel, then they asked to see you. The Director suggested, or rather ordered me, to introduce them. They claim to have something to show you."

However imperious and rebellious he felt, Musa realized he must still observe diplomatic, or in this case, mercantile protocol. "Bring them to the study," he said resignedly.

Musa greeted the two scholars by simply announcing his name and looked at them with casual interest.

"I'm very busy, rabbis, but what is it you want?"

Ben Mar wasted no time. "We were told by ben Paltoi of Fallujah, head rabbi of the Jewish academy there, that you are a renowned translator. His father knew yours, and they exchanged letters on philosophic questions."

Musa managed a half smile. "What have you to show me?"

Ben Mar had been entrusted by Eldad to carry his precious book to the House of Wisdom, but it must not leave his custody. He also carried the long leather scroll from Palmyra, one of its two columns of indecipherable writing bearing some resemblance to the symbols in his book.

He handed the leather-bound pages to Musa, whose eyes narrowed as he studied the second page.

Rabbi Simhah started to tell the translator of the remarkable man who brought them to Baghdad, but he seemed far away, thoroughly absorbed in the carefully inscribed symbols. He began slowly shaking his head, his lips tightened in frustration.

"These wedge-shaped symbols, I have seen them only once before. In my father's effects I found a clay tablet and remembered his copying its markings on paper. He believed the writing was from the Chaldeans of Ur. He was never able to read it though."

Musa sighed, and seemed to surprise himself with his own humility. He reached in a drawer and handed a palm-sized clay fragment to ben Mar. "And neither have I," he said. "My first and only linguistic failure."

Ben Mar took one look at the tablet. "The symbols are so like the left column of the scroll!" he exclaimed.

"*Scroll*. What scroll?" demanded Musa.

Simhah traded the roll of leather for the book, and Musa carefully spread its two-foot length on his desk, placing the roughly circular tablet beside it.

His eyes widened, almost shouting, "I see it! Yes, I see it! The scroll's left column looks similar to the writing on the tablet, but *exactly* like the script of the book. Its writing is more refined, more *drawn* than written. That is to be expected from an illiterate copyist."

Ben Mar disliked the condescension. "But honored scholar, is it not true that in this language, whatever it may be, we are *all* illiterate?"

Musa looked at ben Mar, and with a slight nod of his head, seemed to acknowledge that wisdom he had heard, but then immediately he continued scanning the two vertical columns of strange writing on the scroll. He sat at his desk without speaking for some minutes, the sunlight spilling onto the leather document before him. The highly polished leather surface seemed to glow from beneath the thousands of mysterious symbols.

Ben Mar looked over Musa's shoulder. "I have tried to imagine why there are adjacent columns in different languages." He pointed. "Do you think that each tongue might tell the same story, or perhaps a bilingual decree?"

Musa didn't answer, which led ben Mar to conclude that the possibility had not yet occurred to him.

Isaac was sure that it irked Musa to think a Jew was one step ahead. "I have taught using arrangements of Hebrew and Persian in vertical columns like these," he explained.

"What you say is possible, Rabbi. I'll steal this idea from you and give you no credit whatsoever!" Clearly, he was only half joking.

Rabbi Simhah and ben Mar both laughed heartily.

"As to the matter of credit," Simhah said, "we are authorized to offer you payment for your efforts to translate Eldad's family book."

"Ah, you Jews are cunning in catching me at a moment when I am drunk with intrigue. As you may know, family riches have supplied all my wants, so I shall attempt to do this, not for the gold I shall surely ring out of you, but for the chance at a chariot ride back to where our written words began."

64

Adiva was aching to be alone with her beloved, but this was made impossible by the too-full ben Aaron dwelling, made even more crowded by the arrival of her brother Hillel and their cousin Yosef. They had come to assist her father with a serious scouring of available buildings in Baghdad's Jewish Quarter for the new yeshiva.

The reunion with Yosef and Hillel had been joyous and heart-felt, their affection and respect for Eldad quite obvious. Adiva was sure that the scene was not lost on her parents and hoped that they might begin to accept Eldad as family.

They walked in silence from the Gate of Sweepings toward the massive gates leading to the inner city.

Eldad read her mind. "They're worried, aren't they."

She reassured him. "I think they are torn. We must let them get accustomed to the fact that although I wish their respect and approval, I am a grown woman."

They crossed the bridge over the Nahr Bazzazin, the Canal of the Clothes Merchants, and pushed their way through the throngs in the ever-boisterous streets.

"But let us not bring things to a head too soon," Adiva said.

She knew she wasn't as confident as she sounded. "Yet, when they leave Baghdad in a few days, we shall not see them for a time, as I will not return to Fallujah."

"Then I must talk with your father without delay," Eldad said resolutely.

Adiva smiled, nodding in acknowledgment. She grabbed Eldad's arm.

"But listen to me. No power on earth can take you from me.

Something cries out from inside me that I *must* have you, and it is louder than any whispers of caution, or even cries of alarm we may hear."

Eldad nodded, but Adiva could tell that he was still thinking. She was right.

"I expect them to raise the issue of children," he said, "both their color and their faith. They may be dark or light but will look like none in my tribe or yours."

Adiva was thrilled by the mention of children-their children.

"My mother will adore them, no matter. She will see to it that father does as well. Besides he's easily enchanted by a toddler's laugh. Still, we're getting ahead of ourselves, as I so wish we could."

Eldad's smile told her that he completely understood.

They were by now through the Mart and approaching the inner gate of the Round City.

Something was wrong. Through the twenty-foot double gates, they could see horsemen in the inner city.

"Only the Caliph's or Regent's horses are allowed in the inner city," Adiva whispered. "Having mounted royal soldiers visible from this distance is nothing but trouble."

They saw other soldiers with battle weaponry on foot, some leading their steeds, all looking grim.

"This is the way men look when preparing for battle," Eldad noted. "I have seen this many times."

They passed through the fourth gate, its nearly thirty-foot gold leaf tiled archway still reflecting the splendor of al Mansur's visionary Round City and were confronted with unsettling sight. Dense clusters of royal soldiers carpeted all open spaces in the half mile plaza leading to the Palace of the Golden Gate.

The couple had intended to follow directions they had through the maze of arcades just within the towering city wall to a renowned apothecary shop, where Eldad could sample the healing herbs of Babylon. They were told that the century-old shop was the first privately-owned apothecary anywhere in the world, dating from the time when Arabic medicine separated physicians from the drudgery of acquiring and processing healing medicines. This shop and others like it specialized in syrups that disguised the bitter taste of medicines, preserving an art invented by the Roman physician, Galen, half a millennium earlier.

They could easily see the three-story building, its artfully cantilevered upper stories seeming to float above the swirl of humanity below. They could hear the delighted laughter of children coming from the double-wide door of the shop. An elegantly turbaned and robed older man with sad eyes was handing out stalks of sugarcane to half a dozen children.

When Eldad and Adiva entered the stall, they were surprised at its spaciousness, but quickly realized the absence of anything in the many containers strewn about meant *emptiness*. Even the elegant glass jugs that once held soothing syrups and medicines dissolved in alcohol were uncorked and lying on their sides.

"I might as well give away what's left after the soldiers came this morning," the apothecary owner said with resignation. "One of them started admiring my robe, and I thought I'd be stripped of herbs *and* my clothes."

Adiva introduced her servant, Eldad, explaining his knowledge as an herbalist.

The shopkeeper accepted this without comment. "These oafs came by orders of the Regent's son, who calls himself *General* Abu'l Abbas, our exalted hero in the victory over the slaves in the Zanj Rebellion. It only took him *four* years."

"Yes, we saw one of the vanquished, or rather his head, as we crossed over the outer canal," Adiva recalled with a shiver.

"They just took everything but the sugarcane," the shopkeeper said giving the last of it to the children. He shooed them away.

He turned to Eldad. "You must know how wonderfully healing these plants can be, and how deadly if used wrong. They stripped batches and bundles out of their labeled containers, and they wouldn't know cinchona bark from deadly night shade."

"Do you know what is going on?" Eldad asked.

"*They* don't seem to know. I did hear one of the older troops lecturing on and on to his younger charges about *why* the army was going on this secret mission."

"This seems quite ominous," Adiva said. "What did our pretend historian teach the young thieves?"

The shopkeeper continued, "The soldier cursed the Egyptian ibn Tulun and the seed of his groin, Khumarawayh. He then recounted how our Caliph al-Mu'tamid tried to escape from Samarra seeking the protection of Ibn Tulun, but was caught by his brother, al-Muwaffaq, who has since kept the powerless Caliph under house arrest."

"When was this?" Adiva asked.

"About two years ago."

The shopkeeper took a deep breath and spoke. "That Ibn Tulun would even consider sheltering the Caliph threw oil on the fire of al Muwaffaq's hatred. Egypt still controls upper Syria and the frontier zone with the Byzantine Empire, yet they pay no tribute to Baghdad for any of it, and neither for Egyptian lands."

When the young soldiers pressed as to why their huge army was being assembled in inner Baghdad, the older soldier told them that it was 'none of their business' what plan General Abu'l Abbas had for their futures."

"All this talk of Egypt," Adiva said, "do you think Abbas plans to strike the fortresses on the Syrian frontier?"

The herbalist was pensive. "An attack on northern Syria would alert and mobilize Khumarawayh. Though he may be months in coming, to be sure the Egyptian will mount a furious counteroffensive and will fight for every inch of Aleppo. It is an ancient city worth many sacrifices."

He turned back to Eldad. "Where did you learn your healing arts?"

Eldad once again related his family's long history of being the Tribe's healers, and their knowledge of plant medicines. "We were always taught to carry wherever we went small packets of medicinal plant seeds. I am aggrieved to have lost those of my family's herb garden, from plants passed down by countless generations. I came to you hoping to find some of these. The mighty warriors robbed me as well as you."

"Take the seeds left in the containers. I do not grow things, only sell them, and now, thanks to the general, I have nothing to sell. The captain of the soldiers who sacked my shop was grumbling to an underling about being dragged so far away he'd be an old man when next he saw Babylon. He said, 'There is jihad in the west, and we shall strike at its beating heart.'"

Adiva knew the only holy war declared on Regent al-Muwaffaq was by the rebel Egyptian governor, Ibn Tulun, pursued no less zealously by his son, Khumarawayh.

"They mean to attack the fortress at Cairo," Adiva concluded. "Once it is overrun, nothing will stop their vengeance on our beloved city Fustat. Our friends, our adopted family, our assets, all are in peril."

Against her will, she could feel tears welling up in her eyes.

If the herbalist saw her pain, he did not show it. "Whatever General Abbas' plans are, the sheer size of the force, and their provisioning for a very long journey, point to a major battle in a distant land. I have trading partners in Egypt, in the village that hugs the pyramids. If only I could warn them."

"Perhaps we can," Eldad said with some determination. "But our warning must be based on solid information, not what we guess from the ramblings of an embittered officer showing off for his men."

"They are not ready to move," said the shop owner with some certainty. "Conversation I overheard before the robbery indicated their frustration with waiting for a large contingent of Baghdad's soldiers who are returning from harassing and robbing the Marsh Arabs, who claimed they were the last descendants of the Sumerians of most ancient times. My grandmother was one of them. They still lived in the swampy wetlands of the Euphrates Valley on floating islands of reeds dense enough to support their cattle."

"The marshes are no more than a few days away on foot, though I imagine that moving many men and their impediments is always slower," Adiva said.

"How can we come by better information?" Eldad asked.

"Though they will loot along the way, the needs of a moving army would require amounts of gold and silver, and this would involve the Royal Treasury at the Palace of al Mansur. Benei Netira is well aware of financial machinations behind the Golden Door, some of which he arranges."

She stopped, unsure whether to trust the merchant with further details. She decided that she'd have to count on his bitterness.

"We will avenge your loss, but you must keep our intentions from these locusts who have descended on you. Do you have trusted contacts who will not yield to the temptation of rewards for reporting those disloyal to our glorious Regent?"

"Yes. The owners of other apothecaries—may their sweet elixirs turn to vinegar—will talk to me. These men speak to each other, but to no one of any other trade. No doubt they too have been relieved of their merchandise, and I am certain they will speak most willingly. I shall leave you two out of my tale, but say I overheard soldiers talking."

He lowered his voice. "This is how I shall do it. The two shops by the Bridge to the Hospital have owners who say almost nothing. Except for their wives who do nothing but talk, hungering for secrets they are sworn not to reveal, yet always do so."

The shopkeeper winked. "But just to one or two close friends, who won't say a thing to *anyone*. No, I'm certain we will learn the information we need."

They told the herbalist the location of the ben Aaron home and asked him to send a runner if his sources were revealing. They agreed to avoid written documents, but rather, vague references the messenger himself would not understand.

Given a dozen palm-sized leather pouches, Eldad hurriedly filled each with the seeds of medicinal plants he recognized, including chamomile and opium poppies.

They again expressed their regret for the owner's circumstances and hurried away toward the Anbar Road and the Syrian Gate. Throngs of soldiers clogged the streets and shops, but these men of great curiosity had no money and no hesitation to steal what they wished. Many merchants just folded their tents to avoid them, but the prostitutes–the Round City teemed with them–were thriving. To no one's surprise, the troops somehow found money for *that*.

65

Esther and Ashot waited for the door to open. They were expected, but Esther was a little surprised to be seemingly facing the mistress of the house and not a slave.

The woman smiled. "Ah, the bookseller's wife. Come in."

Esther thought to introduce Ashot, but before that, he took a step back, declining to enter farther than the home's outer stone arch at the street. From there he could observe most of the perimeter of the home, which he casually scanned along with every passer-by.

"I am Esther."

"And I am Sana. Welcome to my home."

Her elegant and colorful robe contrasted with Esther's drab, honey-colored robe, that as a Jew she was expected to wear.

"Musa has mentioned your gracious hospitality the day he spent in your home. This is extremely rare for him, but don't expect to hear much gratitude from my husband."

Esther took note of the woman's bluntness. She smiled. "He has behaved well, except for ignoring *everyone* but our guest from Africa."

"He came home entirely preoccupied with one of his *moments,* as he puts it. Unexpected insights into some linguistic mystery that has gripped him, but he shuts out his surroundings."

"I *did* notice at meals he will stop talking long enough to hear others, then go on talking about his own subject," Esther said, "One thing about your husband, he is *always* interesting."

"I so wish at times he could be just ordinary and predictable. Last night, believe it or not, he had nearly all our slaves out on the streets of Baghdad looking for anyone who looked *Egyptian.* Of the half dozen Egyptians they rounded up, there was one who was *literate*. I had him for the evening meal, and they worked into the night. All my husband would say was it had something to do with the scroll of the African Jew. The poor man is still asleep upstairs, and Musa has issued one of his orders that when he awakens, he is not to be allowed to leave. Pay gold dinars on the spot, but I was not to let him get away."

Sana ordered slaves to bring tea and rolls, directing Esther to colorful overstuffed chairs in a warm nook off the dining room. The morning air carried contrasting aromas of food and farm, heavy with the bawling of the sellers and braying of the sold.

"There's too much of everything in this city, too many people, too many animals, and too many people who act like animals," Sana bemoaned. "And, too many soldiers. The Turkish guards are bad enough-they say there are over 5,000 of them-but now the invasion of the Regent's army makes those guards seem like treasured guests."

"Speaking of guests, this is the reason I am here," Esther said. "As you know, the African Jew carries a book no one can read. Your husband is the last chance the young man has to understand what story it tells. He believes he can."

"My husband believes he can do *anything*. He comes from wealth and has a peculiar belief in his invincibility, as well."

Esther placed her hand lightly on the women's arm. "It seems our husbands have *that* in common."

A laugh of recognition escaped Sana's mouth. "Have you been listening at our door?" she quipped. "If you had, you would have heard my fruitless warnings that Musa had no right, no matter *whose* son he was, to speak his own opinions on our holy faith."

"Ironic," Esther said, wondering as she spoke if she was revealing too much. "We can speak openly about our faith, at least amongst ourselves, but as Jews can express little else."

Sana nodded with understanding. Esther decided that it was an appropriate time to bring up the reason for the visit.

"Your husband showed up this morning having traversed all of Baghdad unaccompanied, as he refused to wait for Ashot, as

previously agreed. He was agitated, said he'd been robbed, and
wouldn't explain why he'd made his way to our house in the dark."

Sana registered no surprise. She shook her head. "Unfortunately, he will continue to act as though he is invulnerable. He's like a
two-year old, wandering off after a butterfly he's seen."

Esther went on. "The young African, Eldad, will not part with
the book he wishes translated. It is too precious to him. Finally, it
was suggested to attempt the translation in Eldad's presence, but
Jews are not allowed to remain at the House of Wisdom or anywhere else nearby. Your husband tried to argue that it would be
safe, but with all the soldiers in the city, everyone else agreed it
was too dangerous."

"I think so too," Sana interjected, calling to the slave to remove
the tea and bring wine.

"Everybody thinks the task is probably beyond even your
husband's remarkable skills."

"I'm sure he doesn't think that."

Esther smiled without comment. "In the unlikely event he
can translate the strange words, I'm wondering how you would
feel about Musa staying for a short while in a Jewish household?"

Sana was quiet, then suddenly brightened. "Do you want us
to be friends, Esther?"

Startled, friendships being rare between Jews and Muslims, Esther stammered, "yes." After a moment, she recovered. "Of course."

"Then *please* take my genius, and keep him, as long as you
can stand him!"

The wine was poured, and two women of different worlds
drank it along with the nectar of vibrant companionship, till morning became afternoon. Esther left with Ashot carrying a leather bag
with carefully folded clothes.

"He always looks like he's gotten dressed in the dark," Sana
said, calling after her departing guest.

At this same time, the Joseph ben Aaron household was re-
acting to their distinguished guest as a foot to a burr in its sandal.
Mercurial as always, Musa had, in a single afternoon, alienated

nearly everyone except the bookseller himself. He didn't mind the master translator's demands for his attention and was now being given a lesson in linguistics.

"Sometimes answers stare you in the face, but you can't see them," Musa told the bookseller.

"And you see something now?" Joseph asked.

"When I first saw the scroll at the House of Wisdom, I immediately observed the striking similarity of the symbols in the right-hand column to ancient Egyptian script. As you may know," he added with a now familiar immodesty, "I translate books in seven languages for the House of Wisdom, but this Egyptian script was not familiar to me. This presented the greatest challenge of the scroll, as I know only alphabetic languages spoken today. The Egyptian miller told me that the right-hand column was written in his native Egyptian which, although incredibly old, it is still readable by him. He called it Demotic.

"What does the scroll say?" Joseph asked eagerly. He had to admit to himself that a mercantile impulse raced side by side with a hunger for history, for a connection with the mysterious past. He knew it was the book, not the two-foot scroll, that was precious to Eldad.

"I do not yet know, but before the Egyptian miller fell asleep on the table, he made it clear the first, very densely written section is a syllabary, a catalogue of syllables."

"Just syllables?"

"No. The bottom quarter of the right-hand column appears to be a compilation of ten prescriptions, herbs, and procedures for wound care."

"Finally the miller says beneath a small gap in the document, there is a long list of common words in Demotic. Although as yet incomprehensible, the left -hand column of the wedge-shaped writing may match the Egyptian words as well."

"Rabbi ben Mar told me he thought each column told the same story. Might the word lists be the same?"

"Yes, and by the way, I see little difference between the peculiar wedge-shaped symbols in the African's book and those of the left column of the scroll. It must have been why he bought it, without knowing it could be the key to his family's oldest mystery."

"Perhaps," Joseph said. "Eldad is an herbalist and will be fascinated to see these ancient remedies. You must get him to recite three things, which he believes may relate to the book. One is from a recent, quite vivid, dream, and another, a curious vision when he crossed the Tigris to Baghdad. The third is from a mystical woman who altered his awareness with a plant substance, during which time she recited from a book she could not otherwise read. I asked Eldad to write this summary of these fragmentary stories." He handed the translator a small parchment which Eldad had written in his Hebrew.

Musa sniffed. "These are very unlikely to be of any value, but I'm interested nevertheless."

Esther returned with the gypsy bearing a woven sack containing several sets of clothes, some scrolls and manuscripts and a note from Musa's wife. Musa glanced at it and quickly put it aside. "The woman talks too much," he said to no one in particular.

 Musa took the leather bag and removed the scrolls he needed. He handed it to Joseph, and said, "With the help of our miller, this will provide a rich vocabulary in Demotic, likely enough to understand all of the left column of the African's scroll. Let's hope the wedge-shaped writing is a syllabic language, and ben Mar was right about each column repeating the same text."

"There are so many ifs," Joseph noted.

"But imagine if we're able to read a story from millennia ago. If it is anything like the dream fragments he wrote for me, it will be a story to rival 1001 Arabian Nights." With that, Musa began to pace around the courtyard, nearly running into low-hanging branches of the orange trees. "Where *is* he? Why doesn't he come here? Only halfway into his rant about how impossible his goal was to reach without *some* cooperation, without naming *who* was not cooperating, the miller arrived, his apron and beard crusted with today's fine grain dust. The nearly deaf slave woman, unresponsive to the master translator's indignant objections, whisked their Egyptian guest to a wash closet, from which he emerged quite refreshed. And well it was, as he would soon be enveloped by the intense surround of energy generated by a genius at work.

Musa exploded resentfully when the old slave brought food and fresh water, but she ignored him and served them both, standing there, a frail intruder, until both he and the Egyptian ate and drank. Something about this little person standing up to his bluster moved him to soften his tone.

The old slave watched them struggle into the night with the unfamiliar task and fed the two men a second meal at midnight. She did not need to hear or understand the strange words to see the men believed they were succeeding so resoundingly that their energy level rose rather than fell as morning grew near.

In first light, the House of Wisdom's greatest translator triumphantly called Joseph to his side. He had written the words he could translate. "See here," he said, pointing. *"Sift and knead together, all in one turtle shell, the sprouting naga plant and mustard; wash the sick spot with quality beer and hot water; scrub the sick spot with all the kneaded mixture; after scrubbing, rub with vegetable oil and cover with pulverized fir."*

Joseph now realized that Musa had opened the door into the ancient wedge-shaped Akkadian writing. There was at least a glimmer of hope that the mysterious tale, so often capturing the Danite's dreams, might speak from the distant corridors of time.

66

The heat of the day seeped, then poured its humid blanket over everything. Summer had come with storm-like suddenness, but the shaded courtyard with fountain and waterfall made it still feel like spring. Rabbi Zemah ben Paltoi felt the tension and frustration of the day ease in the cool mist from water falling eight feet to artful stone lily pads chiseled into the floor. With both his wife and daughter resting, he welcomed the time alone. The search for a new site for Pumbedita's yeshiva had been worse than fruitless. Two of the most promising properties were both beyond repair and their allotted funds.

In the soothing quiet, Zemah knew it was the time he must confront the family's dilemma. It was clear his daughter's plan was to include this African man, but nothing so definite had been expressed. Off to themselves, mother and daughter talked a lot, but Dinah would only reveal vague outlines of what was said. Being told *nothing* of what is going on sometimes reveals *everything* of what is going on, at least according to his wife.

The white sound of the falling water kept him from hearing soft steps behind him, and he was startled. It was Eldad.

"I'm sorry to disturb your peaceful time," he said in his unmistakable, deep, resonant voice. "May I join you?"

"Oh, yes, most certainly," he smiled, welcoming the young man. He motioned to one of the four leather chairs around the waterfall.

"Adiva told of your disappointment with your property search. She said you have only a few more days before returning to Pumbedita."

Zemah nodded. "Sometimes I feel tempted to pick up my

family and my books and leave Babylon. But where would we go? For 1500 years, Babylon has been more of a cradle of our Jewish civilization than Jerusalem."

"I was told by one of the men who freed me of his tribe of Jews on the southwestern shore of India, who live in harmony and respect with the ruling people, Hindus I believe they are called. It seems there are Jews in many places."

"Yes. I have heard of them. The descendants of Israel have been scattered across the world. Until the Almghty wills that we shall return and gather again in Eretz Yisrael, it is here, Babylon, that Jews look to for guidance and spiritual sustenance. Even in our promised land, which the Romans long ago renamed Palestina, the Jews fiercely cling to the land, but are so few in number."

"I have a lot to learn" Eldad said.

Zemah smiled. He had warmed to this young man. To a point.

Zemah pointed to the yellow cloth square on Eldad's robe required of a Jew's slave.

"The role you have willingly taken for deception's sake is similar to the status of Jews everywhere. To the Mohammedans, we are dhimmi, protected people, which only means we have the right to be safe. For a fee. The Christians can't decide if we are to be valued as an older sibling or reviled as the killer of their savior."

Zemah sighed, suddenly feeling very weary. "Or both."

"I do not understand either of these concepts," Eldad said. "At least not yet. But it is not mere oppression but *annihilation* I fear for my people if they do not fight valiantly for our lands."

"I understand" Zemah said softly. It pained him to hear of this suffering.

He decided to make this conversation a little more personal.

"Do you long to return to your people?"

Eldad seemed unconcerned with the question though he must surely understand where Zemah was headed.

"Rabbi Zemah, please let us speak candidly. I know my sudden appearance in the life of your daughter is unsettling to you, and what I truthfully say may make it more so. But to begin with, no,

I shall not return to my people. My family and the tribe of Dan are precious to me, but the survival value of having blood lines far from the perils of tribal life is well understood by them."

Eldad paused. "If Judaism had not survived the bondage in the Holy Land and Babylon, perhaps it would have been our four Tribes on the high plains of east Africa that were the sole survivors of the children of Jacob."

"Perhaps," Zemah said. "Who is to say but God?"

The rabbi took a deep breath, reminding himself not to be drawn into deep philosophical discussion.

He needed to be a father far more than a rabbi. Obviously, Eldad wished to be part of his family. Consciously, and remembering his wife's wise counsel, he knew he must give him the benefit of the doubt. Still, he felt he must protect his precious Adiva.

"You might have noticed that my daughter is somewhat headstrong."

"Yes, I have," Eldad said smiling broadly.

"Like her mother," Zemah said, matter of factly. "And intelligent."

"And courageous," Eldad interrupted.

Zemah nodded. Only recently had he learned from the gypsy of Adiva's extraordinary exploits.

"I tried to give her all the knowledge that our society permits and even some that it does not."

The shadows were lengthening in the courtyard. A comely young slave girl arrived with wine. She could not keep her fascinated gaze off the young guest, nearly spilling the cups. Zemah watched Eldad's reaction, his eyes and expression as the girl poured, but saw no sign of interest.

Zemah watched her leave before continuing. "I wished her to become betrothed to a scholar, someone with the potential to become a great rabbi, maybe even follow in my footsteps."

"And then you showed up..."

Eldad was clearly a little uncomfortable. "Sir, if I may interrupt. When I first met you and your wife, you could not help but register shock. Was it the color of my skin?"

Zemah looked around to confirm they were still alone.

"Since you suggested we speak frankly, I have to say that yes, we were taken by surprise with your appearance. No one, and that includes us, has seen Jews that are black in skin tone, though some families in the Dar Yahud own slaves as dark as you, but with African features."

"I have no doubt that our skin has changed over time. We have mixed with many peoples since our exile, after all. It is only Torah that remains constant."

Eldad had a peculiar look on his face. Zemah wasn't sure what exactly it signified.

He soon found out. And dreaded its arrival.

"I am very much in love with your daughter, Rabbi." Eldad said quietly.

Zemah shouldn't have been at all surprised, but he was nevertheless stunned into silence.

Finally, he managed, "You have given Adiva's mother and me much to consider. I can see you are a sincere man, intelligent and giving. I now know what was perfectly obvious to Dinah that you intend to ask for Adiva's hand in marriage."

When Eldad started to speak, Zemah held up a restraining hand. "Please, not immediately. Try to understand how complex this is for the family. If I am being honest, I remember vividly the passions of your age, and how urgent it seems to enter this new cycle of life. I only ask what my daughter will likewise be unhappy to grant, which is a little more time for us to absorb this reality."

"That is most dearly put, Rabbi. Under ordinary circumstances, an indefinite delay might be reasonable, but these are not reasonable times. No one knows this better than you. Your daughter and I have twice faced death together and have vowed now to face *life* together. You would not wish this to be less than the *fierce* determination I assure you it is."

Zemah was again taken with the young man's straightforwardness. Clearly, he wished for the Gaon's blessing, but there were too many unanswered questions before he could do so without reservation. One he need not ask is whether the strong young black man before him loved his daughter with every fiber of his being. He wisely reminded himself the strength of this was greater than the need for *anyone's* approval.

Eldest daughter Adiva had always been more independent than most Jewish parents could tolerate, but he and Dinah admitted to each other their secret admiration of her adventuresome nature. Her younger brother, Hillel, had been swept along to manhood in the wake of their daughter's exploits. Now, as if her life had not already cast off many traditions that stifled other intelligent women, her parents needed to accept her permanent bond to a mysterious man from beyond the world and time they know, and from a tribe seemingly lost to all but ancient history.

They sat quietly a few moments before a commotion of slaves at the front door brought everyone in the house, except the slave who couldn't hear and the master translator who didn't care.

Dinah appeared in the archway. "Benei Netira has come on some urgent matter and must speak to you both without delay." Independent of the fact that Netira was the major benefactor of the Academy at Pumbedita, he was also deeply embedded, albeit secretly, in the financial affairs of Baghdad's royal palace.

He wasn't alone. Netira's face was tense and lined with worry, but he waited patiently for the slaves to pour the obligatory tea, then spoke just above a whisper.

"My Christian banking partner, the Caliphate's other royal banker, came to me in turmoil, telling of edicts from the Regent I had not yet received. He suddenly demands loans to the Caliphate of exceptionally large sums of gold, quite beyond even our considerable, easily accessible assets. He and I have *never* loaned to anyone, no matter the usurious interest, without knowing what the gold was for. Now, we are told it is a crime to know, or even ask, the purpose of this transaction."

He paused and sighed heavily, then said, "I must tell you I endanger you both by what I am about to say, and you *may* choose not to hear it. You who listen will be as guilty as I who speak."

The rabbi and Eldad looked at one another and nodded with somber expressions, "Tell us what we need to know," Zemah said.

"When this banker was writing out the 'documents of under-standing'—we cannot call them 'interest bearing loan papers'—he was ordered to include provisions that would have us forfeiting our assets if we reveal their purpose."

Zemah shook his head. "This sounds very much like you're being *ordered* to trust al-Muwaffaq, that he will repay his debts with interest. Perhaps he'll do so by seizing and selling more property of Jews. Would it not be a terrible irony, Benei, if he steals the property of your bank purportedly to repay your bank!"

"Though this concern is real, it is not why I am here. There's a grave danger to the people we cherish, and anything of value they possess."

"Here, in this place, now?" Eldad asked.

"Not in Baghdad, though we must always be prepared for it to come to that." Then the banker scanned the courtyard.

Zemah knew Netira to be a man of utmost directness. He could not help but notice his uncharacteristic vagueness.

"At times like this a man could use an elder brother to talk with," Netira said. "What ails us a physician friend of Chiam can remedy with words to the right ears of those in the royal compound of Cairo."

"Adiva and I met a man in Baghdad who lost all his medicines to this scourge of soldiers. He is bitter, alert and determined to inform us when it has begun to move. A runner will come to this home."

"By then, it may be too late," Benei worried. "There are two problems. The first is how do we prove what we warn against, and second, to whom. There is incalculable danger in this warning being discovered, thus altering their plan of attack. It is clear, from the extreme secrecy and massive concentration of soldiers, that they plan a surprise assault with overwhelming force. No matter the outcome, our families, and the 7,000 or more of our people in Fustat must know what is coming, not to mention the rest of the peaceful souls of the great city. We must find a way to be believed by the forces in arms."

"Only certainty in what we know will convince them. What certainty do we have?" Zemah asked.

"In the absolute sense, none, but I call your attention to these facts: The Regent's final victory in the slave rebellion emboldened him to retake control of *all* the Caliphate's lands. Al-Muwaffaq is assembling a vast expeditionary force, and my Christian banking partner tells me it is being provisioned for a very long journey. Coming here today I passed the dromedary house where royal troops were collecting every camel in sight."

"That likely means the army will cross broad stretches of arid land, or desert, like the Silk Road route to Palmyra," Eldad said.

"Besides disbursements ordered for these beasts, a sizeable sum was paid for large leather water bags, demanded in such numbers as to require merchants to raid from warehouses of other Tigris and Euphrates river cities."

"More sure indications of desert crossing," Eldad said, standing to calm a sudden restlessness. "There can be only one objective, and the richest of prizes it is—the enslavement of Fustat and the destruction of the Tulun army in Cairo."

"We thrive in Egypt, one of the only places in the civilized world where Jews are free to follow all professions and trades, worship freely, and mingle with ease," the rabbi added gloomily.

"But, dear friend," Benei said, "The Regent and his General Abu'l Abbas care less about infidels, though they will murder them at will, than they do about bleeding the great wealth of Fustat. Revenge for the treachery in abetting his brother, Caliph al-Mu'tamid's attempted escape to Egypt, but also word of jihad declared against al-Muwaffaq by ibn Tulun, the ruler of Egypt, in mosques throughout the land, are pretexts for first, robbery, then annual tribute of hundreds of thousands of gold dinars. And from whose assets do you think such payments will come?"

"Your people in Fustat, they were so kind to my daughter," Zemah said.

"Yes, they were, beyond what even blood relatives could expect," came Adiva's voice from behind them. So absorbed were they, no one noticed her waiting behind the thick-trunked date palms.

Ruefully, Netira said to her, "Now, you too have violated new edicts by overhearing this."

"Is there a way we can make a difference for our loved ones in Egypt?" Rabbi Zemah asked. "I feel a great responsibility for Fustat, one of the few safe harbors for the Jews of the world."

"The armies created by ibn Tulun are mighty, but may perish if attacked by surprise," Benei Netira answered, "There is only one way we can protect our Egyptian loved ones, and that is we must present to them credible evidence that the threat of annihilation by al-Muwaffaq is imminent. There can be no written document to that effect since the bearer would face a gruesome death if apprehended. On the other hand, if the messenger convinces the Egyptian Regent, Khumarawayh, and his generals in Cairo to mobilize fully for an attack that does not come, it will not garner kindly treatment for him."

"And her," Adiva said firmly. "Hear me out. The Danite and I have fully resolved to take this risk. Our gypsy Ashot met us on the Bridge of the Jews and is eager to join us."

The expected objections led by fears for their safety flowed freely, none louder than from Zemah. For each, they responded in the reasoned way they indicated to Zemah anyway, they had planned for this or at least something similar.

Eldad was the first to speak. "As to the uncertainty of the assault on Fustat, I feel none. There is no other seat of power within the lands claimed by the Baghdad Caliphate that would *require* an army of this magnitude to subdue. We need not fear reprisal for false warnings."

Adiva followed, "As you know, Benei, your beloved brother Chiam lives next door and is quite close to the head physician of the royal compound at Cairo. This man, who is most trusted by the Tulun army, will approach those who have the ear of their leader."

"But something this momentous will not be accepted second-hand," Zemah interjected. "You will both be taken in and questioned by the authorities. It shall not be the doctor, but *you* who must convince them."

"But even if we fail," Adiva said, "my adopted family *will* believe us and prepare to find safety."

"There is a substantial concentration of our family's banking and mercantile assets in Fustat," Benei Netira said, "There was even a plan to move assets a few miles north to the new town growing up around the Cairo compound. It seems now, rather than *lend* gold, we must *hide* it."

"Much of the wealth I acquired in my journey, and as the reward from the family for bringing your assets from Aden, has been hidden at Uncle Chiam's direction near Fustat. I know this place is one of those used to secure business and banking gold, silver and precious gems, which back the letters of credit."

Benei nodded knowingly. "He has a peculiar system for remembering the locations. Three persons are involved: Chiam, another man known in banking circles who knows only the name of the third man, a Christian banker who also knows all locations."

"I know of two Silk Roads across the breadth of Syria, and the royal expedition is more likely to take the southern route through Palmyra," Eldad said. "In advance of the main body of the army, they may block travel on the road for security reasons. I am told the road through the north of Syria is over more forbidding terrain many hundreds of miles to Aleppo."

"I know from my messengers who have been through this ancient city that it is a three-day camel ride from there to the ports of Tripoli or Tyre," Netira said. "Remember the royal soldiers will commandeer all the available boats for their invasion force and may do so before the army arrives at the coast."

Dinah had entered the room, sent for by her daughter, who quickly recounted the troubling developments. Zemah knew that she would focus on the trivial to avoid the troubling and had already expressed her worry about the month her daughter and this exotic man would be in highly intimate contact on this journey. "There are things yet to be resolved here," Dinah said.

Her husband spoke up. "Eldad and I have spoken of many things, some needing more time before putting them into words."

"We may *have* no more time," Adiva said emphatically. "If word arrives, we shall depart quickly. Ashot is in the countryside finding four camels. He is masterful in handling them. He will wait with the beasts among the gypsies, a good source for the travel provisions he shall have at the ready."

"This is moving too fast," Dinah declared. Zemah could feel her glare upon him for not slowing everything down, a quite impossible task.

Netira interjected, somewhat forcefully, "Time is the important element, but truthfully, I wish there were an alternative to sending these three. Adiva has already rescued my family from significant damage in Aden and should not be asked to do more."

"I was *not* asked, and I do this not for you but for *me*. Mother and Father, you must understand my burning desire to protect not only those who were so good to me, but a civilization that shall be good *for* me. Before I saw the wonderful freedom of Christians and Jews in a Muslim city, I thought Jews must be timid, colorless, and as invisible as possible. Instead, I find them to be a positive, moving force. Just as the ancient Hebrews fled oppression *from* Egypt, we," she said without hesitation, "shall flee oppression *to* Egypt. This mission only allows us to do what we had planned before leaving Fustat."

Acting as though it had been thoroughly settled, Netira said, "The northern Silk Road will take you two or three days longer to reach the Sea than the southern. Three weeks into your journey, you will see a landmark, a small mountain above the flat terrain strewn with ruins of some unknown ancient civilization. I am told there is a well there, probably as old as the ruins themselves, whose waters are pure and are said to have healing properties. No one lives at Tell Mardikh, as the surrounding land is windswept sand and dust. From there, it is a day and a half by camel to Aleppo."

"I may know this place or at least the name of it," Eldad said.

"The clear and insistent voice in my dream at Palmyra declared 'Go north to Ebla.'"

Zemah was at last, resigned. Dinah however still appeared quite troubled.

Eldad must have noticed. "Time is so short that things better said in due course need to be said now. We gain nothing by not speaking our hearts and minds."

"Again, young Danite, you show us your grace," Zemah began. "Everything is *incomplete* in our knowledge of you, all except for the obvious love you feel for my daughter. However, we can't be happy you are taking her away from the relative safety of Babylon to a city likely soon under siege."

"Dear Father, *he* is not taking me away, *I* am."

"Knowing what is coming gives us time to prepare an escape from Fustat, should the authorities not fortify the city," Eldad said. "If they are unconvinced, I know I can persuade Chiam Netira to hire village boys to watch from atop the tallest pyramid, from which, I learned from him, one can see as far as the Port of Suez. He will also be encouraged to employ horsemen to rapidly bring word if the force appears at the Port of Alexandria."

Dinah asked anxiously, "But then where will you go?"

"If they invade by sea, it is more likely to be the Mediterranean Port of Alexandria, but they will quickly occupy Suez as well. Chiam and I discussed this one night and he began a rambling discourse about making our way far up the Nile River, to a land with four rivers that nourish the Nile. Chiam believed that this African place, rather than Dilmun in southern Babylon, was the true Garden of Eden. He has business acquaintances in these far reaches of the Egyptian lands where we can seek shelter." He looked intently at the woman he hoped would accept him into the family, and said, "I can always provide for her, even if resources are meager, as I know both edible and medicinal plants. No matter who we encounter, they will seek me out for my knowledge of medicines and other healing advice. This I trade for food and shelter."

"But if we must leave Fustat, it will not be empty handed," Adiva said.

"There is something more I wish you to understand," Eldad said, looking mostly to Adiva's mother.

"I will, without hesitation, lay down my life to protect your daughter."

The quiet and solemnity of the moment was shattered by the jarring appearance of master translator, Musa ibn Ishaq. Gleeful, red-faced, and agitated, he blurted, "I have found something in the African's book wholly unexpected and never seen before in all the world!" The visiting rabbis stared slack-jawed at the intruder until ben Aaron demanded, "What *could* you have found to warrant such a..."

"Now all of you hear me out and do not speak until I have finished! The Danite's dream, so faithfully recorded, which he believed to be from his mysterious book, is in fact an almost-verbatim rendering of the passage I have just finished translating." Musa stopped, silently demanding their questions. Sensing they were being toyed with, Rabbi ben Paltoi said impatiently, *"And?"*

"And, as your Hebrew scholars well know, Abraham, venerable prophet of Islam, Christianity, and Judaism, is known only from your Hebrew bible. There has been no extra-biblical, contemporaneous account that proves he ever lived." He paused, breathing heavily, then in a calm and steady voice, he said to Eldad, "From the mist of ages, your Sumanu records not only being rescued but also blessed by the hands of Abraham."

"I believe in almost nothing, but I am now quite certain of the reality of this man blessed by God to bring His enlightenment to our world."

67

The messenger, youngest son of the herbalist, arrived while everyone was deeply asleep. The bookseller himself opened the door. Welcoming his guest, he instructed a servant to wake the others.

"Gently," he admonished. "We don't want a commotion for the neighbors to hear."

The guest was offered a seat, but he shook his head, preferring to stand. "My father told me to speak plainly as time is of utmost importance."

Joseph ben Aaron agreed.

"Thousands of troops arrived at dusk, fresh from their murderous campaign in the southern marshes. My father is certain this was the contingent the Regent awaited before striking out to the west."

The household was soon fully awake and the messenger was asked to repeat himself.

"Is there a timetable?" Benei Netira asked,

"This is why I have come now," the herbalist's son answered. "Though none of the soldiers know their mission, all are aware they will be gone for months. They freely discussed a peculiar order that four days hence, a quarter of their number are to depart through each of our city's four gates. Nobody can figure which direction the army is moving. My father assumes this is by design."

"One more thing. There is no good reason for us to know your plans, but you should be aware that once the army is assembled, it is rumored that they may cordon off the Anbar Road, blocking the way west. They have not yet done so, as that would announce their intentions." And with that, he was out the door and disappeared back into the shrouded night.

Now the household responded to the urgency, everyone contributing what they could to the preparation for a long and perilous journey.

Adiva was surprised to see her father, the Gaon of Pumbedita, ask for writing materials from a servant and immediately begin penning a letter.

"This should be delivered to the rabbi in Fustat," he explained to Adiva's quizzical expression. "It contains important instructions he should have." He sealed it with wax and handed it to her.

"A *Responsa?*" she said, taking it from him.

He did not respond. Adiva could see in the flickering candlelight her father's face, sad and full of worry.

"Abba," she said, feeling like a little girl, "I want..." But she could not continue when her father wiped a tear that had formed on her cheek. She wrapped her arms around him and was comforted when he held her tight.

The letter was joined with the other things being hastily assembled, including a variety of preserved foods the slaves packed in tightly woven bags. They worked without asking questions, but they probably knew everything anyway.

Eldad had little in the way of possessions to gather, giving him time to develop a plan with Netira and newly-arrived Ashot. The four camels could be heard snorting and groaning, tethered at the front gate. A voluptuous gypsy woman stood with them, not in attendance it seemed, but waiting for the man who had brought her.

Adiva couldn't wait to hear all about who she was.

Netira unrolled maps, which serially revealed stretches of the 700 miles they were to cross.

"This will be barren and barely inhabited," Netira said, pointing at the third scroll. "You are in more danger on this part of the Road from dying of thirst than from thieves."

Ashot added a rare comment. "I know survival under these conditions, and I can keep the animals alive as well." He suddenly drew his long knife, and, in a blur, it whizzed over their heads. "As to thieves, they will find me most hospitable."

It took a moment for the two men to regain their composure, Eldad sooner since he knew the gypsy, at least as well as this mysterious man, on whose combative skills they would depend, could *be* known.

Adiva noticed first. Musa, the scholar, had appeared in the room.

"What goes on here?" he nearly shouted.

Everyone froze, unsure how much to reveal to this Moslem. Adiva felt he could be trusted, but was it a shared opinion?

"We are leaving Baghdad," Adiva said, "likely in the next few hours."

Musa's expression was pained, as if he knew what was coming next.

"I must take my precious book with me," Eldad said. "I do not know when I shall return."

"No, no, no!" erupted Musa, "If you do this, I shall give you nothing of what I have already translated."

He held up a sheaf of parchment papers and shook it at them, then turned to Adiva's father. "Have you told them *nothing* of our discussions?" he asked, clearly exasperated.

The Gaon shook his head. "Go on. You should tell them your-self of the *extraordinary* discovery."

Flattered, Musa nodded, "I have managed to translate what appears to be the final words on the last page of Eldad's book. I don't know its meaning, but if I have read it accurately, the wedge-shaped symbols said, *"We were to be the first Hebrews. And we had singing hearts."*

Eldad appeared stunned. Adiva waited for him to speak but he was silent.

"Therefore, I must be allowed to continue," Musa insisted. "If you remove this book from this household, I am coming with it!"

Adiva immediately thought of Musa's wife and what she might say about this situation. But before she could let his thoughts drift any further, her father, the Gaon, stepped forward.

"Honored scholar, please. What you are suggesting is not possible. For a number of reasons."

Musa was about to protest, but Zemah put his hand up to cut off any attempt.

"The bookseller and I discussed this very situation. But we did not have enough time to advance it."

He took a deep breath and exhaled slowly, looking at Eldad. "Perhaps, if—and only if—the Danite agrees, the precious document could remain in this house where we will guarantee its safety and preservation."

Now Musa was also looking at Eldad. There was hope in his eyes.

But Eldad was looking at Adiva. He seemed a little over-whelmed. She decided that she must say something, offer support.

"It would be safer, of course," she said. "We don't know what awaits us on our journey. But it is your decision. And I will support it without hesitation"

Eldad was about to speak, but Musa interrupted. "Excuse me," he said, exhibiting more diplomacy than he had so far shown. He handed Eldad a tightly folded page. "This is a copy of all my early notes on the content of your family's book. I believe it may be part of a larger story of great antiquity. Though I admit not yet know-ing, the story may have originated a millennium *before* your Torah. The prescription on the scroll was originally written in the ancient Semitic language of Akkadian, long gone before your alphabetic script we know as Hebrew."

Eldad nodded. "It is agreed. The book shall remain with Joseph the bookseller, but here, alone. Even though I am told Muslims have the right to *demand* and receive lodging from any Jew, the kindly treatment by the family and their slaves should be rewarded by giving them the choice as to how long you stay."

"Joseph said I should stay as long as it takes to finish the task," he said. "And that could be forever!"

The old woman slave, dwarfed beside the rotund translator, moaned, and everyone, even Musa, laughed.

"Still, we have not discussed payment for my services," Musa interjected.

"You were offered gold dinars," Adiva said, "but refused. But now you have a price in mind?"

"Not a price, but a reward: a scholar's reward."

For the first time Eldad smiled. "I understand," he said, "The leather scroll was a curiosity, which I purchased without realizing its uniqueness, but it had little meaning to me until your linguistic insights. I now believe you, and you alone, have begun to read the words of my family's most ancient history. The way you scoff at gold means you need do *nothing* for money. Your delight and zealous attack on my book's mysteries deserves to be richly rewarded. The bi-language scroll is yours, whether or not you succeed."

Musa ibn Ishaq beamed. "Thank you. You are most generous."

Adiva was surprised that his familiar arrogance didn't surface. This covered a deeper excitement, centering on something he had discovered in the book, which too much wine and his irrepressible wish to impress had caused him to reveal to Rabbi ben Paltoi.

Settling with the translator, the couple hurried to finish their preparations to leave Baghdad that very night. Departing at midnight would have drawn no special notice, since at all hours the main city gates were streams of caravans bound for the four corners of the known world. There were group goodbyes and private moments for Adiva and her parents, while Ashot and Eldad finished loading the camels. This done, Ashot took the waiting gypsy woman by the hand and led her out of sight to a clump of trees behind the house. Ashot was still sweating profusely when he came back alone, saying nothing.

Adiva had learned nothing about this woman, save that she was a widow that he had met while living with his Roma people encamped a mile from the Round City's outer walls. Her intuition told her that the gypsy woman had become important to him.

Adiva, already dressed in the drab costume of Jews in Baghdad and tired of drying tears from saying goodbye to her parents, insisted they leave immediately.

Mounting the camels, the three crossed the Bridge of the Jews and through the human and animal refuse-strewn plaza of the Gate of Sweepings, the sight of it obscured by darkness, which only magnified its stench. They would now follow the southern bank of the rapid flowing Dujayl Canal 40 miles west into the Euphrates Valley. Their urgent journey to warn loved ones and protect the future of Fustat and Cairo would take them through the river cities of Fallujah, then Ramadi and Hadithah. Adiva's family home was on the heights overlooking the Pumbedita River where it joined the mighty Euphrates. But there was no time to leave the trail on the west bank of the river.

The morning of the third day found them a few miles north of Fallujah, making their way through a river forest of wormwood and other trees Eldad had never seen. Where north and west river trails met, Ashot hesitated, then dismounted, motioning for silence. Drawing his weapon, he moved towards the rustling that they all could now hear.

Before a minute had passed, he returned, smiling. The reason was standing behind him.

"Hello sister."

"Hillel. What are you doing here?"

Hillel slapped Eldad on the arm. "I just had a feeling you weren't going to make it to our home in Pumbedita. When I got to Baghdad, Netira told me of your sudden departure and why. He told me of your route and I decided to offer my help. If you'll have me."

"But our father?"

"He *and* mother gave their blessing. The academy has plenty of supporters to help with the move. I am neither scholar nor rabbi. They know my destiny resides elsewhere."

"What of our little sister, Sari?"

"She so wanted to spend time with you. She's become a beautiful young woman since the last time you saw her."

"I'm sure."

"Father probably didn't have time to tell you."

"Tell me what?"

"It's not official. She is about to become betrothed."

"Who is it?

"One of father's prized pupils. Sari knows him and likes him. I think.

"Just one problem. He comes from very poor circumstances. Our parents would help but that only goes so far. There are many wealthy suitors that would love to be married to the daughter of the great Gaon." Adiva couldn't decide if he was being sarcastic. It didn't really matter.

"So, what changed? You said the engagement is to be announced."

"Our little sister suddenly has a large dowry. Nobody knows from where. Father didn't even know. He wouldn't have allowed it. But it is under the control of Chaim Netira."

Adiva saw Eldad observing her quizzically. She lowered her eyes.

Hillel turned to the Danite. "And you, my friend. How did it go with the Gaon and his wife? Are we to be family?"

"As far as I'm concerned," Eldad said, "we are already brothers. Whether your father agrees, well, that will have to wait. And it is obvious your dear parents will have to accept someone about as different from their expectations as this forest is from the desert across the river. They are wise and will follow their good hearts."

He paused. "And if they do not, we will follow ours."

Hillel nodded. "I understand."

"What will you do in the future? If any Jew has one," Adiva asked. "These are perilous times."

"I must return to the sea. It pulls me toward its embrace. India, maybe. The great ocean. I'm confident someone will give me a ship to command."

Adiva looked at her brother. "Are you for hire, Captain?"

"Of course." Hillel replied. "But where is the ship?"

Adiva shrugged. "When we get to the water, we will have to quietly secure transport down the coast."

"Why do you not simply pay passage on one of the swarm of boats between Tyre and Alexandria?"

"Our mission is secret," Eldad said. "Our Captain may have to *borrow* his first command."

"Sounds very dangerous."

"It is," Adiva answered. "Although it might not come to that. I'll fill you in in the next few days."

"Just don't borrow a pirate ship."

They all laughed hardily. It felt good, Adiva admitted to herself.

Ashot broke the mood, insisting that they waste no more time.

A faint breeze off the river, flowing opposite the direction they followed, failed to cool them in the noonday sun, and their party of four sought the shade at a way station with its usual cluster of peddlers.

It was the first of weeks of sundowns on the great river and they were disquieted by leaving its reassuring presence at Raqqah. The terrain had become a desert, with only patches of irrigated farmland close to the river.

"A week and a day," had been an Assyrian camel driver's guess when asked the distance to Aleppo. He said there were a *few* oases on this northern Silk Road and that some places are desolate but have life-giving wells. At first, reluctant to say exactly where these were, his tongue quickly loosened at the sight of a gold dinar.

"My family," he said, "raised goats for generations on the scrubby vegetation a day's ride south of Aleppo. Our goats were unusually robust, and my grandfather believed it was because of the abundant water we had from a stone well amid a mountain of ruins. He thought an ancient civilization had built a great city there, now hidden by the sands of time."

"What did your family call this place?" Eldad asked. He squinted as if he were trying to see something very far away.

"The locals call this great mound Tel Mardikh, but my family has a different name, passed down through generations." He paused, cocking his head to one side, as though struck with an inexplicable recognition, and leaned close to the Danite.

"I *know* you were at Ebla."

68

The brilliant white limestone uplift was visible from miles away against the stunted sand dunes stretching out in every direction. The road they followed had changed, becoming more solid under foot with short stretches hewn from base rock. After one of these, the trail was an engineered straight line to the gap between 200' mounds of stone and sand, half a mile long at their limestone bases. They had celebrated, as well as they could, three Sabbaths since leaving Baghdad and yearned for the next in civilized surroundings.

"The cameleer told us to find a path up to the middle of the mountain over there," Ashot, said, sounding uncertain. "He said we should look for the well at the west end of the Tel."

The party's supply of water was nearly gone, and they were counting on finding the promised well hidden among the ruins. If they could not, they would have to backtrack several miles to the tiny village of Mardikh. Dusk, and the merciful relief from the relentless desert sun, were nearly an hour away when Ashot found the trail, choosing one among several by its abundant camel dung.

Eldad barely noticed. The strange feelings had returned. From the moment the trail turned toward Tel Mardikh, this area that he had never seen before seemed familiar. The first time this had happened occurred in the middle of the Tigris, when he recognized the old healer and the young scribe of Ur.

They soon came upon the well, and marveled at the nearly perfect circular opening cut by hands ages past to sustain man and beast. Wooden buckets, some battered by banging against the sides of the 40 foot well, were left attached to tightly woven ropes for anyone's use.

Shallow basins cut into the rock could be easily filled, and quickly emptied, by camels and other beasts, and Ashot saw to this before he drank the clear, cold water himself.

Relieved at the abundance of water, Adiva became playful. Standing beside the well, having quenched her immediate thirst, Adiva suddenly lifted a full bucket and threw it on a startled Eldad. And brother Hillel seeing this, could not resist dousing his squealing older sister, whose effort at escape ran her into a face-full of Eldad's retaliation. The camels stopped their voracious slurping of water and stared dripping-faced at the band of laughing children with dripping faces.

In a moment each had refilled a bucket and stood at the ready for the other's next move. From the corners of their eyes, they could see the still-dry gypsy's stealthy movements to fill *his own* vessel, and with no visible cue, they dumped on him in unison. Though all were thoroughly doused, this barely cut into the grime of a month on dusty roads. After their laughter had subsided, Adiva promptly ordered the men to explore out of sight of the well and find a campsite for the night. Ashot unloaded dry clothes from the lead camel, walking the four well-watered beasts to a patch of saltbush 50 yards down the trail they had come up. This thorny plant was ignored by most animals, but relished by dromedaries, and a person could stay alive by eating its seeds and leaves, which stored life-giving salt.

Hillel set about building a little hearth with stones scattered near the large patch of saltbush, and then he unburdened one camel of its bundles of firewood. He would light the fire in an hour, near sundown, in celebration of the Sabbath.

Eldad loosed the leather thongs binding a rigid leather case beneath the camel's outer baggage, containing the master translator's notes. He had been patiently waiting for a good time to consider them.

Seated on a mound of stones, Eldad unfolded the parchment and began reading the letter written to him by Musa in perfect Hebrew:

Danite, this task bedevils me in the slowness of it, but I find myself strangely drawn into the world of the story's narrator, who speaks in the first person. A portion from the middle of your book says that, while in captivity, the narrator found a fragment of a clay tablet at a shrine beside a spring in Haran. It records the words: 'At this place, God first spoke to me.' He also read from the fragment the name Shem and Amathlai, daughter of Karnebo. Then he admonishes his disciples to have 'a benign eye and a humble spirit.'

The first passages of your book have an eerie similarity to what the mystic woman described and you recorded in your notes. Of course, not all words match, but the writer describes himself as an 'A-su', or healer, of Ebla'. The tablet fragment is his most treasured possession, which he knows will surely be lost if he does not secure it for all time. He speaks of the western boundary stone of a place called Ebla, where, as a very old man, he buried the tablet, leaving it as a gift to the ages. I personally doubt such a tablet exists, and the scholars here consider an ancient civilization known as Ebla to be little more than rumor.

Eldad smiled broadly to himself. The scholars must not be very good at traveling, he thought. Everyone they have encountered so far knows the area where he was now resting was once a great city called Ebla.

Musa's letter continued: *I can safely say the story told is very old, or it could not have been written in this archaic language. I suspect it has been a millennium since anyone could read or write it. Remarkably, the book was preserved in your family for many generations by their faithfully redrawing the symbols they could not read, just as you did before you left your tribe. I shall engage scribes to copy every mark on the book's pages and I shall retain their work in The House of Wisdom.*

Eldad smiled again at the translator's sense of entitlement. He didn't ask for permission to share this personal document with anyone.

For a moment Eldad felt quite annoyed, but then, perhaps influenced by the uncertainty he would face, reasoned that it was better for too many to know than no one at all.

From higher up on the trail, Adiva called to the men that she was finished bathing, and she most strongly suggested they do as well, especially because this Sabbath they would give thanks for safe passage in this journey that seems without end. Revived and refreshed, the young woman had clothed herself in silken pants, blouse and robe, all of shimmering lavender silk that highlighted her golden hair.

At the sight of her so clean and fresh, Eldad felt himself becoming aroused. He yearned to be behind closed doors with her, dwelling on the depths of her full beauty. Instead, he must be satisfied with brief kisses and stolen touches.

"Let's walk," Adiva said, pointing to the widening path, then when those two have finished, you too should bathe."

Eldad nodded.

They walked down the western slope of Tel Mardikh. Now the trail was a road, constructed of worn blocks of limestone from unknown ages ago.

A few hundred yards further they ventured into sandier terrain, wishing perhaps some feature of the surroundings would offer them privacy, but they saw only flattened dunes, some with rocks sticking up at odd angles.

Turning back toward the Tel, Eldad saw, no felt, something that stopped his movement, and for a moment, his breathing; an overwhelming sense of knowing that somehow before him was a missing part of his real being. Rising a modest few feet above its grainy surround was a perfectly straight four-sided obelisk of highly polished granite. Even at a distance it seemed to be the tip of a larger, buried structure.

Once again, Eldad could see the old man of his dream. Everything was in vivid detail, including the glint of the rising sun off the western boundary stone of Ebla.

"What is it?" Adiva said, touching lightly on his arm.

"This place, that carved granite sticking up on the third mound from here, this is all the landscape of my dream. I haven't yet been able to tell you, the letter from the translator says the author of my book wrote of burying a treasured possession beneath the western boundary stone of ancient Ebla."

They walked faster the 50 yards to the black obelisk and were standing before it when the setting sun struck the polished front face, and a rock of ages bathed their faces in a blessing of light.

"Here?" Eldad said, mostly to himself.

"What are you going to do?" Adiva asked.

"Every fiber of my being tells me this stone is where the old healer buried his most treasured object. Truthfully, I really must know if it is *not* here. Something too deep in me to understand will not rest until I know."

Studying the obelisk, Adiva observed, "Each of the four sharp edges tapers gradually outward, and the granite doesn't even seem weathered."

"Maybe it was covered until some recent time," Eldad said. "Whatever it is, I won't see the base of it unless I dig now." With that, he moved to the east face, dropped to his knees, scooping sand away from the polished black surface. In my dream, Sumanu said he buried it in the first light of dawn, coming from over his shoulder."

Adiva stood silently. Eldad could tell by the look on her face that she was skeptical.

"I'll bring the men," she finally said. Then she laughed. "You're *really* going to need a bath after this!"

The light was failing, but the three men went on digging with fortuitously shaped pieces of firewood down toward the base of the ever-enlarging stone, and by a bright moon they came to a change in the stone's east face, from highly smooth to roughhewn. They were spent, but dragged themselves back after a short rest, encouraged by Eldad's excitement without knowing they were but a few inches of hard-packed earth from finding a treasured record of human faith.

Now clad in rough-cut clothes, Adiva appeared with tight bundles of dried brush for torches and lamb jerky she had soaked soft and heated in the well water. One of their goat skin water bags bumped on her hip.

"You will eat now or be unable to go on."

A fraternity of grumbles was soon silenced at the smell of the hot ribbons of lamb. She watched with curious satisfaction these famished animals devour much of the party's remaining food. She had observed that the hungrier men are, the less they talk, until they have their fill. She wondered if the opposite was true of making love.

Adiva could plainly see their exhaustion, and without rest, they would be worthless in the early morning when they must push on to Aleppo. No one knew how fast the Regent could move his army overland to the Sea, and if the southern Silk Road to Tyre was days shorter, they may be intercepted and never reach the port. Armies take what they want and the party's four young camels would be prized.

This time there was no resistance when she told them the work must stop. They had moved their campfire near the obelisk, and Eldad returned from the well, freshly robed and groomed, including using the sharp flint stone to shave his face smooth. Adiva could not help but find this or that reason to touch his face and wiry muscled arms. The desert grew colder but troubled no one's sleep on the soft palates of lamb's wool rolled out by the fire. This was comfort compared to times they'd shivered through nights of blowing dust.

Eldad slept the dead part of sleep, without which the body dies, then dreams, some with scenes but no words, others, only a clear dream voice. Its timbre and cadence familiar to the deeply asleep young man, the same voice had urged him to go 'north to Ebla.'

Now the dreamscape was suffused in the silver grey of predawn light, and a slightly stooped older man wearing a white toga made his way along a road wide enough for two carts. He is speaking. To Eldad? To himself?

There is something painful I must do, but not before much thought. Though we live in the tolerant times of the Amorite kingdom of Ebla, two other great civilizations rose and fell here long ago, taking the knowledge of their treasured things with them. Can my family secure the treasure from generation to generation? Will they continue to believe in its significance?

The old man stands before a black stone, nearly as tall as him, its sculpted crown a foot-square pyramid of highly polished granite. Trained in his youth as a royal scribe, he was one of the very few who could read what had been chiseled just above the roughhewn base: Ibbit-Lim, Amorite

King of Ebla. Kneeling, he began to dig beneath the two-cubit wide base of the shiny black stone.

Eldad turned to cover his exposed shoulder, disturbing the vision, but, mercifully, not awakening him from vital rest. His dream resumed immediately, spilling from some mysterious well of ages past.

"The tablet is safe only if it is hidden, and my family, for as many generations who care, shall alone know its exact location. They shall know this from the story on these kiln-baked clay tablets. My survival to this great age was so improbable, there had to be a reason for it. Perhaps it was to tell those who come after of the man of my time who shall be remembered for all time."

It was before dawn when Eldad awoke with a start, fully aware of what he must do. It was cold, but he knew the punishing heat would arrive on the sandy plain not too long after sunrise. Moving quietly to not wake the others, he made his way to their dig at the base of the obelisk.

In the inky darkness he found the lowest point they'd uncovered, where the sand had become hard-packed, on its way to stone. He realized he must stay focused. At dawn they must leave if they hoped to reach Aleppo before the next sunset.

Urgently, he hacked and scraped for a few inches and he came upon what seemed to be another dreaded rock, like those they struggled with last night. A right-angle edge of the obstruction could be felt, but not yet seen, and he used the wooden wedge he found to follow the edge downward. He regretted that he had not taken the time to make a torch from the smoldering hearth fire and he could not tell how long it would be till dawn.

His excitement grew as he freed one side of the object's smooth surface, a little longer that his forearm. Testing it with a push from his fingers, Eldad cried out in alarm when his hand broke into a cavernous space, the interior of a crumbling clay pot. Resisting the reflexive withdrawal of his hand, it closed around a waxy bundle, and he carefully worked it out through the hole in the pot.

His outcry had roused Adiva, Ashot and Hillel who hurried to the stone, launching a chorus of whispering concerns. Eldad stood motionless in the spoils of the dig, barely able to hold in one hand a square bundle of glazed clay tiles, and with the other, he held in his palm up a single, more irregularly shaped tablet.

As the first rays of dawn warmed their faces, they now saw the glazed rust-colored surface of the object in Eldad's hand and stood mesmerized. It was pitted with regular rows of lines, crescents, and triangles. The same ancient symbols as in Eldad's book. Even Ashot, who was mostly disinterested about such things, couldn't avert his eyes.

A glint of sunlight off the object that called Eldad's attention to its center point, where he could see a symbol he instantly recognized from something his grandfather had taught him. Zav had said the first written word recorded a heavenly starburst so awesome that permanently imprinted on mankind. The symbol stood alone, unlike all others that were in pairs or longer. Three sharply etched lines intersected to create a six-pointed starburst.

"See here," Eldad pointed, "This is the symbol for God, inscribed on this tablet, which was buried long ago. The family story has told us *where* it is, but not yet *what* it is. I hope these other tablets are the missing details of my family's story. I yearn to know the man who lived so very long ago; what he thought, and felt, and saw."

"Who?" Adiva said.

"The one who left this here." Eldad didn't quite know how to explain just now.

"We must take them with us," Adiva said. Ashot and Hillel nodded in agreement.

But Eldad shook his head. "The old one who buried it believed his treasure would be lost unless hidden where anyone could see yet no one would look. And only family would know. He chose the boundary stone because it was massive and more permanent than anything else in the ancient city."

He studied the several rows of symbols on the hand-size object, all in larger script than the others. "We shall take the bundle of tablets, but I believe I have a duty to preserve and protect this sacred object, though we do not know what it says. One can imagine an endless number of possibilities in which it could be lost or destroyed if we take it from here. I can in a short time copy these symbols, perhaps only a few hours to draw them carefully.

"Can we afford to wait?" Ashot asked

"I know we cannot delay, so you must leave me with the youngest camel free of burdens and I'll find you before sundown."

Adiva spoke up immediately, "No. We shall not leave until you have finished what you must do. Aleppo is ten miles beyond what we can reach in a day, and an extra half day's rest now will benefit man and beast."

Eldad retrieved parchment paper, pen, ink, and a foot square of thin board, which he sat on his lap. Each symbol required great concentration to reproduce accurately, but he was accustomed to this task from the year it took him to make two copies of his grandfather's deteriorating manuscript. He remembered his vow, made almost daily during that tedious effort, that he would push through the fog of the unknown and come to understand the meaning behind his task.

Now the practiced hand easily recorded symbol after symbol, working outward from the starburst at the center. Ashot brought food and water to him while he worked, which he accepted without looking up. He felt a familiarity with this task, in this place, but from another time. He had known from the moment he touched this object it was different from the other tablets; that *they* were merely a story, but *this* is history.

By mid-morning, the transcription was complete. Eldad wrapped the object in thick leather, sealing the edges in wax, and knelt where he had found the treasure. Placing the bundle into the urn, he sealed the defect with a curved pottery shard, and methodically began covering the exposed base of the great black obelisk. The men silently joined in replacing all they had removed, till the east face of the stone looked like all others, undisturbed by anything but storms of sand and eons of neglect. As he placed the last handfuls of sand, he again felt the presence of Sumanu, the aged physician of Ebla who buried this tablet three thousand years ago. Before he rose from the sand, Eldad ha Dani remembered the words the mystic woman read from the book and recited them aloud.

"By the first rays of the dawning day, I read for the last time the words inscribed on my most precious possession: The Tablet of Abram."

Eldad was overcome with sadness, recalling the ancient healer's final words, burned into his memory and still vivid:

"I feel once again swept into the dust of creation; through space, past time, beyond imagination...Back to where it all began."

69

No unusual activity greeted them at the Port of Tyre as boats of many sizes competed for passengers needing transport south to Alexandria.

Adiva took Ashot with her to find a suitable ship. Nonchalant about their urgency, Adiva bargained lazily with the Berber captain of a two-masted ship, who boasted of the swiftest passage on the sea. Indeed, favorable winds and calm waters had them in sight of the Egyptian port earlier than expected, but not a moment too soon for the four weary travelers. The enforced passivity at sea did allow them some rejuvenating rest, but they immediately left from Alexandria the afternoon they arrived, for what the caravan master said was five days to Fustat.

They all felt the rising anticipation of coming home, though this capital of Egypt was home to none of them. They could dress as they wished, ride horses with impunity, and bear arms in self-defense, all forbidden them in Babylon. If the Regent's forces ever seized control of Fustat, all would be prohibited, especially for Jews.

Their unexpected arrival led to a boisterous celebration at Chiam Netira's house, and inevitably this spread to neighbors, the Bukhtishus, physicians to the court of Tulun. Adiva and Hillel had given other explanations for their unplanned journey until the younger and elder doctors appeared. Netira and his son, Amos, along with the Bukhtishus were pried away from the gathering and herded into the young banker's private office.

"We have vital information for authorities in Cairo," Eldad revealed, "but we must find a way for it to be believed." He broadly sketched for them how their discovery of this unfolded, stressing the urgency of their mission.

"But Eldad and Adiva, you can't simply appear at the Palace." Chiam Netira said. "Even if admitted, you will speak only to low level functionaries who won't trust you and are unlikely to be believed by superiors anyway. You could as easily be seen as some agents of Baghdad, sowing panic and unrest."

After a few moments, the older Bukhtishus spoke up. "Ahmad ibn Tulun fell ill when he took personal command of his army in Syria. Since his death, his forces are dispirited, and his son is inexperienced in battle.

"And Chiam is right."

He paused. "The only time in recent memory, I'm sure."

He smiled and shook his head. "No young man, you won't be believed. I, on the other hand, most certainly shall be."

"How can you be so sure?" Chiam asked.

"Because one of the Tulun generals owes me his life. I once saved him—years ago—by drilling a hole in his head, letting out blood pressing on his brain. Yes, Sa'd al-Aysar will listen to me, and will believe, at least, that I believe the intelligence."

"Then we must go to this man, now," Adiva said. It was late morning, and they could be at the royal compound at Cairo in an hour.

"No, our arriving at the palace gates as a group is too complicated. Everyone not known to them is questioned, and this takes much time. We have no way of knowing if al-Aysar is even in Cairo. The chief of the palace guards will tell me. If the general accepts what I say, then he will want to also hear it from your mouths." With that, Doctor Bukhtishus summoned his manservant, who soon produced a four-wheel cart pulled by a mule. His obvious difficulty in walking made his son frown with concern.

There was nothing to do now but wait. Adiva wanted to ask Chiam Netira a few questions and had been waiting for the proper time. For a moment, she wondered if she should let the younger Doctor Bukhtishus overhear but decided that if the situation in Fustat became grim, they would surely all have to face it together.

"Uncle Chiam, apart from the dwelling I purchased, everything I own is entrusted to your care. In the not unrealistic event that Fustat is overrun, how are my assets secured?"

Chaim smiled faintly "Our word,"

"Your word?" asked the somewhat stunned young doctor.

424 ALLEN CHILDS

Adiva quickly surmised that his family's considerable wealth was also in the hands of the Netira family.

Chiam Netira ignored him, looking around to be certain they were not being overheard.

"Over the years since my brother Benei helped amass our family's great mercantile wealth, he has used this to ensure suitable financial transactions everywhere in the Muslim world, from the Red Sea to the Persian Gulf. We are the custodians, true, but the people who entrust us are never told where, or even how the gold or other assets they give us are secured. In a world of unpredictable circumstances and unseen treachery, trust is more valuable than gold. That is why others, Jews and Christians alike, leave their family assets in our keeping."

The Netiras kept only a small stash of gold, in the range of a thousand dinars, to immediately redeem most letters of credit. On the rare occasions when more was demanded, they drew on the gold reserves of two Christian banking families.

"There are two sets of records, both at secret locations. If the Regent's forces sack our beloved city, we can be robbed, but not ruined."

Along with these records of financial dealings were deeds to properties in Fustat, land grants from the caliphate, and titles to dozens of ships at the Port of Alexandria.

Adiva nodded her head and smiled. She felt reassured and could tell that the young doctor did as well.

The rest of the group had rejoined her. Adiva did not even know where they had gone. She would ask later,

"Good. You're all here." Chiam said. "There's nothing to do now but wait for the doctor's return. I'll have a meal prepared."

"How is our rabbi?" Adiva asked on the way. "I carry a letter for him from my father."

"His reputation must be gaining importance if no less than the Gaon writes to him. I must say, his pronouncements and opinions are unsettling to some, but to me, they clean the air like a rainstorm."

Adiva smiled, saying nothing.

They were served an afternoon meal of luxuriant Nile River vegetables, steamed with chunks of spicy beef and served over long rice.

After they had finished, Chiam stood up. "And now, I must rest. You too must be weary from your travels."

They nodded in unison.

"Hillel, this is your first visit to our home, I think." Chiam said. "A servant will show you where to lay your head for a time."

"Thank you, Uncle Chiam. But first I think I'll go and meet the rabbi and deliver my father's letter. I have a small store of energy left and will rest later."

Chiam nodded his agreement." Adiva, my dear, you remember where your room is? We have not yet replaced you," he said smiling broadly.

"That's comforting to know," she replied, laughing. Adiva could not help but notice that their host had not even mentioned Eldad.

Chiam leaned over to Adiva. "I noticed your gypsy companion did not join us. You know he is welcome."

"Of course, your hospitality is legendary. He prefers to be among his own or left alone"

"I see. Very well." He called a servant to his side. "The man outside. Make sure he is adequately provisioned for a few days."

Hillel stood outside, letting the air blowing off the nearby desert sands caress his face. It was dry but hot, a time of day when those who could retreated to cool inner caverns of their homes, and many shops had cellars that stayed comfortable despite the punishing heat above. For an instant he was enveloped by sunlight mirrored off the highly-polished finishing stones of the largest structures ever built on earth. Standing in front of the Netira house, he could see the reflected light from the pyramid bathe the open courtyard at the top, a curious phenomenon he'd been told happened at this time of day, in this season.

He saw Ashot. "I am heading into town. Would you like to join me?"

"No," the Gypsy replied, "Not unless you need me. I think I'll see what the local courtesans have to offer."

"Good luck," Hillel said, turning away toward Fustat's lush gardens and parks, and the bustle of thousands pursuing their destiny.

Adiva and Eldad suddenly found themselves alone. Without a word, Adiva led her Eldad to the second story room where she had stayed. Chiam was right. It remained as she had left it. Tree-shaded windows collected the little breeze that stirred through the rippling heat.

She closed the door—and opened her robe.

70

Their sweet rest was rudely invaded by voices from the floor below. Quickly dressing, Adiva, followed by Eldad, descended the double flight of stairs.

The old doctor had returned. With him was the source of the loud voice that had roused them, General Al-Aysar, a tall, grey bearded man with piercing green eyes and chiseled features earned over many years.

The doctor tried to introduce him, but he went right on with his rant.

"And to make matters worse," the general shouted, "one of his most experienced generals, the whore's son, Muhammad al-Wasiti, has defected to al-Muwaffaq, and urges him to attack."

The elder Bukhtishus shifted awkwardly waiting for an opening, "These are the people I spoke of, General al-Aysar. They come at great risk to themselves and will confirm what I have told you."

The general grunted an introduction and demanded they immediately tell him everything they knew. Eldad stepped forward and gave a brief summary. This did not take long, and al-Aysar waved his hands dismissively when they mentioned their surmise that Abu'l Abbas would move his army by water to the Egyptian coast.

"No, Abbas will surely use the Via Maris. The Way of the Sea, has connected Damascus and Fustat for two thousand years. It is there on these coastal plains we must stop him, before he crosses into the Jordan Valley."

"So you will have the ear of the young ruler of Egypt, Khumarawayh ibn Ahmad ibn Tulum?" the doctor asked.

At this, the aging general could not restrain his anger, spitting out his words. "Unlike his father, he does not listen, or if he does, it is to the wrong people, such as our former General al-Wasiti. Unfortunately, this traitor knows our weakness, in spite of our ability to conscript large numbers of men. I have warned that these men are just men, not warriors, unless trained and disciplined. And it takes time to weave individual soldiers into a group, willing to fight for one another. As to my command, our leader has demoted me to his reserve forces."

He paused, sounding more conciliatory. "Fortunately, he allowed me to choose which units will make up these few thousand, and I have waded through his army's swollen ranks, finding men who *want* to fight."

The General stood facing Eldad and Adiva. "You have done our nation a noble service, for which you will never be recognized, but that is as it must be."

The general walked toward the front entrance. "And now, I must prepare for war and convince other generals to do so. I fear they do not know how to organize the large numbers of men they'll conscript to fight the Babylonians. If they delay, Damascus and the rest of Syria will be lost, but that is only the beginning. If we are defeated on the coastal plains of the Holy Land, take what you can carry and flee." With that, the aging general was gone into a twilight that briefly turned Fustat's stone streets to gold.

The servants had not finished lighting the multitude of oil lamps, when a rapid and determined knock on the tall heavy wooden door announced Hillel and a smiling man many inches shorter, Moshe, the rabbi of the Fustat bet ha-kneset. The rabbi clutched, as though he feared he would loose it, the letter from the Gaon of Pumbedita. He could not contain his exuberance. "Our congregation has been honored with this personal letter from Rabbi Zemah ben Paltoi, whose word in matters of faith we regard as preeminent. Actually, it is in two parts, one more recently inscribed than the other." He smiled. "So perhaps we are doubly honored."

The rabbi sighed awkwardly, pausing to look at both Adiva and Eldad. "Would you like to know the Gaon's thoughts about you?"

"*We?*" Adiva asked.

"Yes, but it was left to my judgment, and to a lesser degree, your actions, whether to read to you *some* of it, or *all* of it. I have been asked not to reveal the preconditions to reading all of it."

He gave a helpless shrug. "First he wrote of each of you separately, beginning with you," he said not taking his eyes off Adiva. He took a chair near a bank of large candles aligned in front of highly-polished silver plates that mirrored their light and read aloud.

"'Most esteemed Rabbi Moshe:

That you are reading this letter means its bearers have arrived safely in the land of the Pharaohs. I understand you know my gracious daughter, Adiva, and you must permit a father's pride to spill over into this otherwise formal response. When she was a baby, and until all three women in my family silenced me, I called her *my flower of Zion*.'"

Hearing this, Adiva shook her head with bemused resignation at her father's unpredictable playfulness, always lurking where least expected. "'Tradition would place me in a position of authority in her major life decisions, but a decade ago I had to accept her single-minded determination, such as her insistence she learn what most girls never know, not even as women. She always seemed to be racing ahead of life, not waiting for it to unfold but *demanding* it do so. My daughter's adventures have rewarded her with material wealth, as well as the sinewy fiber of womanliness. Her mother and I admire her strength, intellect and tenacity, but cannot help worrying over some of her decisions. However, unlike so many parents, though, we acknowledge her absolute right to make them. Our hope is that our beloved flower of Zion will live a life of peace and contentment.'"

Adiva wiped away a tear forming on her cheeks. The rabbi paused to allow the moment to be felt.

"The next part of this letter concerns you, Eldad ha Dani, and it is, to me anyway, most intriguing."

Adiva could sense Eldad's rising anxiety. He managed a jest, "At least I've not been ignored!"

"Rabbi ben Paltoi writes, 'You have by now met the young African man accompanying my daughter. The story he tells is like no other I ever heard, bordering on the improbable, yet much of it is confirmed by my daughter who shared part of his experiences. In my conclusions about this man, I considered the scholarly observations of the Sura Yeshiva's Rabbis Simhah and ben Mar, as well as the House of Wisdom scholar, Musa ibn-Ishaq, who has, quite remarkably, begun to translate the book the young man carried with him from his east African land. Ibn-Ishaq intimated to me a startling find early in his efforts to penetrate the mystery of the book's extinct language. He believes it tells a story of a young Sumerian scribe's adventure in a most ancient time, who is rescued by an extraordinary leader from Urfa in the Anatolian region of Harran, what we know as our Torah's Ur of the Chaldees. Bearing in mind this translator is entirely skeptical, if not blasphemously non-believing, about his own Muslim religion and all others as well, he let slip his translation of something he found hard to *disbelieve.* He starts by questioning how it could be true, as there are no other written records of this man, outside of our sacred texts. Ibn-Ishaq fears if he revealed to others what he read in the Danite's family journal, he might be accused of blaspheming the memory of our Patriarch. He was unsteady from too much quality wine when he told me he had gone over and over the sentence in the text, but it continued to read the *Tablet of Avram.* The translator said notes he gave to the young man describe where to find this most ancient record of the Father of many nations, whom God the Almighty One would call *Abraham.*'"

Now Eldad knew the meaning of his dreams, that there was a man whose story told of the Patriarch, and from the time of the Prophet. He could not escape the feeling that some unseen hand guided him when he faithfully reproduced the ancient manuscript.

Rabbi Moshe continued reading, "'The young man himself has given a credible account of his knowledge of ancient Jewish law, as the Torah was interpreted two millennia ago. He has written down these halakah in a dialect of Hebrew none of us has ever seen, and this leaves me little doubt that he is from a hitherto unknown outpost of black Jews. I have for obvious reasons had to ask myself, is this man, who knows nothing of our rabbinic and Talmudic tradition, really Jewish? Is he different from the Karaites who reject both? I am aware that he deeply believes in the eternal values that have sustained our people for countless generations, and these mean more than changes in custom and ritual. I have come to understand that an uncompromising attitude is necessary only in matters of ethical responsibility. I see the ethics of this young man, who *asks* instead of *takes*. The answer to the question is, therefore, *yes*, this man is a Jew, a visitor from the distant past of our faith, as far away in time as his homeland is in space. Almost as breathtaking as the *Tablet* is the young man's report of the Lost Tribes of Israel. He bears witness to the continued existence of six of the ten: Issachar, Reuben, Gad, Naphtali, Asher and his own tribe of Dan. In addition, he has been told of the Tribes of Manasseh and Simeon, living where the Roman historian Ptolemy said they would be found, on the shores of the Caspian Sea. There may be *many* ways of being Jewish, and meeting Eldad ha Dani has made me ask myself if Judaism is only a religion, or is it also a *civilization*, achieving *unity* through diversity. Are we not stronger because our fabric is woven of so many different threads?"

The rabbi stopped reading. He sighed. "Now here I am reluctant. There is next an instruction that the last paragraphs of the missive be seen or heard only under specified circumstances which I am asked not to reveal."

"My father is a dear man, yet complex and at times demanding. We'll not press you, Rabbi."

"That is not quite true, my beloved Adiva," Eldad said. "I am honored by the Gaon's acceptance of my authenticity, but he leaves unanswered questions, which I must now ask. As you recall, Rabbi, we have spoken of our decision, which grows in certainty by the hour."

"Yes, I remember. And what do you wish me to do?"

"Marry us now, Rabbi. The Gaon would not allow me to ask

for his daughter's hand, saying he needed more time. He never said 'no', only 'wait.' The coming war with Baghdad makes all our futures uncertain, and we shall not be kept apart for want of a blessing, no matter how precious."

Quite unexpectedly, Moshe laughed aloud, quickly recovering his composure. He placed a reassuring hand on each of them.

"You won't have to be. Because you have both asked me to marry you, the condition for reading the final words in the Gaon's letter has been satisfied. The end of the letter is to both of you, and it says, 'That these words are read aloud or in silence means you have asked this Rabbi to marry you. Had you not done so, there would be no need for them. You will leave Baghdad together on a perilous journey in a few hours, and I must speak to you from my heart. This moment in time I once feared, but now welcome, as your mother and I realize the strength and goodness of the man you have chosen. We open our arms to enfold him into our family.'

"And to you, Eldad ha Dani, we entrust our Flower of Zion, though we know she is more like a mighty cedar of Lebanon. May she be a tree of life unto you."

"And to you both, be blessed in this marriage. And may the flame of your love forever light your way in darkness and warm you in its glow."

A deep quiet and stillness fell on all who heard the rabbi's voice, including the servants, who now crowded the study. Raising his head, Eldad gave a great laugh of relief, grabbed Adiva around her waist and hooked the rabbi with his other long arm and began dancing up and down. In a moment, all ten in the room were entwined in the tribal dance of joy, unchanged from ages past when voices and hands joined around hearths of dancing flames.

71

The weary physician Bukhtishus, the elder, could not believe what was unfolding before him, in the royal compound in Cairo, where he was treating the flood of badly wounded soldiers from a battle gone terribly wrong.

Most of the physicians of Fustat, Jew and Christians, active or not, were rounded up and sent to the Palace. Bukhtishus was among the first, and, knowing of Eldad's experience, took him along.

Every visible advantage had belonged to the Egyptians, they were assured, who built an elaborate campsite at a strategic cross-road on the Via Maris, where it met the road from Jerusalem to the Port of Jaffa.

Eldad looked at the doctor, observing the strain on his face. The moans and cries of agony grew louder by the hour. The blood and smells of putrid flesh only contributed to his despair. Eldad too had reached his limits, relying only on his training and the remnant of youthful vigor to keep going.

In a moment of relative quiet, Eldad turned to the doctor, "These wounds, whether on limb or torso, are all in the *backs* of the warriors."

One of the soldiers described the battle: "After a week of forced marching, we were halted in the center of Filastin, the holy land of the Christians and Jews. We were there to defend the lush gardens and abundant waters of Ramla. We knew by then we were to face Abu'l Abbas and the Regent's troops from Baghdad, but not when or where. At Tawahin, the spearhead of the Babylonian attack easily broke through the thin ring of sentries and seeing them flee panicked the whole of the encamped Egyptian army who lost their nerve to fight."

The man groaned, pleading for something to relieve his pain. Eldad observed the arrow hole behind the man's knee, carefully raised his leg, then cleaned and bandaged the oozing gash with a stinging green paste he'd made from his herbs.

The old physician stood behind him, observing. He did his best to smile.

"Now I'm learning from *you!*"

Eldad nodded his acknowledgment and continued with his work. It had occurred to him that his knowledge of healing may be needed among the Jews of Fustat, but this was before the news of the military disaster reached them yesterday.

He and Adiva had decided to be wed in September, before the holy days arrived, and when the merciless heat had stolen back into the desert. But overnight, their world changed. With no effective forces standing between Fustat and the Regent's army, conquest of the richest city on earth, at one level of violence or another, was inevitable. What would follow in many ways would be worse, the Jews and Christians of Egypt knew full well. Their churches and synagogues would be gutted and turned into mosques. No public display of their worship would be permitted, not even singing in wedding processions.

As she waited for Eldad's return from Cairo, Adiva began separating valuables that would travel discretely from those difficult to conceal. Ashot soon joined her at the earthen-walled bungalow and volunteered to sew the heavy link gold chains to the inner surfaces of goatskin wine and water bags. When Eldad had been whisked away with Bukhtishus along with all of his medicinal herbs, he was told to expect to be in the royal compound for at least three days.

Before leaving, Eldad grabbed Adiva by the arm and pulled her away. "I'm sure you understand what this means," he said. "This urgent call for help, and no hint of victory celebration. I had prayed I would never again see the aftermath of tribal war."

"If we do not move quickly and wisely," Adiva replied, "*we* shall be the victims of tribal war. We talked about how we would make ready, but not where we would go, nor how."

"We expect the gypsy soon. You and he must go to Chiam Netira for his advice, especially about his assets at the Port of Suez."

The doctor's servant shuffled his feet impatiently.

Eldad sounded calm, but Adiva knew he was worried, "If we are separated, my love, I shall find you once again at the Red Sea." He turned and was gone into the middle of a moonless night.

With no one near, she began to cry softly. Each time they were forced to be separated, the fears returned. She wiped her cheek, chastising herself for being so childlike. She must be strong, she reminded herself.

Ashot and she waited till sunup and made their way to the imposing house. Both households seemed to be in turmoil, but on careful inspection, all the movements of slave and master were purposeful. The elder Netira's wife, usually quiet and unassuming, exactly the opposite of her boisterous husband, was speaking over the ambient din of movement, with such admonitions as 'hurry *slowly!*'

They found Chiam Netira two flights up in his study, conferring with his son. They were sorting stacks of parchment documents. The younger man nodded a greeting, but barely took notice, focusing on his father's instructions.

"These deeds are signed by Ibn Tulun," Chiam said, "but they may be worthless since the battle, and it would no doubt delight al-Muwaffaq to void every scrap of paper the object of his jihad signed." Sure that his son understood, Chiam finally turned his attention to Adiva and the gypsy. He looked worried, tense.

"Now, how are you coping with this sudden shock, my dear?"

"My intended has been stolen by your old friend, who is not at this moment my favorite person. On the other hand, the Danite is eager and able to help."

"Of course," Chiam said, doing his best to smile. "We've been expecting you. You're here for two reasons, the least important of which is the security of your investments. Would you address that, son?"

The younger Netira was impatient, but also appeared eager to earn his father's confidence.

"We have gathered these letters of credit, anticipating your request for them. Be reassured that the assets represented here are entirely safe from whatever is coming at us from Baghdad. From the standpoint of the Netira network, it has not changed, even under the malevolent rule of al-Muwaffaq, who remains dependent on, as he puts it, 'the Jew money changers'. My Uncle Benei in Baghdad, whom I think you know, has spent years insulating the family banking assets from the vicissitudes of changing rulers. When al-Muwaffaq imprisoned his caliph brother he tried to seize our banking assets, but none could be found. Now that we are facing conquest from a vengeful Babylon, which will seize everything it wants..." The young banker picked up letters of credit, waving them in the air. But they will find only paper.

"We acquired a fleet of ships at the ports of Suez and Alexandria, converting the bank's assets into vessels." Chiam added. "Captain Tushar's boat, which he believes belongs to mysterious Chinese investors, is one of our twelve ships plying the Red Sea, the Indian Ocean and the Persian Gulf. Your assets are hidden on the open seas since nothing there is as menacing as the treachery everywhere on land. I took the liberty of sending word to our agent in Suez, whose runner tells me that Tushar's ship is due at the Port within the week. But Tushar will not linger there when he gets news of the disaster on the Via Maris, even if he has to leave without a cargo. He paused. "It's bad for business but our floating bank will be safe at sea."

Most uncommonly, Ashot spoke up, having become impatient with discussions of money. Adiva was grateful for the assistance.

"This information may offer an answer to our other question," Ashot said. "Which is where do we go?"

Amos Netira didn't hesitate, "Captain Tushar's is one of our four merchant ships that dock at Suez at least twice a year for repairs and resupply. Each captain is part owner of his vessel, but knows only his partner's representative, who receives reports, but gives no orders. Unknown to anyone on board, each ship has a secret watertight compartment hidden within the frame, containing gold, precious stones, and, most importantly, coded records of all major transactions of the Netira network, these updated biannually, during unaccompanied 'inspections' demanded by the silent partner."

Adiva noticed the pride showing on Chiam's face. His son had learned well. "Go on," she said, returning her attention to Amos.

"Every location, even those in threatened places like Baghdad and now Damascus, has its own copies of these meticulous records of such information as to whom we issued letters of credit."

The younger Netira paused, awkwardly shifting his feet. There is a plan for all of us. It has been in place for some time..."

"No!" the old man thundered. "*I* am not leaving. Nor is my head slave. And don't tell me, son, that my most loyal servant is not as sturdy as he once was. We do just fine."

Amos rolled his eyes but otherwise ignored his father.

"If we must leave Egypt, let us not be like the children of Israel, forced to wander the desert for forty years. This is why we must leave by sea. *All* of us."

"We will travel in secret."

"Like you once did for us, Adiva," Chiam interjected.

"And we cannot reveal to the captain our identities as this could bring unwanted attention, Amos continued. "We have already sent word to our agents that any of our vessels must be held in port and prepared with extra provisions for a long period at sea."

"That's just the problem with your plan, my dear son. *Where* will we go? Flawed though this place may become, it is *our* world, an important and safe place for Jews, as it has been for many generations. A unique expression of the human spirit. If it dies on the vine, I shall die with it."

"We will find a place, father."

"Where? Babylon is in disarray. Isn't that right, Adiva?"

Adiva reluctantly agreed.

He became quite agitated. "Eretz Yisrael is a place for pious old to spend their final days among the ruins of our ancestors. No. Jerusalem will *not* be rebuilt in our days, no matter how much we pray for it."

Perhaps the old man is right, Adiva thought to herself. Maybe, like her own father, there comes a time when it is too late to rip away one's life story.

She changed the subject. "I cannot say where my betrothed will wish to go if we must leave Fustat. Our circumstances keep changing, erasing our imagined future and giving us few choices. One choice we shall not surrender to time or circumstance is the *real* reason I came to you today, *Uncle* Chiam."

She paused for the endearment to light up the old man. "We want you to be one of our two witnesses for our wedding."

Beaming, Chiam asked, "And who might the other be?"

"We have not yet been able to talk about that. Things are coming upon us so suddenly. I alone am deciding things we should decide together. But tomorrow will be our blessed day. My loyal Ashot and I must hurry away to the bet ha-tefilla to see the rabbi. I pray your physician neighbors will emancipate my Danite, in time." She picked up her letters of credit and left.

Rabbi Ben Moshe was not surprised by Adiva's request that he marry them right away. "Many young Jews—or maybe their parents—see their options closing."

He sighed. "Perhaps they're right." He thought of having multiple marriages at once but decided against it.

He explained that the sages had determined that a rabbi must be involved in the kiddushin, the betrothal, to insure it is sanctified. A man and woman may marry without a rabbi present, having only two witnesses, and saying the proper words, but it was really the same thing. This was the *only* kind of ceremony Eldad knew, since people had no rabbis.

Abruptly summoned by a group of husky workmen carrying boxes of books from the geniza on the synagogue's second floor, he warned them not to drop these sacred texts, lest they be required to fast a week. Not being Jewish, they thought he was joking, but he made clear he was not.

He returned to Adiva and said soberly, "I know what the Babylonians do to synagogues and churches, and this structure has been both. They will surely desecrate our holy books. Perhaps it is fitting that we spend the waning days of this house of worship celebrating joyous unions." He was again called away when a wagon arrived at the entrance to the synagogue.

"One other thing. Eldad must have a ring to give you. It must not be yours. Perhaps your brother, or the gypsy here, can quickly procure one."

Adiva and Ashot made their way through increasingly crowded streets to Adiva's home a half mile distant. Everything seemed to be offered for sale, and clamoring merchants could be seen packing what they couldn't unload. Arriving at the outer gate of the house, they were alarmed to find it ajar, and the gypsy drew his knife.

Advancing silently, they listened at the open doorway to the inner courtyard onto which all the rooms opened. Adiva and Ashot looked at each other, eyes wide in perplexity as they heard a chorus of heavy snoring, three throats strong. Peering into the first of the home's six rooms, a servant's quarters, they beheld an enormous pair of thickly calloused feet jutting from the end of the bed.

"I know those feet!" the gypsy whooped and launched himself at the fully covered figure spilling from the too-small bed. A great grunt, then a howl of protest was followed by the supine giant flipping over, sending the gypsy flying onto the floor. With remarkable agility, the black-bearded man was on his feet fully prepared for combat, but instead, he just burst out laughing.

In a blur, the nimble first mate Rafik appeared, leaping from the shadows onto the back of the stout gypsy. After swinging the three of them in a circle, Kasim set them down and they laughed like playing children. This commotion roused Eldad from a canyon-deep sleep, but bleariness cleared rapidly, and pointing to Kasim and Rafik, said, "These strays came to the door. What was I to do?"

The reconnection between these loyal friends who had together weathered so many storms was short-lived. To Adiva's immediate and profound relief, Eldad had arrived, looking haggard, but uninjured. Eldad finally took notice of Rafik and Kasim. "I am delighted to see you, my dear friends, but how..?"

"They have come for our wedding," said Adiva.

"If we even have *that* long."

The Netira family's agent at Port Suez had delivered a message to Captain Tushar's carpenter and first mate. They left the ship immediately for Fustat, a two-day trek inland from the Red Sea. Learning of the military disaster at Ramia, they realized Tushar would not linger long in port with hostile Babylonian forces likely to seize control within days to weeks.

Adiva placed her arm around Eldad's waist. "Tomorrow, in the afternoon, we shall all be together to share a sacred moment in our lives. You blessed friends make our world whole again, bringing the best of the past into our future."

"And now we must rest," said Adiva and had her guests shown to sleeping quarters. Finally, they could rest. But Eldad was too anxious for sleep.

"We must leave this glorious place immediately after our wedding, lest we be trapped in Fustat under siege by the Regent's army. Captain Tushar's vessel will sail south in the Gulf of Suez, then north in the Gulf of Aqaba to Eilat. Rafik and Kasim tell me it is a peaceful port, but of course, we will be prepared to seek other sanctuary if it is not."

Having a concrete plan formed a thin cover over a multitude of worries about all that *could* go wrong in the next two days, including the premature arrival of a victorious General Abu'l Abbas to claim his spoils of war.

The afternoon shadows were lengthening when Adiva tore herself away from her men and dutifully reported to the Netira home, there to undergo the preparations to become a Jewish bride. The tiniest details were attended to, like trimming her nails and immersion in a ritual bath, all symbols of bridal purity. She was to be escorted in the short walk from the banker's house to the Ben Ezra synagogue by a royal entourage, since this was her day to be a queen, and royalty was to be attended every step. Her bridal gown of white silk seemed to possess an interior light of its own, flowing from her shoulders like the Cataracts of the Nile.

The night was mostly sleepless, as she was flooded with memories of high arousal, and anticipation of even more. In the quiet, hungry solitude, she forced herself to ask if her yearning for this enticing young man clouded her judgment. Would her Danite wish to continue his exploration of known, and perhaps unknown, worlds? He had spoken glowingly of the Lost Tribe of Issachar, the scholars, and teachers in the mountains of Persia. Will he feel caged by my world, or I by his? Then she realized these questions were the same as so many brides asked their private selves. She would not speak of these concerns, even with the pointed questions from the women, particularly the younger Netira.

Now alone in the darkness, Adiva smiled and tried to take this last revelation to sleep with her, but the anticipation only added to the heady mix of thoughts on parade keeping her awake. Then, as though a blessing descended upon her, she answered her most compelling questions as she remembered the passage from the Book of Ruth: "Do not urge me to leave you or turn back from you. Where you go, I will go and where you stay, I will stay." The rest of the beautiful verse was lost to merciful sleep that cradled her away from the twilight of the old, toward the dawn of the new.

72

The sweltering Egyptian night added to the sweat of dreams wetting an outline of his recumbent body on the silken coverlet beneath him. He would remember only two images on awakening, both of indelible sight and smell and touch. He knew the dream voice, which always seemed to speak from a deeper knowledge than his. It sometimes revealed, often lectured, and tonight had a pointed message for the dreamer. His much-loved childhood friend Saul, lost forever to the savagery of cannibals, appeared as he did at his best, weighty but muscular, teasing Eldad. Would he *ever* think of him and not be stabbed by grief?

Then one after another of the people he loved and longed to see, each a different hue in the rainbow of his life. Texture, grit, sinew—they had all these, and his grandfather appeared first, flooding him with memories of the centenarian's cautious guidance into the deeper mysteries of life. Sav believed God could not be understood by any feat of intellect, though many, if not most, pretended to do so. He said there could as well be *not-being* as *being,* and since there is being, there has to be a reason for it. Within each of us, Sav taught, is the 'white-hot spark of the divine.' "You are more than your body and conscious thoughts." Such talk was met with skepticism by Mahli, Eldad's highly practical father. An Elder in the Tribe of Dan, Mahli accepted this honor after the Council said Sav was *too elderly* to be an elder! Eldad's gentle mother appeared beside his father, and lingered unhurriedly, as they never would have in the waking world. Kind and endlessly energetic, they tended to the sicknesses and injuries of many hundreds of Danites. He spoke to them without words, and they told him not to agonize if he did not see them again in this life, as he would in another reality. Without understanding this, his spirit was aglow with certainty, and for a dreamscape moment, his mind was filled with light.

Then after a time, a sudden darkness descended in which he stood holding the tablets he had recovered at Ebla. He yearned to know their meaning and with dreamer's logic believed he *could* read them, if he only had the *light*. The dream voice said, "Use your touch," and he held one of the tablets so the tip of his finger could sense the crescent shaped pits on its surface. He heard the voice of him who wrote these words three thousand years before, saying, "If you read this, I know you were at Ebla. The tablets are my story; how I came to be a scribe, then a healer, of precious love lost, then found."

As it always does, the waking world came smashing through the thinning veil of sleep, with a persistent tugging at his shoulder, and an unknown female voice commanding. "You up! You go get married!"

Still not yet out of the dream world, Eldad managed, "Why are you still here?"

The seamstress supervised baths for each of them in the court-yard fountain pool, with no regard for their modesty, as though they were children. Dissatisfied with scrubbing technique, or rather its absence, led her to seize soapy rags and attack from behind. In a few minutes, the bear stopped grumbling and seemed to enjoy being washed, something he had never experienced before. Too quickly they were dried and given clean clothes which appeared to be never worn.

Out into the sunshine, the ordinarily pristine streets of Fustat, paved and kept clear of refuse, were now showing signs of sudden neglect, people carelessly discarding unwanted things that could not be sold or easily moved on the river of pack animals flooding the byways.

But it was the fear on the people's faces that Eldad noticed most, then the children demanding to know where they were going and their inconsolable crying when the questions went unanswered.

Everybody moved more quickly, but without any real purpose of destination. Those with coin were bartering for a place on a cart or at least the back of an ass. Prostitutes offered their bodies to sweeten the deal.

The tension was made worse by the fact that nobody knew what was to come. Eldad could hear excited discussions as they walked along. A conquering army would be in their midst in a day or two, or even hours, one said. He ignored them all and focused on his destiny with Adiva.

The bet ha-tefilla came into view. The square in front of the Hanging Church next door was jammed with merchants and travelers, and they saw a cart bearing books from the geneza pull away from the ornate entrance of the synagogue. Eldad realized his writings, a more or less complete rendering of the dietary laws of the Danites, were with these books and papers now being hidden from the Babylonians. He could not escape the irony that so many documents being hidden, like worn-out copies of the Passover haggada and the Talmudic writings had *come* from Babylon.

They entered. At once they were met by Hillel. "There you are, my brother," he said warmly.

Hillel must have sensed Eldad's surprise. "I have been staying at Chiam Netira's, help them to organize. For what exactly, I'm not sure."

"Nobody is," Eldad replied. "At least we are together."

Eldad looked around. He pointed to the grandeur of the synagogue's interior with its double row of five marble columns supporting the open balcony of the second floor. Rafik and Kasim followed the grey and cream-hued columns of marble continuing from the balcony to support arches of alternating light and dark stone. Light poured in through large windows that brightened both floors, and the intricately inlaid tile of the domed ceiling sparkled with a rainbow of colors. They were clearly impressed. Even Ashot was staring.

All four stood silently when they beheld the beauty of the curving marble staircase leading to the bimah at the center of the synagogue, and the raised north end of the sanctuary enclosed the dazzling Aron Kodeash. Its doors were inlaid with gold leaf, mother-of-pearl and semiprecious stones of many hues, evoking images of Eden. The carpenter's practiced eye saw immediately that the eight inch hinges, attaching the doors to the tile walls were loosened for quick removal along with the precious contents of the Arc.

"Here put this on," Hillel said, handing Eldad a small hat. "It is customary here for a Jew to wear a head covering in a house of worship. It's like that back home as well."

Eldad did as he was directed.

Men were milling about the first floor, many more than Eldad expected.

"I'm sure some are left over from the numerous wedding ceremonies performed this morning. Yours is the last my friend," he said. "I've heard people in the community wanted to honor the great Gaon's daughter in some way. My father has that effect on people. At least by reputation."

Eldad nodded, smiling at the recollection of his discussions with Adiva's father and his struggle for acceptance. "Adiva also, I expect."

"Of course. The Netira family alone could fill this room."

"Perhaps," Eldad said, "they are merely here to pray."

"You may be right," Hillel said.

Even inside this beautiful place of worship, Eldad couldn't help but notice the anxiety in the room. He had learned enough to know that in many parts of the world, when the people faced danger, the Jews suffered first. But here in Fustat, most Jews had never experienced this and this only added to panic, and their sense of doom.

"My friend," Hillel said, "come with me to quickly sign your marriage contract. Adiva signed the ketubah earlier."

Eldad, followed Hillel into a small room. Hillel placed the document on the table. Two other men were waiting.

He could make out some of the language but was not sure of the rest. Hillel noticed his confusion.

"Here, let me read it for you. It's in Aramaic, I am standing in for my father, the Gaon, whom you are addressing in this sacred document."

"I came to your house for you to give me your daughter, Adiva, to wife: she is my wife, and I am her husband from this day and forward."

"The rest of the document mostly concerns Adiva's rights to property and to divorce. I am sure Adiva has no need of either. She may be the wealthiest woman in Fustat."

Eldad smiled.

"But come now, we have little time to waste."

Cream-colored marble covered the raised platform and the smiling rabbi, looking very tired, stood alone to the right. He met Eldad's eyes as he stood just inside the sanctuary's main entrance and motioned for him to come forward.

Satisfied that his instruction was being followed, the rabbi turned to the left, repeating the invitation toward a curtained anteroom. Adiva walked into a shaft of light which seemed to illuminate her path to the platform steps. The white silk of her gown shimmered in the light, adding it to the even brighter radiance from within Adiva which blinded Eldad for a moment.

The rabbi beckoned them to stand together under the makeshift chuppah, held aloft by four men.

Standing across from his beloved, Eldad slowly lifted the veil that covered Adiva's face, avoiding the trickery that was foisted on their Patriarch Jacob.

But there was no trick. Even at this moment, Eldad was stunned by her beauty.

The rabbi pronounced a blessing of wine and they both took a sip.

Hillel handed him a simple ring and he placed it on Adiva's index finger.

"*Mekudeshet,* be sanctified to me with this ring in accordance with the law of Moshe and Israel."

They patiently waited while seven blessings, the sheva b'rachot, were recited. This honor was given to Chiam Netira, who looked like a proud father, himself.

"Perhaps all marriages face the challenges of their times," the rabbi said, "but few must weather such a storm as fast approaches from the east. And there are other headwinds from ancient times blowing hard against you: traditions from our fathers, that sometimes conflict with those of perhaps ten generations or more ago, between worlds that spring from different epochs of man. But remember, we all heard the Torah at Mt. Sinai. And so, may the spark of your love kindle the trash of ages past and light the way for mankind. There is strength in the difference between you, as a cloth of wool and silk is stronger than a weave of either thread alone."

"The experiences of your young lives have taught you to *accept*, but no longer *fear* uncertainty. In spite of the tumult of the world around you, find the quiet place between you, the flowing spring that satisfies your deepest wishes."

Adiva vowed to remember this moment, her mind cleared of doubt, when there seemed to be a perfect resonance between her inner and outer worlds. The last time she could remember such bliss she was 8 years old. Illusion or not, it suddenly become an ideal to seek after. For that, she sadly realized, they would need to find a better world. She knew she must cling to the fragile hope there was one, where the peace of her inner self would match a just and kind surrounding.

Her senses heightened, colors becoming more vivid, sounds louder, and light brighter. She realized such perceptions would herald madness in ordinary days, but this was like no other moment in her life. Unlike all her other decisions, she was taking a step from which there was no retraction and wondered if a bit of madness wasn't the wind bringing two ships together on a storm-tossed sea.

Her thoughts were interrupted by the sounds of thunder.

Others heard it too, but the as the noise grew louder, it became a continuous roar, not thunder at all.

"Horses," Eldad shouted. *"Soldiers."*

The once joyous congregation was in a panic.

"Rabbi, have someone take the sefer Torah to a safe place," Hillel said. "Have you weapons?"

The rabbi shrugged, answering without words.

Eldad grabbed two rods from the chuppah, handing one to Hillel.

Hillel shook his head. "I'll find our crewmates. Find a way out."

Adiva faced her husband. She must will herself to remain serene. Staring into Eldad's beautiful blue eyes, she was determined to remain happy in his presence.

"We are married, my love." She smiled. "No matter what happens, we will be together for eternity."

Eldad smiled back. "At this moment, I realize how abundantly the Lord has blessed me."

They made their way towards the entrance. The sound of galloping horses had ceased. Only the noise of the Jews inside remained.

The soldiers had arrived.

Adiva caught a glimpse of Ashot, his ever-present dagger at the ready. She shook her head, wordlessly conveying a message. No, my friend this is not the time for a fight. He seemed to understand.

The door swung open fully and, in the sunlight, she could only make out the outline of soldiers, first two, then ten, maybe more, their swords glimmering.

Their eyes slowly adjusted. "Those are palace guards," Eldad said. "What are *they* doing here?"

The rabbi did not wait to find out. He rushed to the door. "Welcome to our house of worship," he said, "what can we do for you?"

The guard looked at him with a hint of contempt in his expression. "Stand aside," he nearly shouted.

Before anyone could react, more guards entered, splitting the room, creating a clearly defined pathway. This caused the anxiety of the assembled to rise even more.

Into this void, a young man entered. Some people lowered their heads, but Adiva thought it was an apparition and continued to stare in disbelief.

It was none other than Khumarawayh ibn Ahmad ibn Tulun, the ruler of Egypt.

As if the Regent's appearance at a synagogue weren't stunning enough, he smiled, his face almost joyous. He seemed to be enjoying the confusion he had created.

By now, the streets had begun to fill behind him. He turned slightly so that he could be heard by them as well.

"You many have heard," he said "when we went to confront our enemies, the soldiers at the vanguard, though vastly superior in numbers to Abbas' army, panicked and ran when the time came."

He sighed. "Sadly, this is true. Their general believed I, too, had fled and was well on my way back to Cairo."

He laughed heartily. "This was not so. We allowed the heady-with-victory Babylonians to settle into our quarters which they proceeded to pillage. General Sa'd al-Aysar waited with my reserve force a few miles from Ramia. Baghdad's 4,000 soldiers were drunk with celebration, with chants of 'On to Cairo' when the old general's surprise attack tore them to pieces. Nearly all commanders were slain, and the traitor al-Wasiti as well."

The crowd had grown even bigger and more festive forcing the regent to raise his voice even louder. "Now you may think it strange that I have come to this Jewish house of prayer to announce our great victory."

He paused to allow the crowd to contemplate this. Indeed, most of the Jews were puzzled as well.

"It has come to my attention that we would not have even know about the danger we faced if not for two people: A child of Babylon, the daughter of a great Jewish scholar and an African who is also a Jew. At great risk, it is they who made us aware of the great peril we faced?"

Adiva smiled at Eldad, who grabbed her hand squeezing tight.

"Thanks to these two brave people, Egypt remains free. We owe them a debt. I understand today is the day of their marriage. I will make sure that suitable gift is presented on behalf of all my people."

The crowd, Muslims and Christians alike, erupted with joy and celebration.

The victorious son of Ibn Tulun abruptly left the synagogue, pushing through the cheering throng ringed by his soldiers. One of the regent's spokesmen appeared on the balcony of the church next door praising the young leader for his glorious victory over

Baghdad's treacherous al-Muwaffaq, whose so called 'wonder general' son had now withdrawn from Syria entirely.

The change in the streets of Fustat was as though an unbearable heat had been suddenly cooled by a life-giving rain, and discarded items in the tree-lined streets were magically disappearing to their previous owners and the city's ever-present scavengers.

With Hillel clearing a path, the bride and groom, glowing with their shared inner light, made their way through hearty pats and hugs. Adiva was grateful to have her brother near, but had an unexpected moment of sadness when she thought of her dear parents. Would she ever see them again?

Kasim, Ashot and Rafik had joined them and Adiva smiled, knowing that this was family now. They opened their circle and surrounded the couple with three concentric rings of enveloping arms pressing against them from all sides. They all felt the warmth and security, swaying as a tribe in the noisy sea of humanity that crowded the sanctuary. Then everyone spoke at once, until Eldad interrupted, "Tonight we shall finish this celebration, loved ones, but for now, I am stealing my bride away."

He paused, as Kasim used his bulk to move people aside. "Or is *she* stealing me? My cries for help are not likely to be heeded, are they?"

Adiva was thrilled when Eldad, obviously more self-assured, swept his arm around her waist, leading them through the throng that seemed to grow by the minute. Jostling their way to a side street, they soon found the wider byway that led the half-mile to the banks of the river.

The road was wide and paved with flat stones, many worn smooth by ages of feet shuffling down to the banks of the mighty river. Stately palms, 40 to 60 feet in height, lined the ancient byway which aligned precisely with the largest of the three pyramids. They walked unhurriedly, perhaps for the first time, Adiva thought, there *was* time to be easy in step and peaceful in mind. They slowed everything to find the natural rhythm of this unforgettable day so filled with life-changing moments and breathtaking surprises. They had not let go of each other's hands since leaving the celebrating multitude. Hungry for the bonding that would deepen that very night, she knew there would be no restraint in their intimacy. They would not hurry those moments either.

"I look back on the assignment that Hillel and Yosef and I accepted from the Netira family," she said, "the risk we so willingly took, and I wonder what madness possessed me. I was restless in the restrictive life of a Jewish woman in Babylon, but I almost traded it for one of human bondage, or for no life at all."

Eldad held her tight. "And I, too, risked my life to find one free of tribal conflict. Yet even here I see the wounds of battle and smell the death of war. It is well for us to anchor here for now, yet always realize our world must change, for good or ill, but it never remains the same."

They could now smell the earthy black silt, laden with life-sustaining nutrients from the rainstorms in the Ethiopian highlands. Eldad wondered if the Danites' mythical river Sambation, beyond which the Lost Tribes of Israel were banished, flowed into the mile-wide river they were fast approaching. Swollen, but not yet over its banks, the Nile air was heavy with an invigorating mist, fertile and mysterious.

Adiva stopped a moment to take in the shimmering images of the three largest manmade objects on earth, still six miles distant. "Around here they have a saying: 'Man fears time, but time fears only the pyramids.' Your love has, my darling Danite, taken from me my fear of time. My anguish was it would pass without my ever knowing the wonder of a man like you. You are brave like a lion, gentle as a woman, and you comfort everyone who touches you." She stepped in front of him and, with quick reassurance, brought his face down to hers, there to begin the lingering kiss that had been interrupted by the arrival of the Regent. She marveled at how every time she kissed this beautiful man, it was like the first.

Sitting a few feet above the water line on the haphazard stones that lined the east bank of the vast river, Eldad took Adiva's hand, and, looking into her eyes, said, "Our lives are finite flames, and we accept this, together rejoicing in the light and warmth God has given us. We are more thankful after the terrible storms failed to steal our youth. Wouldn't it be lovely if *nothing* happens for a time?"

Adiva kissed him. "When nothing is happening, *everything* can!" she replied.

The heat of the Egyptian summer day was beginning to dissipate as the sun had dipped behind the pyramids, illuminating them in a yellow haze.

Gazing at the north-flowing Nile, Eldad wondered, "Now, how would a child of Israel escape his dreadful Egyptian enslavement?"

"Dreadful *Babylonian* enslavement, if you please," Adiva corrected.

"The poor beast could flee south on the great river, moving ever higher to the Blue Nile in search of his tribe. Or he could drift north with the flow of the river, taking the Roetta branch west to the Mediterranean Sea."

"He could hide awhile from his mistress, but how long from *himself?*"

They were quiet then, basking in the light of a sunset on the Nile. The air was fresh, cleared of desert dust yet earthy from the mist above swirling waters. A few yards from shore, the sunlight glinted off the water's surface, and Adiva pointed urgently at the reflected ball of light, for there, cruising in their direction, glistened the elongated heads with wide-spaced predator eyes of two Nile crocodiles. With the quick reactions and agility of youth, they sprang to the top of the rocky embankment. Peals of laughter issued from two muddied adolescent boys fishing at the water's edge, apparently unconcerned about the lurking man-eaters, and thoroughly delighted by the panicked lovers. They were soon laughing, too, the beginning of a life they so hoped would be filled with laughter, a life to the full and sweet.

They stood for a moment, then turned toward home and the quiet place between them. And they had singing hearts.